Whispered Sins

The CEO's Secret Baby

Rebecca Baker

Translated by: Heartbeat Publishing / www.heartbeat-publishing.de

***

Sign up for my newsletter and receive a **free romance novel:**

https://www.subscribepage.com/rebecca-baker-english

Chapter 1

ADDISON

I smoothed my blouse with my hands as I studied myself in the mirror. I let out a sigh as I took in my reflection, critiquing with a harsh eye. The gray tweed skirt I found on sale last week dug into my stomach, even after I tried doing squats and various exercises to get it to give a little. I must have looked ridiculous huffing and puffing on my bed, trying to squeeze the dang thing on. Thankfully, I lived alone and no one was there to bear witness.

I gave myself one more glance in the mirror and shrugged. I guessed I just had to suck it in and smile through the pain of a size eight. It was a wishful thinking purchase, and one that I needed to make for this afternoon's meeting. I had to look the part of a professional businesswoman, even though I was really more of a sweatpants kind of girl who worked for a nonprofit. It wasn't the most glamorous job, but it was a passion. An underpaid one at that. Hence my tiny Brooklyn loft that could pass as a closet. It was cramped, but it was cozy. I didn't need much.

Anyway, I didn't take this job for the money. I took it to help those in need, and I remind myself of that as I grab my purse from the kitchen counter and look back at the brick-walled box I lived in. Locking the door behind me,

I startled at something brushing against my legs. I jumped back and looked down, expecting to see a rat, but it was just my landlord's cat, Beatrice. I let out a little sigh of relief and bent down to run my hand across her smooth coat. She purred with pleasure and closed her eyes.

"Beatrice!" I heard echoing up the stairwell.

"She's here," I called back.

My landlord emerged at the top of the stairs, catching her breath and clutching her heart as if she had just run up ten flights of stairs, when it really was only two. She had a flair for the dramatic.

"There you are," she said, rushing toward her cat that was in no distress at all. In fact, she may as well have been asleep.

"Hey Elma," I said, standing up as she scooped up her precious feline.

"Addison." She nodded, looking me over. "You look...nice."

I caught a note of surprise in her voice.

"Thanks," I replied, smoothing my skirt once more, even though nothing was going to smooth out the rolls I've taken on from one too many orders at Ling's Dynasty on the corner.

"Where are you off to?" she asked.

"I have a meeting with a potential donor."

"Anyone I would know?" Elma asked, raising a curious brow. She did love to be in everyone's business. She was a fifty-year-old woman who lived alone with her cat. I didn't mind entertaining her, though. I figured it was the least I could do for not raising rent on my loft, like the other surrounding buildings.

"Daniel Jacobs?" I asked with a shrug, even though I knew the reaction that would elicit.

At the name, Elma nearly drops Beatrice, who wakes up with a start, her paws jutting into the air like she'd been electrocuted. Another one with a flair for the dramatic. The two were made for each other.

"*The* Daniel Jacobs?" she asked.

"Yeah. I guess. The big wig on Fifth Avenue."

"Do you even know what you're walking into?" she asked with a narrow voice.

I thought I did. My boss had provided me a lengthy portfolio to study Daniel Jacobs. *The* Daniel Jacobs, as Elma put it. He was the typical New York wealthy businessman, like I had dealt with before. But this guy was in a different league. He was the wealthiest businessman on the East Coast, running a tech company with his brother.

I tried to pass the meeting off to someone else, but my boss was adamant that I take it. I didn't know why. It wasn't like I had outstanding people skills. They were mediocre at best. Whatever the reason, I spent the last month preparing for this meeting, so I wasn't going to let Elma get my nerves in a tizzy. They were already doing a fantastic job of that themselves.

"Nothing I can't handle, I'm sure," I said, feigning a confidence I hoped convinced her.

"Oh, honey..." she started, shaking her head.

"What?" I asked, trying to hide my exasperation, but also letting my curiosity get the best of me.

"He was New York's most eligible bachelor. And he knows it. He was like the Leonardo DiCaprio of the tech world."

"I'm not going on a date with him, Elma." I laughed.

"Obviously. He only dates supermodels."

Ouch.

"I hear he took three women out in one night," she continued. "Or was it four?"

She furrowed her brow as if trying to remember what she read in some gossip magazine.

"I really should be going, Elma."

I politely squeezed past her and made my way to the stairwell.

"Good luck," she called after me.

As I walked down the stairs, I could have sworn I heard her say something under her breath. Something like, "He is going to eat you alive."

Outside, the bright afternoon sun beat down on me as I stepped the sidewalk toward the subway. Elma's words were repeating in my ears like whispering echoes pounding at the outer parts of my brain.

He is going to eat you alive.

Thank you for the vote of confidence, Elma.

I checked the time on my phone and realized I was cutting it close for the next train into the city. I started my descent down the stairs to the subway, taking the stairs two at a time. It was a wonder this skirt let me do it. On the platform, I saw my train already filling up and pushed my way through the doors just as they closed behind me. I breathed a sigh of relief and found a place to stand in the crowd. The last thing I needed was to be late.

Twenty minutes later, I reached my stop and stepped out onto the platform where I felt like I could breathe again outside of the crammed car. I made my way to the stairs and began my ascent to the city awaiting above, the sounds of taxis and live music drifting down the stairwell. Up in the sunshine once more, I checked my phone. I'd be early, but that was better than late.

As I strolled down the sidewalk, a large glass building came into view. It was the largest one on the block, and was most likely the one I'd be entering in just a few moments. Reaching into my purse, I checked the address I had scribbled on a piece of paper this morning and confirmed it. Then I took a deep breath as I walked up to the large glass doors. I went to push one, but the doors automatically slid open, causing me to stumble slightly into the vast lobby. The security guard gave me an amused nod as I walked past him toward the front desk.

"How can I help you?" asked the blonde in the crisp white suit that only she could pull off.

"I have a meeting with Mr. Jacobs at four. I'm a little early."

She checked her computer and nodded. "He is in a meeting at the moment, but I will let him know you're here. If you like, I can have someone escort you up where you can wait."

"Sure. Thank you."

She waved over the security guard who watched me stumble in here, and he led me to an elevator. We rode in silence to the 90th floor. I could feel my stomach rise to my throat as the numbers kept ticking by and we still hadn't reached our destination. Finally, I let out a slow breath as the elevator doors opened to another lobby. I thanked the security guard and stepped onto solid ground, the doors closing behind me.

I approached another desk and a woman impeccably dressed in a black suit to match her raven hair. This place really did a number on my confidence.

"Hello, Ms. Heartly. Mr. Jacobs will be with you shortly. In the meantime, you can help yourself to coffee and pastries. Or you can explore the rooftop garden while you wait." She waved at a buffet table full of croissants and Danishes that she probably didn't eat herself, and then to two large doors that opened onto a large terrace.

"Thank you," I said, opting for the garden.

I doubted this skirt would give any more for a cheese Danish, even though they looked mouth wateringly good. I stepped onto the terrace and was immediately hit with the lush smells of roses and jasmine. I breathed in deeply and took in my surroundings. It was breathtaking. I didn't realize anything so beautiful and so alive could be this high up from the concrete jungle below.

I strolled down one of the pathways, gently running my fingertips over the flowers. If anything was going to calm my nerves, it was this. I found a bench in the shape of a butterfly and sat down. I closed my eyes and began going over the script I had been memorizing for the past week. I didn't like bringing notes to these things. It felt like I was unprepared, and I wanted to look like I knew what I was doing, especially with these big wigs.

I heard someone clear their throat and snapped my eyes open to see a man standing on the other side of the bench. I squinted and tried to allow them to adjust to the stranger before me, the sun beaming behind him. He looked slightly older than me, wearing a pair of gray slacks and a white button-down. His eyes were a piercing blue. A violent contrast against his tan skin and dark hair. He was honestly breathtaking, which was why I hadn't found my voice yet.

"Hello," he said, smiling down at me curiously.

That smile. If I couldn't speak before, there was a slim chance I could now.

"Uh..." I stammered, pushing myself to stand.

He studied me with an amused expression as I finally got an actual word out.

"I'm Addison. I have a meeting with your boss," I said. Judging from his more casual attire, I just assumed he was Daniel's assistant.

He raised an eyebrow momentarily before it settled back into place on his perfect face.

"Oh?" he asked.

"Yeah. I'm early. I'm a little nervous, actually." The words came out like I'd had three glasses of wine at the bar with my best friend. Literal word vomit. The nerves were getting to me. I wasn't sure if they were because of my meeting or this stranger who just turned up.

"Why is that?" he asked, crossing his arms.

"I've been researching him for the past month. I know just about everything there is to know businesswise, but then my landlord sprang some gossip on me before I left for this meeting. She told me he was some playboy who's seen with a different woman every night. Hell, multiple at that."

This was really not anything I should be discussing with his assistant, but it was too late. The words had already toppled out of me.

I noticed the amused smile on his face waver momentarily, but then he let out a laugh that rang in my ears like a favorite song I could play over and over.

"Is that so?" he asked.

"It must be. I mean, just judging by the women who work here. He probably sleeps with them, too."

He studied me for a moment before looking out toward the city, but it was really not the city he was looking at. It was just sky because this was one of its tallest buildings. I had a moment to study his profile, which was ridiculously chiseled. I wondered what he was thinking about, and worried I might not even have a meeting anymore. Why did I have to open my dumb mouth?

Chapter 2

DANIEL

I looked out over the edge of the terrace wall, wondering if I should be offended or amused by what this woman said to me. Maybe I should be proud of how my reputation precedes me. Either way, she had no idea who I was. I liked that. I was going to run with it.

I turned toward her and my eyes quickly wandered, as they'd been known to do. I couldn't help it. I loved women, and the one who stood before me was striking. She wasn't my usual type. Addison, was it? I think that was why I found her so captivating. Rather than being stick-thin with blonde hair and a tan I was never sure was natural, nor did I really care to find out, Addison was different.

Her body curved in places I'd like to place my hands on, my fingertips pressing into places I wondered when were last touched. I couldn't tell if her dark hair was brown or a warm shade of black. It was pulled into a bun that said she tried, but not too hard by the way unruly strands fell around her face. That face, though. It was in the shape of a heart that matched perfectly with the rosy pout of her lips. Right above her top lip was a kiss of a mole, which my eyes couldn't help but be drawn to.

She seemed to notice where my eyes had stopped and covered her mouth shyly, chewing on her thumbnail. She was self-conscious of it when it might have been the sexiest thing about her. She didn't even know it, which made her all the more attractive.

The woman cleared her throat nervously and my eyes caught hers. They were a warm brown and searching mine to see if perhaps she went too far. I decided to put her mind at ease, but also have a little fun.

"You'll be fine. But entertain me. What else have you heard about my boss?" I asked with a playful smirk. I might as well play the part of whoever she assumed I was.

"That he only dates models. He thinks he is Leonardo DiCaprio."

Ouch. I was only thirty-two, and I took out women over the age of twenty-five.

"Hmm. What else?"

It was interesting to gain perspective on myself from a complete stranger.

"That's all Elma said." She shrugged.

"Elma?"

"My landlord."

"Ah." I nodded.

"She loves to gossip," said Addison. "The last thing she said was he was going to eat me alive. What do you think she meant by that?"

I fought back a smile because her landlord seemed to know me quite well for never having met me, because that was exactly what I'd like to do, among other things. My imagination was already running wild.

"Maybe she thinks my boss tends to get what he wants..." I quipped.

"Well, I highly doubt he wants me."

You doubt wrong. Very wrong.

"Plus, I'm not that kind of girl," she added.

"And what kind of girl is that?"

"The kind that sleeps around with some rich playboy."

She said it firmly, and I was already taking this as a challenge. *Game on.*

I watched as she pulled out her phone and checked the time, her brow furrowing.

"His meeting must be running late..." she said, looking around the terrace.

Just then, I heard the *click-clack* of heels coming down the stone pathway. I saw my assistant appear from behind the large pink rose bush. The jig was up.

"Oh, Mr. Jacobs. There you are. I see you've already met your four o'clock," she said, spotting us by the bench.

I heard Addison suck in a sharp breath and saw her shoot me a nervous look.

"Thank you, Margaret. I'll take her to my office," I said, dismissing her.

Margaret nodded before heading back down the pathway.

I turned toward Addison, whose eyes were wide and her lips parted slightly. I saw she'd put it together. I gave her a sheepish smile.

"*You're* Daniel Jacobs?" she asked in an almost whisper.

"The one and only." I hold my arms out.

"I-I am so sorry," she stammered. "I had no idea. You must think I'm a total idiot."

"Not at all. It was quite all right," I said, waving her off.

She put her face in her hands and looked at me through the slits of her fingers.

"Why didn't you say anything?" she groaned.

"You just assumed I was...someone else. Who *did* you think I was?"

"His assistant. I don't know. Oh my God. This is mortifying."

She slid her hands down her face and looked at me remorsefully.

"It's okay. Really. I like roleplaying, anyway."

I saw her cheeks turn crimson as her mouth dropped open. She let out a strained sound before shutting it quickly. She broke our gaze and looked at the floor, fumbling with her purse. My words got to her. I liked seeing her squirm.

"Shall we?" I asked, nodding toward the building.

"Wait. You still want to have the meeting? Even after everything I said?" she asked, surprised.

"Why not?"

"Okay," she replied hesitantly.

She fell into step beside me. I noticed the warm vanilla-scented perfume she wore somehow competed with the surrounding flowers. I breathed it in as we walked through the opened doors.

"This way," I said, leading her down the long hallway to my office.

Margaret eyed us curiously. Despite what Addison thought, I hadn't slept with her or anyone in the building. I just liked having pretty things to look at. I knew better than to mix business with pleasure, although in this moment, with this new acquaintance, I wasn't so sure.

I opened the door to my office just enough so she had to brush past me. I closed the door gently behind me with a click and watched as she took in her surroundings. The marble floors. The high ceilings. The floor-to-ceiling windows. Not many buildings in the city were this high up or lent such a grand view of the sky and city below.

"This is incredible," she said as she spun slowly in a circle.

My eyes couldn't help but fall to her backside as she turned. That gray skirt did wonders for her. I wondered what was underneath.

"May I get you anything? Water? Coffee?" I asked.

She turned to me and shook her head. "I'm fine, thank you."

"Well, let's get started."

I gestured to the leather armchair and took a seat behind my desk across from her.

She sat and smoothed her hands down her skirt. I saw no ring. She was fair game. Not that a ring had ever stopped me in the past.

I could see she was nervous after what happened in the garden because she was chewing on her bottom lip and looking anywhere but at me. I couldn't stop staring at her mouth. Her lip tucked under her teeth, fighting to break free. I wished it were my teeth biting into her fleshy pout.

"So...what can I do for you?" I asked, ignoring my wandering thoughts. I leaned back in my chair and crossed my hands in front of me. This was business, after all. Mostly.

"Well, first of all, I again want to apologize for what I said out on the terrace. I don't know what came over me. Whatever someone's lifestyle is, is no business of mine. I hope we can still have a successful meeting despite our initial one."

"Let's pretend it didn't happen."

Even though I was still replaying her words in my head. I could listen to her talk about sex all day. If we weren't interrupted by Margaret, I would have pushed further to hear what else she heard about *the* Daniel Jacobs. The way *playboy* rolled off her tongue like that. It was like porn for my ears. And the way she said she wasn't *that* type of girl. It was already a challenge I had accepted in my head. We would see about that.

"Let's start over. Would that help?" I offered.

She gave me a weak smile.

"That would be great," she replied.

"I'm Daniel Jacobs," I said, holding my hand out.

"Addison Heartly," she said, placing her hand in mine.

It was soft and small, and her touch caused the hairs on my neck to stand up. *This is new*, I thought to myself. I shook her hand and reluctantly released it. Her eyes fell to her hand and I wondered if she felt the same sort of electric shock I had. It took me a moment to collect myself before I spoke.

"So, what can I do for you today, Ms. Heartly?"

Her name was made for her.

"Well, I'm with Leading to Learn. We're a nonprofit that provides learning toys for children in third-world countries. Have you heard of it?"

"I have."

I haven't.

"Then you know our mission is to make learning and education accessible for all children, despite their location or economic situation."

I didn't know that, but I was doing my best to pretend like I was listening intently when really all I was thinking about was getting her into bed. Hell, on this desk. Anywhere she'd have me. I was probably an awful person for thinking about sex when she was pouring her heart out about kids who had nothing, but I couldn't help it.

She was still talking about their mission and my eyes were straying to the small amount of cleavage that was peeping out of her white button-down top. I noticed the white lace trim of her bra. I felt myself growing hard and was glad there was a desk in front of me at this moment. I liked women, but they didn't normally have this much of an effect on me.

I noticed she stopped talking and my eyes snapped up to hers, hoping she wasn't onto me or my lack of self-control in this moment.

"What you're doing is very admirable," I said, playing the part. This seemed to appease her.

"Thank you. I think everyone has a right to the opportunity to learn."

"I agree."

"Every child we've helped so far has been so incredibly grateful for even the smallest of toys. To see the looks on their faces when they're introduced to something new, yet something so ordinary to us, it's magical. It really puts things into perspective."

I could see this meant a lot to her and wasn't just a job to her. Or else she was one hell of a sales pitcher. I was going with the former.

"I can see this means a lot to you. So, what can I do for you?"

"Well, your company is the current leader in tech, making you one of the most profitable enterprises on the East Coast. We could use a donor of your stature. Our toys, up until now, have been mostly manipulatives, but we want to begin incorporating books and possible digital items for the villages that have access to electricity. As a nonprofit, we rely on donors to make what we do possible."

I did the usual signs of active listening. I nodded and mused and furrowed my brow like I was in deep thought. I pretended to be thinking about what she said, even though I'd already internally agreed to whatever she asked for. It wasn't like I'd miss a couple hundred thousand dollars. Hell, even a couple million. Whatever she needed. But I couldn't make it that easy. I needed more time with her.

"It would look good for your company. I could see *Forbes* writing up a noble article," she offered, her words rolling off her tongue as if she was dangling a piece of candy in front of me. Little did she know, she was the candy. And I'd like to taste her sweetness in my mouth.

Chapter 3

ADDISON

I watched Daniel as he took in what I said. I was surprised anything was coming out right at all. In fact, I wasn't sure exactly what I was saying, but it must have sounded good, judging by the ponderous look on his face. I hoped I was sticking to the script.

It was just that his good looks were incredibly distracting, and I had to will my eyes to stay on his, and not wander to his mouth or his sharp jawline. There was a little stubble along the angles of his face and I wondered what it would feel like against my skin. My face. My legs.

How could I have not known he was Daniel Jacobs? It couldn't be more obvious. He had an effect on me. On women. This guy could get anyone he wanted. He wasn't Leonardo DiCaprio. He was better. No wonder he had the reputation he did.

The thought of him sleeping around was a turn-off before I realized it was him, and now I was hot just thinking about him in bed and what he was capable of. His hands probably knew exactly where to touch a woman, and his mouth probably knew exactly how to kiss a woman.

I swallowed hard and tried to focus on what I was saying. I thought I was on the part about how it could be a generous tax write-off. It was like I'd had too much wine, and he was the bottle.

I finished my pitch and sat back in my chair, waiting for him to speak.

"Well, it sounds like it could be a good opportunity for the both of us," he said. I watched as he ran his fingers along his jaw.

"I believe it could be."

"I'd have to visit the project first. Maybe have a tour of the place. See more of what you do. I want to make sure it's a good fit."

"Of course," I said, nodding eagerly. Too eagerly.

Did I really just possibly land our biggest donor yet? Maybe I was a better people person than I thought. My boss did assign this meeting to me. And here I thought it was because most everyone was going out of town for the Fourth. Maybe he saw something in me that I didn't.

"But the tour has to be with you," said Daniel firmly.

"Me?" I asked with surprise.

I felt like I was flailing in midair.

"I don't really... I mean, I'm sure my boss would be better suited to..." I stammered.

Daniel shook his head. "I'm not interested in what your boss has to say. I'm interested in what *you* have to say. The tour has to be with you."

I sucked in a deep breath, trying to calm the hammering of my heart. This was unexpected. I didn't really think I would see him again after today. Hell, I didn't think he was going to give me a dime. Yet, here we were.

"Okay," I said after a pause. "I'll give you the tour."

He *did* get what he wanted.

And for some reason, he wanted me.

I laughed to myself. That was ridiculous. This wealthy, handsome businessman didn't want me.

"Is something funny?" he asked, cocking a brow as a small smile spread across his lips.

Shit. Did I laugh out loud?

"Oh, no. Nothing," I said, waving him off, feeling my cheeks burn.

"All right. Well, then it's settled. I'll have Margaret set up a time that aligns with both our schedules."

"Okay. Thank you," I said, reluctantly pulling myself to my feet.

I almost wished he had more questions or that he wasn't so willing to work with me, so I could push further. It would mean more time with him. I wanted more time. Needed more time. What was going on with me?

He stood and walked around his desk toward me. He held out his hand and I wondered if the initial spark I felt the first time I shook his hand would run shockwaves through me again. I shook his hand firmly, noting how large his was in how it enveloped mine like a warm blanket. There was that electricity again.

I pulled my hand away and headed toward the door, feeling his presence behind me like my own shadow. He pushed it open and allowed me to slide past.

"I look forward to seeing you soon," he said after me.

I was able to muster an "mhmm," but I didn't dare look back.

I stopped and saw Margaret at the front desk.

"Hello. Daniel. Er, Mr. Jacobs, said to set up a follow-up meeting. He wants to visit our offices."

She scanned her computer screen and I willed it to have an opening soon. I noticed her eyes were a brilliant shade of green that played off her jet-black bob. I couldn't help but feel self-conscious. And weirdly jealous. There was no way she hadn't slept with him.

"It looks like he's free tomorrow morning. Does ten a.m. work?" she asked, looking at me expectantly.

"Uh, yes. That should work."

That was soon. Sooner than I expected. My nerves had hardly settled from just a minute ago, and now they were playing ping-pong through my whole body knowing I would be seeing him again in less than twenty-four hours.

"Perfect. I'll put it in the calendar. Can I have the address, please?"

She slid me a pen and a piece of paper and I jotted down the address for the Leading to Learn office building. I thanked her and headed to the elevator. As the elevator began its long descent down to the lobby, it felt as if a piece of me was still on the top floor.

I was being crazy. I was not this type of girl. I said it myself, and now I was eating my words. As I walked out of the lobby, I breathed in the fresh air and felt the sunshine on my face. I tried to ground myself, but before I headed toward the subway, I looked up at the building I had just exited. I could see a peep of foliage hanging over the top terrace and smiled to myself as I walked down Fifth.

There was something about Daniel that was so captivating, it made me forget who I was. I was not usually attracted to men like him. I knew the type. Rich and only cared about themselves. I'd tried pitching to enough of them to know. They didn't care about a nonprofit or helping children, let alone anyone. I could hardly get anything out of them. They were cold and calculated, unless they wanted something from you. And usually that was getting you into bed with them.

Here I was, thinking about what it would be like to be in bed with *him*. Despite this ridiculous fantasy, he seemed interested. Sure, it was probably for the tax write-off, or the accolades or the *Forbes* article that would surely be printed. Either way, my boss would be happy.

Before descending down the stairs to the subway and the land of no service, I typed out a quick email to my boss. I let him know the meeting went better than expected, and that Mr. Jacobs would be visiting the offices tomorrow morning, but had requested the tour be with me. I hit *send* before tucking my phone in my purse and making my way downstairs to the platform.

My train arrived five minutes later. I found a seat and leaned my head against the window as it jolted to life and made its way back to Brooklyn. A place that seemed far from Daniel Jacobs in more ways than one.

As I trudged up the stairs to my apartment, I noticed Elma's door was open. I could sense her waiting to pounce, like her cat. I snuck past silently, wanting to avoid any questions about my meeting with Daniel. I made it successfully up to my apartment. As I searched for my keys, my phone rang in my purse. I slid it out. It was my boss.

"Hey, Brian. Did you get my email?" I answered, holding the phone between my cheek and shoulder.

"Yeah, I did. Uh, what's with this tour tomorrow?"

"Oh, Mr. Jacobs just wants to see more of what we are about before he makes a decision, but I'm confident he will be our newest donor."

"That's all well and good, but what's this about the tour being with you?" he asked skeptically.

"I don't know. He was adamant about it."

Brian paused on the other line. "All right. Don't screw this up, Heartly."

I rolled my eyes. I had gotten us this far.

"I won't. See you tomorrow."

Hanging up, I unlocked my door, stepped inside and kicked off my shoes, looking around my small abode. Daniel's office was five times the size of this. We were definitely worlds apart.

I unzipped the back of my hellish skirt and slid it off, tossing it on the floor by my bed. I didn't plan on wearing that again any time soon. When Daniel came to the office tomorrow, he would see we don't really do office attire there. It was more like a smart casual dress code. One that didn't require tweed skirts with no give, thank God.

I walked to the kitchen in just my button-down and underwear and pulled a bottle of cabernet from the wine rack. While I normally didn't drink during the week, tonight, I could use a glass or two. I took my wine opener and unscrewed the cork, the familiar sound soft popping from the opening. I took a swig from the bottle before grabbing a glass from the cabinet.

After I poured a somewhat generous serving, I moved to sit on the couch, grabbing my laptop on the way. I plopped down and took another sip of wine before opening my laptop. I had some Googling to do. I typed *Daniel Jacobs* into my search bar and his face popped up immediately. It was such a common name, but he took precedence in the search results. His pictures didn't do him justice. They were good, but he was better in the flesh.

I scrolled through, seeing nothing new that I hadn't read in the file Brian had given me. I switched over to the "news" tab and intermixed with articles on his latest business deals were tabloid articles. This was what I was looking for.

The headlines read:

Three Girls in One Night? Daniel Jacobs At It Again!
Will New York's Biggest Playboy Ever Settle Down?
Caught With a New Leading Lady!

I read through the tabloids and studied the paparazzi photos glaring at me from the screen. All the women he was with were stunning, and never the same ones in the photos. My stomach growled as it craved Ling's Dynasty. I wondered if these women were ever as hungry as I was. If they were, they sure didn't show it. I noticed their slender arms and long legs on display in skintight dresses that hugged their small midsections.

I saw his fingers interlaced with theirs. His hand on the smalls of their backs. His lips on their ears, exchanging intimate secrets. I felt that familiar pang of jealousy I had earlier while scheduling my meeting with his assistant, Margaret. I closed my laptop and slid it across the couch with a sigh.

I took another swig of wine before calling in a takeout order for Chinese food. Then I laughed to myself as I sprawled out on the couch. Daniel Jacobs would never be interested in me. It seemed to calm my nerves slightly for tomorrow's meeting.

Chapter 4

DANIEL

There was a knock at my office door and I prayed it wasn't a meeting I overlooked or Margaret with another question. She was new, so it was to be expected. While she was mostly smart, I didn't really hire her for her professional skills. I glanced at my watch and let out a frustrated sigh before acknowledging whoever was at my door.

"Yes, come in," I said, leaning back in my chair and preparing to give another mini tutorial of my digital calendar.

The door swung open and my brother strolled inside like he owned the place, which he did. Well, half, anyway.

"Hey, bro," he greeted with a smirk.

I rolled my eyes and watched as he leaned against the wall and crossed his arms, looking at me like he had something up his sleeve. It was never good.

"What is it, Brody?" I asked.

"Hey, can't I just come and see my big bro?" he asked, putting his hands up innocently.

Doubtful, I thought to myself.

"I'm just about to head out."

"Gotta rush home and get ready for tonight, right?"

I wanted to wipe that smirk off his face. I loved my brother, but he was the definition of the annoying younger sibling, and it had only gotten worse with age.

"Yes, Brody. I know the auction is tonight."

"And?"

"And what?" I snapped, standing up from my chair and grabbing my jacket.

I slid it on and grabbed my briefcase, avoiding my brother's amused expression.

"Don't tell me you forgot about the bet. You lost, Daniel."

"I didn't forget."

"Okay, good. Because I invited my friends and we are looking for some entertainment tonight."

"It's a charity event, Brody. Not a frat party."

"I know that. It's just a few buddies from college."

I pinched the bridge of my nose and tried to be patient. My brother was my COO, and while I would think he would be able to differentiate work from his social life, it wasn't always the case. It was probably because he didn't always have to be on his best behavior, like I did. Even though that was seldom the case. I was just better at being private about it, except for those damn paparazzi. All eyes were on me all the time.

"Fine," I said, walking toward the door.

"Don't be such a sore loser, bro." Brody patted me on the back as he followed me out into the hallway.

"I'll see you tonight," I said, shrugging him off and walking toward the elevator.

I was in no mood to pay my dues tonight, but he was right. I had lost the bet we made a few weeks ago. It was stupid really, but that was what happened when you'd had a few double whiskeys on the rocks.

I couldn't remember whose idea it was, but the bet was to see who could get this particular girl in bed first. She was a smoking-hot redhead who was doing bottle service at a club in New York. We were there on business. Pleasure, too. Brody took her back to his hotel room, but I called bullshit because I was pretty sure he paid her to leave her post early. It must have been a generous sum of money because she most likely lost her job. We should have come up with better terms, but I didn't think prostitution was on the table.

Either way, I lost. And now I was to be auctioned off at tonight's charity function. It was one of our biggest fundraisers of the year. Turned out the rich, older women of New York threw down lots of money to have a day or night with eligible CEOs. While I wasn't really in the mood to stand up on stage in a penguin suit waiting to see what unfortunate fate I ended up with, I knew it would look good in the press.

I needed that right now. Again, those damn paparazzi. My latest scandal was splashed all over the papers and gossip pages on Instagram. I shouldn't be that surprised. I had been caught leaving the club with three busty blondes, and they were photographed leaving my hotel the next morning. All their eyes rimmed with mascara, like little platinum blonde raccoons squinting their eyes in the harsh reality of the morning.

As I rode the elevator down to the lobby, I smiled to myself thinking about that night. I'd been with several women before, but three at the same time was a first. I couldn't keep their names straight, but there wasn't much talking, anyway. I was just happy that the hotel room had a California King bed.

Despite the backlash in the press, I still thought it was worth it. But now there was damage control to do. The money we raised tonight would be a perfect Band-Aid, until some other scandal arose. Hopefully, it wouldn't be mine.

The elevator doors opened to the lobby cast in an orange glow, as the sun was setting. I nodded to the front desk as I passed. The security guard opened the door and I stepped out onto the sidewalk where my driver waited. He opened the car door and I slid into the backseat. A glass of whiskey with a large steel ice cube sat in the cupholder. He knew me so well.

"Thank you, Armand," I said, taking a sip as he slid into the driver's seat.

"Of course, Mr. Daniels. Home?"

"Yes, please."

The car slowly pulled away from the curb and began the five-minute drive to my condo, which sat high above the city. My phone pinged in my jacket pocket. I slid it out and saw it was a calendar notification Margaret forwarded me. I was surprised she even knew how to do that.

Tomorrow. 10 AM meeting at the Leading to Learn offices.

That was fast. I wasn't expecting to see Addison so soon, but I wasn't complaining. I wanted to know more about her. The ins and outs. I was excited just thinking about it. The effect she had on me was new. It was intoxicating. I took a sip of whiskey and leaned my head back, closing my eyes and trying to remember the lines of her, curving in all the right places.

Soon, the car pulled into the parking garage, the carriage overcome with darkness as we descended to my private level. Armand parked by the elevators and came around to open the door for me.

"Thank you, Armand. Be back here at seven. In the meantime, go grab some dinner."

I handed him a one-hundred-dollar bill. He nodded gratefully as I strode past him. I rode up to the top floor, the elevator doors sliding open to reveal my condo. The city lights fought to compete with the sunset that was now turning to a purply dusk.

I had an hour before I had to head to the auction. It was being held at the Met. Traffic would be a bitch, and I didn't want to be late. I walked down the dim hallway to my master bedroom and found my tux lying on the bed, freshly pressed. My housekeeper must have dropped it off earlier.

I'd rather put on a pair of sweats than this thing, but duty called. I quickly took a shower and dressed. After I made sure my bowtie was straight, I ran some gel through my damp hair, and sprayed a generous amount of cologne.

I decided to make myself another drink to calm my nerves. Whiskey neat. The usual. Before I knew it, it was time to leave. I rode the elevator down, and as the doors opened, I caught Armand tossing a bag of McDonald's in the trash. It wouldn't have been my first choice if I had a hundred to spend, but I knew he had mouths to feed at home. I pretended like I didn't see and waited for him to open the car door.

Like I expected, traffic was awful, but we still managed to get to the Met in time. The red carpet was already alive with some of New York's wealthiest businessmen and women. I never wanted to be the first one on that thing, so I was glad we were arriving when we did. As the car pulled up and Armand rounded the back to open the door, I saw the paparazzi whip their heads around.

I took a deep breath and plastered a smile on my face as the car door opened. I gave a wave and made my way up the steps toward the red carpet. The camera flashes were blinding, but I was used to it. Almost.

I posed for a few photos on the red carpet before excusing myself and making my way inside. Cocktail tables with crisp white linen were sprinkled around the vast room. Chilled champagne was being passed around on silver strays. A jazz band played upbeat music on the stage I'd be standing on in a short while.

I made small talk with a few guests before heading to the banquet table to load a plate with hors d'oeuvres. My stomach felt unsettled. Maybe it was the whiskey on an empty stomach. I was starting to think Armand had the right idea with a Big Mac. As I made a meal out of the caviar and bruschetta, I spotted my ex-girlfriend. Kiera.

Her long blonde hair was pulled into a tight updo that sat atop her head, revealing the smooth skin of her back that was exposed in a plunging, backless, emerald-green dress. She looked good. Part of me wanted to go to her. We always had fun, but I knew better.

I turned my head to avoid her searching gaze as she looked in my direction. I should have known she'd be here. She was usually at these events, especially if I was hosting. Hell, I probably invited her. I couldn't remember the guest list. It wasn't like we ended on bad terms or anything. We're friendly. I knew she wanted more, but I wasn't looking to get married any more than she was looking for anything other than my money.

Kiera had already been married and divorced. Twice. To two successful businessmen on the East Coast. Not as successful of me, of course, but successful enough to earn her a decent sum of money. One that most people wouldn't see in a lifetime. Still, it didn't seem to be enough for her. She wanted the next big fish, and that would be me.

I heard the auctioneer come on the microphone, announcing the auction was about to begin. I saw my brother and his friends snickering in the corner as they waited for me to take the stage. I was sure I'd be saved for last. Enough time to have more caviar, and another drink.

At the bar, I heard eligible bachelors going for thousands of dollars. Even tens of thousands of dollars. It was ridiculous, but at least we were raising money. The inner city youth clubs would be happy, even if the money was earned in this humiliating way. This wasn't exactly a kid-friendly type of fundraiser. It was practically escorting.

I heard the auctioneer over the speakers.

"And now, ladies and gentlemen, but mostly you ladies. We have our final bachelor of the night. I've saved the best for last. Daniel Jacobs, make your way to the stage."

I put on a grin that I hoped was convincing and walked up the steps. I saw hands flying up in the air and obscene amounts of money being shouted out quickly. I could hardly keep up with what was going on. After a few minutes, the auctioneer slammed his gavel down and shouted, "Sold!" I squinted out at the crowd to see who my buyer was, and that was when I saw Kiera making her way to the stage to claim her prize.

Chapter 5

ADDISON

I woke up and saw it was still dark out, and wondered what time it was. I was in that weird state where I was curious to know what time it actually was, but scared it would say it was about to be morning. I wondered if I even slept at all with all the tossing and turning last night. Maybe it was because of the combination of Chinese food and wine. It usually made for some strange dreams. However, this time I was pretty sure Daniel was in them.

I rolled over and reached for my phone to check the time. As I picked it up, the glare of the screen was blinding. It was just as I feared: 5 a.m. Now that I knew it was morning and I had to be up in an hour anyway, there was no way I'd be able to go back to sleep, if that was what I was doing anyway.

Sighing, I rolled onto my back and stared at my ceiling. Maybe I couldn't sleep because I was going to see Daniel again in a few hours. The thought of our meeting sent my heart into high gear. I inhaled a deep breath.

"Chill out, Heart," I whispered to myself.

Heart was what my family and closest friends called me. An easy nickname, given my last name was Heartly.

I pushed the covers off me and swung my legs so my feet met the cool hardwood floor. The sun's rays begin to peek out over the buildings in dull orange and pink colors behind the clouds.

I padded to the kitchen and put on a pot of coffee, the smell of freshly ground beans rising up to greet and wake me up. I picked them up yesterday from my favorite coffee shop. The coffee began to brew and I looked through the calendar on my phone. There wasn't much going on today besides the meeting with Daniel, which was somehow synced in my phone with his. It felt oddly intimate to have our calendars so friendly.

I poured myself a cup of coffee and curled up on the couch. I switched on the lamp next to me, its warm glow covered me and the corner of the couch. I reached for my book on the coffee table. It was a romance novel I'd practically devoured. I had to get love where I could, and for a while now, it had been in the pages of books.

For the next hour, I got lost in my book, turning the pages quickly to see what happened next. I was just about to get to the end when there was a knock at my door. I jumped slightly. Who would be here this early in the morning? I folded the ear of my page before closing my book, and tossed it on the couch.

"Who is it?" I called out.

"It's me!" my friend Monica called through the door.

Shit. I forgot we said we would go on an early morning run. It was my idea. My stupid idea.

"Coming," I said as I walked to the door.

I opened it and found her in leggings and a workout top. Her strawberry blonde hair was pulled back in a ponytail. She gave me a once-over in my striped pajamas and furrowed her brow.

"You forgot, didn't you?"

"I did," I said, pushing the door open and letting her into my apartment.

She helped herself to a cup of coffee, making herself right at home. As usual.

"I think I was a little tipsy when I came up with the idea," I admitted.

I had been all gung-ho about starting a workout routine and eating healthy on our last girls' night out. Over wine and bruschetta, it oddly seemed like a good idea to get into fitness.

"Do you want a croissant?" I offered, reaching for the box of pastries I had picked up yesterday with the coffee beans.

"Hmm...running or a croissant..." she said, scrunching up her face as if deep in thought.

She held out her hand. I laughed as I put an almond croissant on a plate and handed it to her. She took a bite and closed her eyes in appreciation for the flaky sweetness that I was about to bite into myself.

We took our pastries to the couch and sat down.

"We could take up running another day," I offered.

She shot me a look like she didn't believe me. Then her eyes fell to the book next to her on the couch.

"Reading my competition, huh?" she asked, picking it up and inspecting the cover.

Monica was a romance writer. A good one. She was popular in the indie scene, but hadn't made it big just yet. She was always looking for her next story, but it was too bad I couldn't lend her any inspiration.

"What do you think of it so far?" she asked, turning the book over in her hands.

"I'm practically finished. It's really good. You know I love the enemies to lovers trope."

She nodded.

"But it wasn't as good as yours," I added quickly.

"Oh, stop," she said, waving me off. "It was good. I read it last month. I've been trying to find inspiration anywhere and everywhere. I'm in a writer's rut."

"Well, I wish I could help you out with that..." I sighed.

"I wish I could help myself out." She laughed.

She took a sip of coffee and turned to me as if remembering something. "Hey, how did your meeting go yesterday?"

"Good," I said, hoping the high pitch of my voice didn't give me away.

She raised an eyebrow at me. She knew me too well.

"What's up with you?" she asked.

"Nothing." My voice was even more shrill.

"Spill."

I sucked in a breath before letting it go through my lips. "I had a meeting with this big wig. His name was Daniel Jacobs, and—"

"Wait. *The* Daniel Jacobs?"

Why did everyone keep saying that?

"Yeah..."

"The like hottest man in New York."

"See, how does everyone know this, but me?" I fell back into the couch and crossed my arms as if I hadn't been invited to some imaginary party.

"He is like on every gossip site."

"You know I don't care about that kind of stuff."

"Well, neither do I, but it makes for some good book inspo sometimes. Hey, maybe I could write about him. What's he like?"

"He's...a businessman," I answered nonchalantly as I avoided her gaze.

"Oh my God. You have a thing for him," said Monica excitedly.

"I do not." I could feel the smile creeping over my lips, giving my lie away.

I couldn't have a thing for him. I barely knew him. Although, he did keep me up all night. Well, the thought of him did.

Monica clapped her hands excitedly like a baby seal, and I couldn't help but laugh at how ridiculous she was.

"This is so exciting," she squealed.

"Nothing happened, Monica," I defend.

"Yet."

I rolled my eyes before giving her a little morsel that I knew would indulge her.

"I do have another meeting with him this morning. He wanted to tour Leading to Learn, and he kind of insisted that I be his guide."

"Oh my God," she squealed. "He is into you."

"No, he is not." I laughed.

She stood up quickly and grabbed my hand, pulling me from the couch.

"To the closet! We have to get you ready!"

I struggled to keep up with my manic best friend as she pulled me into my tiny closet that I was surprised we both fit in. She began pulling hangers and clothes frantically from the rack, tossing most of them on the ground. She finally landed on a camel-colored leather skirt and a sleeveless blouse, paired with ballet flats.

"This is it," she said, shoving the clothes at me.

I stumbled backward out of the closet.

"Put it on," she demanded.

I knew there was no use in arguing. When Monica had her mind on something, there was really no getting out of it. I shimmied out of my pajamas and pulled the blouse over my head, and slid the skirt on. This was more a girls' night out outfit than a work outfit, but after I glanced in the mirror, I had to admit I looked pretty good.

I spun to appease her.

"That's it. That's it right there," she said with an approving nod.

I took another look in the mirror and was brought back to reality. After looking through the paparazzi photos of Daniel and his many conquests, my confidence took a dive. Even in this outfit, he would never be interested in me. The doubt must have been transparent on my face because Monica took a step toward me.

"What's wrong?" she asked.

"This was just stupid. I hardly know the guy, and even if I did like him or think he was handsome, he would never go for me."

"Why not?"

"Because I'm not stick-thin and don't walk on a runway."

"Who wants a girl who only eats romaine lettuce, anyway?" Monica rolled her eyes.

I laughed softly. "We're not in the same tax bracket. Hell, we're not even on the same planet."

Monica put her hands on my shoulders and turned me toward her for one of her famous pep talks.

"You are beautiful. You are smart. You are worthy," she said, her eyes narrowing.

I smiled and shook my head.

"Say it," she demanded.

"Seriously?"

"Say it."

"I am beautiful. I am smart. I am worthy," I mumbled, feeling like a total idiot.

"That's more like it," she said, releasing me.

"I should probably finish getting ready. I don't want to be late, and I have to prepare my office."

"Yeah, you do. You're going to get busy on your desk," quipped Monica, doing a little booty shake.

I reached down and picked up a pair of jeans, throwing them at her. She laughed as she walked toward the door.

"I want a full report later," she sing-songed, opening the door and stepping out into the hallway.

"There won't be anything to report," I called after her in the same voice.

I finished my cup of coffee and walked to the bathroom. I brushed my teeth. Twice. And moisturized my face before adding some light makeup. Concealer, mascara, and a swipe of gloss. I didn't want it to look like I was trying too hard. I ran a brush through my hair and pulled it into a low bun. I gave myself a little nod, as if it were a stamp of approval, and headed for the door.

I made the 8 a.m. train and began my ride into the city, my nerves growing as each stop passed. I repeated Monica's little pep talk over and over in my head. I could do this. It was just a meeting. I'd done it before. I'd do it again. I just needed to land him as a donor, and then I didn't have to see him again.

When I arrived at the office twenty minutes later, Bryan found me quickly to ensure I was prepared. I could tell he was a little irked that he was not running the tour, but it wasn't in my hands. After our quick brief, he left my office. I started doing a fast tidy- up, making sure everything looked organized and professional. Before I knew it, it was 9:45. He would be here in fifteen minutes.

I sat at my desk and tried to calm my beating heart that felt like it was about to escape my throat. Taking a sip of water, I drummed my fingers nervously on the surface of my desk. I glanced around and laughed to myself. Look how different our offices were. We had absolutely nothing in common. In a way, it helped ease my nerves. If I had no chance, then what was there to be so scared of?

Soon, there was a knock at my door.

"Yes?" I asked, my voice jumping an octave.

The girl from the front desk poked her head in.

"Your ten o'clock is here."

I nodded, and she pushed the door open to reveal Daniel standing there. There was no mistaking who he was today. He was in a freshly pressed navy suit and a white button-down. His hair was pushed effortlessly to the side and there was an unreadable expression across his full lips.

My breath hitched and my knees felt weak, but I pushed myself to stand as he entered my office. I took a step toward him and held out my hand, but then faltered when I saw he was not alone.

Chapter 6

DANIEL

I saw Addison hesitate as she noticed Kiera enter the room behind me. It was only for a moment before she put a smile, one that I knew was not genuine, and held out her hand again for me to shake. I took it and firmly shook it, reluctant to let go as that same electricity flowed through my fingertips and the rest of my body.

There was no way she didn't feel it too, that she didn't feel it yesterday. Was that why there was a look of disappointment to see I had brought another woman with me today?

It wasn't by choice. I was following the auction rules, which stated I had to spend an entire day with the woman who bid the most on me. Of course, that woman was Kiera. I was still trying to get back in the public's good graces, so I had to play along.

Kiera was a stubborn one. I was not her boyfriend anymore, but that didn't mean she wouldn't stop at any means to nudge her way into my life. Even if it did cost her $200,000. It was an exorbitant amount of money, but I had no interest in entertaining her today, no matter how much she spent. The auction rules didn't state what we had to do, so she was at work with me for the day.

It almost felt like a *bring your child to work* kind of day, and my child was a stuck-up brat who ironically enough had called me "daddy" in the bedroom.

"Mr. Jacobs, please come in. Excuse my small office. I have to find another chair for your, er, guest."

Addison quickly slid past Kiera and me and out into the hallway, leaving Kiera and me alone.

"What is this place, Daniel? I thought we were going to do something fun," griped Kiera, shooting me a look.

"It's a work day." I shrugged. "Not all of us can live off divorce money and shop at Barney's all day."

Kiera rolled her eyes and leaned against the doorframe. She looked ridiculous in a champagne slip dress and strappy heels. Where did she think I was taking her on a Tuesday morning? Then a thought came to me. She probably looked like this for the paparazzi who had been staking out my place since after last night's auction. They'd already taken several photos of us since—leaving my place, to getting coffee, to coming here. While I didn't want the public thinking Kiera and I were an item again, at least visiting a nonprofit would look good for me.

I ignored Kiera and took a look around Addison's office, trying to find little things that would tell me more about her. I didn't have time though because I heard a grunt outside the door and glanced up to see Addison carrying a heavy armchair. She set it down with a loud clunk and I couldn't help but notice the little bit of cleavage that peeked through her blouse. I wondered if they were real. If so, she was blessed.

I got my mind out of the gutter and walked toward her as she caught her breath.

"Here, let me," I offered.

I grabbed the chair and lifted it with ease through the doorway of her office, setting it down across from her desk.

"Thank you," she said, tucking a strand of hair behind her ear. "Please, sit down."

I sat down and watched as she walked to her seat, ignoring Kiera, who huffed beside me. Addison wore a camel skirt. It was shorter than the one she wore yesterday, revealing her creamy thighs. I imagined my hands sliding up them, feeling their smoothness, but then she slid behind her desk and my train of thought was broken.

Addison looked from me to Kiera, and I realized I hadn't introduced the two of them.

"Addison, this is Kiera. Kiera, this is Addison."

I decided to keep it simple because explaining that Kiera was my ex was not something I wanted to get into, and explaining the ridiculous notion of auctioning myself off was embarrassing. Kiera gave Addison a curt smile, which Addison took with grace.

"Very nice to meet you," she said.

"I'm hoping you can tell me a little more about Leading to Learn and what you do here," I said, leaning forward and placing my hands on the desk. I caught a whiff of her vanilla perfume again. Sweet, but also with a note of spice I hadn't noticed yesterday.

"Of course. Well, as you know, we are a nonprofit. We were formed around five years ago after our founder traveled abroad on his honeymoon. While traveling, he had come across several regions that were underdeveloped, leading to a lack of education for the children who resided there. He wanted to give back, and that's how we came about."

"Who would want to honeymoon in poor countries?" asked Kiera. "Sounds like a nightmare."

Addison looked at Kiera, and I saw a small amount of disdain cross her face before she answered sweetly.

"Our founder is fond of giving back. They planned their honeymoon so there was a mix of pleasure and charity work."

"That poor wife."

"Actually, it was her idea," said Addison.

Kiera let out a small laugh through her nose and inspected her nails.

"I like that idea," I said to Addison, hoping she didn't think I shared the same lack of values as Kiera. I was no saint, but I also was not a total asshole.

Addison gave me a smile and continued to tell me more about the nonprofit, and I did my best to concentrate. The way her mouth moved was distracting. Her lips were almost too pouty to fully close, and they were lacquered with a shiny gloss I wish I could taste. Plus, there was that small mole above her lip that was sexy as hell. I wondered if she knew it.

"Would you like the tour now?" asked Addison.

I met her gaze and wondered if she knew my eyes had been wandering, and my thoughts had wandered even further.

"A tour?" huffed Kiera.

"That would be great," I replied.

I wished Kiera would just stay in the office so I could have time alone with Addison. That was why I had set up this whole meeting in the first place. I heard the *click-clack* of Kiera's heels behind me as I followed Addison around the building. I watched as her hips swished back and forth in the leather skirt that hugged her like it loved the hell out of her.

I met a few people around the office and saw others' curious expressions as we passed by. I didn't blame them. Here was a billionaire CEO who probably looked like a drooling dog following their coworker, and behind him was a heavily Botoxed woman dressed as if she was going to a cocktail party.

We ended the tour back in Addison's office, where she looked at me hopefully. I realized all I wanted to do was please her, in more ways than one.

"Well, what do you think?" she asked.

"I like it here. I think this could be a very good fit for me," I said, a smile spreading across my lips. I hoped she caught my subtle innuendo.

I saw Addison's cheeks turn a rosy pink. She did.

"Th-that's great," she stammered, shuffling some papers on her desk.

I had her flustered.

"I'll meet with my financial advisor and draw up papers sometime this week," I commented.

"Sure. Okay. Thank you so much. This is really going to benefit so many kids."

Kiera made a sound that was full of disgust.

Addison and I looked at her, as if we had forgotten she was here.

"Oh, I just don't like kids," defended Kiera with a shrug.

"Well, we should be going," I said, standing from my chair and eager to get out of there before Kiera embarrassed me further.

Addison stood and followed us to the door.

"It was a pleasure meeting you," she said.

"The pleasure was mine."

I held her gaze for a moment too long, because Kiera cleared her throat loudly, breaking whatever spell we were under. I followed Kiera down the hallway, the sound of *click- clacking* echoing as we went. I turned to get another glance of Addison, but she was already closing her office door. An unfamiliar feeling of disappointment washed over me. I didn't like it.

Outside the office, Kiera had wiped off her sour expression and was all smiles at the familiar sounds of cameras flashing surrounding us. I nodded solemnly at the paparazzi and made a beeline for my car where Armand waited. He quickly opened the door and I slid inside. A few seconds later, Kiera joined me.

"Could we do something *fun* now?" she whined, crossing her arms like a pouting child.

"Like what?"

"Shopping and then lunch at the Ritz sounds nice," she offered.

We spent the next couple of hours shopping at Bloomingdales. Kiera dragged me to the fitting rooms with her as she tried on gowns, shoes, and jewelry. We were offered a bottle of champagne, which made Kiera giddy, even though I knew it was just a tactic to get you to buy more when you were all boozed up.

"I think you'll like this next one," called out Kiera from the fitting room.

I took another miserable sip of champagne as I waited for her to come out. She pushed the curtains open and strutted out in a red lacy set of lingerie. She looked good. Too good. Her breasts were lifted high and I could make out the soft color of her nipples through the lace. Her matching stockings were connected to the tiniest lace fabric, leaving very little to the imagination. I felt myself getting aroused. I had to hand it to her, she knew how to work a man. She did a turn and stumbled slightly, tipsy from the champagne. She plopped down in my lap.

"Let's skip dinner and go to your place," she whispered in my ear.

A part of me wanted to take her right here in the dressing room. It wasn't like I hadn't done it before. But another part of me couldn't get my mind off Addison. I wondered what she would feel like on my lap, my hands against her skin, feeling the lace of lingerie hugging her in all the right places.

Kiera noticed my hesitation and pounced.

"Or you could follow me in that dressing room and I would give you the best blow job of your life," she whispered before her teeth surrounded my earlobe and pulled lightly.

I swallowed hard before placing my hands on her hips and guiding her off me.

"We should probably get some food in you and get you home," I said, trying to hide the reluctance in my voice.

It was rare I turned down sex. I was honestly questioning who I was in this moment, but my thoughts were somewhere else. With someone else.

Kiera stumbled backward and looked at me with a scrutinizing look before going back into the fitting room. But not before she called me an asshole.

Chapter 7

ADDISON

I heard a knock at my door that broke me from whatever daze I'd been in for the past few hours since Daniel left my office with that awful woman. The whole meeting had put me into a bad mood, which was ridiculous because I practically landed him as our newest donor. Our biggest one yet.

Still, I couldn't help but feel slighted by the morning. Here I was thinking it was going to be something more, when in fact, it couldn't have been more the opposite. I felt foolish for being swept up in whatever fantasy I had thought up. I blamed Monica for putting her silly romance plot inside my head.

Another knock sounded at my door.

"Come in," I said, pretending to busy myself with something on my laptop.

Brian poked his head in before the rest of him followed. "How did it go?" he asked, taking a seat across from me.

I mustered up the proudest smile I could. "Daniel Jacobs is Leading to Learn's newest donor."

Brian slapped his hand on the desk loudly before leaning back in his chair and looking at me in awe.

"Holy shit, Addison," he said.

"I know." I shook my head because I still couldn't believe it.

"You did it."

I didn't like the sort of disbelief in his tone of voice, but I ignored it because I was somewhat in disbelief myself.

"I guess so." I shrugged.

"You should celebrate. Go home early."

I didn't feel like there was really anything to celebrate, but it would be better to be miserable in the comfort of my loft than here in my office.

"Really?" I asked.

"Really."

Brian stood and headed out the door. "Good job today," he said before slipping out.

I gathered my things and stood to leave, my leather skirt loudly peeling from the surface of my chair. I looked down and thought how ridiculous this outfit choice was. I let out a sigh and shut my laptop before heading out the door.

As I walked toward the subway station, my phone pinged in my purse. It was Monica:

How was it?

I wasn't in the mood to talk about it, so I slipped my phone back in my purse before descending the stairs to the platform below. The train to Brooklyn blurred past me. I missed it. I frustratedly plopped down in a row of metal chairs, the chill of the metal biting into my bare skin. This skirt was way too short.

I wondered for a millisecond if that was why I landed this deal, but quickly shook it off. Daniel Jacobs was a businessman. A majorly successful CEO. He didn't make deals based on how short a woman's skirt was. Plus, even if he did, I wasn't his type. That was made crystal clear when I saw Kiera. Even her name screamed classes above mine.

The only thing that made me feel better was knowing I was a good person. As much as I kept it together during our meeting, I could feel a fire of slight rage growing inside me brought on by Kiera's privileged attitude. I couldn't believe the way she rolled her eyes or looked down on people who wanted to make a difference in the lives of those less fortunate than them.

I wondered how Daniel could stand to be around someone like that, but maybe that was just how rich people were. Really, I was better off not knowing him, or being involved with him in whatever fantasy I had conjured in my head. Still, I couldn't help but think about the moments our hands had touched, creating their own kind of fire in the pit of my stomach.

There were times today I could have sworn his eyes lingered a little too long in places they probably shouldn't have. I didn't even feel upset by it. If it was desire from him, it only made me want him more. It was over now, though.

The next train to Brooklyn rumbled down the tracks, causing the platform to shake slightly. I stood up and walked toward it, the breeze from the fast train blowing against my face. I looked around at my fellow commuters. This was just another reminder of how different mine and Daniel Jacobs's worlds were.

When I arrived home to my apartment, I turned my phone off. I decided to take a true afternoon off. From work, from the world, from Monica's questioning. I'd disappoint her tomorrow with the news that I wouldn't be the inspiration for her next romance novel.

I drew a hot bubble bath and peeled the leather skirt off of my body, tossing it on the floor next to the gray one from yesterday. Two things I wouldn't be wearing again for a long time. I stepped into the tub and inhaled a deep breath as the hot water surrounded me like a cozy sweater. I read the rest of my book, and while the ending gave me the happily ever after I desired, I couldn't help but feel sorry for myself.

Finished, I tossed it aside, watching it skid across the tile floor until it came to a stop against the wall with a dull *thunk*. I sucked in a breath before I submerged my head underwater, thoroughly washing the day away.

The rest of the evening I spent on my couch watching horror movies and eating leftover Chinese food from the night before. I bit down on a soggy egg roll as I watched the killer slowly stalk toward his next victim, a helpless prom queen getting ready for the big dance. Probably not the best thing to watch when I lived alone, but I couldn't take another romcom. Not today.

The next morning, on my way to work, I stopped by the newsstands for today's paper. I saw the racks were plastered with Daniel's face and a headline that made my stomach sink:

Is NYC's Infamous Bachelor Finally Settling Down?

I snatched it off the shelf quickly and slid a few bucks across the small counter to the attendant. I jogged down the stairs of the subway station and quickly hopped onto the train to Manhattan. Luckily, I spotted a seat and quickly claimed it before opening up today's paper.

I frantically turned the pages until I landed on the article I was looking for. There were Daniel and Kiera walking into Bloomingdale's together. This must be from yesterday because he was wearing that same well-fitted suit and his hair was perfectly in place. I stared at him for a moment before my eyes landed on her in that obnoxiously slinky dress that hugged her petite body perfectly. A ridiculous thing to wear to a work meeting, but she practically came alive on the pages of a newspaper. I wondered if it was an intentional wardrobe choice.

I noticed in the picture that she was all smiles. Not in a cheesy, toothy-grinned kind of way, but in a sly, close-lipped way that said she was holding onto a secret. Daniel, on the other hand, looked perturbed. His lips pressed together tightly. He looked like he wanted to be anywhere else, but that could just be because of the paparazzi. I couldn't imagine being followed day and night by the flash and sounds of cameras.

My eyes reluctantly left his face and landed on the title of the article:

Daniel Jacobs and Kiera Shipley Are Back On!

The couple made their first public debut yesterday when they were spotted leaving Jacobs' penthouse apartment in the mid-morning hours. Shipley wore a champagne-colored, floor-length gown, and Jacob wore a custom suit. The couple were sharply dressed as they stopped for coffee at a nearby café. They sat by the window and looked deep in conversation, and were very touchy-feely.

I swallowed hard as I read that last part, and saw the photo that accompanied it. Kiera's hands were on Daniel's arm as he took a sip of coffee. She looked completely enamored by him. And why wouldn't she be? He made drinking coffee look like it was a freaking ad for Gucci.

I continued reading:

As we know, the couple has been on and off since they met in college. She was there through his come-up, and seems deserving of taking the role of leading lady in his life.

While we weren't able to get a statement from Jacobs, we were able to get in touch with Kiera's publicist to ask a few questions.

You and Daniel seem to have a history that you can't seem to let go of. Could you tell us more about that?

I met Daniel in college. I was a sophomore. He was a senior. I'm completely enamored by him and his drive. I mean, look where it has gotten him. We've lost each other a few times since then, but we always seem to find our way back to each other.

And where do the two of you stand now?

We're getting to know each other in this current stage of life. Timing is everything. This may just be our time.

With your somewhat unlucky past with love, could marriage be in the cards?

I think Daniel was always my person. As far as getting married again goes, I never say never.

I closed the paper a little too abruptly, startling the older man sitting next to me.

"Sorry," I mumbled.

I couldn't believe how worked up I was about this. About someone I hardly even knew.

The train slowed to a stop. I realized it was already my stop. I had gotten so wrapped up in the article, I hadn't been paying attention. Tucking the paper under my arm, I slung my purse over my shoulder, exiting the train.

As I emerged onto the sidewalk, my phone rang. It was Monica. I groaned. I had ignored her text from yesterday, and then a call from this morning after I turned my phone back on.

"Hello?" I answered as brightly as I could.

"Uh, hello. Where have you been?" she asked with a tinge of annoyance.

"Sorry, I decided to unplug yesterday. Brian let me go home early."

"Oh no! Are you feeling okay?"

"Oh, I'm fine. I'm not sick. I actually think I got Mr. Jacobs to make a deal with us, so Brian let me leave early as a reward or something."

"Mr. Jacobs..." said Monica slowly, as if she was processing it. "Well, holy shit, Heart. That's amazing. I told you that leather skirt would work."

"Oh, come on. Couldn't you chalk it up to my outstanding people skills?"

I heard her laugh on the other line before falling silent again.

"But what's with this morning's papers? I thought he had a thing for you?"

"Uh, no. He doesn't. You assumed he did because that's how a romance writer's brain works."

"Pfft. Whatever."

"He actually brought Kiera with him to the meeting, so I would say it's pretty serious."

"Wait, she was there?" asked Monica loudly.

"Yep."

"What the hell?"

"I know. She was not the nicest person in the world either."

"Spill."

I told Monica about the snarky way Kiera greeted me, if you could even call it that. And about her attitude toward charity work and children.

"She sounds nice," said Monica sarcastically.

"I don't know what he sees in her," I agreed.

"Boobs. He sees boobs."

I laughed out loud. Monica always made me feel better. I should have just talked to her yesterday before I fell into a stupid depression with egg rolls and slasher films.

"Well, I'm sorry, Heart. Clearly the guy lives up to his reputation," said Monica.

"It's okay. I'm actually getting to the office now. Back to reality. Sorry I couldn't be the material you needed for your bestseller."

"You're my best friend. That's all I need."

I smiled as I said goodbye and walked through the door to my work. At least I had this as a distraction.

Chapter 8

DANIEL

I slammed this morning's paper down on my desk, startling Margaret, who had just appeared in my doorway holding a cup of coffee. I saw it spill slightly on her cream skirt, but she ignored it before walking over to set it on my desk.

"Sorry," I muttered.

I pulled the checker-print handkerchief from my jacket pocket and offered it to her. She took it gratefully and dabbed at the coffee that seeped into the fabric of her skirt. It was a useless attempt, but at least I didn't look like a total asshole.

She eyed me warily before speaking. "Is everything okay, Mr. Jacobs?"

I sighed and leaned back in my chair, placing my hands behind my head and pressing my head against them.

"Not really," I replied.

I watched as her eyes traveled to the paper on my desk and saw no surprise. She already read it, along with all of New York City. She forced a smile and handed me back my handkerchief.

"Thank you," she said softly.

"No problem."

She lingered, as if waiting for further instruction. Or maybe she wanted to get more out of me. Or maybe this was finally the moment she made her move. Either way, I wanted to be alone.

"Thanks for the coffee," I said dismissively, hoping she got the hint.

She did. She nodded disappointedly and turned to walk out the door, but not before saying, "I think it was a very romantic write-up, for what it's worth."

I could see Margaret getting swept up in the words of the article and the carefully crafted half-truths Kiera has spun. God. Had the rest of New York been swept up in this bullshit?

I scoffed as the door closed behind her, reaching for the paper again. My eyes scanned over the article before I tossed it aside. There was no mention of the charity auction and how I was obligated to spend the day with Kiera.

I should have known Kiera would talk to the press. Her image was all she really cared about, and this got her on the front page of the papers. I had hardly touched her all day, but the photographers knew how to work angles. And Kiera knew how to work them, as well.

The article didn't even mention my visit to the Leading to Learn offices. If anything, I thought that would be in there, since they followed us all damn day. But no, they had their own version of the story they want to spin, and me being painted out to be a good guy wasn't part of it. I let out a frustrated sigh.

My phone pinged on my desk. I picked it up and saw a text from Kiera:

We look pretty cute in today's paper.

I rolled my eyes and thought of a few choice words to send back, but opted not to. Right now, I didn't want to get on her bad side. She was pissed enough yesterday when I turned her down. Maybe that was why she ran to the press.

Instead of texting her back, I texted my best friend, Freddy:

Drinks at Bemelmans tonight?

I saw three dots appear and bounce just for a moment.

Freddy: *Hell yes. Meet you after work.*

Now, if only I could get through the next seven hours of work, then I could unwind with a glass of top-shelf whiskey and good company. Company I could trust. They were few and far between these days.

I had known Freddy since childhood. We both grew up on the same tree-lined street in upstate New York. Our parents worked a lot, so we had to entertain ourselves. It wasn't hard. In our younger years, we played GI Joes in his treehouse or rode bikes until the streetlights came on. In our teenage years, we raided my dad's liquor cabinet and rode golf carts to the clubhouse to sneak into the pool.

Now, we were in our early thirties, but I wasn't sure how much we'd grown up. It sometimes felt like we were using play money and running around town picking up women. He was the Upper West Side's renowned gynecologist, a field I never imagined him getting into. He said he loved it though. I could kind of see why.

Work seemed to drag on. There were meetings, emails, calls from the press that Margaret tried to dodge for me, but some still snuck their way through. I found myself growing frustrated that nothing I was doing at my company mattered. The only thing people wanted to focus on was who was in my bed. Maybe I did it to myself. I earned this reputation.

There was a knock at my door.

"Come in," I said.

Brody strolled in with a shit-eating grin. "Made the papers again, huh?" he asked

"Shut up," I snapped.

"When do I get to call her my sister-in-law?"

"I mean it, Brody."

He put his hands up in defense. I looked at him and seethed even more. This was all his fault. If we hadn't made that stupid bet at the club, none of this would have happened. I wouldn't have been up for auction, and Kiera wouldn't have been able to force her way into my life again, and then have it splashed all over the papers.

"This was *your* fault," I groused.

"How was it my fault?" he asked, plopping down in the armchair across from me, kicking his feet up on my desk.

I rolled my eyes. "If it wasn't for your stupid bet, I wouldn't be in this situation."

"It wasn't my fault the redhead wanted me." He shrugged. "Plus, I'm pretty sure the bet was *your* idea."

Could be. I couldn't remember.

"You're lucky, you know," I commented.

"How's that?"

"The press doesn't go after you like they do me."

He finally wiped the grin off his face and looked at me seriously.

"You're CEO. I'm COO. I'm the less interesting younger brother. That's not really fun either."

I never really thought about it like that. I may have all eyes on me, but I also got all the recognition.

"It was the life we signed up for, big bro," he said, swinging his feet from my desk and standing up.

I nodded solemnly.

"You'll be old news tomorrow," he remarked, heading out the door.

I better be.

I checked the time and realized it was just after five. Thank God.

**

I arrived at Bemelmans at 5:15. I chose to walk, sneaking out the back door of the building to avoid the paparazzi. I had Armand trail me in case I needed a fast exit. Thankfully, I was left alone. I needed that time to clear my head. Sometimes the noise of the city helped.

I pushed my way through the doors and walked into the dimly lit lounge. I didn't see Freddy yet, so I took a seat at the bar. The soft sounds of the piano trickled through the place, along with the hushed conversations of other patrons. The bartender spotted me and made her way over. Her honey blonde hair fell in loose curls at her shoulders and she moved with confidence in her black and white cocktail dress. She had waited on me before.

"Mr. Jacobs, it's nice to see you again," she said, leaning against the bar in a carefully crafted way that was not only casual, but also gave me a bird's eye view down her low-cut dress. An immediate way to get twenty percent more of a tip.

"Danielle, is it?" I asked, giving her a smile that lifted one side of my mouth.

"That's right. Daniel. Danielle. Remember?" she said, pointing between the two of us.

"Of course," I replied. I was surprised I remembered that.

"What can I get you?" she asked, her blue eyes intent on mine.

"Double whiskey. Neat."

"Long day?" she asked, reaching for a bottle above her, so her breasts were at my eye level. I didn't even hide my stare. On her way back down, she noticed, but didn't mind. In fact, she smiled. She knew what she was doing.

"Very," I answered as she slid the drink toward me.

"Well, I feel privileged you chose to spend the last of it here at Bemelmans. Hopefully, I can make it better."

"You already are," I said before taking a sip of my drink, not breaking eye contact.

"Are you already harassing the staff?" I heard Freddy ask as he took the seat beside me.

"Hi, Freddy," said Danielle, shaking her head.

I guessed we came here often.

"Danielle." He nodded. "The usual, please."

She gave him a lippy smirk before turning to make his old fashioned.

"What's up, man?" he asked, patting me on the back. "I saw the papers..."

"Yeah," I grumbled.

"Tell me you're not really back with her?"

I glared at him, incredulous. "You're not serious."

He shrugged. "I never know with you and Kiera. You guys have always been complicated."

"No, that hasn't been a thing in a while."

"Good. Because honestly, Daniel, she is the worst."

"I know."

I slid my hands down my face and felt the stubble against my palms.

Danielle was back and slid over Freddy's drink. He lifted his glass to her and took a long sip before turning to me.

"It will blow over," he said. "Don't worry."

"Yeah..."

But it wouldn't really. The only thing that would make that headline go away was another one with me and a different woman. I glanced at Danielle, wondering if she could be the one to make all this go away and to show everyone I wasn't really with Kiera. That would be a big blow to her ego. I took a satisfying sip of my drink just thinking about it.

Bringing the honey-haired bartender home with me would be easy, but I realized she was not who I wanted. Ever since I met Addison two days ago in the garden, she hadn't left my mind. She was not like anyone I'd ever met, and I hardly even knew her. I just had this feeling about her.

I mean, most of the women I knew were rich or just trying to be rich. Addison was different. She actually cared about something other than herself, rather than chasing the dollar, or someone else's dollar. She was too good for me, and because of that she was a challenge. Maybe that was why I couldn't get her off my mind. Once I found a conquest, in business or with women, I had to win.

I had to find a way to see her again. It shouldn't be too hard, since I'd be giving her nonprofit hundreds of thousands of dollars. She wouldn't be able to refuse a meeting with me, even though our last one went so poorly, thanks to Kiera. I decided to check my phone calendar to see if another meeting had been scheduled, but I saw nothing.

Disappointed, I signaled for Danielle to bring me another drink. Freddy looked at my empty glass.

"You really are pissed about this whole thing."

I shrugged and took a look around the bar. The whiskey helped, but I needed a distraction. Just for tonight. Most of the tables were filled with businessmen and women half their age. I noticed the door open and did a double-take. Talk about wishful thinking.

Addison stood at the hostess stand. She wore a strapless black dress that she tugged at as she looked around with uncertainty. Her hair was down and parted to the side, flowing just past her shoulder blades. The hostess gestured to the bar and Addison walked to the opposite end of the bar from me. She sat on a barstool, the hem of her black dress riding up as she crossed her legs. I noticed strappy heels that tied at her ankles. She looked sexy as hell.

I thought to myself, *game on.*

Chapter 9

ADDISON

I sat stiffly in the wooden barstool and looked around for a drink menu. I wondered if it was happy hour, or if they even did that sort of thing at this type of place. When my coworker, Shelley, suggested coming to Bemelman's for birthday drinks, I was surprised. It wasn't like we made an exorbitant salary to be able to shell out $40 for a single cocktail, but we had chosen a different spot for dinner. Somewhere far cheaper, so I figured one drink wouldn't hurt.

I tried to find a comfortable position. It's not my seat, it was the damn dress. I swear, I just needed to accept that I was a size up and buy some new clothes. Squeezing into dresses and skirts felt like a workout each morning. I practically rearranged my insides to fit in this black dress. It felt far too sexy for drinks with my coworkers, but I wasn't sure of the dress code here.

As I looked around, I saw other women wearing similar attire, all cozied up to men twice their age in suits. It made me feel even more uncomfortable. I pulled at the hem of my dress to cover more leg, but ended up showing more cleavage. I couldn't win. Giving up, I signaled for the bartender to come give my self-consciousness some relief.

She was stunning with her light, warm hair and tiny cocktail dress. I couldn't help but stare and when she was in front of me, I realized I didn't even know what I wanted to drink. I just knew I needed one.

"What can I get you, hun?" she asked.

"Ummm...I-I'm sorry. I didn't get a chance to look at a drink menu."

She reached under the counter and slid one over. "First time here?" she asked.

It must have been obvious.

I nodded as my eyes skimmed the menu.

"Might I suggest our Cosmopolitan? It has passionfruit-infused vodka and a champagne float. It's a popular choice."

"Sure, I'll have that."

For that price, I might as well have two drinks in one. I handed her back the menu and glanced toward the door. I wondered where my coworkers were. I checked the time on my phone. It was nearly 6:30 p.m. I drummed my fingertips on the bar top and glanced around the place.

It was beautiful. The lights were dim but warm, casting an orange glow over the tables. It felt incredibly intimate in here with small tables and corner booths. I could see why these men brought their dates here. You had no choice but to be pressed up against one another with a fancy cocktail in hand.

My eyes grazed to the end of the bar where they stopped suddenly on none other than Daniel Jacobs. I sucked in a quick breath and looked down at the bar top, hoping he didn't see me, even though I could feel his gaze on me.

Please, don't come over. Please, don't come over, I thought.

I wasn't sure I could handle being in his presence, especially if I had a drink in me. It would only lower my guard. With him, my guard was already practically at my feet. The last thing I needed to do was feel tipsy and brave, leading me to fail at flirting with a guy who was practically engaged and had no interest in me.

The pretty bartender slid my drink toward me. It looked beautiful. I didn't think cocktails could be that pretty. It was pink and bubbly and had edible flowers floating on top of the champagne.

"Thank you," I said, admiring it.

"Would you like to start a tab?" she asked.

"This one is on me," Daniel said. "In fact, all of her drinks are on me."

He was right beside me and I could smell his cologne, and it screamed expensive and incredibly sexy. I hadn't noticed it during the whole two times I had seen him. I suddenly wanted it on my skin, so I could bring it home with me.

I turned to him and feigned surprise. "Daniel," I said, putting my hand to my heart for effect. "What a surprise."

"A pleasant one, I hope," he quipped, raising an eyebrow.

Very.

"Thank you for the drink. You didn't have to do that."

He waved me off, like it was no problem at all. He probably did this for everyone. *You're not special,* I reminded myself. He lifted up his glass. I lifted mine to meet his and listened as they clinked lightly together.

"Cheers to a fate," he said, his eyes intently focused on mine.

I'm not sure what he meant by that, but it sounded awfully flirtatious. I ignored it.

"And cheers to your new girlfriend," I said with a curt nod.

It sounded snarkier than I intended. I hoped he couldn't sense the icy notes of jealousy that spilled off my tongue. *Oof.* I hadn't even had a sip of my drink yet. I broke his gaze, and looked toward the bottles of liquor lined on the shelves at the back of the bar. I lifted my glass to my lips and took a long, heavenly sip. The drink was sweet and strong. I was in trouble.

Daniel looked ahead, too, taking a long pull of his amber-colored drink. There was a moment of awkward silence before he spoke again.

"She's not my girlfriend, just so you know." There was a gruffness to his voice, and I couldn't tell if he was upset or angry. I found his voice rumbling in my core.

"Oh, I'm sorry. The papers…"

"Fuck the papers."

Oh, he was angry. And was a hot kind of angry. I took another long sip of my drink, the bubbles dancing their way down my throat.

"Sorry," he said, turning to me.

"It's fine. It's none of my business."

I hadn't turned to face him, but I could feel his eyes on me. It felt like there were words he was holding in his throat, like he was afraid to set them free just yet. I was afraid, too, because they could possibly undo me.

I looked toward the door, hoping my friends had finally arrived to save me from whatever this situation was. I didn't see them. I let out a sigh of frustration.

"Are you waiting for someone?" asked Daniel curiously, following my gaze to the door.

"Yeah, but they're late."

"Is it a date?"

I looked at him, surprised that he'd asked that.

"Um, no. It's my coworker's birthday."

Was it just me, or did he look relieved? That drink was playing tricks on me. I reached in my purse. "I'm just going to text her."

Daniel nodded and stood next to me patiently. I noticed he hadn't taken a seat, but he still lingered beside me. I wasn't complaining, though. He was here. And he wasn't with that snooty girl after all.

I typed out a quick text to Shelley.

Me: *Where are you? I'm at Bemelman's.*

Shelley: *Oh, shit, Heart. I thought Brian told you I was sick.*

Me: *He did, but I thought you were just playing hooky.*

Shelley: *I wish. I'm so sorry! Raincheck?*

I looked down at my phone before locking it, the screen going dark. I was here alone. Well, not entirely alone. Daniel was here, but I still felt so out of place. I chewed on my bottom lip as I thought of what to do next.

"Is she not coming?" he asked, leaning against the bar.

"Um, no. I guess not. She's sick."

I looked down at my half-full drink. Part of me wanted to chug it and get the hell out of there, but part of me wanted to stay.

"Would you like to join us?" asked Daniel, gesturing toward his friend at the other end of the bar. I peeked over and saw him flirting with the pretty bartender.

"Oh, that's okay. I don't want to intrude."

"I insist."

Daniel held out his hand and looked at me expectantly. Before I placed my hand in his, I braced myself for that familiar feeling I got when our hands touched. When my palm met his, there it was. This time it ran across my skin like tiny electric kisses. He helped me down from the barstool and I trailed behind him holding his hand, balancing my drink in my other.

"Freddy. I'd like you to meet Addison," said Daniel as we sat down.

"Addison, huh? Nice to meet you," replied Freddy, holding out his hand.

"Likewise," I said, shaking his hand firmly.

It was an entirely different feeling than having Daniel's hand in mine.

"So, how do you two know each other?" asked Freddy, pointing between the two of us.

"Addison here works at the nonprofit, Leading to Learn. They're doing amazing things. I've decided to become a donor."

"Which we are very grateful for. Thank you," I added.

Daniel looked to my drink, and signaled for the bartender.

"Can we get another round, please?"

"Of course, Mr. Jacobs."

I noticed her eyes linger a little too long and the careful batting of her eyelashes. Could I blame her? He probably had that effect on everyone. I noticed he seemed unfazed as he turned back to me.

"So, do you usually come to Bemelman's on a Wednesday night?"

"No. Never. This is my first time here."

"Well, lucky us," said Freddy with a grin.

"Lucky us," Daniel agreed.

The bartender brought over another round of drinks, even though I hadn't finished my first one yet. I gulped it down in two sips. If I thought I was in trouble before, I certainly was now. There was a reckless feeling coming over me. I didn't know if it was the vodka and champagne, or the way it felt like I was living a double life in this fancy bar, or being in this close of proximity to the powerful force of Daniel Jacobs. Probably a combination of all three.

"How do you two know each other?" I asked, looking at Freddy, and carefully avoiding looking at Daniel.

"We grew up together," he said. "Childhood buddies."

"Wow, that's amazing. And what do you do, Freddy?"

"I'm an OBGYN. If you ever need one, here's my card," he said, flipping open his wallet and handing a matte white card to me.

"Er, thank you." I couldn't help but laugh a little.

"Seriously, man?" Daniel asked.

I could see his cheeks had turned a rosy pink, which made me giggle more. Daniel Jacobs, uncomfortable? Never thought I'd see the day.

"What?" Freddy shrugged.

Daniel shook his head and took a sip of his drink. He turned his back to Freddy, who was back to flirting with the bartender.

"Sorry," he mouthed.

I waved him off. "It's fine," I whispered.

I felt his knee graze against mine and stay there. I sucked in a quiet breath as his eyes traveled to where our bodies touched. They stayed there for a minute before finding mine again. They looked icy blue, which was a stark contrast to the dim, yellow lighting of the bar.

"You look really nice tonight, in case I hadn't told you," he said.

I realized I had been holding my breath.

"Thank you," I let out breathlessly.

Freddy slapped the bar with the palm of his hand, breaking whatever trance I was in. I jumped a little in my seat and curiously looked over.

"Sorry. Stocks took a dive." He glanced up from his phone.

Daniel took in a frustrated breath through his nose and turned his back to me. I saw something register on Freddy's face, and wondered what silent exchange had just occurred. Freddy yawned dramatically and stretched his back.

"I think I'm going to call it a night, you two," he said, tossing a few hundred-dollar bills on the bar top. "It was nice to meet you, Addison."

He patted Daniel on the back, and just like that, he was gone, and I was suddenly very aware of how I somehow ended up alone at a bar with Daniel Jacobs.

Chapter 10

DANIEL

I was relieved to see Freddy walk out the door of the bar. He had gotten the hint, as if the look on my face didn't scream "get the fuck out of here." I loved the guy, but he could be a total idiot sometimes. I mean, did he really offer to be Addison's woman doctor? I didn't want him or anyone else exploring the places I had yet to. The places I hoped to.

I watched as her pillowy pink lips wrapped around the rim of her martini glass, and then my eyes trailed down and grazed across the top of her strapless dress. I couldn't help myself.

Addison cleared her throat, bringing my attention back up to her face. There was a sharpness to the look she gave me. Could she really blame me? She had herself on a delicious display.

"Sorry, what were you saying?" I asked with a sheepish grin.

"I was saying, I'm sorry about this morning's paper. You seemed upset."

I leaned back in my seat and looked down into my drink.

"It's just this life. I guess I asked for it, but sometimes I think everything gets so misconstrued."

"Like the three women in one night? Let me guess, you were just playing board games up there…"

She had looked me up. I smiled at the thought.

"You've done your research…" I took a sip of my drink.

"I had to know who I was getting into business with," she said, but I could tell from the flush of her cheeks that wasn't the only reason she had searched my name on the internet.

I set my glass down on the bar top and looked at her. I figured I might as well be honest with her.

"Look, I won't lie to you. I have a reputation. Some of it is lies. Most of it is true. But I am proud of the company I've built. I wish my work could be a headline, rather than the woman I'm seeing."

She looked thoughtful for a moment. "That must be frustrating," she said. "I'm sorry."

"Very. The whole thing with Kiera was bogus. I had to spend the day with her because of some stupid charity auction where I was up for bid."

Addison shook her head and let out a laugh through her nose.

"What?" I asked.

"Rich people problems."

I laughed. It did sound ridiculous.

"How much did you go for?" she asked, raising a brow.

"You don't want to know," I groaned.

"Tell me." She nudged me playfully with her shoulder.

She was flirting with me. I'd play along.

"No way."

She turned in her seat so she was fully facing me.

"Tell me," she demanded, leaning in close.

"Fiiiine," I said, before leaning in. "Two hundred thousand dollars."

"Shut the fuck up," she blurted out loudly. Some patrons at the bar looked up curiously. She quickly covered her mouth with her hand in embarrassment.

I let out a laugh. A genuine one that I hadn't had because of a woman in a long time.

"I know. It's ridiculous," I said, running my hand through my hair.

She sat in a bewildered silence for a moment.

"So, that's what it costs to spend a night with Daniel Jacobs. Well, I hate to break it to you, but I don't have that kind of money," she said with a smirk.

"I better be going then." I pretended to stand.

Her eyes widened before she reached over and slapped me lightly on the thigh.

"You are the worst," she said with a laugh.

Her hand was still on my thigh and I felt my blood coursing through my veins as if it were boiling water. I looked down at her hand and she nervously pulled it away. She reached for her drink and finished it in one impressive gulp.

Now or never, I thought.

I glanced at my watch. It was only 8 p.m.

"It's still early," I said. "Do you maybe want to come back to my place?"

She stared at her empty drink and I could see she was considering it.

"Is there food?" she asked.

I wasn't expecting that.

"Food? Uh, yeah."

"Good, because I'm starving."

I laughed and tossed some cash on the bar.

Outside on the sidewalk, she went to hail a cab before she noticed I had a car waiting. Armand opened the door for us, and she scooched her way inside the town car, with me following behind her. I noticed she slid all the way to the other side and was practically pressed up against the door. She was keeping her distance. For now.

"Do you like pizza?" I offered.

"Obviously," she said.

"Armand, can you get some pizzas from Di Fara's delivered?"

"Yes, sir." He gave me a nod through the rearview mirror.

I leaned back in my seat and looked over at Addison. She gazed out the window, the city lights passing by us in a blur. I could see by her reflection in the window that she was maybe second-guessing herself. She was unlike most women, who practically straddled me seconds after getting in the car.

"Pizza should be there in about forty minutes, sir," Armand called back.

"Thank you."

Minutes later, we pulled into the parking garage of my building. Armand parked in front of the elevators, and I got out before he could open the door.

I wanted to be the one who opened the door for Addison, to show her I could be a gentleman.

I held out my hand and she hesitated before taking it, allowing me to help her out. Armand stood back with an amused expression. This was a first.

"Have a good evening, sir," he said, before getting back into the car.

I punched in the code for the elevator and the doors immediately opened. It was my private elevator, so no surprise there. Addison stepped inside and leaned against the back corner, again keeping her distance. We rode up in silence, her avoidant gaze looking anywhere but at me.

The doors opened to the entryway of my penthouse, and I stepped inside. I didn't hear the sound of Addison's heels behind me, so I turned and found her gaping from the inside the elevator. She stepped out and slowly followed me into the living room, taking everything in. I liked the feeling of impressing her. Knowing I could give her what most men couldn't.

"Drink?" I asked, gesturing to the bar behind the couch.

"Are you trying to get me drunk?" she asked coyly.

Maybe.

"Me? Never."

"Good. Because just so you know, I'm not that kind of girl."

"I know. You told me."

She gave me a puzzled look.

"Out on the terrace. When we first met."

Her cheeks flushed. I went to the bar and heard her footsteps follow behind me.

"Champagne?" I asked.

"Okay." She leaned her back against the marble bar top.

I pulled a bottle from the fridge and eased the cork off with a dull pop. I poured two glasses and handed her one. She took a small sip and looked out the large windows to the city below.

"If you aren't that type of girl, what are you doing here?" I asked.

"I just came for the pizza." She shrugged.

I could see she fought back a smile.

"Well, we still have about thirty minutes," I pointed out, taking a step toward her. I placed my hands on her arms. Her eyes raised to mine and she inhaled a shaky breath.

"What do you want to do until then?" she asked, already damn well knowing the answer.

"I have a few ideas."

I leaned in closer and watched as her eyes fluttered closed. Instead of going for her mouth, I pressed my lips against her jaw, leaving a trail of kisses. She leaned her head back, exposing her neck and I gladly took her invitation. I trailed my lips down the nape of her neck, tasting her with my tongue.

My hands reached for her waist, gripping it before quickly turning her to face the counter. I pressed myself against her, finding myself already growing hard against the small of her back. She turned her head and looked at me over her bare shoulder. I leaned in and kissed her softly at first before needing more almost immediately. I ran my tongue over her lips and she parted them to let me explore her mouth. She tasted like champagne as she massaged her tongue against mine.

She reached her arms up and around my neck, leaving my hands free to explore. They wrapped around her, cupping her breasts through the silky fabric of her dress. They felt full as I massaged them, our mouths quickening their pace against one another. I moved my hands lower, across her abdomen, down her hips until they reached the short hem of her dress.

As I started to pull up her dress, she broke free from our kiss and looked at me, searching my eyes. Was I moving too fast? I paused my movements, waiting for some sort sign. For permission. She looked at me for a moment longer before pulling me in for another kiss. A deeper kiss than before. She spread her legs slightly.

Permission granted, I thought.

With her dress up at her hips, my fingers grazed against the lace fabric of her underwear, and she shuddered at my touch. I wondered how long it had been since someone touched her. I trailed her panty line with my fingers before peeling back the lace. I tucked a finger inside of her, finding her warm and wet, eager for me. Her back arched into me and her breaths became shorter, more ragged as I moved my finger in and out of her.

She suddenly reached down and grabbed at my hand, pulling it from her, her moisture covering my fingers. She turned around to face me, a desperate look on her face. I could tell, she wanted more. She reached up and grabbed my jacket, pulling it free. Her fingers quickly stumbled over the buttons of my shirt, until my chest was bare in front of her. Her eyes grazed over me as I peeled my shirt off.

I reached around and found the zipper of her dress, pulling it down so that her dress fell to the floor. Her breasts spilled out, and I leaned in to taste them, surrounding her nipples with the warmth of my mouth. She let out a moan as her hands desperately pulled at my waistband, unbuttoning and unzipping, my pants and briefs falling to my ankles.

I released her breast from my mouth and saw her gaze on my erection. She looked up at me nervously, and then with her eyes never leaving mine, she pulled down the waistband of her lace panties, and she kicked them to the side.

She stood there completely naked and completely beautiful. Her creamy curves were exposed before me. Mine for the taking. I lifted her onto the countertop. She opened her legs and I sucked in a breath. Holy shit. She bit her lip as she watched me take her in with my gaze, and that right there sent me over the edge.

I slid her to the edge of the counter until the tip of my cock was against her wet opening. She spread her legs even further. I could feel her pulsing against me, begging me to enter. I placed my hand just above her perfect ass and pulled her in, my dick dipping into her inch by inch. She let out a throaty moan and threw her head back.

I pulled out of her slowly before plunging back into her, her walls hugging me tightly. As I moved inside her, I took her breast in my mouth, sucking her nipple as her hands grasped the countertop tightly, her knuckles turning white. I moved quicker, with vigor, fucking her harder. I could feel her convulsing around me and then she screamed, climaxing on me as I exploded into her.

Chapter 11

ADDISON

My eyes felt heavy as I tried to pry them open. I could feel the morning light warm against my face and wasn't sure if I was ready to welcome it in yet. My head pounded dully. The consequence of too much expensive champagne on an empty stomach.

My eyes adjusted to the morning that felt like it was cruelly laughing at my hangover. I saw Daniel sleeping next to me and sucked in a breath. So, this happened. It wasn't a dream. I watched him sleep for a moment. He looked so peaceful. His breath was slow and steady, his eyelids fluttering in a dreamlike state.

My eyes wandered down his bare chest to the silky, white sheet tucked around him just at the V of his lower abdomen. Holy shit, he was hot. The urge to wake him up and go again bloomed inside of me. I reluctantly rolled onto my back and stared at the ceiling instead.

I replayed our night, bits and pieces vibrant in my mind. Others somewhat blurry. Like the pizza. I wonder what happened to the delivery guy. Poor guy was probably scared off by the noises coming from the other side of the door.

I didn't blame him. The screams I let out were primal. I barely recognized the sounds coming from my mouth.

Besides the blurry bits, like how many times we had sex last night, there were images that replayed in high contrast. Daniel's large hands grabbing me. Everywhere. His fingertips pressing into my skin and entering places that had been neglected by a man for far too long. His mouth on my neck. His tongue on my breasts. His teeth on my earlobe. The way he entered me. His slow, steady thrusts becoming frantic and swift. How he filled me, his body shuddering around me with pleasure.

As I lay there next to the most beautiful man I had ever seen in the wake of him ravaging me, I could feel my insides pulsing for more. I went to reach for him, but my brain took over. This was a bad idea. Last night was a bad idea. I had to nip this now before getting in too deep.

Did Daniel even get deep? He was honest about his reputation last night. I was just another woman he could add to his list. While it wasn't the best feeling, I was the one who wanted this. I got swept up in the moment. It was stupid, but also probably the best night of my life. And it was over now. Back to reality.

I pulled the cool sheets from my body, noting that I would never have anything this nice on my skin again. I carefully pushed myself from the bed, so as not to wake him. The last thing I needed was the awkward morning after thing. That, or falling into the oceans he had for eyes and feeling my heart break knowing I was just another girl on his roster. Nothing more. Either would be too much to bear.

I searched the floor for my dress or my shoes, but found nothing. I remembered we didn't start here in the bedroom. We ended here. Where this all began was at the bar. I tiptoed out of his bedroom, feeling suddenly aware of how naked I was. In the living room, I spotted my dress and strappy shoes in a pile on the floor. I shimmied the dress on and slid on my heels, tying the straps at my ankle. My underwear. I needed those.

I found them hanging like an ornament on the wine fridge just underneath the bar. I held the counter as I slipped them on, careful not to snag the lace on my heels. This was a ridiculous outfit to go home in at 7 a.m. If this didn't scream *walk of shame*, I didn't know what did.

I grabbed my purse from the entryway table and pressed the button for the elevator, then looked back one more time, a feeling of slight sadness washing over me. I didn't feel regret for what happened. No, I felt regret that it wouldn't happen again. Daniel was like a drug, and I had to stop before I was addicted.

Taking a deep breath, I gave myself a nod of mustered certainty and stepped into the elevator. I pressed the button for the lobby and closed my eyes as I began the descent. Soon, the elevator doors opened and I stepped into a grand lobby. Quickly, I strode through it, the *click-clack* of my heels echoing against the marble floors. I pushed the large glass doors open to the street and hurriedly hailed a cab. I hardly ever took cabs, especially all the way to Brooklyn, but there was no way in hell I was stepping onto the subway looking like this.

As I slid into the backseat, I could feel the driver's eyes on me. I avoided his amused expression and gave him my address. As I stared out the window and watched the buildings change when we crossed the bridge into Brooklyn, I couldn't feel further from Daniel than I did now.

I wondered what he would think when he woke up. I wondered if he would even think of me at all.

Back home, I practically ran up the stairs of my apartment, nearly breaking an ankle. The last thing I needed was Elma catching me in last night's dress. In the safety and privacy of my apartment, I kicked off my shoes and removed my dress. I kind of felt like Cinderella coming home from the ball, except she didn't get laid and there was no Prince Charming.

I had an hour before I had to be at work. I looked at my bed longingly and considered calling in sick, but decided against it. I wasn't going to let Daniel Jacobs derail my life, even just for a day. I hopped in the shower, and washed his touch and kisses away. The water circled the drain, as if it were our nonexistent relationship.

Out of the shower, I quickly dressed in a pair of faded jeans and a white button-down. This was me. No more suffocating skirts or strapless dresses. I had no one to impress, and felt foolish for even trying to impress Daniel in his custom suits and shiny shoes. What a fool I had been.

I put on a pot of coffee and poured it into a thermos before making my way to the subway station. As I rode the 8:40 train back into the city, I desperately tried to block memories of last night from popping into my brain like little bubbles. *Pop. Pop. Pop.* It was really no use.

I made it to the office at 9 a.m. on the dot.

"Addison, can you come in here?" I heard Brian call as I walked past his door.

For a moment I felt scared he knew what happened, but I shook it off. I was just being paranoid.

"Yes, Brian?" I said as I stepped inside his office.

"I wanted to see where we were on signing papers with Mr. Jacobs."

"He was having the papers drawn up to sign this week."

"Well, can you check in with him?"

That was the last thing I wanted to do.

"Uh, sure. I'll get right on that."

"Good." Brian nodded and went back to typing on his computer.

I walked into my office, closing the door behind me. I sat at my desk and put my head in my hands. I felt so stupid. There was a reason they said not to mix business with pleasure. There was no way I could continue working with him when I knew what he looked like naked. I had to find someone to take over. It would mean losing the credit for landing such a prominent donor, but I didn't care.

I picked up my office phone and dialed Shelley's extension, hoping she was back in the office today and feeling better after yesterday. It rang three times before she picked up.

"Hello?"

"Shelley! You're back. How are you feeling?"

"Better today. I think it was food poisoning. I'm so sorry for standing you up last night."

"It's totally fine."

If she hadn't, then I wouldn't have been in this mess, but I had to let it go.

"Can you come to my office when you have a chance? There's something I want to run by you."

"Sure. I can pop over in thirty."

"Thanks, Shelley."

For the next half hour, I nursed my hangover with the black coffee in my thermos and snacks from the office kitchen.

There was a knock at my door and Shelley popped her head in. "Hey Addison, what's up?"

"Come in. Take a seat." I gestured to the chair in front of my desk.

Shelley looked at me expectantly.

"So, I don't know if you've heard, but we landed Mr. Jacobs as a donor."

"I heard! That's huge! Congrats on getting him."

Oh, how that could mean so many things.

"Uh, right," I said. "I'm actually wondering if you could take over for me?"

"Wait. Seriously?" Shelley's eyebrows rose in surprise.

"Yeah, I'm just bogged down with so much work. I just think it would be better for someone else to take him on and give this deal the attention it deserves."

Shelley eyed me curiously, as if she wasn't buying it.

"I mean if you don't want to..." I started, looking thoughtful.

She would be a fool not to take this opportunity.

"No, no. I can do it." She nodded firmly.

"Great. I'll send you all the contact info and our email threads. Thank you, Shelley."

"Thank *you*."

I breathed a sigh of relief as she walked out the door. With relief came a small pang in my heart, knowing that I would no longer have anything to do with Daniel. *It's better this way,* I told myself.

For the next few weeks, I threw myself into work. I renegotiated previous agreements with donors, came up with fundraising ideas, and worked out a new quarterly budget. I wanted to look like I was busy so Brian wouldn't ask any questions about me passing on the deal with Daniel. Thankfully, he didn't.

I did hear from Shelley that she was working with one of Daniel's foundation staff members. He had apparently passed it onto them around the same time I had passed it onto Shelley. Clearly, he wanted nothing to do with me. To say it didn't sting would be a lie. But who was I to say anything? I had done the same.

As much as I didn't want to, I often thought of our night together. I hadn't shared what had happened with anyone. Not even Monica. I wanted to hold on to it like a secret because I didn't want anyone to taint it. Even though it ended the way it did, what I felt in that night was unlike anything I had or probably would experience again. It was a sacred little part of my life I held to, especially on lonely nights.

One night, after a long day at work, I poured myself a glass of red wine and watched it slosh up the sides of the glass. As I went to sit on the couch and wrap myself up in a cozy blanket, my normal weeknight routine, a thought occurred to me. I checked the date on my phone and a feeling of unease crept over me like a fog rolling in.

I quickly grabbed my phone and opened my Google calendar. I went back through the weeks and panic set in. There was a missing red calendar day. It couldn't be. I quickly went through the weeks again, frantically swiping with my fingertip. I stopped and stared at my phone before sucking in a slow, shaky breath as the realization hit me.

I had missed my period.

Chapter 12

DANIEL

I took a sip of black coffee that sat steaming in the mug on my desk. The heat swished to the back of my tongue and down my throat as I willed for the caffeine to enter my system at a rapid pace. I rubbed my eyes and leaned back in my desk chair. I was exhausted.

Going out with Freddy last night had been a bad idea, especially with the slew of work meetings I had lined up for the day. I wasn't thinking. I was desperate for some sort of distraction from the strange void that formed since my night with Addison.

Our night together was all I thought about for the past month. Having her made me hungry for more, and made everything else I had tasted in the past seem dull and flavorless. What transpired that night at the bar, on my couch, in my bed—it was reckless abandon. I had become completely lost in her, and her in me. Or so I thought.

She had left without a word the next morning, which would normally put my mind at ease. I didn't have to have the inevitable conversation of, "You're really great, but I'm not looking for anything serious." Or the awkward feeling when I want them to leave, but they were just not getting the hint. That was the worst. That's if they were even lucky to stay over, which was rare.

That night, I had gone to bed with my arms wrapped around Addison, and I wasn't a cuddler. For some reason, no matter which way I had her into the late hours of the night, I needed more. My hands were desperate to touch her smooth skin. My lungs needed to breathe her in. Vanilla and beads of sweet sweat. She fell asleep pressed against me, and her quiet, steady breathing somehow lulled me to sleep, even though I was ready to go for a fourth helping.

When I rolled over, already aroused and hoping to go again, I found my bed empty. I was humbled to realize she had left sometime in the early morning hours. To say it wasn't a blow to my pride would be a lie. I should have felt on top of the world. I had conquered my conquest. Challenge completed. Instead of feeling like a winner, I couldn't help feeling at a loss.

For someone who was so high on her pedestal of not being "that type of girl," she made it clear that what happened between us was a one-time thing. I had never been on that side of it before. I'd had plenty of one-night stands. Hell, that was all I'd really ever had. But I was usually the one to leave. Being left was foreign to me.

When I got to the office that morning, I had an email at the top of my inbox. I quickly opened it when I saw it was from Leading to Learn. I assumed it was Addison with some sort of excuse as to why she left, but it was quite the opposite. She had passed our business deal off to a coworker named Shelley. I didn't want Shelley. I wanted Addison. And I thought I had made that clear, but that was before I had learned what she tasted like. I had broken my own rule of not mixing business with pleasure.

After that email. I grew annoyed. Instead of fighting for her, I took the hint and handed the deal to one of my foundation members. If she didn't want anything to do with me, then I wanted nothing to do with her. That was my pride taking over.

And it was that same pride that had kept me from reaching out to her, and instead went searching for something, someone, to replace what I felt with her that night. Turned out, pure ecstasy wasn't exactly easy to come by.

My night out with Freddy last night was filled with predictable women who didn't spark my interest or my arousal. We had gone to a new club opening. Bottle service. Cocktail waitresses in barely-there uniforms. Women in tight dresses eager to get a free drink with shameless flirting and dancing that was more dry humping than rhythmic.

I sat in our booth probably looking miserable as I sipped on straight vodka.

"What is up with you, man?" asked Freddy as a redhead slung her arm around his neck. Her friend was sidled up beside me, her legs thrown over mine. I didn't remember her name. I didn't care.

I shrugged, looking down into my drink. Usually, my hands would be up this girl's short skirt already, but instead my fingers stayed wrapped around my cocktail glass. It wasn't like I wanted to be like this. I couldn't help it.

"Is it work?" asked Freddy.

I shook my head.

"Brody?"

"Nah."

"Is it a woman?" he asked with a tone of disbelief.

I felt the blonde shoot me a look.

"You're joking, right?" I asked with a sarcastic laugh. I wrapped my arm around the blonde, hoping it would be enough to hide that he had figured me out.

It didn't work. His eyes widened as he leaned in close, the redhead slipping onto his lap like some sort of barnacle.

"Holy shit, man. Who is she?" he asked, his eyes narrowed.

"It's no one, Freddy."

"Is it that girl from the bar? Big tits? Dark hair? Black dress one size too small?"

I took a sip of my drink, holding it in my mouth to feel the burn before swallowing it slowly.

"Whatever happened with that?" asked Freddy. The redhead was now nibbling on his earlobe, making it hard for him to concentrate. Hell, it was making it hard for me to concentrate.

"Nothing."

"Bullshit."

"If there was anything there, do you think I'd be here with..."

Shit, I didn't know her name.

"Rebecca," she muttered.

"Rebecca. I knew that," I said.

Freddy let out a laugh as Rebecca removed her legs from my lap. Whatever. I wasn't interested anyway. I removed my arm from her shoulders and checked the time on my watch.

It was 1 a.m. I was already fucked for tomorrow. I didn't need to make it worse.

"I think I'm going to head out," I said.

"What? We still have half a bottle left," said Freddy, pulling the bottle from the ice bucket.

"Have at it."

Rebecca rolled her eyes and slunk against the seat of the booth. I slid on my jacket and gave them a single wave before heading toward the door. I carefully pushed my way through the crowd and out onto the sidewalk. There, I heard the disappointed murmurs of the paparazzi who had been waiting outside all night. Nothing to see here. No woman, or women, on my arm. I gave them a shit-eating grin and got in my town car.

When I got home, I could barely sleep. I kept thinking about Addison and how empty my bed was. I hadn't brought anyone home since that night. It was a new record for me. Of course, the paparazzi didn't report on that. A playboy is much more interesting than a guy who spends his nights alone. Plus, Kiera was still playing the angle that we were headed for an engagement. I hadn't cared enough to set things straight. People assumed things all the time.

After maybe getting only four hours of sleep, I headed miserably into the office this morning. CEOs don't have the luxury of sick days. Now I was struggling to keep my eyes open. There was a knock at my office door, waking me up slightly.

"Come in," I said, but it was more of a quiet groan.

Margaret popped her head in. "I sent you a push notification on your Google calendar. Did you see it?"

"No. I've been...busy."

"Oh, it's just a Ms. Heartly called earlier and wanted to schedule a meeting with you."

My ears perked up.

"Wait, Ms. Heartly? As in Addison Heartly?"

"Yes. That's right."

I sat there in a few seconds of quiet disbelief.

Margaret cleared her throat. "So, do you want me to set that up for you?"

"Did she say what she wanted?"

"No, sir. She just said she needed to get in to see you as soon as possible."

"Thank you, Margaret. I'll handle it." I dismissed her.

She nodded before closing the door behind her.

I smoothed my fingers over my chin in thought. It had been a month since our night together. I ran through a list of reasons why she would want to meet with me. Was it because she couldn't stop thinking about that night either? Or did it have to do with the business deal? There was only one way to find out.

I checked my calendar for the day, but I had no openings for a meeting. I had one available for tomorrow, but I didn't think I could wait that long. My curiosity was at its peak. I would have to call her. But I refused to give her the satisfaction of sounding too eager.

I found her number within an email thread, and dialed.

It rang three times before she picked up.

"Addison Heartly," she said.

I hadn't realized I was holding my breath.

"Hello," I said, breathing it out slowly.

"Hello? Who is this?"

"It's Daniel. Daniel Jacobs."

"Oh, um, hi. I called earlier hoping to schedule a meeting."

"I heard," I replied with a crispness to my voice.

There was a pause on the other line.

"Well, when is your next availability?" she asked.

"I'm pretty booked up," I commented.

"Daniel. Mr. Jacobs. Please," she came back, sounding desperate.

Good.

"Look, anything that has to do with the donations can be handled through my foundation."

"It's not about that..."

"Then what is it, Ms. Heartly?"

She inhaled a shaky breath. "I'm pregnant."

I felt like someone had punched me in the gut. I placed my elbows on the desk for support as I replayed those two words in my head. Was she saying what I thought she was saying? I couldn't believe it. Panic began to set in.

"What are you trying to say?" I whispered.

"I think you know what I'm trying to say."

Shit. Fuck. Shit.

"How do you know I'm the father?" I blurted out.

"Are you serious?" she asked, her voice a warning.

"I don't know. Maybe it's someone else's—"

"I can't even believe what you're suggesting!"

"Why? I hardly know you. I don't know what you do in your spare time."

"I told you I'm not that kind of girl."

"Well, you were that night with me."

I regretted the words as soon as they left my mouth. The silence that followed rang in my ears as if I could feel her anger through the line.

"Go to hell," she snapped.

I heard the click of the phone on the other line. I slammed my phone down and put my head in my hands. Heat creeped up the back of my neck. What the hell just happened? Could I really be the father?

Theoretically, yes. I could be. I had been too in the moment to slip on a condom, which was incredibly careless looking back. We were both lost in the moment. She hadn't asked or protested. Hell, she invited me in when she spread those beautiful legs of hers. I didn't hesitate. I just wanted her. All of her. I figured she was on the pill or something.

This couldn't be happening. My office started to spin. It felt like my world was closing in around me. This feeling of being out of control was not one I was used to. I had to get out of here. I slid on my jacket and quickly grabbed my briefcase. On my way out I told Margaret to cancel my meetings for the day, and left her sitting there in a state of shock. Work would have to wait. I needed to think.

Chapter 13

ADDISON

I stared at my phone as tears formed in my eyes, threatening to leave salty trails down my cheeks. I hated that I was letting someone like Daniel Jacobs make me cry, but I couldn't help it. The tears came and they didn't stop. Angry, devastated drops fell on my pillow as I clutched my sheets around me.

I wanted to tell him in person, but as soon as I heard his voice, I just had to get it out. The words came tumbling out of me so quickly I couldn't grab hold of them and were met with a coldness I wasn't expecting. I didn't know what I was expecting, but it wasn't that.

His iciness on the phone before I even dropped the bomb on him was biting. I knew there was a slim chance he was upset by how I snuck out of his place the morning after our night together, but I doubted it. Wasn't that what a guy like him would want? Sex without repercussion or awkward morning goodbyes.

Well, this was one hell of a repercussion, whether he wanted to believe me or not. I couldn't believe he had the nerve to ask if it was his. As if I was someone to go home with a different guy each week.

I sighed heavily and fell back into my pillow. I *had* gone home with him, and I had let things go too far, too quickly. Deliciously too far. It was so unlike me, but there was a pull toward him that I couldn't deny. Hell, I had been the one who practically begged him to take me on that bar counter. My cheeks burned red as I remembered it.

How could I have been so irresponsible? I was on the pill, but I had definitely missed a day or two. It was hard to remember to take a tiny white pill when your sex life was nonexistent.

My phone buzzed and I quickly read the screen, hoping it was him calling back. It wasn't.

Shelley: *Hey. You okay? We missed you at this morning's meeting.*

Me: *Yeah, just a little under the weather. Thanks for checking in.*

Shelley: *Feel better soon!*

I locked my phone and tossed it on the bed next to me.

I had called out sick from work, which was a rarity, but when I saw the two lines on the pregnancy test, I practically felt sick. I had run out to the store to grab two more boxes because I didn't believe it. It had to be faulty. Four tests later, and there were more lines and the word *pregnant* clear as day.

I looked over at my bathroom counter where they sat in a neat row. They were practically screaming at me. I felt like I was going to throw up. Was it too early for morning sickness? I threw the covers off and dry-heaved into the toilet. Panic began to set in, pulsing through my body and making me feel flushed. I tried to catch my breath, but felt like there was a limited supply.

I crawled back over to my bed, reaching for my phone. With my back against the mattress, I called Monica.

"Hello?" she answered.

"Monica."

"Heart? Are you okay? What's wrong?"

"Can you come over?"

"I'm on my way."

Twenty minutes later, she was knocking on my door. I opened it and smiled weakly at her before bursting into tears.

She pulled me into a hug. "I'm here. I'm here."

After a few minutes of crying in my doorway, she followed me to the couch. My panic became more of a dull pulse and I felt like I could breathe again.

Monica looked at me with concern on her face, her eyebrows drawn together.

"What's going on, Heart?" she asked, reaching for my hand.

I took a deep breath.

"I'm pregnant," I said, not being able to meet her eye.

"Oh my gosh, Heart," she said in disbelief.

"I know."

"Wait, whose is it?"

I had been keeping my night with Daniel a secret, and normally we didn't keep secrets from each other, especially when it came to men. Even though they were pretty rare in my life, I usually spilled everything to Monica over a few glasses of wine. I had planned on telling her eventually. I just wanted it to be my little secret a little longer. Time to give it up.

"Daniel's," I said.

Monica nearly choked. "Wait, what? Daniel. As in Daniel Jacobs?"

I finally met her eye and nodded.

"Holy shit, Heart. When did this happen?"

She seemed excited, like it was some sort of plot twist in one of her novels. It was the first time I felt like smiling all morning. I actually let out a soft laugh. "Whoa, calm down."

"Sorry, sorry." She put her hands up and took a deep breath.

"I kind of ran into him at a bar weeks ago. I think it's been just over a month. I had a few expensive drinks and got carried away."

"What woman wouldn't?" Monica gave me a sly smile.

"Well, he invited me back to his place and one thing led to another...and another..."

"And another?" Monica raised her brow at me.

I couldn't help but laugh before putting my face in my hands.

"This is crazy, Heart."

"I know," I groaned.

"Hey, it's going to be okay." She scooched closer and pulled my hands from my face.

"Is it? Because I just told him and it was awful."

"Oh, my God. What did he say?"

"He asked if it was his."

"Asshole!" Monica said loudly.

"I know, but he doesn't know me. We hardly know each other. He probably just panicked."

I was trying to see it more from his point of view.

"Well, screw him," said Monica.

"I can't do this alone..."

"You're not alone."

We spent the next few hours searching for doctor's offices in Brooklyn and in the city. Monica insisted we needed the best of the best, which was terrifying for my wallet, but I was happy to have someone who cared when I was too shocked to. Thankfully, we found one in Manhattan that was highly rated and took my insurance.

It was too early to come in for an ultrasound, but we scheduled an appointment for two weeks from then. It felt like an eternity to wait that long to receive hard proof that this thing was real. Until then, I had to rely on the white plastic tests on my bathroom counter to tell me there was most likely a baby growing inside me.

The two weeks dragged on. I didn't hear from Daniel again, and figured he was out of my life for good. The realization started to set in that I was doing this on my own. *If* I was to go through with it. I could barely afford to keep myself alive, let alone a child. The thought kept me up at night.

On the day of my appointment, I took a personal day at work and Monica met me at my apartment. She rode the subway with me into Manhattan, babbling on about her newest plot for a book. I was surprised she wasn't taking this whole mess and turning it into a bestseller. It had the surprise element. Maybe she could write the happy ending that I wouldn't have.

We arrived at the doctor's office with five minutes to spare. The waiting room was bright white with white leather chairs. It felt sterile and cold. I noticed women with growing bellies sitting with pearls around their necks and Louis Vuitton handbags at their feet, with their doting husbands in suits beside them. They looked up curiously when Monica and I walked in wearing leggings and oversized t-shirts.

Even the front desk woman looked me up and down before greeting me with her best attempt to be friendly.

"Hello, may I help you?" she asked. Her smile was so ungenuine, she may as well not have even tried.

"Um, hi. Yes, I have an appointment at 9:30 for an ultrasound."

"Name?"

"Oh right. Heartly. Addison Heartly."

"And who is this?" She side-eyed Monica.

"Her best friend," said Monica with authority, stepping up closer to the counter.

"Riiight. Okay, well, I have a few forms for you to fill out. You can just skip over the 'father' section, if you need to."

That was a bold assumption, but I hated that I would have to prove her right.

"Thanks," I muttered.

"Highly rated, my ass," said Monica as we sat down.

"We're in the upper East Side. What did you expect?" I whispered as I jotted down my information.

We waited for fifteen minutes before a woman in scrubs poked her head out of a nearby door and called my name. I shakily stood from my chair and followed her through the door and down the hallway. We entered a small, white room that felt just as cold as the waiting room.

She handed me a pink hospital gown.

"Go ahead and put this on and make yourself comfortable. I'll be right back."

She slipped out the door and I quickly undressed. I slid the pink gown over my head and sat back on the examination table. Monica pulled her chair up beside me. I looked over at the computer and video monitor. It all started to feel very real.

A knock sounded at the door and the woman stepped inside.

"Are you ready?" she asked.

I nodded. My throat felt dry.

The woman busied herself with typing my information in the computer and getting the white wand prepped with a clear jelly.

"Okay, it will feel cold at first and maybe a little uncomfortable. But since it's early, we have to do it this way. Here on out, ultrasounds will be done externally."

"Okay," I said softly.

Monica reached for my hand and held it.

A few uncomfortable seconds later, the nurse pointed to the video monitor. She explained the different things we were seeing on the screen. I wondered where the baby was. Maybe the tests had been wrong. But then she stopped moving the wand and pointed at the screen.

"And there is your baby," she said.

I felt my breath catch as I looked at the tiny blob on the screen.

"Oh, my gosh," I whispered.

"I'll snap a few pictures for your ultrasound now."

I looked over at Monica and saw her eyes were watery as she watched the screen.

"And now, we can try to hear baby's heartbeat. It's not guaranteed this early...but oh, no. There it is."

The sound of dull thumping filled my ears and I couldn't help it, but I started crying. That was my baby. Every doubt I had before then was washed away like a crashing wave on the shore. Every piece of me was now that baby's. I was all theirs.

"You can get cleaned up now. I'll be back with your photos," she commented before stepping out of the room.

I sat up and held my stomach, a dreamy smile across my lips.

"I'm going to be a mom," I said softly.

"The best mom," said Monica, standing and putting her hand over mine.

I was quiet for a moment.

"A single mom," I said, reminding myself of my reality.

"Remember, you are not alone. Ever. I will be there every step of the way."

I nodded to her gratefully before easing myself off the table and getting dressed.

The lady knocked and stepped back in the room.

"Here are your photos. Please stop by the front desk on your way out," she said before disappearing down the hallway.

I looked down at the photos in awe. For being a blob, the baby was perfect in every way.

I handed Monica one of the copies. "Here."

"Really?" she asked, her eyes watering again.

"Of course. You're Auntie Monica now."

She took the photo and burst into tears. As happy as I was she was here, I couldn't help but wonder what it would have been like if Daniel had been with me.

Chapter 14

DANIEL

"Earth to Daniel," said Brody, waving his hand in front of my face.

I broke out of whatever trance I was under, blinking a few times as I remembered where I was. It shouldn't have been hard to forget I was prepping for one of our biggest board meetings, but my mind had been anywhere else but here lately.

It was like an audio recording had been jammed inside my head, and all that played over and over again was Addison's voice.

"I'm pregnant. I'm pregnant. I'm pregnant."

I shook my head, hoping the words would get the hint and make their exit. "Sorry, bro," I said.

"What the hell is going on with you?" asked Brody, settling back in the armchair across from my desk, crossing his arms as he studied me cautiously.

"I didn't get much sleep." I shrugged.

It was partly true. Partly a lie. I hadn't been sleeping very well, but I also hadn't been able to focus on work or anything since Addison had dropped that bomb on me.

"And what was your excuse yesterday? And the day before?" he asked.

"You know me. I've just been having fun."

"Really? Because I haven't seen you in the tabloids…"

"That's a good thing," I said defensively.

"Yeah, well, I've also run into Freddy a few times, and he said you'd been declining his calls."

I could see he wasn't letting this go. I had to come up with something, but I didn't want to share the news of me possibly being a father with my brother, or Freddy, or anyone. Not until I had everything figured everything out.

"Maybe I'm seeing someone," I lied. "Can you get back to minding your business?"

Brody raised a skeptical eyebrow. "Fine, as long as you get your damn head in the game. You've missed deadlines, shown up late for meetings, and everything I'm saying is going in one ear and out the other."

"What the hell? Are you keeping tabs on me?"

"Someone has to."

I was annoyed, but he was right. I had to get my head on straight, especially for today's board meeting with our shareholders. When did Brody become the sensible one?

"Okay," I said. "I'm here."

Brody gave me an affirmative nod before sliding over a stack of papers. I looked through them and hopelessly tried to focus, or at least look like I was.

I couldn't go on like this much longer when my company's reputation was at stake—I had to talk to Addison and know what was going on. I hated how we had left things after our phone call and I'd been kicking myself for how I had responded ever since.

For the past two weeks, I had tried emailing and calling, but she ignored my emails and calls. I knew I had hurt her by questioning her and my legitimacy as the father. I just panicked. It didn't seem real, so I questioned it, and insulted her in the end.

Deep down, I felt like I knew what kind of girl Addison was. That was what drew me to her. She was different. Driven. Caring. Had no idea who I was, and I wasn't sure she cared. She didn't seem like the type to sleep around. I was a one-off. I got lucky. But now I had to fix things, especially considering I might be a father.

"The goals for the upcoming year look good. Have any of the shareholders raised any concerns?" I said, stacking the papers neatly and handing them back to Brody.

"Not that I know of, but you never know what they could spring on us today."

I nodded. "We'll be ready."

And I prayed we would be.

I checked my watch. The meeting was to start in just a few minutes.

"We better head to the meeting room," I said, standing from my chair.

Before following Brody out of the door, I refreshed my inbox in hopes there would be something from Addison. I made another attempt to get hold of her this morning, but there was nothing from her.

The board meeting went surprisingly well. The shareholders had no real concerns. Maybe it was because my face hadn't been splashed over the morning papers in a while, or the fact that the paparazzi had become bored with me. I had to admit it was a nice change for me, even though it also meant I wasn't getting laid.

I was impressed with Brody and how he came prepared. For how much I doubted my little brother sometimes, I never forgot why he was COO. I should have a little more faith in him.

After the meeting, Brody slapped me on the back enthusiastically. "That went really well, bro," he said.

"Until next year," I said.

"We should celebrate! Maybe head to Bemelman's for lunch?"

The name alone made my breath catch. I hadn't been there since Addison strolled in and changed my entire life.

"Can we do a raincheck? I have somewhere to be."

Brody looked disappointed. "Tomorrow night?" he suggested.

"Tomorrow it is."

I watched Brody walk down the hallway to his office before I stopped at Margaret's desk.

"May I help you, Mr. Jacobs?"

"I was hoping you could find the address for one of our associates."

"Which one?" she asked, placing her pale pink-painted fingertips on the keyboard.

"Addison Heartly."

A few clicks of the keyboard sounded.

"Ah, yes. The Leading to Learn office. I can write the address down for you."

She reached for a post-it.

"Um, no. Actually, I was in need of her home address."

Margaret looked at me curiously before looking back at her computer screen. She scrolled the screen and then back up.

"I'm sorry. I don't have her personal information on file."

"Well, can you find it?" I asked, drumming my fingers on the desktop.

"I could try..." she replied.

"Thank you. I'll be in my office."

I walked down the hallway and into my office. I sat in my chair and refreshed my inbox again. There was still nothing from Addison. I scrolled through all of my sent emails to her and suddenly felt embarrassed. There were thirteen total. All sitting and staring at me as reminders of how badly I had screwed this up.

I sighed and looked out the window. I felt desperate and out of control. Two feelings I despised.

A knock sounded at my door.

"Come in," I said eagerly.

Margaret stepped inside holding a bright yellow post-it. I felt hopeful for the first time in a long time.

"I have that address for you, Mr. Jacobs," she said.

She held out the sticky piece of paper proudly. I took it from her and read the words silently. I guessed I was heading to Brooklyn.

"Thank you, Margaret. I'll be heading out now. Please hold my calls."

"Of course, sir," she said before slipping out the door.

I grabbed my jacket, sliding it on over my shoulders before heading out the door. Downstairs at the curb, Armand waited. I wondered if he ever did anything else besides wait on me.

"Where to, Mr. Jacobs?" he asked as he opened the back door.

"Brooklyn," I replied, sliding into the car.

Once Armand was up front, I read him the address and sat back as he put the car into drive. I couldn't remember the last time I had gone to Brooklyn.

It wasn't far, but felt like a whole other world from the high rises and wealth of the upper East Side.

Forty-five minutes later, we pulled up to a small, brick apartment building. Armand walked around the side of the car and opened my door. I thanked him as I stepped out onto the curb. I looked down at the address in my hand. Apartment 2B.

I noticed a pizza delivery guy exiting the building and jogged up to catch the door to let myself inside. I walked down the hallway toward the stairs and noticed a fluffy white cat at my feet. As I stopped to greet her, she weaved her way between my legs.

"Hello there," I said, bending down to pet her.

"Beatrice!" I heard someone call.

I looked up and saw an older woman clutching a fluffy pink robe around herself, her gray hair rolled tightly in pink sponge rollers.

"Beatrice. There you are!" she said, walking over.

I picked up the cat and stood.

"Cute cat," I said, extending my arms out to give her cat back.

The woman took it and cradled it before looking at me. I noticed her eyes widen slightly. She looked me up and down, her mouth open in surprise.

She scrunched her eyebrows together. "Aren't you..."

"I really should be going," I said.

I headed toward the stairs and began climbing them. I could hear the woman mumbling to herself. It wasn't unusual to be recognized, but I didn't need anyone knowing I was in Brooklyn or what business I was on.

I walked down the hallway and stopped in front of apartment 2B. I took a deep breath before knocking. My nerves caused waves of nausea to roll through my stomach. The last time I had seen Addison was when she was sleeping in my bed. I didn't know how much I would end up missing her. Missing someone was not something I did.

I heard the numerous locks of the door click before it finally opened. To my disappointment, it wasn't Addison standing there. I checked the address on the post-it. This was the place.

"May I help you?" asked the woman standing there. She was short with a brown angled bob that hit just above her shoulders. Judging by the scowl on her face, she didn't look too pleased to see me.

"I'm looking for Addison Heartly," I said.

"Heart's not here right now."

"Heart?"

"Yeah, that's what her *close* friends call her."

Ah. I was dealing with the protective best friend. Fuck me.

"Well, will you let her know I stopped by?"

"And you are?" she asked, even though her icy stare made it clear she knew exactly who I was.

"Daniel Jacobs."

"I don't think she wants to see you."

"Please."

"No. I think you should go."

I desperately wanted to call out Addison's name. Heart's name. Whatever she was called. I just wanted to see her. But clearly she didn't want to see me.

She started to close the door.

"Wait. Please," I said.

Not knowing what else to do, I reached into my jacket pocket and pulled out my checkbook and a pen. The girl eyed me suspiciously as I began writing a check with a whole lot of zeroes. I ripped it from my checkbook and handed it to her.

Her gaze scanned over the check and her eyes widened as they landed on the amount.

"Please, make sure she gets this. I want to help. She can do whatever she wants with the money."

The girl looked from the check to me, as if she was struggling to find the words. She stepped inside the apartment and closed the door, leaving me standing outside like a complete idiot. I kicked at the floor as I turned and started walking down the hallway.

"Wait!" I heard a voice call out.

I turned around and saw her friend walking swiftly toward me. She pushed a piece of glossy paper into my chest.

"If you want to be involved, you need to be sure," she said sternly.

I looked down at the piece of paper and saw it was an ultrasound. Addison's ultrasound. Our baby's first picture. It was real. So fucking real.

I stared at the picture speechless, for I didn't know how long before realizing I was standing alone in the hallway. I carefully slid the photo in my jacket pocket and somehow walked down the stairs. My legs felt like they were going to give out on me every step of the way.

Chapter 15

ADDISON

"What did he want?" I asked, peeping out from behind the kitchen counter.

Monica closed the door behind her and looked around until she spotted me on all fours on the black and white tile. She shook her head at me and let out a soft laugh.

"You're ridiculous," she said.

"No, I'm not."

She raised an eyebrow. Okay, I was being ridiculous. But Daniel showing up at my apartment was not on my bingo card for the day. Being pregnant with his baby wasn't either, but here we were.

When I heard the knock at my door, I assumed it was Elma. What I saw through my peephole was Daniel looking like some freaking GQ model in a charcoal gray suit with his hair pushed back. My stomach did several backflips, as if it were competing for the gold medal in gymnastics. I stumbled backward and told Monica to answer the door in a commanding whisper.

A small part of me wanted to go out there and tell him off. A larger part of me, and the more stupid part of me, just wanted to hear his voice and feel his blue eyes on me again. But I couldn't face him, hence me being tucked away in my tiny kitchen.

Monica walked over and offered me her hand. She pulled me to stand and leaned against the counter, staring straight ahead.

"So?" I asked. "What did he say?"

"He wanted to see you."

She shrugged so nonchalantly that I just wanted to shake whatever information she had out of her. She had just walked back in the door and I was already feeling my patience growing thin.

"And?" I asked, my voice rising slightly.

"That's it. It's not like we went out for coffee, Heart. The guy was here for maybe a minute. I wasn't exactly welcoming."

"Monica!" I said, exasperated.

"What?" she asked. "You expect me to be friendly to the guy?"

I could just see her tough guy act now. No wonder Daniel high-tailed it out of here. I loved my best friend to death. Her protectiveness of me was endearing, but I half-hoped there would be more to Daniel's visit. Like her digging for answers, or him pushing past her and barging in here looking for me. I leaned against the counter, feeling disappointed.

The truth was, I didn't know what I wanted. This whole time I had been pushing Daniel away since I told him I was pregnant. That phone call had been a complete disaster, and his reaction had nearly broken my heart in two.

It wasn't like I was in love with the guy. Hell, I didn't even know if I liked him all that much. We had spent more time having sex than we had talking in the short time we had known each other. Good sex. Amazing sex. But still. I just didn't expect my start to motherhood to be like this.

I had been ignoring his emails. Thirteen to be exact. I'd be lying if I said I hadn't read them over and over again, looking for some unsaid thing behind his professional verbiage. He was a businessman through and through. He had called, too, but never left a voicemail. It was probably better that way. Hearing his voice would probably make me lose all resolve. I was determined to stay strong.

Now, he was showing up at my apartment. I wondered where he had gotten my address. I was also surprised he had made the drive out to Brooklyn.

I looked over at Monica who seemed like she was in her head.

"What aren't you telling me?" I asked, eyeing her suspiciously.

"Nothing."

Her voice was an octave higher. Liar.

I spotted something in her hand.

"What is that?" I asked, nodding to her hand that suddenly tightened its grip.

She looked up at the ceiling and sighed before opening her hand. She held it out to me and I saw a folded piece of paper. I picked it up and unfolded it carefully. It was a check for more than I would make in ten years at Leading to Learn. Daniel's name was in the upper right-hand corner. I sucked in a sharp breath.

"Holy shit," I whispered.

"Yeah," said Monica softly.

"He just gave this to you?"

"Yeah, he wrote it right by the stairs and handed it over. He said he wanted to help and that you could do whatever you wanted with the money."

I suddenly felt angry and sad. Two emotions that had been on rotation for weeks now. I was really hoping happiness would take a turn soon. The only glimpse of happiness I had was hearing my baby's heartbeat, but then sadness took over. And fear.

I could feel hot tears forming at the backs of my eyes. I was angry at myself for avoiding him the past few weeks when maybe he was trying to turn things around. But if his way of making things better was writing a big fat check, then he wasn't ready to be a father. I couldn't fault him for that. I wasn't ready to be a mother, but I was going to try my hardest for my baby.

I knew Daniel didn't ask for this. I hadn't either. I guessed I just expected more. I was stupid for expecting anything at all. I was stupid for going home with him in the first place. Did I really think we were going to just talk and get to know each other?

I wished so badly that I could turn back time and never have stepped foot into Bemelman's. But then I wouldn't have this baby growing inside me. I had never felt so torn in my life.

I sunk back down to the kitchen floor and leaned my head against the cabinets.

Monica slid down beside me. I looked at the check again.

"*This* is how he wants to help?" I asked, shaking it in front of Monica's face.

"Maybe it's the only way he knows how," she said.

"Well, I don't need it."

"Heart—" started Monica.

"No!"

My voice was shaky as I held the check in front of me, ready to rip it into pieces. I was sure I didn't need anything from Daniel Jacobs. I could do this on my own.

Before I could so much as put a small tear in the check, Monica snatched it out of my hands.

"Hey!" I yelled, reaching for it.

"Don't do this," said Monica firmly. "Whether you keep this baby or not, it would be stupid to throw this away. It's chump change to him, but it could be life-changing for you. Or if you decide not to use it for yourself, you could put it into the nonprofit."

I blinked back tears as I tried to swallow down my anger toward Monica. Toward Daniel. Toward this whole messy situation. As much as I wanted to tell my best friend off, I knew she was being practical and I was being emotional.

I put my head in my hands and the quiet sobs came. Monica put her arm around me and we sat in silence for several minutes. I knew I needed money. I knew the reality of living in a tiny loft in Brooklyn and living on one salary that I already scraped by on. Also, I knew that I had my best friend to lean on, but it wasn't enough. At the end of the day, I would be raising this baby by myself. How was I going to support myself and a tiny human?

I lifted my head when the tears stopped coming and sniffled.

"You're going to be okay, Heart," said Monica.

"Maybe," I said. "I have to make a call."

Monica looked at me, confused.

"Daniel?" she asked.

I shook my head. "My parents."

I was sure that response shocked her more than if I would have said Daniel.

I hadn't spoken to my parents in years. Our relationship hadn't always been the best. I always felt like I wasn't good enough for them. I felt like I wasn't doing enough. Every little thing I did seemed to disappoint them. I didn't know what made them have such high standards for me, but it was exhausting.

Things really went south when I got a job at the nonprofit. They didn't understand why I took a job that paid so little. When I explained to them that it wasn't about the money, and it was about helping others, they scoffed. They told me I would regret it.

It was then that I felt empowered enough to put distance between us. I was an adult and capable of making my own decisions. I no longer needed their support or their roof over my head. I was free.

Gradually, the void between us grew. I began skipping trips home for the holidays, and eventually stopped visiting at all. The calls stopped too, on my end and theirs.

As I pulled my phone from the back pocket of my jeans, Monica stood and quietly excused herself to the living room to give me privacy. As if there could be privacy in my apartment.

I inhaled a shaky breath as I scrolled through my contacts and found the number to my parents' house. I pressed the green *send* button and closed my eyes as the rings trilled.

"Hello?" I heard my mother answer.

I held my breath and struggled to speak.

"Hello?" she asked again.

"Mom?" I asked softly.

I paused.

"Addison? Is that you?"

I heard the quiet disbelief in her voice.

"Yeah, it's me."

"Wow. Um, how are you? Wait. Wait. Let me get your dad on the line."

"Oh, you don't have to—"

I heard her hand cover the receiver and muffled words. She was probably coaxing my dad out of his recliner in the living room where he sat and watched the news all day. I could see it now. It almost made me miss them. Almost.

I heard the click of another phone pick up.

"Addison?" my dad asked, just as disbelieving as my mom.

"Hey, Dad."

"This is a surprise."

"Yeah...listen. I have some news."

I just wanted to cut right to it. We were never very good at small talk anyway.

"Okay..." my mom said hesitantly.

"I'm pregnant."

There was silence on the other line. I looked at my phone, wondering if we had lost connection. We hadn't.

"Hello?" I asked.

"Pregnant? Wow," said my mom unenthusiastically.

"Um, and your boyfriend or husband..." started my dad.

"The dad isn't in the picture actually," I replied, trying to keep my voice from shaking.

I could have sworn I heard my mother mutter something under her breath. Something like "Of course, he isn't."

"Addison...how are you going to do this?" asked my dad. At least there was a hint of concern in his voice.

"I'm figuring it out."

"By calling us..." said my mom. I could hear the sneer in her voice.

This had been an incredibly stupid idea on my part. Did I really expect them to be happy for me? Did I really expect them to help me?

"I just thought—"

"We're not millionaires, Addison," said my mom.

"I know that. I just thought..."

"Thought what? You could call up your parents, who you cut out of your life, and ask for help with your mistake?" She laughed sarcastically.

"Nancy..." my dad warned. I could tell he was torn.

"Don't 'Nancy' me. She's not getting a dime out of us."

"Maybe we could—"

"No, John. We could not."

They continued to bicker, completely forgetting I was on the phone at all. I shook my head and ended the call.

"How did *that* go?" asked Monica, peeping over the countertop.

"As you'd imagine," I said.

"I'm sorry, Heart."

"Me too."

Chapter 16

DANIEL

On the drive back to Manhattan, I stared at the ultrasound in my hands. I knew nothing about babies, but I assumed the little white blob in the bigger black blob was the baby. My baby. Our baby. My heart felt like it had somehow grown as soon as that girl handed me this piece of glossy paper. I could only imagine what Addison felt. Heart. Whoever she was.

Heart seemed more fitting. Part of me wanted to earn the right to call her that.

God, I had been a total asshole when she gave me the most important news of her life. Of our life.

We hadn't even talked about anything yet, but my uncertainty around me being the father or not had diminished completely. Staring down at the little white blob, I knew it was mine. He. She. Whichever.

I had to see Addison again. I wondered if she was in her apartment. She probably was. She probably sent her bulldog friend out to grill me and stay the hell away from her. As she should have. But knowing she was so close, yet so far was pulling me apart.

Maybe I should have tried harder to see her.

I would try harder. I would come back tomorrow and I would make sure she couldn't ignore me.

My phone rang just then, and I half-hoped it was her. To my disappointment, it was Freddy.

"Hey, man," he said when I picked up.

"Hey," I said, trying not to sound annoyed that it wasn't Addison.

"Are you coming out tonight?" he asked.

"For what?"

"Uh, my birthday."

Shit. I forgot. That was the last thing I wanted to do when I had this much on my mind.

"I don't know—"

"Yes, you do. You are. Lavo. 11 o'clock. If you don't, I will officially disown you as my best friend."

I rolled my eyes. He was so dramatic. Still, I had never missed Freddy's birthday. Not since we were kids.

"Fine. I'll be there."

I hung up and tossed my phone on the seat beside me.

The rest of the ride back to Manhattan, I stared at the ultrasound and felt a small chance of hope I might see Addison tomorrow.

When 11 o'clock rolled around, I rode the elevator down to the parking garage where Armand waited with the car. I was late, but I didn't care. At least I was going at all.

I arrived at Lavo twenty minutes later and Freddy was already three drinks in and feeling friendly. There were four women surrounding him in his private booth. Normally, this would entice me, but this was the last place I wanted to be.

"Look who showed up!" said Freddy excitedly.

"Happy Birthday," I said, sitting at the edge of the booth and keeping my distance from the vultures in little black dresses who had spotted their next prey.

It was funny how things changed. I used to relish in the fact that women were impressed by my money. It turned me on. I liked the idea of taking care of a woman, and her being eager to take care of me. Now, I couldn't care less about impressing anyone.

Brody handed me a drink from the tray before whispering flirtatiously to the cocktail waitress, who eagerly giggled. I took a sip. A lemon drop. My worst nightmare. But whatever. I'd be a good sport for Freddy's birthday.

I spent the next hour pretending to be interested in what anyone was saying, all the while thinking about the ultrasound sitting in my jacket pocket. It was a risky move bringing it with me, but for some reason I wanted it with me. It was like this quiet reminder of what really mattered. None of what was happening in this club did.

As soon as Freddy had his tongue down someone's throat, I took my chance to leave. He would be busy for the rest of the night. He would hardly miss me. Plus, I wanted to get to bed, so I could get out to Brooklyn early the next morning.

"Freddy, I'm going to head out."

He pulled away from the platinum blonde who was now straddling him.

"Yeah, I have an early work meeting. But this was...fun. Happy Birthday."

He gave me a small salute and went back to jamming his tongue down the girl's throat.

I laughed as I began pushing my way through the crowd. That was when I spotted Kiera on the dance floor. I tried to avert my gaze, but she latched onto my eyes and made her way over. She wore a white dress with a plunging neckline and I would be lying if I said it was hard to look at her face.

She slung her arms around my neck and moved her body to the music.

"This is a surprise," she said in a sing-song voice.

"Sure is," I said.

"Do you like my dress?" She let go of me and did a twirl, stumbling slightly.

"It sure is something," I replied, steadying her.

She was drunk.

"Who are you here with?" I asked, looking around. I wanted to make sure she was taken care of before I left. Despite our history, I still cared about her.

She looked around and squinted one eye. The classic Kiera's wasted face.

"I don't know." She shrugged. "I forgot."

She giggled before slinging her arms around me once more.

"Let's get you home, Kiera."

I wrapped my arm around her waist and half carried her through the club. Before going outside, I called Armand to bring the car around. The last thing I needed was to be seen in the papers with Kiera in a white dress. They'd probably claim it was our engagement party.

The doorman let Armand in and I passed Kiera off to him.

"See that she gets home, please," I said.

"And you, sir?" asked Armand, raising his brows.

"I'll Uber."

"You're not coming?" asked Kiera with a pouty face.

"Not tonight, sweetheart. Get home safe, okay?"

The doors to the club swung open and I could see the flashes of cameras instantly go off. I was happy to be hidden inside the darkness of the club.

After a short Uber ride home, I took a hot shower and washed the day away before climbing into bed. I thought my nerves would keep me up, but it was actually the opposite. Knowing I would possibly see Addison in the morning made me fall asleep quickly. I wanted the morning to get there as fast as possible.

The next morning, I woke up at six and quickly dressed for the day. I met Armand down in the parking garage. On our way out of Manhattan, I had him stop at a coffee shop. I had the idea of bringing some tea for Addison. I read that it helped with morning sickness.

I had been Googling various things about pregnancy while I ate my dinner last night at home, before going to Freddy's party. I wasn't sure if Addison had any symptoms yet, but I saw the tea as some sort of peace offering.

We arrived at her apartment just past seven. I had no idea when she left for work, but figured it wasn't this early. I had Armand park out front and felt odd for staking out the place, but I would do whatever I could to at least talk to her. Thankfully, Armand didn't ask questions. He never did, which was why I liked him so much.

Time ticked by slowly. I was going restless in the car, but I knew if I went up to her apartment again, there was a chance she wouldn't answer the door. Or worse, she'd send her friend out. I wasn't sure if it was her roommate or what the situation was. It was better to wait down here.

Finally at 8:20, the door to her building opened and I saw her step outside into the warm sunlight. She wore a pair of faded jeans and a pin-striped blue button-down. I smiled to myself. I had never seen her dressed down, but I liked it. Then my nerves caught up with me. I took a deep breath as I opened the car door. She had already begun to walk down the sidewalk.

"Addison," I called.

She stopped and turned around. Her face dropped when she saw me. I half expected her to turn and keep walking, but she stayed put. I climbed out of the car, grabbing the tea from the cupholder and walked toward her.

"What are you doing here?" she asked, looking around like I had just flown across the world when really I had just driven over a bridge.

"I had to see you. I stopped by yesterday, but..."

"I know," she said sharply.

"Look, I'm so sorry for being such a dick. I was just surprised and didn't know how to handle the news."

She didn't say anything.

"I brought you tea," I said, holding up the cup that now was lukewarm at best.

She looked from me to the cup.

"It's going to take a lot more than tea to get me to talk to you." She turned and began walking away.

"Wait. Please. Have you thought about names?" I blurted out.

She stopped walking, but didn't turn around.

"Please, Heart." I tried again.

"You haven't earned the right to call me that yet," she said softly as she turned around.

The 'yet' made me feel hopeful.

I nodded. "I have to head back to Manhattan for work. Can I give you a ride?" I asked.

As I watched her consider my offer, I was reminded of how beautiful she really was. Her dark hair was pulled into a high ponytail and her brown eyes were caramel in the sun.

"Okay," she said.

"Really?" I asked a little too eagerly.

She shot me a look and I reminded myself not to get too ahead of myself. I walked past her and opened the door for her before Armand could. She slid inside the car and I followed, closing the door behind me.

Again, she sat as far away from me as she could. All I wanted to do was be close to her, but I understood her coolness toward me.

"You look nice," I said.

"Er, thanks." She looked out the window as the car pulled away from the curb.

Even though we had at least an hour's drive back to the city, I felt like the minutes were fleeting.

"Here," I said, handing her the tea. "It's probably not very hot anymore."

She gave the faintest smile and took it from my hands, avoiding any contact with my fingers.

She took a sip. "Thank you," she said softly.

"How are you feeling?" I asked.

"Fine."

"No symptoms? I read morning sickness can start around six weeks."

She bit back a smile, and my eyes fixated toward her lips. It was the first time I had felt any real arousal in weeks. Jesus.

Pull it together, Daniel.

"I've been a little nauseous here and there, but nothing too bad."

"Good. That's good."

"Did you get a baby book or something?" she asked, raising an eyebrow.

I laughed. "No, just Google."

"Hmm," she murmured.

"Is that a good 'hmm' or a bad 'hmm?'"

"It's just a hmm."

I could see her mouth lift into a smile as she turned and looked out the window again. My eyes traveled from her face to the buttons of her blouse, which were pulled taught against her breasts. They stayed there for a while as I wondered if they had gotten bigger since our night together. I read that was the first sign of possibly being pregnant. I hoped I could find out. Probably not any time soon, but her accepting to ride with me was a step in the direction I wanted to go.

Chapter 17

ADDISON

I took a sip of the lukewarm tea, hoping it would calm the incessant jitters in my stomach. I didn't have morning sickness yet, but I wondered if this was what it felt like. A mixture of nausea and anxiety.

As cold as I tried to come off because I knew that Daniel deserved it, my heart was playing tug-of-war with my head. I wanted to be angry at him, and I was, but I also felt my resolve weakening. I wouldn't be able to stay angry for long. Why did he have to be so damn charming?

I knew I should have walked away when he surprised me outside of my apartment, and I almost did, but the sound of his voice when he asked if I had names picked out for the baby stopped me right in my tracks. He was either a really good actor, or he actually cared.

I mean, the guy showed up with herbal tea. And he'd been Googling about pregnancy? It didn't sound like something he would do if he was trying to buy my silence. But still, I kept my guard up, or at least tried to.

Now I was in a closed space with him and the walls of the car seemed to be closing in, making my urge to be closer to him even greater. It didn't help that his cologne smelled so damn good or that he wore the same suit I had taken off him during our night together. I wondered if he had strategically worn it. Smart move.

I continued staring out the window as we weaved our way through the traffic of Manhattan. I was surprised how quickly we had gotten to the city. I knew we would be at my office soon, and I was already dreading saying goodbye. I didn't know when I would see him again, or if I even wanted to. Or if he even wanted to see me again. Maybe this was just his way of trying to be decent by apologizing before wiping his hands clean of me.

As we turned down the street of Leading to Learn, my heart began fluttering in my chest in a panic. Maybe this was the last time I would see him and I had just completely blown it on the hour-long car ride here. It was funny how the heart worked. Here I was supposed to be upset with him, and now I was upset with myself for ruining a chance I didn't even think I had.

The car came to a stop at the curb. I finally turned to him and saw his eyes were already intently on me. Had he been looking at me for long? I cleared my throat nervously.

"Well, this is me," I said, looking up at the building, as if he hadn't told his driver to come here.

"Right," he nodded.

We sat there awkwardly for a few seconds before I reached for the door, but it was already opening. His driver smiled down at me and waited for me to get out.

"Thank you," I said to Daniel softly.

He didn't say anything, but his eyes were on mine.

More than anything, I wanted to reach over and grab his hand or hug him or touch him in any way, but instead I slid out of the car and walked toward my building without looking back. I figured goodbye would be easier that way. As I stepped through the door, I felt tears stinging my eyes.

Out of sight of the car, I leaned against the wall, let out a long breath, and wiped at the tears that threatened to fall. I was completely undone. Everything I had held against Daniel over the past few weeks had dissipated like mist when the sun comes up. All the reasons I had convinced myself to hate him seemed invalid now. I shook my head, trying to knock the sense back into me.

"Addison?" I heard a voice say.

I looked up and saw Brian staring at me with a curious expression as he stood by the elevators.

"Oh, hey, Brian," I said casually, pushing myself from the wall.

"Uh, you okay?"

"Yeah, totally fine. I think I just got something in my eye. I'm good now."

He didn't look convinced, but also didn't press me further. He pressed the button for the elevators and we stepped through the doors as they slid open.

"Did you Uber today?" he asked.

He must have seen me get out of Daniel's town car. I felt a slight panic set in. There were strict rules about starting relationships within the office or with associates outside of the office. It wasn't like Daniel and I were in a relationship, but having a baby certainly complicated things.

"Yeah," I lied. "I couldn't find my subway pass."

It was a stupid lie of an excuse, but he seemed to buy it.

When the elevators reached our floor, I said goodbye and walked swiftly to my office. My stomach was in knots, and remained that way for the rest of the day. It was hard to focus on work or my meetings. I just kept thinking about Daniel, after I had worked so hard to forget him. Or at least tried to.

Monica came by on my lunch break and we went to the deli on the corner. I ordered a veggie sandwich, even though I would have loved some cold cuts piled on. I wanted to do everything right by the baby, so instead I sat there and chewed on cucumber and lettuces smooshed between two halves of French bread as I told her about the morning.

"You mean he just was waiting for you?" asked Monica between bites of her sandwich.

"I guess." I shrugged.

"What did he want?"

"To apologize. Then he offered me a ride to work..."

"And you said, 'hell no.' Right?"

I reached in my bag of chips and popped one in my mouth, avoiding her gaze as it crunched.

"Heart..."

"I don't know, Monica. He seemed different."

She let out a solitary laugh, its sarcasm biting.

"I doubt I will ever see him again," I said, looking out the window to the bustling sidewalk, hoping it wasn't true.

Little did I know.

When I walked out the door of my apartment building the following morning, I saw him leaning against his town car with another cup of tea in hand. I swore he could hear my heart pounding in my chest as I walked toward him.

"You're back," I said.

"I hope that's okay." He handed me the cup of tea.

"It's hot today," I said after taking a sip.

He gave me a smile. One I hadn't seen before from him. It was genuine and warm. He opened the back door and gestured for me to get inside. I hesitated just for a second before realizing there was no place I would rather be than next to him in that car. I slid inside and he followed behind me.

"How are you feeling today?" he asked as the car pulled away from the curb.

"I'm okay. Just tired," I said. I wasn't sure if it was from pregnancy or the thought of him that kept me up last night.

"That's normal," he mused.

"What, are you some sort of expert now?" I asked, a smirk trailing across my lips.

"Trying to be," he said.

His eyes looked at mine and fell to my lips where they stayed for a delicious moment too long. I wondered what he was thinking and if it was the same thing as me. How it would feel to taste each other again.

Again, we arrived in Manhattan too quickly for my liking. I was actually begging for there to be traffic. Wasn't that what New York was known for anyway? I begrudgingly said goodbye and got out of the car, looking around cautiously to make sure no one saw me.

The work day dragged on as I thought about the possibility of seeing Daniel again. It seemed ridiculous that he would make the drive out to Brooklyn each morning just to bring me tea and drive me to work, but that was exactly what he did.

Each morning, I found him leaning against the town car in that sexy, relaxed way of his, holding a steaming cup of tea. Because of this, I took extra time getting ready. I didn't squeeze myself into tight skirts or dresses, but an extra spritz of perfume and a swipe of lip gloss wouldn't hurt.

Each morning, he told me I looked nice, and the way his eyes took me in made my skin break out in goosebumps. It was as if he was imagining what was underneath, as if he didn't already know. We didn't fall into this complicated situation by staying clothed.

This morning, I wore a white linen dress that skimmed just above my knees. I had pulled my hair back into a braid that fell down my back. When Daniel saw me, his eyes wandered and he didn't even try to hide it.

It felt good to feel wanted. I had struggled with feeling confident for so long, but with him, he made me feel different. I felt desired. Beautiful. Sexy. Also, very pregnant. The morning sickness had finally hit me.

As he opened the car door for me, I felt his touch for what felt like the first time in years. His hand grazed my lower back as he guided me inside the car. That one touch unraveled me and I wanted more. I made the conscious choice to not scooch to the far end of the car. As he slid in next to me, I didn't pull away when his thigh grazed against mine. I felt his eyes meet where our bodies touched and a small smile crossed his lips.

"How are you feeling today?" he asked.

"Tired. A little nauseous. And my boobs hurt."

He laughed. "They look bigger," he said, holding back a smile.

"Daniel!" I said, slugging him playfully in the arm.

"What? It's hard not to look."

I felt my cheeks burning.

"You make a really hot pregnant woman."

"You're ridiculous," I said, shaking my head.

The word pregnant coming from his mouth made it all the more real. I was carrying a baby. Our baby. While I didn't know exactly what our situation was, I was grateful he was here. It might just be a ride to the city and a supposed cure to morning sickness, but it meant so much more to me than that. This was him showing up when I was convinced he was walking out.

We hadn't talked about the logistics of anything, or about if or how he would be a part of the baby's life. I didn't know where we stood. We talked about anything and everything else, and that was enough for me. For now.

I was seeing a new side to Daniel. He didn't seem like the same man I had met all those weeks ago. Yes, he was still incredibly sexy and charming and made it easy to see why I had gone home with him in the first place. The man didn't have the reputation he did for nothing.

But he was also funny. Sweet. Pensive. Genuine. It was as if his cool guy façade had fallen away and I could see the man behind the millions. I wondered if it was a side many had seen or if I was just lucky. Either way, it was hard not to fall for him.

Knowing I was carrying his baby just added to my attraction for him. It seemed incredibly stupid, but I couldn't help wondering if there could somehow be a happy ending for us. I hoped for it. For the baby. For me.

Chapter 18

DANIEL

I noticed Addison's eyes on me and for the first time in a few days I didn't see anger or fear or sadness. All things I wished I hadn't caused her. I didn't know what I saw in that glance, but it made her brown eyes come alive. I held her gaze until she looked away coyly. I realized we were on her block and our time was almost up.

As the car came to a stop outside her work, I felt the same disappointment I felt every day when it was time to say goodbye. On top of that, I felt a franticness that it would possibly be the last time I saw her. Maybe she would change her mind and this short time together would end. An hour or so was not enough time together, but it was all I could get right now. All I attempted to get. All I probably deserved to get after what I had put her through.

"Well, this is me," she said softly, grabbing her purse and putting her hand on the door.

I gave a solemn nod as Armand rounded the car and opened her door for her. She was almost out of the car, and then she turned around and slid back across the seat toward me. I sucked in a shallow breath as I wondered what she was doing. Eager for whatever was bringing her closer to me.

She leaned in and whispered in my ear, "Thank you."

Those two simple words entered my skull and sent shivers down the length of my spine, forcing me to close my eyes as if it was a reflex to her close proximity. She then pressed her soft lips to my cheek before pulling away. Then she was gone.

As soon as her lips left my cheek, a burn took place of where her kiss had been. I could have sworn it was a touch that would scar me in a way I would want to remember. Like a scar on your knee from when you first learned to ride a bike. It was exciting and new, and without the pain.

I watched as she walked up to her work, parts of her white dress swishing as she walked, while others clung to her curves. She didn't look back, but my eyes didn't falter from her until she disappeared through the doors. Today was the first time we had touched in the week I had been picking her up from Brooklyn. I had taken a chance by placing my hand on the small of her back today as she got into the car.

I couldn't help it. She was like a magnet, and I no longer had the strength to avoid her pull. It seemed to open a door I thought had surely been shut.

This morning felt different. Driving her to Manhattan had become some sort of unspoken agreement between the two of us. Every morning, she would walk out of her brick building and look around as if she doubted I was there again, but then her eyes would find me and a slow smile would spread across her lips. It got me every time.

Every car ride, I felt her walls start to come down a little. I wondered if I would eventually get the chance to call her Heart. It had become a new challenge for me.

In the five-ish or so hours we had spent together the past week, we hadn't talked much about the baby or what the future looked like, other than how she was feeling and what symptoms were new. The boobs were definitely new. They were good before, but now I knew they'd spill out of my hands, and the thought was tantalizing.

It was as if we knew that talking about the baby would mean talking about us, and we were just barely figuring each other out. After doing everything backward, we were now at the getting to know you stage.

We had nine months to figure everything else out. Or was it eight?

I learned that she was smart. Not in an "I went to an Ivy League," but more in a street-smart way that I found incredibly attractive. You could go to Harvard and still not know shit about the world. I knew plenty of people like that, and they failed to impress me in the way Addison did.

I felt oddly insignificant next to her, which was saying something coming from the guy who had his ego fed by everyone around him. What she did mattered more than anything I had contributed to the world.

She was worldly in a way that most weren't. She'd been to places I couldn't even imagine because of her work with the nonprofit. Places people would never go to willingly. The way she talked about her job and the things she'd seen spoke volumes about her character. Her heart. Which was why her name was so fitting, and why I wanted it to be a normal thing rolling off of my tongue.

All of her brains and her passion were wrapped in a package I was dying to get my hands on again. To slowly unwrap her like the gift she was. It was all I could think about lately, which was why my eyes couldn't help but wander over the white number she put on today.

The buttons struggling to contain her creamy breasts, the hem of her skirt riding up slightly as she slid across the leather seat. It was beginning to feel like torture being in such a confined space with someone I had once peeked inside. I closed my eyes, remembering her spread open on my bar, her nails digging into my back.

I heard Armand clear his throat, breaking me out of my thoughts. I looked up and caught his eye in the rearview mirror, a smile on his face.

"To work, sir?"

"Yes, please. Thank you, Armand."

He nodded and pulled away from the curb. I watched as Addison's office began to fade away with the distance. It just hit me that I wouldn't see her the next morning. It was Friday, which meant I didn't have a reason to drive to Brooklyn. Now I wished I had realized it sooner. I could have asked her to lunch or to dinner. I sighed. It was going to be a long weekend.

My phone buzzed just then. I pulled it from my jacket pocket and saw Kiera's name flash across the screen. I rolled my eyes and debated answering. I went against my better judgment and hit the green button.

"Hello?" I answered.

"My knight in shining armor," said Kiera, nearly purring.

"Excuse me?"

"The other night...at the club..."

I had done the gentlemanly thing and made sure she got her wasted ass home after I left Freddy's birthday party early.

"Oh, right. I'm glad you got home okay."

"Thanks to you."

"Well, thanks to my driver."

"Either way, I was completely wasted. I barely even remember leaving. If it weren't for you, I don't know where I would have ended up."

Probably in some billionaire's bed, which was how she ended up getting married the first two times.

"I do what I can," I said.

"Well, I want to say thank you."

"You just did."

"No, silly. I want to take you out, so I can *really* say thank you."

I knew that voice. It was the one she used to get anything she wanted. It was almost whispery, and dripping with sex. It had worked on me too many times to count in the past.

"That's not necessary," I said.

"Daniel..."

"How about the next time I'm up for bid at a charity auction, you can bid on me."

I heard her huff on the other line.

I had no plans on being up for bid ever again. As much money as it raised, the salacious press that followed wasn't worth it.

"You can play hard to get all you want, but you know I always end up getting what I want," she said before hanging up.

I looked at my phone and smiled. I had pissed her off. She wasn't a girl who was used to being turned down, and she was zero for two with me. It was new for me too. Even though we broke up over a year ago, we hadn't exactly wiped our hands of each other. We had remained friendly. Maybe too friendly. She would sometimes make her way into my bed if we ran into each other at an event.

I couldn't help myself. With Kiera it was familiar, and the sex was good. But now, things were different.

Armand pulled up to the large glass building that was practically my second home and opened the door for me. I slid out of the car and saw my brother walking up to the entrance.

"Brody," I said, jogging up next to him with a grin on my face.

"Hey, bro," he said, pushing the doors open.

"How are you?"

"Fine, I guess."

"Nice day out, huh?"

"Uh, yeah. Real nice." He looked at me curiously as we walked through the spacious lobby toward the elevators.

"You're extra cheery today," he said, pressing the button.

"It's Friday." I shrugged.

"Riiiight."

The elevator doors opened and we stepped inside.

"Did you get a really good lay last night or something?" asked Brody, raising a questioning eyebrow at me.

"Can't a guy just be happy?" I asked.

"Sure, but that guy is usually not you."

"That's not true."

"Uh, yeah it is. You're either stressed about work or getting bored of supermodels most guys would be damn lucky just to get a passing glance from."

Okay, that was true.

"Speaking of supermodels, it's been a while since I've seen you on TMZ..." he quipped.

"And that's a bad thing?"

"Nah, it's good. Our stocks are up." He laughed.

It was true. In the absence of any scandal with my name in it, our numbers were up. It had been over a month since I had been in the papers. The last time had been when Kiera and I were photographed on our "date" and she went on to claim that wedding bells were in our future. Little did I know it would actually be footie pajamas and a crib.

I couldn't imagine the field day the press would have if they caught wind I was going to be a father. Thankfully, I trusted Addison enough to keep this under wraps until we figured everything out. I hardly knew her, and I trusted her more than Kiera who I had known for years.

Brody and I stepped out onto our floor and went our separate ways to our offices. He was on one end of the long marble hallway, and I on the other. As I started to make my way down the hallway, Margaret called me over to the front desk.

"Good morning, Mr. Jacobs."

"Morning, Margaret."

"Your dinner meeting canceled this evening. They just called to reschedule."

Shit. That was a big client I had planned on schmoozing over steak and expensive red wine.

"Did they say why?" I asked, trying to hide my annoyance.

"Their baby is sick." She shrugged.

I suddenly felt a little more empathy. I wondered if I would ever be in the position where I had to reschedule or cancel because I was being a dad to a sick baby.

With my night free, I suddenly had an idea.

"Keep my schedule clear for the night, please," I said, drumming my fingers on the desk.

"Yes, Mr. Jacobs," she replied.

As I walked down the hallway, I started to formulate a plan that would involve seeing Addison tonight. And, if all went well, getting her in bed again. Seeing her naked was all I could think about. I felt like I might combust if I couldn't have her again.

Chapter 19

ADDISON

I walked into the breakroom feeling like I was walking on cloud nine. Despite the lingering nausea in my stomach, my morning with Daniel had distracted me enough from the discomfort of morning sickness. I grabbed a bag of pretzels and a water bottle from the fridge. Small snacks helped my upset stomach.

I sat down at a small round table by the window and listened to the sounds of the city below, wondering what Daniel was doing now. I smiled as I crunched down on a salty pretzel.

"You look awfully happy," someone said.

I looked up and saw Shelley standing in the doorway with a curious smile on her face.

"Just happy it's Friday," I lied.

I wasn't happy it was Friday. It hadn't hit me until I sat down at my desk this morning that I wouldn't see Daniel again until Monday. That was, if he was going to continue chauffeuring me to the city. It was ridiculous, but also incredibly sweet for him to make a two-hour commute each morning on top of his drive to work.

"Any big plans for tonight?" asked Shelley.

"Ice cream and my couch." I shrugged.

She laughed. She knew I was a homebody and practically begged me to come out for her birthday. It was a good thing she did. If it weren't for her, I would never have run into Daniel. I also would never have ended up being pregnant.

"Well, I'm just sorry I didn't get the chance to see you out of the office for once! How was that Bemelman's place, by the way?"

"Fancy! And the drinks were dangerously good."

"Good to know." Shelley grabbed a bag of chips from the basket on the counter before giving me a little wave goodbye.

I finished my bag of pretzels and bottle of water, and walked down the hallway back to my office. As I passed by Brian's office, he called me in.

"Addison, can you come in here for a minute?"

"What's up, Brian?" I asked, leaning against the doorframe.

"We just got in the final numbers from Daniel Jacobs' donation."

Just the sound of his name made my heart bang violently in my chest.

"Oh?" I asked, trying not to let his effect on me show.

"Yeah. They're big. Really big. I don't know how Shelley did it. I've emailed them to you. Can you start working on the new budget?"

"Of course. I'll get right on it."

I walked back to my office wondering exactly how big Daniel's donation was. I sat down at my computer and quickly opened my email. I scrolled through Brian's email and saw the number. The number of zeros made my mouth fall open. It was our biggest donation ever. Hell, it was quadruple our last donation.

I had the urge to email him and say thank you, but decided not to. It's not like he had done it for me. Right?

I started typing up a rough draft of a list of expenses for our next project at Leading to Learn. We were planning to visit Cambodia next and were determining the best toy designs that would educate the children. Thankfully, with Daniel's generous contribution, our budget had greatly expanded, and we were able to pour more money into research on how to best serve the community, and also send more of us down there to help.

I went over the numbers and realized there was more than enough left over to hire on new staff and visit several other countries. My heart was full knowing we could really start making a difference and put Leading to Learn on the map as a major nonprofit. It was unbelievable.

As the "whoosh" of my sent email to Brian sounded from my computer, there was a knock at my door.

"Come in," I said.

The door clicked open and a courier stood in the doorway holding a package.

"I have a delivery for an Addison Heartly."

"Yes, that's me." I stood up and walked to him, eyeing the box in his hands.

It was matte black and I could see the word *Bloomingdale's* etched in gold peeking out from under the black satin ribbon. What in the world? I never got packages delivered to the office, and even if I did, I hadn't ordered anything. Especially not from Bloomingdale's.

I jotted down my signature on the courier's clipboard eagerly before taking the box from him. Once he was gone, I placed the box on my desk and opened the lid. On top of soft, gold tissue paper sat a handwritten note.

Be ready by 7:00 PM.

It wasn't signed, but I would bet it was from Daniel. No one I knew shopped at Bloomingdales. What was he up to? The thought excited me and filled me with nerves.

I set the note aside and peeled back the tissue paper. Underneath was red satin fabric folded neatly. I slipped my hands carefully under it, lifting it out of the box as if it were a piece of fine China that would break. It unfolded in front of me, revealing the most stunning dress I had ever seen.

It probably cost more than my rent. I checked the size and breathed a small sigh of relief. The guy clearly knew women's sizes, which made me feel a tinge of jealousy. I pushed it away as I held the dress up against me. I had never worn anything this nice.

I carefully folded the dress and placed it back in the box. I looked at the note again and bit back a smile. I would be seeing Daniel sooner than I thought. I wondered what he had in store for me. Whatever it was, I knew the rest of the workday was going to drag on.

On my lunch break, I called Monica and filled her in on everything. I told her about the past week with Daniel and about the mystery package. She seemed skeptical at first. Her usual protective self. But when I told her how he seemed interested in my pregnancy and how he seemed like a different person, she began to soften. I promised her I would FaceTime her before I left for the night.

After lunch, the rest of the day went slowly. I caught myself staring at the clock, just watching the minute hand tick painfully to the next number. By five o'clock, I had barely focused on anything but the night ahead. I quickly clocked out, barely saying goodbye to any of my coworkers. I rushed to get to the subway and caught the train back to Brooklyn before it closed its doors. I sat the whole ride home, clutching the Bloomingdale's box tightly on my lap.

By the time I got to my building, I only had an hour and a half to get ready. Normally, it was more than enough time for me. I could get ready in ten minutes, but tonight was different. I had a once in a lifetime dress to wear with *the* Daniel Jacobs.

I clutched the box as I headed toward the stairs to my apartment. I spotted Beatrice meowing at the bottom of the stairwell and let out an annoyed sigh. Elma really needed to keep better track of her cat. I debated leaving her there, but didn't have the heart to.

I scooped up the fluffy cat with one arm and knocked rapidly on Elma's door.

"Coming!" she called out, a tone of annoyance in her voice.

I heard the locks of her door click and she swung it open.

"What is it?" she said sharply.

I held up Beatrice, and Elma's face softened.

"Oh, you escaped again, have you?" she said, taking the cat in her arms. "Sorry, I was catching up on my soaps. Did you know you can record shows now?"

Only for the past twenty years.

"Wow," I said, feigning surprise.

Elma looked me up and down and before I could move the box out of view, her eyes latched on.

"Bloomingdale's, huh?" she asked curiously.

"Oh, yeah. I treated myself after work today."

I could tell by her face she didn't believe me. If I were living here, there was no way I was shopping at Bloomingdale's.

"Is that right?" she asked, unconvinced.

"Yup, I better be going."

"Before you go...there was a gentleman caller here last week. He looked very familiar. Very rich."

"Oh? Weird. Maybe he was lost," I said innocently.

I turned away and walked up the stairs to my apartment. Now, I only had an hour and twenty minutes to get ready.

Inside, I stripped off my clothes and turned the shower on. I tapped my foot impatiently waiting for the water to heat up. As I stood in front of the mirror, I studied my body. Really, the only thing that had changed was the size of my breasts. I wasn't showing in my stomach area yet. I ran my hands over my bare belly and smiled.

The steam fogged up the mirror, signaling it was time to get in the shower. I took my time exfoliating, shaving, deep conditioning. The dress deserved that. At least, that was what I told myself when my mind wandered to what might happen tonight.

Once I was out of the shower, I towel-dried my hair before taking a blow dryer to it. I couldn't remember the last time I had taken the time to style it. I usually just threw it in a bun or a ponytail, so it was out of my face. Now, I struggled with a round brush and my arms were tired.

After I was done, I grabbed my makeup bag and sat on the floor in front of my full-length mirror. I looked inside the bag at my modest makeup collection and started brushing it on carefully. I added a little more blush than usual, an extra coat of mascara, and shakily drew a cat eye with liner. Lastly, I swiped on a coat of rosy lipstick.

Now it was time for the dress. The thing I was most nervous for. There was a chance it wouldn't fit. I carefully removed the tag and stepped into the pool of satin at my feet, sliding it up my body and over my arms. I held my breath as I arched to reach the back zipper and slowly zipped it up. I let out a sigh of relief. It fit.

I rummaged through my closet to find the one pair of heels I owned. The same strappy black ones I had worn my first night with Daniel. I tied the straps and I looked at myself in the mirror. I couldn't help but feel like an imposter.

My nerves started to kick in, so I picked up my phone and FaceTimed Monica.

"Hello!" she answered, holding a glass of wine.

"Please tell me I don't look ridiculous," I said, turning my phone to face the mirror.

"Holy shit, Heart!" she practically yelled.

"Shhhh." I giggled.

"You look like you might get pregnant again."

We both burst out laughing. I already felt better.

"You have to tell me everything tomorrow. Promise?"

"Promise."

"Go get him, girl."

I ended the call and checked the time. It was seven on the dot. I slid the phone in my small black clutch and walked out into the hallway, locking up behind me. I slowly walked down the stairs, not wanting to trip. At the door, I took a deep breath, as if everything in my life was about to change.

I pushed open the door and stepped out into the cool night. In front of me stood Daniel leaning against his town car with a single rose. For a moment, I felt like I couldn't breathe. He wore a black suit, his hair pushed back just right, and a smile that melted me into a pool of liquid that I wanted him to dive into.

Chapter 20

DANIEL

My hand clutching the red rose began to shake slightly as I watched Addison walk toward me. It was like she was moving in slow motion as my eyes drank her in. Her hair was down, hanging past her shoulders in dark, loose waves that I wanted to run my fingers through. I noticed she had more makeup on, but not in a caked-on way, but in a way that brought out her brown eyes and her plump lips. I didn't want to tear my eyes away from hers, but I had to see the dress.

I had spent an hour in Bloomingdales on my lunch break trying to find the perfect dress for her. The saleswoman was patient with me as I looked through her rack of selections, pushing through them dismissively until I landed on this one. I thought it would be perfect. And it was.

The red satin clung to Addison's body in the way I hoped. It tugged across her voluminous breasts and hugged her waist until it broke into a carefully placed slit that exposed her upper thigh. As much as I hoped she would feel good in it, I selfishly chose it for me to stare at her in it all night.

As she took one last step toward me, she did a slow spin and I instinctively brought my hand to my chest. I had just had the air knocked out of me. I gathered my wits about me and handed her the rose.

"You look...incredible," I said softly before leaning in to kiss her on the cheek.

"Thank you," she replied. "For everything. This dress..."

"Was made for you."

I wanted so badly to reach out and place my hands on her waist, running my hands up the smooth fabric against her body. Instead, I turned and opened the door.

"Shall we?" I asked, gesturing to the car.

She nodded as she stepped inside the car before I slid in after her. I closed the door gently behind us and the sound of soft jazz music filled the car. *Nice touch, Armand.* I caught his eye in the rearview mirror and he gave me a wink.

"Where are we going?" asked Addison as the car pulled away from the curb.

"You'll see," I answered with a sly smile.

The conversation didn't flow as easily as it had the past week. I wondered if she was feeling the same nerves I was as we made our way to Manhattan. We, instead, settled into a comfortable silence with careful glances and small smiles. Whenever I got the chance, I let my eyes wander without her knowing in the darkness of the town car. Even in the dark, I could see the flesh of her breasts illuminated by passing cars. I would take her right here in this car if she would let me.

But I had plans for us tonight, and I couldn't be selfish. I wanted to treat her to a night she would never forget. I might have to hide my arousal all damn night, but it would be worth it. Knowing I could do something special for her made her even more intoxicating to me.

The car slowed to a stop outside of Le CouCou. I opened the car door and slid out, then held my hand out for Addison. She placed her hand gently in mine and I helped her out of the car, but didn't let go. I couldn't. That charged feeling ran through me and I didn't want it to end.

The large, arched windows cast their warm glow onto the sidewalk before us. I led her in the large black doors and into the restaurant. I watched as Addison looked around at the large chandeliers hanging from the high ceilings, and the brick walls that lined the large bar area surrounded by lush flowers. I smiled as she did a circle, taking everything in.

"May I help you?" asked the hostess.

"I have a reservation under Jacobs."

She scanned her computer screen before grabbing two menus.

"Right this way, Mr. Jacobs."

We followed her to a small corner booth that was tucked away from the rest of the patrons. I had requested seating that was more intimate, and they had delivered. Addison scooched into the navy velvet seat of the booth and I took the seat across from her. The hostess placed our menus on the table before excusing herself.

"This place is beautiful," said Addison, looking at me.

"Wait until you try the food," I said.

She smiled and looked down at her menu. I watched as she scanned the words, furrowing her brows slightly.

"I don't know what any of this means," she said with a soft laugh.

"Would you like me to order for you?" I offered.

"Yes, please. If I tried to order, I would butcher every word."

"What *don't* you like?" I asked.

"I'm not picky." She shrugged.

When the waitress came around for our order, I did my best attempt at French and ordered their most popular dishes, along with a few of my favorites. As we handed the menus back to the waiter, Addison looked at me with a smile.

"What?" I asked.

"I'm impressed." She sat back against the plush seat of the booth and crossed her arms, studying me. I marveled how she pressed her breasts together.

"Me too," I said with a smirk.

"Oh my God, Daniel," she said, covering herself self-consciously.

"Well, don't do that."

She shook her head and fought back a smile. "I can't handle you."

"No, I can't handle *you.*"

Her face flushed and she reached for her glass of water, taking a sip.

"So, what did you order? In English, please," she asked, changing the subject.

"Salad with scallops. Chicken and roasted plum. Lamb and eggplant. And the sweet bread basket."

"Wow. That sounds amazing."

"I think you'll enjoy it."

And she did. When the food started to come out, I watched as she bit into everything and her eyes either closed or danced with satisfaction. I could have gone the whole meal without eating and gotten full off of her reaction to every bite. When we were finished with our main courses, I read the dessert menu to her. She chose the chocolate mousse to share.

While we waited for the dessert, she looked at me intently.

"I wanted to say thank you for the generous contribution you made to Leading to Learn," she said.

"Oh, it was no problem at all. I'm happy to contribute."

"Daniel, you just changed the entire trajectory of our company. I don't think you realize."

What I had donated was hardly missing from my bank account, but I knew it was a significant amount for the company. I was happy to do it. I'd like to say it was because I wanted to help the children, which I did. Truly. But I had mostly done it for the beautiful woman who sat across from me.

"I know how much your job means to you. How much helping others means to you. I was happy to do it."

She looked at me for a moment before speaking so softly I could barely hear her. "You did it for me?"

"Well, yes. And for the kids, too," I added quickly.

"Why?"

I sat back in my chair and looked at her thoughtfully before speaking.

"I've never met anyone as passionate as you about helping anyone other than themselves. It's entirely new to me. I find it incredibly intriguing."

I watched as my words landed and the effect they had on her. I hadn't meant for it to be a line. I was being honest.

"Your chocolate mousse," said the waiter, as he placed the decadent dessert in front of us before leaving the table.

We both picked up a spoon and took a bite. The chocolate melted on my tongue as the tanginess of the raspberries bit through the sweetness. It was the perfect balance. I watched as Addison experienced the same thing, her eyes closing in satisfaction. I remembered that same look in my bed and felt myself growing hard against my pants.

Calm down, boy.

"Good?" I asked.

"That was the best meal I've ever had," she said. "I'm surprised this dress still fits."

"Oh, stop. You look incredible."

I reached in my jacket pocket and checked the time. We had to get going. I pulled out a few hundred-dollar bills, setting them on the table before the waiter had even brought the check. Addison looked at me curiously.

"Are you ready for the next thing?"

"There's more?" she asked with surprise.

"The night is just getting started," I said, standing and holding out my hand.

She placed her hand in mind excitedly and followed me from the booth and out of the restaurant where Armand waited with the car. Inside the car, she closed the distance between us. Her shoulder was pressed up against mine. I placed my hand on her exposed thigh, feeling the smoothness of her skin against my fingers. She stared straight ahead, but I heard her breath quicken just for a moment.

"Where to, sir?" asked Armand.

I wanted to tell him to take us back to my place, as my hand resisted the urge to explore and graze up under Addison's dress. But I restrained myself.

"West 46th Street, please," I said.

"Where are you taking me, Mr. Jacobs?" whispered Addison, looking up at me.

I smiled down at her, her eyes eager to know what came next.

"You'll see."

I gave her leg a gentle squeeze and she laid her head on my shoulder.

As we weaved through traffic to get to the Broadway district, I couldn't remember the last time I had planned a date like this for anyone. Hell, I hadn't been on a date in a while. Unless, you considered bottle service at the club and bringing a woman back to a suite at a hotel a date. For some women, that was enough.

Normally, I would find this type of thing cheesy. A fancy dinner at a French restaurant and a Broadway show. It was typical. Most women I slept with had been there, done that. But Addison hadn't. I could tell by the way her eyes took in the restaurant. How her mouth chewed the food slowly, savoring it. How her eyes excitedly looked at the passing theatres and what shows were playing.

"Are we seeing a show?" she asked, lifting her head from my shoulder and looking at me with wide eyes.

"I hope that's okay."

"Oh, wow. I've never been to a show."

"Wait, are you serious?" I asked, genuinely surprised.

"I know, I know. I've lived in New York for years, and have never made it down here." She shrugged, somewhat embarrassed.

"Well, I'm happy to be the one you experience it with."

The car slowed to a stop in front of the theater. I went to open the door, but she grabbed my arm gently and stopped me. I turned to face her.

"Thank you," she said, her tone genuine and full of wonder. "For everything."

I leaned in and kissed her on the cheek.

"It's my pleasure," I whispered in her ear before pulling away.

And it was. I enjoyed spoiling her. She was the mother of my child after all, which I had become more comfortable saying to myself over the past week. I was still scared shitless, but doing this with her took a little bit of the fear away.

As we walked to the box office, I slid my hand down her back and settled it against her lower back. I only had to wait three more hours to see if she would let me touch the places I had been imagining over the past month. It was going to be torture, but I would do it for her to experience something for the first time.

Chapter 21

ADDISON

As I watched Daniel converse with the box office attendant outside the theater, I could tell I wasn't the only one completely enamored by him. The young woman behind the glass window could barely tear her eyes away from him to retrieve our tickets. Could I blame her?

His words practically oozed off his tongue in that deep, but somehow gentle voice of his. The way he ran his hand through his dark hair as he waited patiently. It was effortlessly sexy because he didn't even know he was doing it. The suit helped, too. It hugged him in all the right places as if it were made for him, which it probably was.

A part of me felt pride in knowing that I was here as his date. I slightly tightened the grip on his hand that had found its way in mine on more than one occasion tonight.

He looked at me and gave me that megawatt smile that made my knees feel weak. The box office attendant slid the tickets through the small opening in the window and told him to enjoy the show. I wondered if she made the conscious decision to leave me out of that sentiment. I laughed softly as Daniel led me to the entrance of the theater.

"Shit," I heard him whisper suddenly.

I looked up and gave him a questioning look, but then I saw them. A few men with cameras slung around their necks peering over at us from the side alley of the theater. Paparazzi. I suddenly felt on edge, and I could tell Daniel did, too. He led me into the line of people waiting to enter the theater, concealing us behind the other theatergoers.

"How did they find you?" I asked, looking over my shoulder and back at him.

He shrugged. "They always do. Maybe someone tipped them off after our dinner at Le CouCou. It wouldn't be the first time."

"That's insane," I said.

"I'm sorry," he said softly.

"It's not your fault."

To me, being followed around by cameramen all day felt like such an intrusion of privacy. I didn't understand how it could be okay to take photos of people without their permission and sell them on the internet. I felt sorry for Daniel, even though I had been sucked in by the tabloids and gossip pages with his photos.

There were hundreds, and most of them were with women. All different ones, except for that awful woman, Kiera. I tried to shake her image from my head. Her honey blonde hair and wispy limbs that fit into any outfit seamlessly. Hell, she would look good in a potato sack. I suddenly felt very insignificant as I played a mental slideshow of Daniel and his various conquests.

"If we are among the crowd, it's harder for them to sell photos," said Daniel, ducking down. His six-foot frame was hard to miss. It made me laugh to see him try to make himself small when he was one of the tallest and sought-after men in this crowd. I laughed softly.

"What?" he asked, raising an eyebrow.

"You couldn't fit in if you tried," I said.

"Neither could you," he quipped.

"Yeah, right."

"I mean it. You don't see it. But even if you didn't have that red dress on that's made every man in Manhattan get whiplash tonight, you'd still have everyone's attention."

I swallowed hard as I felt heat creep up toward my cheeks. No one had ever given me a compliment like that. His words had swallowed me whole and I didn't want to come up for air. I could just happily replay what he said in my head for the rest of time.

The line started moving forward and soon we were in the safety of the theater. I had seen a couple of flashes go off, but I doubted they got anything good. Daniel seemed relieved as we made our way through the lobby and to our seats.

We walked down the aisle until we stopped just before the pit of the orchestra.

"Here we are," said Daniel, pulling me gently behind him as he found our seats at the center of the stage.

"*These* are our seats?" I asked, looking wide-eyed.

"Do you like them?"

I leaned over the railing and looked at the orchestra below as they were busy turning their composition pages and preparing their instruments. I turned to Daniel and shook my head in awe.

"Daniel, this is incredible."

A look of pride overtook his perfect face. I could tell he was enjoying this. Wining and dining me. It made it all the more special.

"I'm glad you think so," he said.

We both sat down in the plush chairs, and I took everything in. The velvet curtains that hung over the stage matched the deep red of our seats, and gold, braided tassels hung on either side. The ceiling of the theater was covered in stained-glass octagonal panels and the largest chandeliers I had ever seen. I didn't think I had ever been anywhere so beautiful.

After I was done admiring the theater, I turned toward Daniel and noticed his eyes were already on me.

"Thank you for bringing me," I said.

"You already thanked me," he replied with a smile.

"Well, it just didn't seem like enough."

The lights dimmed around us and the soft sounds of the orchestra began to play. I felt Daniel's hand graze my upper thigh and settle comfortably against me. His touch made a shudder roll through my spine from top to bottom. I sucked in a shaky breath as I wondered how I was going to make it through this show without completely losing my head.

All night I had been trying to keep my wits about me, but the way he looked at me, like I was the only one in the room, completely threw me. While his eyes would wander, skimming my breasts or the high cut of my dress, they would always find their way back to mine. The piercing blue filled with an unspoken desire.

And his hands seemed to always find their way to me, whether he was intertwining his fingers with mine or placing his hand on my lower back, or now, holding my thigh. Every touch lit a match in me and I felt like I would catch fire.

I watched as his thumb slowly stroked my inner thigh, and while I felt like I could get off just from that, he stared straight ahead as if he didn't even know he was doing it.

The stage lights came on slowly and the play began. I watched as the performers danced their way around the stage, making the theater come alive. In my seat, I swayed to the music and watched as their colorful costumes swished to the sounds of the orchestra. It was pure magic.

At intermission, Daniel helped me from my seat and led me out to the lobby.

"Are you thirsty?" he asked.

"I could use a water," I answered.

We walked to a small bar area and stood in line. My eyes grazed over a bottle of cabernet longingly. If only I could have a glass. Maybe it would help calm my nerves that had barely let up all night. I wondered if I was confusing nerves for butterflies. Whatever it was, being around Daniel gave me feelings I had never felt before.

"Two waters, please," said Daniel, as he retrieved his wallet from his jacket pocket.

"Are you sure you don't want a drink?" I said, eyeing the cocktail list.

"Nah, I'm good," he replied, putting up his hand.

The cocktail waitress handed him two water bottles, eye-fucking him the whole time. He didn't even seem to notice. He carried our waters to a nearby bench and we sat down.

"You really don't know the effect you have on women, do you?"

"What do you mean?" he asked, looking taken aback.

"That cocktail waitress was ready to take you right there behind the bar." I laughed, nodding toward the bar.

Daniel looked over at her and looked back at me with a puzzled look.

"You're clueless," I said, nudging him.

I took a sip of water and leaned back against the wall, wondering what this man was doing here with me.

"I don't really see anyone else when I'm with you," he leaned in and whispered.

I turned toward him and our noses almost brushed, that was how close he was. I looked from his eyes to his lips and desperately wanted to kiss him right then and there. I had forgotten what he tasted like, and it was something I needed to remember.

His eyes fell to mine as he reached his hand up. He trailed his thumb over my lips that were slick with water. The tip of his thumb stopped as it touched the beauty mark above my right lip.

"I love this," he said.

"Really?" I asked with a little laugh.

"It's one of the first things I noticed about you out in the garden."

It was funny because my mole had always made me feel self-conscious. When I was younger, I would often cover my mouth when I talked, or slightly turn my head. I had grown used to it by now, but had never seen it as something beautiful.

The lights flashed in the lobby and I reluctantly pulled my gaze from his as I looked around with confusion.

"It means the second half is about to start," said Daniel with a smile.

"Oh, right."

Broadway show virgin over here.

We stood from the bench, even though I would have happily missed the second half if it meant more sweet nothings and gentle touches from Daniel. God, I wanted him so badly. I thought being pregnant would hinder my libido, but it was quite the opposite. I wondered how he felt about having sex with a pregnant woman. It wasn't like I was showing. I didn't even have a bump yet.

I was getting ahead of myself. I didn't know where this night was going to lead.

Back in our seats, the theater lights dimmed again. The stage was different now. The set was completely new and the costumes had changed, too. It was even more magical than the first half. I hummed along to one of the songs and I felt Daniel press his lips to the top of my head, bringing me to a still silence. Every touch up until now had an electric charge to it, but that kiss was warm and soft.

It was hard not to become completely lost in him. A part of me wanted to let it all go and lose myself in whatever this was. Another part of me was still skeptical. I hated that part of me. The part that didn't want to get hurt by this man that I hardly knew, with a reputation that everyone knew.

What if this was all an act? Maybe the check and this whole magical night was to keep me quiet about the baby and not tarnish his image. He did hide away from the paparazzi, when in the photos I had seen, he was proudly walking out of hotels and clubs with the latest Victoria's Secret models. I frowned at the thought. I didn't want it to ruin our night.

Still, it was hard for me to believe that he was falling for me. *Me.* A nobody. Except for the fact that I was carrying his baby.

As if he was reading my mind, Daniel reached for my hand and laced his fingers through mine as some sort of quiet reassurance he didn't even know I needed in that moment. I nuzzled my head further into the crook of his neck. *Just enjoy this moment*, I thought to myself.

Chapter 22

DANIEL

I hardly watched the play. I spent most of the time watching Addison watch. The way her face lit up when a song came on or a funny line was delivered, it was better than anything on Broadway. I was happy I had brought her here. Anyone else wouldn't have made this so special. They would have had a "been there, done that" kind of attitude, but this really meant something to her.

As much fun as I had watching her, I also found it extremely difficult to keep my hands on their best behavior in the dark lighting of the theater. They could have easily roamed across her skin and up the smooth hem of her dress that already left so little to the imagination. I didn't want to take away from her first Broadway experience though, so I tortuously held back.

When the show was over, we headed toward the exit of the theater and I saw the preying hyenas with their cameras through the glass doors. There wasn't a big crowd to hide in now as everyone dissipated onto the sidewalks and into cabs.

"Wait, one second," I said to Addison, who looked at me curiously.

I looked around for an attendant and walked over to one who was starting to clean up the playbills that were scattered on the floor.

"Excuse me," I said. "But is there a back entrance we can go through?"

"Uh...it's not really for audience members."

"I understand, but maybe just this once you can make an exception?" I reached for my wallet and pulled out a hundred-dollar bill.

His eyes widened. "Right this way," he said.

"Let me just get my date."

I walked toward Addison, who was waiting by the theater doors.

"I found another way out." I took her hand and we followed the attendant down a long hallway.

It wasn't like I wanted to keep her a secret, but it was nice having whatever this was just between us without the tabloids dissecting it. I didn't want anyone ruining this, or digging for information. The last thing I needed was for anyone finding out about the baby.

I hadn't been in the papers all month, and it was a nice change for me. For business, too. Our stocks had gone up even more without any scandals clouding up stockholder's judgments. I wanted to keep it that way.

We finally reached a back room and the attendant nodded toward the door.

"This will lead you to the back alley," he said.

"Thank you."

I called Armand and let him know where to pick us up.

"This all feels very *Mission Impossible*," said Addison with a little laugh.

"It's kind of fun, huh?"

Kind of sexy.

She nodded.

A few minutes later, I heard a honk outside. I pushed open the doors and led Addison to the car where we quickly clambered inside.

"Where to, sir?" asked Armand, tilting the rearview mirror to meet my eye.

I didn't want to assume that Addison was coming home with me, as much as I wanted her to. I knew things were complicated, but tonight had gone so well. I was torn for a moment before defeatedly telling him to go to Brooklyn.

"Did you have a nice night?" I asked her softly, as I mentally beat myself up inside for not just taking her home.

"Mhmm," she said, chewing on her cheek.

She seemed quiet. Upset. Was she hoping to go home with me?

She leaned against the far side of the car, looking up at the lights of Times Square. Her eyes looked like they were dancing against the red and yellow lights. The red dress rode up, the slit revealing her perfect legs. Her hair hung softly behind her back, revealing the perfect gap between her breasts. We had barely left the theater, and I felt like I was already running out of time to fulfill the urges suddenly coming over me.

I reached over and placed my hand on her smooth knee, hoping to gauge her reaction. She looked away from the window and her eyes fell to my hand that so desperately needed to be between her legs. Then her eyes locked on mine.

I slid my hand further up her leg and stopped just at her inner thigh. I hovered over her now, our breaths growing heavier as they moved in and out of us in sync. She blinked slowly before giving me the smallest of nods.

Game on.

I reached over to the center console and flipped a switch. The divider between the backseat and the front slowly rose.

"I didn't know it did that," whispered Addison. I could sense some nerves in her throat.

I smiled down at her as my hand moved up the rest of her thigh, until my fingertips met the fabric of her panties. They were a soft lace. I wondered if she had worn them for me.

I began moving my fingers in swirling motions against her, as I watched her head fall back and her eyes close. Her neck lay there exposed, as I lowered my lips against her. I trailed my tongue across the nape of her neck as my fingers moved more quickly against her. I could feel her squirm below me.

She lifted her hips and I reached up for the waistband, pulling the lace down her thighs and to her ankles, tossing them aside. My hands slid up the silky fabric of her dress, feeling the smoothness of her body and knowing there was really nothing in my way now. I pulled the fabric of her dress up so it clung just above her hips.

I lowered myself and breathed against her, watching her watch me. I opened my mouth and ran my tongue against her slowly. She was already deliciously wet. I groaned at the sweet taste of her, causing vibrations to run through her. She closed her eyes tightly and grabbed the armrest behind her,

her fingers turning white. I reached up and gripped her hips, pulling her against my open mouth. As I kissed her, I brushed her lips open with my thumb, tasting more of her.

Moans escaped her throat as she grabbed onto my hair. Her legs shivered as I kept my hands firmly on her hips, to keep her from squirming and leaving my hungry mouth. Her grip on my hair tightened as the heat built inside her. I flicked my tongue against her quickly. Knowing the power I had over her in this moment made my erection grow harder against my pants.

I felt her spasm as a throaty moan escaped her and the sweet taste of her filled my mouth. Her legs had stopped reflexively moving and were now weak on either side of my face. I licked my lips and smiled up at her, her eyes dreamlike.

"Fuck," she whispered, releasing her grip from the armrest.

She sat up, pulling at my face to sit up with her. We sat facing each other as she tried to catch her breath. She looked at my lips before pulling me in for a kiss, the taste of her dancing between our tongues. Her hands grazed my thighs, moving up toward my waist. She undid the button with ease and pulled the zipper down slowly. She pushed my chest, my back meeting the seat as she lowered herself to the floor of the car. Never breaking that fuckable eye contact, she grabbed the waistband of my pants and briefs, and pulled them down, my erection on full display.

She sucked in a quiet breath before the warmth of her breath brushed against my cock, causing all my nerves to heighten. She licked her lips before parting them slightly. I closed my eyes as I felt the distance between her mouth and me close. Her lips brushed against my tip and then the wet smoothness of her tongue swirled around me. Tasting me. I felt a spine-tingling jolt run up my spine.

I had to watch. I opened my eyes and watched as her mouth opened wider, her lips moving further down the length of my shaft. Every inch of me disappeared into her mouth, and then reappeared slowly. She moved her mouth up and down, faster now, her tongue licking the bottom base. I clutched the headrest behind me and lifted my hips instinctively, filling her mouth even more. She held me deep in her throat. I let out a growling moan.

"Come here," I whispered.

She pulled her mouth from me and looked up, her lips wet and holding back a coy smile.

"I need to feel you. Now." I said, an animalistic demand to my voice.

She grabbed the seat and pulled herself up so she was face to face with me. I grabbed her hips, tugging her dress up before pulling her on top of me. She placed each leg on either side of me, straddling me. I could feel her wetness against the base of my cock.

She moved up the length of me slowly, teasingly, before moving back down.

I reached up and pulled at the low neckline of her dress. Her breasts easily spilled out in front of me, mine for the taking. They were bigger than the last time. I cupped them in my hands, barely able to hold their entirety. I leaned in and ran my tongue around each of her perfect pink nipples, causing them to harden against my mouth.

She whimpered slightly before continuing to move herself against me, but never letting me inside, in some sort of tortuous slow dance. I could tell she was using me to pleasure herself and it almost made me lose it right there. I watched as her body moved in waves. Her head rolled back slowly. Her breath hitched as my firmness massaged against her just so.

I needed more. My hands made their way to her lower back and gripped her tightly, grinding her against me even harder and faster. She let out a low moan. I could feel her growing even more wet against me. Her lips parted on either side of my cock.

I lifted her up slightly so that the tip of my erection was against her smooth, wet opening. She looked down at me, her eyes pleading. She lowered herself onto my cock, tightly surrounding it, inch by inch until I filled her entirely. Then she stayed there a moment, our eyes locked, her pussy throbbing around me.

She started to move, rolling her body against me, my cock deep inside her. Exploring her with every wave of her body. She threw her head back as she ground against me. She was moving faster now. I reached between us, my thumb finding her clit, and massaged against her as her breasts bounced in front of my face.

"Oh, fuck," she moaned.

My hands found her ass. Her perfect ass. And they squeezed tightly, pressing her firmly against me. I lifted her up slightly and pushed her back down.

She let out a quiet scream. I started thrusting harder and faster, the sounds of our bodies pounding against each other filling the back of the car.

I felt like I was getting close. I reached up and grabbed her neck, forcing her to look down at me as I pushed deeper into her. Her eyes were locked on mine, and they looked as if someone had set them on fire. She wrapped her arms around my neck and I could feel her begin to tremble around me.

My body shook as I released everything I had inside of her, just as she exploded around me. The loud, sweet pleasure took everything out of us as we collapsed against one another in the backseat.

Chapter 23

ADDISON

As I was still wrapped around Daniel in a naked heap, I noticed we were getting close to my apartment in Brooklyn. I let out a shaky sigh of remorse as I unwrapped my arms from his neck and my legs from his body. He looked at me questioningly with sleep in his eyes. We had worn each other out.

"We're almost there," I whispered as I lowered myself to the car floor.

I started looking for my red dress and my underwear. I still had my strappy heels on, but nothing else. I found the satiny fabric in my fingers and blindly slipped it on, hoping I knew which side was up. Daniel watched me with a smile on his face that I could only see when headlights flashed through the car windows.

"These are tinted, right?" I asked, trying to work the clasp of my dress.

He let out a soft laugh as he reached down and pulled up his pants. "Yes, they're tinted."

"And is there any chance this is soundproof?" I knocked on the divider between the backseat and the front seat.

"Hmm, I'm not sure," he said, furrowing his brow.

"Daniel!" I said loudly.

Poor Armand.

I covered my mouth in embarrassment and the neckline of my dress fell, my breasts on full display. I quickly reached for it and pulled it back up, as if he hadn't just seen everything. Or had his mouth on them.

"Let me help you with that." Daniel leaned in and grazed his fingertips up my body until they found the clasp to my dress. I closed my eyes and soaked in his soft touch as he carefully hooked the top.

"Thank you," I said in almost a whisper.

He gave me a quick kiss on the lips and scooped me up, placing me on the seat beside him. I saw my building come into view, and already missed him, even though he was sitting beside me.

"I wish tonight didn't have to end," I murmured as I nestled my head on his shoulder.

He was silent for a moment.

"It doesn't have to..." he said.

I lifted my head up and looked at him.

"I don't have work tomorrow. You don't have work tomorrow." He shrugged.

Armand slowed the car to a stop in front of my building. Was Daniel suggesting he stay the night? I suddenly felt acutely aware of how small my studio apartment was. It was the smallest fraction of his penthouse. I didn't know if I had left it in disarray getting ready for tonight. I was slightly embarrassed, but it would be ridiculous to suggest we go back to his place in Manhattan.

"Would you like to come up?" I asked, biting my lip anxiously.

"I'd love to." He was already reaching for the door.

He grabbed my hand and pulled me from the car before leaning in to talk to Armand through the window. After a moment, he knocked on the top of the roof and I watched as the town car drove away, leaving us alone on the sidewalk.

I looked up at the modest brick building in front of us and took a deep breath, before grabbing my keys from my purse. I unlocked the olive-green door and held it open as he passed by me. I saw that Elma's door was closed. Thank God. I led him up the stairs and stopped outside my door.

"It's not much," I said, fidgeting with my keys.

"I'm sure it's perfect," he said, putting his hand over mine.

He was trying to calm my nerves. I gave him the best smile I could muster and unlocked the door. I stepped inside and switched on the lamp in my living room, a warm glow filling the room. Daniel followed me in. I didn't want to look at his face as he took in the single room I called home.

After a moment, I felt his arms wrap around me and he laid his chin on my shoulder.

"I love it," he said, kissing my neck.

"Liar," I said.

"No, it has real charm. It's quaint. And cozy. And warm. It's *you.*"

He put his hands on my hips and turned me toward him. The sleep in his eyes from earlier had disappeared and now they were icy blue and alive. He reached up and tucked his thumb under my chin, gently tilting my face up toward his. He leaned in and pressed his lips against mine.

It wasn't the desperate, passionate kiss I was used to with him where we were completely devouring each other whole. It was soft. Loving. A side to him I didn't expect. My eyes fluttered closed as we stood there in the middle of my apartment, experiencing something new with each other. It wasn't lust. It was care.

He pulled away and put both his hands against my cheeks.

"Thank you for tonight, Heart," he whispered.

I didn't correct him. Tonight, I would happily let him call me that. For forever, even.

I reached up and took his hand, pulling him with me toward my bed in the corner of the room. We had already ravaged each other, but now, I wanted to make love to this man. Slowly and tenderly. And that was exactly what we did before falling asleep wrapped around each other under the cool sheets.

The next morning, light poured in through the sheer white curtains of the room. I felt the sun warm against my eyelids as I peeled them open slowly. I let out a quiet yawn and turned my head to see Daniel fast asleep beside me. His arm was draped over my bare stomach.

I turned to my side and looked at him, feeling his slow and steady breaths against my face. I reached over and gently ran my fingers down the side of his face, feeling the slight stubble of his five o'clock shadow. He was the best thing I had ever laid eyes on. Handsome even when he slept, his mouth partly open.

Last night had been a complete dream. From the fancy French dinner to the Broadway show to completely losing myself to him in the car. And every moment in between. His eyes finding mine. His fingers interlaced in mine. His hands needing to touch me. I had never felt so wanted or taken care of.

And last night in this bed. We were so connected to each other. Our eyes locked. Our kisses were slow and sensual. Our bodies becoming one. I didn't know there could be so many sides to sex, but last night we had explored a new one. It was vulnerable and real. I refused to believe any other woman had been with the Daniel I had experienced last night. At least I hoped they hadn't.

As I lay in bed, watching him sleep, the doubts crept in. Everything I had read about this man painted him out to be a Casanova. He knew exactly how to get a woman, and clearly knew how to please one. I should know, as I had completely lost my head multiple times. I didn't know it was possible to experience one after another.

The guy wasn't a saint. That much was clear. I knew that going into this. I shuddered knowing I wasn't the only one he had ever laid his hands on. It was clear I would have to push my stupid jealousy of his past aside, if we were ever to have a future. If there was one.

"Are you watching me sleep?" he whispered, breaking me out of my thoughts.

He opened one eye and squinted over at me.

"Sorry." I laughed softly.

"It's okay. I like it," he said, pulling me close to him.

I closed my eyes and would have happily fallen back asleep in his arms, but then my stomach growled loudly.

"Oops," I said, feeling embarrassed.

"Baby is hungry," he commented, opening his eyes and putting his hands on my stomach.

I had almost forgotten after our night together that I had our baby growing inside of me. It felt crazy to know we would always be tied in some way, whether we ended up together or not. I placed my hands over his and searched his eyes for what he was feeling.

Up until now, we still hadn't talked about what our lives would look like moving forward. Even though the baby was barely the size of a plum, according to my pregnancy app, it was still such a huge part of our lives. A part we hadn't brought ourselves to discuss much yet. I wondered if we would brave that conversation now.

"Let's get brunch," said Daniel, kissing my forehead.

I guess not now.

"Okay," I replied.

I peeled the sheets off of me and padded to my closet to get dressed. I heard Daniel whistle behind me. When I turned, he was sitting up in bed, staring at me with a grin on his face. I shook my head at him before stepping into my closet. I slid on a pair of jeans and a white t-shirt. "Do you have anything that would fit me?" Daniel called out in amusement.

"Are you serious?" I asked, peeking around the closet door.

"I think a black suit might be a little much for brunch in Brooklyn."

"True."

I dug through my dresser drawers and found a pair of oversized sweats and a baggy Yankees shirt. I walked over to the bed, holding them up. He took them from me and rolled out of bed, his strong, naked body on display before me. I swallowed hard as I admired him, his back to me.

He slid on the sweats, which were snug and came up past his ankles. I stifled a giggle as he slid the shirt over his head. That was a much better fit, but still a little snug. He turned and looked at me, holding his hands out.

"Well?" he asked, doing a turn.

"You look ridiculous," I said.

He laughed out loud as he ran a hand through his unruly bedhead.

"Here, let me get you a hat or something."

I walked back in my closet and pulled down a baseball cap, loosening the strap to the biggest size. I handed it to him and he tugged it over his head. I had never seen him in anything besides a suit. Despite the ill-fitting clothes, casual looked good on him. Then again, anything would.

"Thanks," he said, leaning in and giving me a kiss on the cheek.

After we washed up in the bathroom, me brushing my teeth and Daniel gargling some mouthwash, we headed outside to the busy sidewalks of Brooklyn on a Saturday morning. We decided to walk to brunch, which was something I assumed he didn't do often, given he had Armand to drive him around. Poor Armand. I didn't think I could ever face him again.

We walked hand-in-hand down several blocks, a comfortable silence between us. I noticed him taking in the different buildings and sights. Now and then, I would point out a few of my favorite places, even though, deep down, I knew they would probably never compare to what he was used to.

Eventually, we made it to one of my favorite brunch places. Buttermilk Channel. Of course, there was a line out the door, but Daniel said he didn't mind waiting. In line, I noticed a few people glance in our direction. I wasn't sure if it was because they recognized him or if it was the sweatpants. Either way, I could tell it made Daniel shift uncomfortably. He pulled his hat lower on his head and kept his back to the crowd.

Was he afraid to be seen with me? I thought back to all the tabloids I had seen. He was photographed confidently with a woman on his arm. Even smiling for the cameras sometimes. I chewed on my cheek as I wondered why I wasn't good enough to be seen with him. Maybe it was because I wasn't a supermodel or someone like Kiera.

Between now and us sneaking out of the back door of the theater last night, I was starting to feel like his dirty little secret.

Chapter 24

DANIEL

After a thirty-minute wait, Heart and I were seated at a table by the window overlooking the busy sidewalk outside. I didn't mind waiting. I enjoyed people-watching. Brooklyn was a whole other vibe. Laid back and cool.

I liked experiencing it with Heart. I also liked that I was able to call her that now. Another challenge I had given myself was accomplished, and this one was the most important yet. This meant she trusted me. At least, I hoped she did.

The restaurant was filled with smells of maple syrup and pancake batter, and then my stomach was grumbling. I shifted in my seat, trying to get comfortable in the too tight of sweatpants Addison had lent me. I second-guessed if this was a good choice as the cotton chafed against me.

"You okay over there?" asked Heart, shooting me an amused look.

"Just fine," I lied.

"I bet your suit sounds real nice right about now." She laughed.

It did. Especially since it was custom made to me by my trusty tailor on Fifth Avenue. But I didn't want to stick out like a sore thumb on a Saturday morning in Brooklyn. Everyone around us was dressed down. I would have been the guy in the suit at a pancake breakfast.

"A little," I said. "So, what's good here?" I eyed the menu. There was plenty to choose from.

"Well, the pecan pie French toast is phenomenal. If you're looking for something savory, the short rib hash is really good. Obviously, they are known for their pancakes."

I watched as she talked animatedly about the menu. She was so sure of herself here. I liked seeing this side of her. I had taken her to my side of town, and now I was here in hers. While our places were very different, I liked being here with her. I would like being anywhere with her.

"Let's get all three," I said, putting my menu down.

"Are you sure?" she asked. "That's a lot of food."

"I have to make sure you and baby are well fed."

A smile crept over her lips before it slowly disappeared again. It was as if she realized something, but I couldn't tell what it was. All I knew was that it seemed to make her sad. I wondered if it was something I had said, and desperately wished I could be in her head.

I knew we should probably talk about us. The baby. What the hell we were going to do. We might have been living in our own little fantasy world for the past twelve hours, but the reality was she was pregnant. Maybe we both weren't ready to face it just yet, and even if we were, talking about it over brunch in a bustling restaurant wasn't the smartest idea. There were eyes and ears everywhere.

Which was part of the reason I also opted for these gray sweatpants and oversized Yankees shirt. I was more of a Mets fan, but I settled for what I got. I didn't need the photos of me in the paper and speculations beginning to stir. Although, I doubted the paparazzi had any idea I was in Brooklyn. Right now, I was enjoying my privacy with Heart. It felt good to be unrecognized. A nobody.

When our food came, we shared it family style across our small little table. I was surprised by how good it was. The pancakes were buttery and melted on my tongue. The corned beef hash was salted to perfection. And the pecans on the French toast added a little crunch to each bite. Hell, it might have been better than Le CouCou last night.

After we finished our meal, I sat back and patted my stomach. I was stuffed to the brim.

"Holy shit," I said. "That was incredible."

"Right?" she asked, giving me a knowing smile.

I loved that smile.

Our server came around and cleared our table, leaving our check behind. Heart reached for her purse and dug out her wallet.

"What are you doing?" I asked.

"I'm buying," she replied, pulling out her credit card.

"Like hell you are," I said.

I reached into the pocket of my sweatpants and fought to pull out my wallet that was crammed tightly inside. Heart watched me struggle for a moment, biting back a smile.

"Right. Well, while you try to do that, I'm going to pay," she said in amusement.

She placed her card down and the server came by and picked it up. I watched him go helplessly. It was the first time a woman had paid for me. I wasn't sure if I loved it or hated it.

"Thank you," I said.

"You should let someone take care of *you* sometimes."

She reached over and squeezed my hand. As if I couldn't like her more, here she was adding to the list of reasons effortlessly.

Maybe I did like it.

An hour later, as we rounded the corner to her apartment after a walk around Brooklyn, I saw my town car waiting at the curb. I had texted Armand after brunch to have him make his way here. As much as I wanted to spend more time with Heart, I didn't want to wear out my welcome. I also had some paperwork to go over. Even though it was the weekend, work never really stopped.

Armand stepped out of the car and looked me up and down. I could tell he was holding back a smile.

"Oh, your suit," said Heart. "Let me go get it for you."

"No, I can go," I said, grabbing her hand and pulling her back toward the car. "It's a lot of stairs."

"It's one flight of stairs," she said with a laugh before leaning in and lowering her voice. "I'm not that far along yet. You can be my knight in shining armor when I'm the size of Shamu. Okay?"

She stood on her tiptoes and gave me a quick kiss on the cheek. Then she gave Armand a nervous wave, her cheeks turning a shade of pink, before disappearing into her building.

"Sir," nodded Armand, eying my sweatpants.

"Not a word," I muttered.

He smiled at me and opened my door. I slid into the car and he closed it behind me. I couldn't wait to take these damn things off.

A moment later Heart was at my window, my suit folded neatly in her arms. I rolled down the window and she handed it to me.

"Thank you," I said.

"Thank *you*," she said, leaning against the window with her elbows.

"Can I see you again soon?" I asked.

"I'd like that."

I reached up and wrapped my hand around the back of her neck, pulling her toward me. I kissed her softly at first, before her lips parted slightly to welcome me in. I felt her tongue against mine as she leaned in closer. She tasted like orange juice and pancakes, and I couldn't get enough. She was making it very hard to leave.

After a moment of getting lost in each other, again, she pulled back with a dreamy look in her eyes. She stepped away from the car and gave a little wave. She was still watching as I reluctantly drove away. I knew I had to see her again. And soon.

***

When Monday morning rolled around, I stopped by my favorite coffee shop in Manhattan. I ordered my usual Americano, along with lattes and pastries for the office. I didn't think I had ever done that, or at least not in a very long time. I was in a giving mood though. After my weekend with Heart, I felt like a new man.

Balancing the coffee holders in one hand and pastry boxes in the other, I entered the large glass doors of my building. I handed out coffee and pastries to the lobby and security staff, who took everything gratefully. I rode up the elevators to the floor of my office and found Margaret standing there with her clipboard, ready to give me the rundown of the day.

I handed her a latte. She looked at me confused.

"For you," I said. "I also have fresh croissants and berry Danishes here."

"Um, thank you, Mr. Jacobs," she said, taking the box and walking it over to the front desk.

"What's this all about?" asked Brody, his voice booming.

"Just thought I would treat the office today. Everyone's been working hard," I said, drumming my fingers on Margaret's desk.

"Oh?" Brody raised an unconvinced brow.

I handed him a latte, still hot in my hands.

He took a sip. "Mmm. Mocha. My favorite. Thanks, bro."

I never understood how he could drink that crap. It was practically chocolate milk with caffeine, but then again, Brody was kind of like a child.

He walked with me down the hallway to my office.

"You're in a good mood today," he commented.

"Am I?" I asked innocently.

"Yeah, you have been for a few weeks now."

"Well, I did close that deal early this morning. The one with London."

I had been up at 4 a.m. on a video call with a leading tech giant overseas. It had gone surprisingly well, and now we were teaming up for a huge collaborative release the following year. We had done work overseas, but nothing like this. This would be a huge foot in the door for European markets.

I took a sip of my Americano, wondering if my brother was going to pry further. It was Brody. Of course, he was going to.

"Yeah, but what about before this morning's deal? You just have had some extra pep in your step or something. Don't tell me it's because of Kiera?"

"I haven't seen her in weeks," I said, irritated.

I wanted to continue telling him there was nothing going on. But I hesitated before going further. I thought I had already told him there was nothing going on there, but if believing I had something going on with Kiera would get him off my back then I could let him think that. I could let the world think that.

It would give me more time to figure out things with Heart. Having a cover like being involved with Kiera would get the press of my back and maybe we could continue living in our private bubble a little longer. At least until we figured out what we are going to do, which should probably be soon. I didn't know when women started showing, but it could be soon. If paparazzi somehow got a picture of us and she had a bump, it would only mess up our situation.

"Okaaay..." said Brody, clearly annoyed with my conspicuousness.

I looked at him for a moment, wondering if I should tell him. He was family after all. He could be a total douche, but I also knew he would have my back. Eventually. At least, I hoped he would.

I let out a small, disappointed sigh before taking another sip of my latte. I just wasn't ready to tell him yet. I didn't need a lecture from my little brother about how I needed to be more careful and how he couldn't believe I knocked up a one-night stand. Even though she was so much more than that now.

Also, I knew if Brody came to me telling me he was in a similar situation, I would rip him a new one. No, it was best to keep the fact that I was going to be a father a secret. At least for a little while longer.

I checked my watch and feigned surprise.

"Wow. Is it almost nine already? I gotta go," I said. "I have a phone meeting."

"Thanks for the coffee," said Brody, a suspicious undertone to his voice.

I stepped in my office and closed the door behind me. I was safe. For now.

Chapter 25

ADDISON

I checked my phone for what felt like the hundredth time, but didn't see anything from Daniel. This was hardly unusual, as we had never texted or talked on the phone before. We had always communicated through email for business or through mysterious notes in Bloomingdale's boxes. Still, after our weekend together, I was hoping there would be a text waiting in my messages.

I sighed as I placed my phone on my desk. Then I reminded myself that it had only been two days since I watched him drive away from my apartment after another passionate kiss. I closed my eyes, remembering his hand on my neck and his tongue in my mouth. You couldn't fake that.

Still, he wasn't on the curb waiting for me this morning. I had grown used to seeing his sleek, black town car in front of my apartment with him waiting for me. I had to swallow down my disappointment as I walked to the subway, feeling like a peasant again. It was as if after our date, the bell had struck midnight and I was back to my regular life again.

I'd had to hold back tears as the subway screeched to life on the tracks, making its way through the tunnel to Manhattan. I felt stupid sitting there blinking back the tears that were threatening to fall down my cheeks in front of strangers. Because what? I didn't get a ride to work. God, these pregnancy hormones were wrecking me.

My eyes snapped open and I shook my head, trying to rid the doubts from my mind. He was probably just busy. He was a freaking CEO of a billion-dollar corporation. I began sifting through the emails that had found their way into my inbox on my lunch break. They were just another reminder that it was Monday.

My phone buzzed then, and I quickly snatched it up. I hated feeling disappointment when I saw it was a text from Monica, and not Daniel.

Monica: *What time is the class tonight?*

Me:*6 PM. Do you want to meet there?*

Monica: *Sure. Dinner after?*

Me: *Definitely. I can't stop eating.*

Monica: *Haha. I love pregnant Heart.*

I smiled weakly at my phone. Tonight was my first birthing class. It felt way too early to even be thinking about how to breathe and push a baby into the world, but I wanted to feel prepared. Everything else I had such little control over, but at least I could feel in control of some things, like taking classes and buying various baby books.

The class suggested I bring a partner. For a millisecond, I thought about inviting Daniel along, but quickly changed my mind. I could only imagine the looks we would get in that classroom. A well-known billionaire helping me breathe through a pretend labor. The thought was almost laughable, if it also didn't make me want to cry.

Not wanting to show up alone, I invited Monica instead. She was so excited. She had even been reading baby books herself. I really didn't know what I would do without her.

My phone buzzed and I picked it up, expecting it to be Monica again. Instead, it was a call from a number I didn't recognize. My heart beat a little faster in my chest as I pressed the green button.

"Hello?" I asked, feeling hopeful.

"I'm sorry I wasn't there this morning."

It was the calm, deep voice of Daniel on the other line.

"Oh, it's okay," I said, my voice jumping an octave.

"I got caught up in a meeting with someone in London. The time difference had me up way too early. Afterward, I actually fell asleep with my face on my laptop."

I laughed. "You did not."

"I did. Just like the movies. I even had the keyboard marks to prove it."

"Aww."

"I hope you don't mind, but I had my assistant find your phone number for me."

"Not at all. I'm happy you called."

"Me too. I can't stop thinking about our night together." His voice was almost a whisper.

I felt my ears burn and I looked around my office to make sure no one was listening. Of course, there wasn't anyone. I was alone and the door was closed. Plus, it wasn't like my cell phone was tapped. Still, it felt almost like this was forbidden, him calling me at work.

"Me neither."

"Do you think I can see you this weekend?" he asked.

"Hmm, let me see…"

I pretended to tap on my keyboard, as if I was checking my embarrassingly free schedule. I didn't want to seem too eager, even though I wanted to yell "yes" and do a happy dance right there in my office.

"I'm free Friday," I said after a moment.

"Friday it is," he said. I could hear the smile behind his voice.

"Oh, I won't be able to get out to Brooklyn this week. This deal with London has a lot of fine print and early mornings at the office. I hope you understand."

I did, but it didn't make me miss him any less.

"I never asked you to be my personal chauffeur," I replied sarcastically, to show that I was more than capable of getting to work myself, even though I wished it were with him.

"I liked it," he said.

"Me too."

"Especially our drive home on Friday night…"

"Daniel!" I exclaimed.

"What?" he asked innocently.

"Don't you start. I'm at work."

"What are you wearing?"

I giggled. "You are a real piece of work, you know that?"

"So they tell me." He chuckled.

I was sure they did.

"I have to go," I said, cupping the phone and looking at my office door feeling paranoid.

"Goodbye, Heart," he said.

Just him saying my name like that made my arms break out into goosebumps. I didn't let many people call me that. Most didn't know that was the name I preferred, but only if you meant something to me. Somehow, Daniel had earned that right, and it sounded best coming from him.

"Goodbye, Daniel."

I hit the *end* button and slid my phone across my desk. I couldn't help but smile. The hold that man had on me was either going to ruin me or change my life forever. I hoped it would be the latter.

After work, I took the subway home and made the short walk back to my apartment. I had just five minutes to change out of my work clothes and get back to the subway to meet Monica at the birthing class. In my apartment, I kicked off my shoes and found a pair of black leggings and slid on an oversized white tee. I wanted to be comfortable.

It felt like I had popped overnight. There was most definitely a little bump. I doubted anyone else could tell, but I could. My clothes fit differently and my belly was bigger. Firmer than my normal pudge. I hoped I could get away with no one noticing for a little while longer. I didn't need anyone asking questions at work.

If the truth came out that I had intimate relations with Daniel, I could lose my job. Then I would be jobless, without benefits, and trying to bring a child into the world. I wasn't sure how I was going to hide this pregnancy from my coworkers or my boss in the months to come. Suddenly, I thought back to the check Daniel had given me. I had almost forgotten until now.

I walked to my nightstand and opened the drawer. Inside was the baby book I was currently reading. I opened the glossy cover and saw the check staring at me with all those zeros that felt like eyes. I still wondered about the motives behind it. A wave of nausea hit me then. I wasn't sure if it was morning sickness, which should really be called 'any time of day sickness,' or the exorbitant amount written on the check. I slammed the book shut and put it back in the drawer. There was no time to think about that now. I was already running late.

On the train, I gave up my seat to a woman who had an adorable baby boy. He giggled as she bounced him on her lap. I couldn't help but stare as I wondered what I was going to have. A boy? A girl? The thought excited me and scared me all at the same time.

I made it to the class with one minute to spare. Monica was standing outside, leaning against the building waiting for me.

"There you are," she said.

"Sorry, I got caught up with Elma. You know how she is."

"That woman is way too invested in the lives of her tenants." Monica rolled her eyes.

"You have *no* idea."

We walked into the class and were met with smiling couples all seated on the floor in a circle. I noticed I was the only one there without their significant other. I tried not to let it get to me as I found an empty seat on the floor, Monica sitting beside me.

The teacher walked us through various breathing exercises and then positioned us into a few birthing positions. I felt ridiculous with Monica sitting behind me with her hands on my stomach, repeating after the teacher.

"Hee-Hee-Hoo," she breathed loudly.

"I think I'm supposed to be doing that," I said with a laugh.

Monica giggled, and the teacher looked over at us curiously.

"God, could you imagine if Mr. Billionaire was here doing this with you?" said Monica, her voice low. "What's going on with you two, anyway? You never told me about your fancy date."

"Oh, Monica, it was amazing. Perfect even. We ate at this amazing French restaurant and he took me to see a Broadway show. You should have seen him. He was dressed to the nines."

"Wow. He's really wining and dining you. Without the wine, of course."

"Unfortunately," I muttered.

"Then what?" she asked.

"Then what, what?"

"How did the night end?"

"Oh…" I said, pausing.

"Oh, my God. You totally did it again, you little floozy," she said, her voice rising.

The teacher looked over at us, now with a frown on her face.

"Shhh!" I said. "You're going to get us in trouble."

"What is this? Middle school? Am I going to get sent to the principal?"

I put my hand over my mouth and stifled a laugh.

"I guess he already got you pregnant. What else could happen?" whispered Monica with a shrug.

"True."

"Did he stay the night?"

I nodded as the teacher instructed us to get on all fours for the next position.

"But the next morning, he asked to borrow my clothes."

"Wait… what?" asked Monica.

"He didn't ask for a pair of heels," I said. "He just didn't want to wear his fancy suit."

"Ah, makes sense."

"Yeah, but I got the feeling he was trying to go incognito. Like he didn't want to be seen with me."

"Get out of your head, Heart. He's into you."

"You're the writer. How is this going to turn out for me?" I asked as I arched my back like the teacher instructed.

"This is a classic bad boy turns good trope."

"This isn't a romance novel. This is my life."

"Well, your life is certainly going to serve as inspiration for my next novel."

I rolled my eyes at her as I arched my back and pressed my hands into the floor.

Monica seemed so sure, but this all felt too good to be true. This stuff didn't really happen. Maybe it did in her literary world, but not in real life.

"So, tell me, is this how he got you pregnant?" whispered Monica.

I burst into laughter and the teacher shot us another warning look. Leave it to Monica to get us kicked out of a Lamaze class.

Chapter 26

DANIEL

My phone buzzed on my desk as I wrapped up signing some documents for the London deal. Everything was in place to start on my newest product to launch, but the fine details were taking longer than I had expected. And the time difference was taking its toll on me. I yawned as I reached over and picked up my phone. It was Freddy calling.

"Hello?" I answered.

"Hey, man. Are we still on for tonight at Royal 35?"

Confused, I opened my calendar on my laptop. Shit. There it was. Friday night. A dinner reservation with Freddy at 7 p.m. I was supposed to take Heart out tonight, and I had no intention of canceling. I hadn't seen her all week. Without our usual morning drives from Brooklyn to Manhattan, I missed her.

"Aw, man. Freddy. I totally forgot. I'm double booked."

"What could be more important than whiskey and a ribeye with your oldest friend?"

I hesitated. I hadn't told Freddy about Heart yet.

"Ohhh...it's a woman," he answered knowingly.

I rubbed the back of my head as I leaned back in my desk chair. "Yeah. I have a date."

"Who is the flavor of the week this time?"

"Uh, it's Heart. Well, Addison. You met her at Bemelmans's that one night."

I heard silence on the other line. I pulled the phone away from my ear to make sure he was still connected.

"Hello? Freddy?" I asked.

"Hi. Yeah. Still here. I'm just trying to process that you've been seeing this same woman for almost two months now..."

I laughed. Little did he know.

"Crazy, right?" I said.

"I think the world has flipped on its axis..."

"Okay. We get it, Freddy."

"And here I thought you were practically engaged to Kiera."

"You believe tabloids now?"

"No, but what else would explain your 'good guy' image?"

"Maybe because I am a *good guy.*"

Freddy laughed a little too hard on the other line.

"Are we done here?" I asked, rolling my eyes.

"No. Why don't we double tonight? I'm sure I could change the reservation to four at the restaurant."

"I don't know..." I said. I wondered what Addison would think. Tonight was supposed to be just us two.

"Come on," Freddy whined on the other line. "I've already met her. It could be fun. Plus, I have a new girl I want you to meet."

"Oh goodie. Another one," I said sarcastically.

"I deserved that," said Freddy.

"Fiiiine. I'll meet you at seven tonight," I caved.

I hoped Addison wouldn't be pissed, but she didn't seem the type. Plus, it would be nice to have her spend more time with the people I was close to in life.

"See you then," he said before hanging up.

At 5 o'clock, I left the office and headed home to freshen up. I took a hot shower and shaved the thick stubble I had been growing out the past week. I ran a small amount of pomade through my hair and spritzed on a few generous sprays of cologne. In my closet, I chose a gray linen suit and a white button-down. Once I was happy with what I saw in the mirror, I grabbed my phone and keys and rode the elevator down to the parking garage where Armand waited.

The drive to Brooklyn took just over an hour. I smiled as Heart's familiar brick building came into view. Once we pulled up to the curb, I walked up to the entrance and buzzed her name. A few moments passed before I heard her voice through the small speaker.

"Hello?" she asked.

"It's me!"

"I'll be right down!"

"Are you sure you don't want me to come up?" I asked.

"No, my nosy landlord might see you. Be down in a jiff."

I strode back to the town car and took my usual spot leaning against it. A few minutes later, Addison pushed open the door to her apartment and stepped out into the warm glow of the sun that had just dipped below the buildings. She was in a long black dress with thin straps. The dress jutted out just before it hit her waist, swishing around her like a dancer. Her hair was pulled up into a bun piled on her head, wavy tendrils framing her face.

"Wow," I said.

She smiled and did a little twirl. I reached for her hand and pulled her toward me. I leaned in and gave her a quick kiss before opening the car door. We both slid inside, closing the door behind me.

"Is this new?" I asked, feeling the skirt of her dress in my fingers.

"Mhmm," she said proudly.

"I like it. A lot."

"I had to do a little shopping. I'm starting to show," she whispered, running her hands over the dress. I could see a small bump protruding as she pulled the dress against her. I sucked in a breath. Seeing her stomach growing made the baby seem all the more real.

"May I?" I asked softly.

She nodded.

I placed my hands gently on her stomach and could feel the firm roundness underneath my hands.

"Wow," I said. "When will I be able to feel it?"

"Not for a while," she said. "I haven't felt anything yet."

I furrowed my brows with worry.

"It's okay," she reassured me. "That's normal. Baby's too small to feel any movement."

I nodded, feeling relieved. "I haven't been keeping up with Googling all things baby."

"It's okay. I've been doing enough reading for the both of us." She squeezed my hand.

"So, where are we going?" she asked, looking at me with excitement in her eyes.

"Well...I hope you don't mind, but I told Freddy we could go on a double date..."

"That sounds fun," said Heart, and the smile on her face was convincing.

"Really?" I asked, letting out a small sigh of relief.

"Yeah. He was really nice. Plus, who else is going to tell me embarrassing stories from your childhood?" She nudged me playfully.

She really was something else. So go with the flow and sincere. She was unlike anyone I had ever met. I leaned in and kissed her on the cheek.

"What was that for?" she asked.

"You. Just being you."

She smiled up at me and she just looked so damn beautiful.

"Let's tell Freddy tonight."

"Wait? What? About the baby?" she asked in surprise.

"Yeah. Why not?" I shrugged.

"I'm just surprised. That's all. I felt like I was kind of your secret or something."

My stomach dropped. I didn't know she felt that way, and the way she said it sounded so sad. I reached for her hands and brought them to my lips, kissing each knuckle.

"I'm sorry you felt that way, Heart. I just...I'm not used to *this*. Whatever this is. I just wanted to protect us. Protect the baby."

She nodded slowly.

"I know what the paparazzi and tabloids can do to people."

"It's okay. I understand," she said softly.

"But I do want to tell my best friend about us. About the pregnancy. If you're okay with that."

"Of course, I am. My best friend already knows everything about you."

Ah, yes. The bulldog from her apartment. I'd have to really try to get in her good graces when I had the chance.

When we arrived at Royal 35, I saw Freddy already seated at a booth with a raven-haired girl on his arm. He spotted Heart and me and waved us over excitedly. I could tell from his smile he had already had his usual whiskey on ice.

When Heart and I approached the table, he stood and patted me on the back before giving Heart a hug.

"Nice to see you again," he said. "This is Virginia."

His date stood and shook our hands firmly. She was naturally pretty and dressed in a sophisticated cream skirt suit. She was different from most of the women I had seen Freddy with. Those were usually in lingerie they tried to pass off as dresses with layers of makeup on.

We all sat at the booth, and the server came around to take our drink order.

"We will have your finest bottle of Cabernet for the table," said Freddy, handing the server back the wine list.

"Oh, um...actually..." I started.

Heart put her hand on my arm and gave it a gentle squeeze. I looked at her and she gave a little nod, as if saying it was fine.

The server left and Freddy was already eying me suspiciously.

"What's going on?" he asked, looking between the two of us.

"Well, I... er... we, kind of have some news," I said nervously. "We're having a baby."

"Shut the fuck up," said Freddy loudly, slapping the table excitedly.

Heart laughed beside me.

"Is he fucking with me?" Freddy asked Heart.

"Nope," she answered, her smile so wide.

"I don't know what to say. Congratulations!" said Freddy excitedly, pulling me in for a hug.

"Thanks, man," I said.

"How far along are you?" asked Virginia, leaning in.

"About two months," said Heart.

"Wow, you look amazing. I'm jealous of your glow!"

"Oh, gosh, no. I feel like a total whale…"

"Not at all!"

"Whoa, whoa, whoa," said Freddy, interrupting their girl talk.

We all looked at him.

"Who is your OBGYN?" he asked, a hint of competition in his voice.

I realized I didn't know the answer to that question. It felt like something I should know.

"Oh, it's this place on Park Avenue. I'm not sure I'll be staying there, though. They're not very friendly. It felt really cold."

I looked at her in slight surprise. She hadn't told me anything about going to the doctor or having a bad experience. Then again, I hadn't asked. I couldn't help feeling a little jealous she hadn't confided in me about it.

"Well, that's bullshit," said Freddy. "If you'd like, I can recommend a few."

"Not *you*," I said, shooting him a look.

"I wasn't suggesting that." Freddy put his hands up in defense.

The server brought the bottle of wine then and began filling the glasses on the table. Freddy told him to just fill two.

I leaned in and whispered in Heart's ear.

"Why didn't you tell me about the doctor?"

She shrugged. "It just never came up."

"I hate that you had to go through that by yourself…"

"I wasn't by myself. I had Monica with me."

I sat back in my seat and grabbed my glass of water, taking a sip. I tried to swallow down my hurt feelings.

For the rest of dinner, Virginia and Heart were deep in conversation about everything baby. They were talking about nursery colors, baby registries, names, and clothes. I tried eavesdropping a little, but Freddy was yapping away and when he wasn't, he kept shooting me these weird, meaningful looks.

Once we were finished with our steaks, the girls excused themselves to go to the bathroom, leaving Freddy and me alone. He took a sip of wine, giving me another weird look of his.

"What?" I asked pointedly.

"This is just…crazy," he said.

"I know."

"Are you really ready for this?" he asked, leaning back in the booth and giving me a curious look.

"Of course, I am. Would I be here with her tonight if I didn't think I was ready? If *we* weren't ready."

"Yeah, but you hardly know each other..."

"We're getting to know each other now." I started to feel defensive.

"Okay," he said, nodding. But I could hear the doubt in his voice.

"I'm ready, Freddy." I said with a chuckle at my rhyme.

"Well, I'm happy for you, man."

I watched as Heart and Freddy's date walked back to the table. Heart laughed, the crease of her eyes fanning out in genuine happiness. I hoped I was ready for this, but doubt was beginning to seep in. Damn you, Freddy.

Chapter 27

ADDISON

After our double date with Freddy and Virginia, Daniel didn't ask me back to his place. I tried not to feel disappointed, but I had hoped the night wouldn't end right after dinner, which was delicious. I had never felt so full. Steak, truffle garlic mashed potatoes, balsamic roasted Brussels sprouts, and crème brûlée. My bump grew three times its size.

I was nervous at first when Daniel sprung the double date on me, and then said he wanted to tell Freddy about the baby. Now it wasn't just a secret between Daniel and me. And Monica. That was another surprise he sprung on me when he said he wanted to share the news. It made it even more real knowing there were people in his bubble who knew we were going to parents. Whether we were parents together, or parents who co-parented, it seemed like we were in this thing together.

Freddy was shocked by the news, which was understandable. As excited and congratulatory as he seemed, I couldn't help but wonder what he really thought about Daniel becoming a dad. And with someone like me. I was sure he had his doubts. I could tell by the face he gave Daniel at one point. There was a flicker of doubt, and I hoped it didn't plant anything in Daniel's head.

But now, as we made our way back to Brooklyn, something seemed to have shifted between us. The excitement he had was gone, and instead, he seemed ponderous as he looked out the window. This was nothing like our drive home after the theater last weekend. His hand didn't find mine, his lips weren't places that made me blush, and his eyes had barely looked at me since we left dinner.

"You okay?" I asked softly.

"Hmm?" he replied, tearing his gaze from the Brooklyn bridge we were crossing over. "Oh, I'm fine."

He reached for my hand and gave it a gentle squeeze.

"Dinner was fun. I really like your friends."

"Yeah, it was a good time," he said. "Sorry I couldn't invite you back to my place tonight. It's just this deal with London is taking everything out of me. I'll probably have to wake up really early, and you need rest."

I chewed on the inside of my cheek as I wondered if I should believe him. It wasn't like we got much sleep any other night we had spent together. It seemed like an excuse, but I didn't know why. The night had started off so perfect.

"It's okay," I said, trying to give him the benefit of the doubt.

The car pulled up outside of my apartment, and I looked disappointedly up at the brick building, knowing I would be entering it alone.

"Well, thank you for tonight," I said.

"Thank *you*." Daniel leaned in and finally closed the distance he had kept between us the entire ride home, giving me a quick, gentle kiss on the lips. "I'll see you soon."

I really hoped he meant it.

Armand opened my door and I stepped out into the coolness of the evening. I gave Daniel a little wave before heading into my building.

The rest of the weekend, I didn't hear from him. I tried to convince myself he was just busy with business or catching up on sleep. I spent Saturday and Sunday on the couch watching a marathon of movies and ordering in Thai food. I was craving anything spicy, and made a mental note to ask my new doctor if it meant anything.

At dinner, Freddy had been able to get me in with a doctor he highly recommended, and she was in Brooklyn, which was convenient. My appointment was on Monday, and I was excited for another ultrasound because it meant I got to see the baby and hear its heartbeat again.

I thought about inviting Daniel with me, especially after he found out about my awful experience with the doctor in Manhattan. He seemed hurt that I hadn't told him, or perhaps that I hadn't invited him. I just didn't know where we stood back then. I still didn't know.

Which was why I invited Monica instead, who was more than eager. I had taken the morning off work, and since she mostly wrote at night, she was able to come with. We walked into the doctor's office and were met with warm wood furniture and framed photos of babies and their moms on the walls. There were toys for siblings to play with and parenting magazines scattered about. It was a completely different vibe than the white-washed walls of the office in Manhattan.

I breathed a sigh of relief as I sat down in a cushy chair with my new patient clipboard.

"This place is way better," said Monica, looking around.

"Thank God," I said.

"How did you find it?"

"Oh, Daniel's friend recommended it."

"His friend knows?"

"Yeah," I nodded as I began jotting down my info. "Daniel wanted to tell him."

"Eeeeh!" said Monica, nudging me. "This is huge, Heart."

"Mhmm," I said warily.

"What's wrong? Your dream guy is sharing the news he's becoming a dad with you."

I set the pen down and looked at her, my eyes watering.

"I don't know, Monica. After dinner the other night, he just seemed to shut down. I don't know what happened. I was actually going to invite him here today, but he was so distracted. So distant. I just don't know..."

Monica put her arm around me as I fought back tears. I had never been this emotional in my life. Was it because of my feelings for Daniel or the hormones? Probably a mix of both.

"Hey now," soothed Monica. "I'm sure it's a lot for him too. Don't count him out just yet."

A nurse called my name from an open door. I quickly scribbled in the last information on my paperwork before handing it to her and following her back to the ultrasound room.

"We will do the ultrasound first, and then you will go to an exam room to meet your new doctor. You're going to love her," said the nurse with a warm smile.

I lay back on the exam table and lifted the flowy blouse I wore. The nurse applied some jelly to the wand and ran it over my stomach, which felt way less invasive than the first time. She found the baby quickly on the screen and I was surprised how much bigger it had gotten.

"Oh, my gosh," I whispered.

"Is this your first?" asked the nurse.

I nodded.

"How exciting! There's nothing like it," said the nurse as she moved the wand around my stomach. "Everything looks on track. I'll get those pictures printed right out for you."

She cleaned my stomach with a paper towel and exited the room. Soon, she was back with a few ultrasound photos that she carefully handed to me. She led us back to an exam room, and a few minutes later, my new doctor entered the room.

With just a simple hello, my doubts diminished. She was so friendly and witty, and there wasn't an ounce of judgment as she met both me and Monica. I asked her a few questions, which she answered patiently and informatively. Soon, we were done with my appointment and walking out onto the sidewalk with pictures of my baby in hand.

I sucked in a deep breath and let it out slowly.

"Way better, huh?" I asked Monica.

"Night and day," she replied, pulling me in for a hug.

"I kind of wish I had invited Daniel. Not that I didn't love having you there..."

"I know, I know," said Monica, waving me away. "I get it."

I kicked at the sidewalk feeling defeated.

"Hey, why don't you go visit him at work? Show him the baby. I'm sure he would love that," suggested Monica.

"You think?" I asked.

"Go," she said, giving me a little shove.

"Thank you," I said as I walked the short distance to the subway.

The ride to Manhattan went quickly and my excitement bubbled inside of me, knowing I was going to see Daniel soon. I would rave about my new doctor and we would both probably ooh and ahh over the ultrasound photos, and I would realize how silly I had been.

Downstairs in the lobby, my excitement came to a halt when I was met with a front desk attendant who wasn't allowing me to go upstairs without an appointment.

"If you just tell him it's Addison. Er... Heart. He will tell you it's fine," I said.

"Which is it? Addison or Heart?"

"Heart," I said.

She looked me up and down curiously before picking up the phone and punching in a few numbers. She turned her back to me so I couldn't hear what she was saying. After a moment, she hung up the phone and turned her chair to face me.

"You may go up, Ms. Heartly. My apologies."

I gave her a smile and a nod before walking toward the elevators. I watched as the floors ticked by, clutching my purse with the ultrasounds tucked inside. The doors opened and I stepped out into the lobby.

Margaret was there to greet me. "Hello, Ms. Heartly. Follow me."

I followed her down the long hallway to Daniel's office, still not over how big his floor was. She stopped outside his door and knocked softly.

"Come in," I heard him say, a bit of gruffness to his voice.

I looked at Margaret unsure, but she opened the door and nodded for me to go inside. I stumbled into his office, the door closing behind me.

Daniel was hunched over his desk with a pile of paperwork surrounding him. His hands were in his hair as his eyes scanned the documents in front of him.

"Hi," I said, hating how meek I sounded.

He looked up surprised, as if he hadn't just given the front desk the okay to send me up.

"Heart. Hi," he said, standing up. He strode toward me and gave me a kiss on the cheek before sitting back down at his desk.

"Sit," he said, getting back to his papers.

I did as he said and pulled the ultrasound photos from my purse.

"Look what I have." I placed the pictures on the papers in front of him.

"Oh, wow," he breathed, his eyes barely grazing over the pictures.

I jerked my head back as I looked at him, my heart starting to break right there in his office. He couldn't seem more uninterested.

"Yeah, I went to that new doctor Freddy recommended…" I started, trying again.

"Oh? How was it?" he asked. His eyes found mine for just a moment before going back to his papers. He pushed the ultrasound pictures gently aside to read one of the documents.

"It would have been better if you were there," I said pointedly. My patience was growing thin, and my excitement in coming all the way over here had left the building completely.

"Well, you didn't invite me," he pointed out, looking at me and raising an eyebrow.

"And why do you think that is?" I asked, my voice raising.

"You tell me."

"Maybe it's because you don't actually give a damn about the baby. Or me, for that matter."

"That's not true…" he started.

"Maybe you're just trying to get on my good side, so I stay quiet. God forbid the press finds out that *the* Daniel Jacobs is going to be a father with some stupid girl from Brooklyn."

"Heart…"

"Don't," I said, putting up my hand. "You don't think I've noticed how you keep me hidden? We had to go out the back alley of the restaurant Friday night. I'm going to be an expert at fire exits by the end of this because you're embarrassed to be seen with me."

The words were rolling out of me, and there was no stopping them.

"I'm sorry that I'm not a supermodel. Or *Kiera*. I'm sorry that I'm not someone you'd proudly have on your arm."

Daniel's eyes watched me intently.

"And I'm sorry that I got pregnant," I said, standing up and grabbing the ultrasounds from his desk.

"Heart…" he said, standing up, too.

"I think it's best if you don't call me. Don't come by. I need some space."

I walked swiftly to the door and slammed it behind me. Not caring what others thought, I raced through the lobby and it wasn't until I was out of the elevator and out of the building that I finally let the tears flow.

Chapter 28

DANIEL

I knew I should have gone after Heart, but I didn't. My feet felt like they were glued to the floor of my office as I helplessly watched her walk out the door, its slam still echoing in my ears. I sunk in my desk chair and ran my hands through my hair, frustrated.

I had never seen her so angry, or heard her voice so sharp. Granted, I was still getting to know her and all the sides of her, but that one hurt. It was a side I didn't ever want to see, and it was one I had caused.

Stupidly, I should have known that sneaking around with her would hurt her. I kept saying it was to protect her. To protect that baby. That was true, but it was also because I wasn't ready to face the judgment of the tabloids. It would ruin my image. My company's image.

It had nothing to do with Heart or where she lived or what she looked like. I didn't care about any of that. I found her to be the most beautiful woman I had ever seen. I hated that my actions had brought out such ugly insecurities.

If the press found out about us and the baby, they wouldn't just tear me apart, they would go after her, too. I didn't want that for her. I wished she could see that. Our worlds were just so different. She would never understand what it was like to be splashed all over newspapers and gossip sites. I didn't want her to ever experience that.

I didn't know she was coming today. I didn't even know what day it was after the weekend I'd had. I spent half the time going over the contracts for the London deal that had important holes in them that had been overlooked in underwriting, and the other half wondering how the hell I was going to be a father.

That was why I didn't invite her back to my place after dinner on Friday, and I could see on her face the flicker of disappointment. Disappointment that I felt, too. More than anything, I wanted to bring her home and get her back in bed and forget everything. But it wasn't that easy. This baby was coming whether we addressed it or not. And I was scared shitless.

It seemed like the only one who had faith in me was Heart, and now I wasn't so sure. Freddy made it clear he didn't think he could do it. The exact words didn't come out of his mouth, but I saw it in the way he eyed me as he took a sip of wine at dinner. He could smile and pat me on the back all he wanted, but deep down he thought this whole thing was crazy. And he was right.

I couldn't be a dad. Hell, I couldn't even be a one-woman kind of guy. At least, I hadn't been up until this point. Now, I had just potentially lost the one woman I wanted to be with because I let my insecurities get the best of me. I had to fix this.

I picked up my phone and tried calling Heart. It rang two times before I was sent to voicemail.

"Fuck," I said, slamming my phone on my desk.

I should have stopped her. Gone after her. I should have looked at the damn ultrasounds. There were a million things I could have done better in the five minutes she was in this office.

I just knew that if I saw the baby, and how it had grown and changed, I would have grown even more attached to it than I already was. I couldn't risk that, not if there was a possibility I wasn't in his or her life. It was more for the baby's benefit than mine. I would probably just screw everything up.

I sat back in my chair and looked up at the ceiling, wondering what I should do. She said she wanted space, and it seemed like she meant it. I just didn't know if I could give it to her.

The following weeks dragged on. I didn't try to call Heart again. I didn't make the drive to Brooklyn that I had grown quite fond of. I gave her what she asked for, but only because I knew we couldn't stay apart for long. We were tied to each other because of the baby. She would have to talk to me eventually. Wouldn't she?

I guessed she had the check. The check that would change her life and allow her to comfortably take care of herself and the baby. I wondered if writing it had been a hasty mistake. I just wanted her to know that I cared. That I was there for her.

A few Fridays after our double date, I was getting ready for a fundraising event that was held every year. As I put on my tux and tightened my bowtie, I thought of all the places I would rather be than schmoozing with the socialites of Manhattan. I wondered what Heart was doing too. Like I had wondered every day since she walked out of my office and left a void in my life.

As Armand pulled up to the Plaza Hotel, the cameras were flashing before I had even exited the car. I sighed in frustration before plastering on a smile as Armand opened my car door. The cameras were blinding as I walked the red carpet, giving a wave and buttoning my tux as my publicist had advised. It looked good for pictures, she said.

The demands and questions began filling my ears as the press shouted.

"Mr. Jacobs! Mr. Jacobs!"

"Over here!"

"To your right, Mr. Jacobs!"

"When is the wedding?"

"Where is Ms. Shipley tonight?"

I just kept a smile on, one that never reached my eyes and continued down the red carpet. I breathed a sigh of relief as I entered the hotel. A cocktail waitress came by with a tray of champagne and I eagerly grabbed two, downing one and keeping the other to sip on as I prepared to socialize.

I found a few associates I had done business with in the past and made my way over. We talked about the usual. Stocks, business deals, and the current economy. Things I had grown accustomed to talking about. It felt all so robotic. So ungenuine. Still, it was best to remain professional. That was the face I had to wear, being the head of my own company.

"Look who just arrived," said one of them, looking toward the door.

It was Kiera. I took a long sip of champagne.

"I hear you two are back together," he said, nudging me. "Lucky guy."

"That's what they're saying," I said. "If you'll excuse me."

I downed the rest of my champagne and grabbed another off a tray as I made my way to a corner of the room where I wouldn't be spotted by Kiera. I leaned against the wall, away from the spotlights of the dance floor. I wanted nothing more than to go up to my room, which was complimentary for the guests tonight. I spent a few minutes people-watching, keeping a close eye on Kiera's whereabouts. And that was when I saw her.

Heart stood across the room, talking to an old associate of mine. I had to do a double-take to be sure it was her. This didn't seem like the kind of place she would be on a Friday night. But there she was.

She wore a strapless pink dress. The tulle skirt was fanned out just at her waist. A clever disguise for her growing belly, but also one of the sexiest things I had ever seen her in. The blush color of her dress almost blended in with her creamy skin, and the bust was barely clinging on to the curves of her breasts. Her hair was down in waves, sleekly parted in the center. I wanted nothing more than to touch her. Feel her surround me.

I watched as she talked to the guy at the bar. He said something and she laughed, putting her hand on his arm. I felt jealousy bubble through my blood. I downed my third glass of champagne and strode over with determination to stop whatever was transpiring here.

"Brock," I said loudly as I patted the guy on the back and prayed that was his name. It had been a while since we had done business together.

He turned and looked at me, registering my face before a smile crossed his.

"Daniel! How the hell are you?" he asked.

I could feel Heart's eyes on me, staring daggers.

"I see you've met Addison," I said, feeling weird about calling her that. "They're doing incredible things over at Leading to Learn."

"So, she's been telling me," he said, smiling down at her. I noticed his eyes skim her cleavage and I wanted to knock him out right there.

"Is that so?" I asked, looking at her. "I'm surprised to see you here, Ms. Heartly."

"Yes, well, Leading to Learn has some items up for bid as part of tonight's silent auction," replied Addison coolly.

"It really is a great organization," said Brock, praise dripping from his tongue. I didn't buy it for a second. He was probably just trying to get close to her.

"That's why I am their newest donor," I said cockily.

"Is that so?" asked Brody, raising an eyebrow. "I was actually just about to write a check."

He pulled out a checkbook from the inside of his tuxedo jacket. I tried my best not to roll my eyes.

"Addison, would you be so kind as to accompany me to a cocktail table so we can do this the right way?" Brody asked, offering his arm.

"I'd love to," she said, taking it, but not before shooting me a look.

I stayed nearby and watched as he wrote out a check, but the whole time he was trying to make conversation with her, her eyes were searching for mine. The guy didn't stand a chance. But right now, I wasn't sure if I did either.

Heart slipped the check into her small beaded clutch, and I watched as she politely excused herself. She began making her way toward me, her face tied up in an expression that wasn't welcoming. She grabbed my arm and pulled me away from the crowd of people.

"What the hell do you think you're doing?" she asked, shoving a finger into my chest.

"What do you mean?" I shrugged innocently.

"You know exactly what I mean."

"That guy is a prick."

"He was perfectly fine," she argued.

She was right. There wasn't anything wrong with him, other than he couldn't keep his eyes off of the parts of her that I desperately wanted. The champagne was clearly going to my head.

"How much did he give you?" I asked.

"Excuse me?" she asked sharply.

"The check. How much was it for?"

"None of your business."

"Probably not as much as mine."

"You are a pompous asshole," she said before turning to go.

She couldn't be more right.

"Heart, wait." I reached for her hand.

She looked down as I intertwined my fingers in hers. I didn't realize how much I missed this until now.

"Let go of me," she said.

"I just wanted to help."

"I don't need your help, Daniel. I'm perfectly capable of doing my job. I'm perfectly capable of doing *everything* without *you*."

She tugged her hand away, but didn't walk away. She just stood there with her arms crossed in a beautiful party dress, staring into the crowd of people.

Chapter 29

ADDISON

I tried to calm down and not show Daniel that I was visibly shaking as I stared out at the crowd of Manhattan's elite all in their thousand-dollar cocktail dresses and custom tuxedos. Seeing them sipping on champagne and tossing money around like it was nothing only made me more aware of how much I wanted to disappear in that moment. I didn't belong here.

I tried getting out of it, but Brian insisted I come and try to schmooze the wealthy while they were a little tipsy and giving money away. Of course, I should have known there was a chance I would see Daniel, but I had no idea he would have the balls to pull off what he just did. In front of a potential donor, no less.

Maybe a part of me *did* know I would run into him, which was why I spent a little more money than I would have liked to on this dress at the consignment store and maybe added a little more rose blush to my cheeks. Now, here he was in front of me, and I had no idea what to do. It wasn't like I had any friends here to lean on.

"Heart," he said softly.

I blinked back hot tears before shooting him a look. "What?" I asked sharply.

"Can we please just talk?" he asked.

"This is hardly the place."

He looked around the banquet room for a moment and then signaled for me to follow him. I hesitated before reluctantly giving in. Would I ever be able to say no to this man?

He pushed open a pair of double doors that led out into an empty hallway. He fidgeted with his tux jacket, buttoning it up and then unbuttoning it. I was growing impatient.

"Well, you have me here. So talk," I said, crossing my arms.

He let out a deep breath through his nose. "Well, it's kind of hard when you're being so..."

"So what?"

"Hostile."

"How else do you expect me to be, Daniel?" I snapped, giving him a pointed look.

"Look, I know I didn't react very well when you came to my office."

"You didn't react at all."

"I just wasn't expecting you, and you know how the deal with London has been." He shrugged.

"I don't care if you're making a goddamn deal with the King of England. I put a picture of our baby on your desk and you hardly looked at it," I stated, my voice rising.

"I know..."

"What is it with you? I feel like my mind is running marathons just trying to keep up with you and your feelings that seem to change on a daily basis."

"And what about you? You seemed awfully flirtatious with that jerk back there," he pointed out.

"Are you serious?" I spat. "It's business."

"Well, I didn't like it."

"Too bad."

He let out a loud sigh before his shoulders fell.

"This is just a lot for me..." he said, looking down at his black shiny shoes.

"And you don't think it's a lot for *me?* I'm growing a baby inside of me and trying to figure out how I'm going to do it all. I don't know if you're in this or not. You want to tell your friends, but then you still want to keep me a secret. Which is it?"

He stayed silent.

"Man the fuck up and decide. Because I don't need to be raising two children."

"Man the fuck up?" he asked, looking up at me, seething.

He took a step toward me.

"Yeah," I said, hating how my voice wavered.

He took another step toward me. I took a step backward until my back was pressed against the wall. I swallowed hard as I felt my legs turn to Jell-O as he closed the distance between us. He put his hands on either side of my head. My eyes fluttered closed, as if that was going to stop what was going to come next.

I felt his lips lower to my ear. "This is me manning up."

His whisper ran through me like ice-cold water, sending a shiver through my entire body. And then his mouth was on my neck and his hands were on my breasts, massaging against the tulle of my dress. I let out a little moan as I leaned my head against the wall and let him touch me in the way I desperately wanted.

His hands made their way to the sides of my head and his fingers became lost in my hair as he pressed his body against me. My arms wrapped around his upper back and my fingers pressed into him as his mouth devoured mine. His tongue moved quickly and with purpose. I felt him growing hard against me, which only made me kiss him harder.

A door opened some distance away and I quickly pushed him away. I smoothed my dress as I watched a server roll a cart into the hallway, completely unaware we were there.

"Come with me," whispered Daniel, grabbing my hand.

He strode quickly down the hall, and I tried to keep up. He pushed open the doors to the hotel lobby and hurried toward the elevators. He hit the button a few times until the doors opened and he pulled me inside. He tapped his foot impatiently as he watched the floors tick by. A few moments later, the doors opened and he led me to a door, quickly pulled out a key card, and held it against the lock. It lit up green and clicked open, and Daniel pulled me inside.

The door had barely closed behind us before his mouth was on mine. I stumbled slightly as he pulled me into the room. He reached to the back of my dress, finding the zipper and pulling it down quickly. The dress fell to my ankles and I stepped out of it as we made our way to the bed.

Daniel turned so my back was toward the bed and I fell onto it, wearing nothing but my heels and a blush-colored thong. He stood above me, drinking me in with his eyes that looked like stormy seas. He slid off his jacket and began unbuttoning his white shirt. Goddamn, he looked good in a tux.

I couldn't help myself. I sat up on the bed and reached for the waistband of his pants, pulling him toward me. Quickly, I unbuttoned them and shoved them down, revealing his large erection. I looked up at him as I swirled my tongue over the tip, watching as his eyes closed and his breath quickened.

Opening my mouth, I ran my wet lips down his shaft slowly until I could feel him in the back of my throat. He groaned softly as I moved my mouth up and down his length. I had missed the way he tasted, and the power I felt when I was in control of him. His hands found my head and his fingers got lost in my hair as my mouth moved faster, my tongue gliding along his base.

"Heart," he whispered desperately.

I pulled my mouth off him and looked up at him with a coy smile. I scooched back on the bed and pushed the lace thong from my hips and down my legs. Then I propped myself up on my elbows, spreading my legs slightly. I watched as Daniel's lips parted slightly as his gaze fell between my legs. I felt myself get wet under his gaze. He inhaled a sharp breath before climbing onto the bed and hovered over me.

He positioned himself against me and I held my breath as he dipped into me slowly. I grabbed the bed sheets and held them tightly as he filled me inch by inch. Daniel's eyes moved from mine to where we met, watching as he slowly pulled out and pushed back into me with ease. He was getting off from watching, and I was getting off from watching him.

He lowered his mouth to my breasts and I could feel his breath against my nipples, causing them to harden. When he parted his lips against my nipples and his tongue flicked against them, I moaned and grabbed at his lower back.

Now he started moving faster, consuming all of me. Filling my walls with his girth, as my fingertips dug into him. I spread my legs even further so they sprawled out on either side of me. I lifted my hips slightly as pleasure built in my chest. It felt like I was going to scream as I tightened around him.

His fingers found my clit and began massaging me as our breathing grew heavy and in sync. He pounded into me and his fingers moved faster. I bit my bottom lip to stop from crying out as euphoric pleasure consumed me. He thrust into me once more, hard and deep. I felt him convulse inside of me as he let out a loud moan before collapsing around me.

We lay there for several minutes, breathless and not saying a word. What the hell had just happened? One second, we were arguing and the next we were completely losing ourselves to each other in a hotel suite. I had completely lost my head and my heart.

I peeled Daniel's arm off of me and stood carefully from the bed, my body still processing the pleasure it had just experienced. I walked to the bathroom to use the toilet and cleaned myself up. When I came back to the room, Daniel was in bed looking at me with a smile on his face.

"Don't look at me like that," I said, holding back a smile.

"That was just...wow," he murmured, running a hand through his hair.

"We really should get back," I said.

"Are you serious?" He sat up and eyed me questioningly.

"I am actually working tonight, Daniel."

I slid on my dress and heard him climb off the bed. His hand found the zipper of my dress and zipped it up.

"Thank you," I murmured.

He kissed my neck before putting on his tux. I could have stayed in that room all night, but I really did have to work. I didn't need Brian asking questions about how I didn't raise any money or socialize with any new associates. However, I hoped we would find ourselves here later tonight. Maybe we would actually talk.

We rode the elevator back down to the lobby and walked back into the hall. The music was now booming and there were questionable dance moves happening on the makeshift dance floor. I giggled at an older man doing the robot before giving Daniel's arm squeeze and heading to the silent auction table.

The next hour, I tried my best to focus on talking business, but seeing Daniel across the room was a major distraction knowing what we just did upstairs. Once the final bids were in for the silent auction, there was little left for me to do, so I went in search of Daniel. I spotted him near the bar, talking with another man.

As I approached, I heard Daniel talking and what he said made me stop in my tracks.

"I'm not really into the whole marriage and white picket fence thing. Kids and a wife. They just tie you down. I have a major business to run."

He laughed as the other man slapped him on the back in agreement.

My stomach did a flip as I slowly backed away. I couldn't believe what I had just heard come out of his mouth. I was a complete fool for falling into bed with him and letting my emotions run rampant, thinking that this time it would be different.

I turned and strode quickly out of the banquet room. It felt like the walls were beginning to close in on me. I was either going to puke or cry and had to get out of there. I ran through the lobby and out the hotel entrance. My mind gave a whisper of goodbye to the man I thought I was just starting to figure out.

Chapter 30

DANIEL

"I feel you, man," said Chuck, as he gave my back another good slap. "I have never understood these guys who end up with one woman."

"What's the fun in that?" I asked.

"Right? No fucking thanks. And then after the woman reels you in, they want a ring. They drop those little hints and take you through Tiffany's innocently." Chuck held his hand out and wiggled his fingers and batted his eyelashes.

"All part of their master plan," I agreed.

"Then they get that. Then they want the big, white wedding, and yadayada. It's always take-take-take."

I nodded and took a sip of champagne, hoping no one would hear me to pretend to agree with this guy. He was a complete prick, but I needed to appeal to his good side for an upcoming business deal. The way he talked about women, it was no wonder he couldn't lock one down. It wasn't because he didn't want to, it was because no one wanted him. His ego would never let him admit the harsh truth, though.

"A wedding in the Hamptons probably."

"Exactly. And then they want babies. God, those things are so loud. Not to mention needy. That whole daddy daycare thing. Leave that to the women."

Oof. He just kept getting worse. If it got me a business deal, I'd play along.

"I wouldn't even know what to do with a baby." I shrugged, half playing along and half pondering my situation with Heart. I really wouldn't know, but the day I would need to was approaching faster than I liked.

"I know what you do. You hand it back to its mother."

I forced a laugh before lifting my glass. "Cheers to the bachelor life," I said.

"Now hold on there," said Chuck, putting his hand up and raising a skeptical eyebrow.

I looked at him curiously.

"You talk a big talk, but I heard you're off the market with that Shipley girl..."

"Oh, that?" I waved him off. "I'm just telling the poor girl what she wants to hear."

"Ahh," said Chuck, impressed. "Well played for a swell lay."

"Exactly."

"Well, cheers to that." Chuck raised his glass and clinked it to mine before he downed it.

"It's nice to meet another businessman with their eye on the prize. We should sit down for a meeting sometime," I offered.

I had cast my line and now I just needed to reel him in.

"I'll have my assistant call yours."

He bit.

"Uh-oh," he said suddenly, looking behind me. "Your *fiancée* is headed this way. Man, does she look like a real dime. You're a lucky man."

"We'll talk soon," I said, shaking his hand firmly.

"Count on it."

I turned and spotted Kiera walking toward me with determination and a martini in her freshly manicured hand. She wore a black silk dress that plunged at the neckline, revealing her sun-kissed tan that was probably sprayed on. Her teeth peeked out from her red lipstick in a seductive smile.

"Daniel," she purred, draping her arms around my neck. "I thought I would run into you here."

"Kiera." I nodded as I looked around the room for Heart. The last thing I needed her to see was Kiera all over me, giving off a very wrong impression. But I didn't see her. I figured I would get this over with quickly and then go find her.

"Not up for bid tonight?" asked Kiera with a smirk.

"Sorry to disappoint," I said.

"I had my checkbook and everything." She pouted.

"There's plenty to bid on tonight. You could put it to use."

"Oh, you know I don't really care about all this charity bullshit," she said, lowering her voice so no one would hear.

Then she leaned in close and whispered. "You know, charity or not...if you liked what you saw, I wouldn't charge you."

"Tempting, but I'm here on business tonight."

She pulled back and rolled her eyes. "When did you become so serious?"

"Probably around the same time you got married for the second time. Or was it the third?"

She gave me a playful shove. "You're the worst."

I put my hands on her upper arms and gave her a gentle squeeze. It probably seemed like a kind gesture, but it was really to hold her back from hanging all over me.

"I really am here on business, but it was great to see you, Kiera."

She pulled herself from my grip and stood on her tiptoes. She was anything if not persistent. She wrapped her hands around my neck before giving me a kiss on the cheek.

"Call me when you want to have some fun," she said before slinking off.

I watched her go and then scanned the room for Heart and the pink dress I had helped take off just over an hour ago. I was ready for round two now that my business was done. I wandered around the room, giving smiles to some acquaintances, while I looked for her. She wasn't at the bar, which was a given. She wasn't at the buffet table. She wasn't at the silent auction table where they were now compiling all the bids.

I didn't know where she was.

I slipped my phone out of my jacket pocket and texted her: *Where are you?* I waited for a few minutes, drumming my fingers against my phone. She didn't reply. I tried calling her, but it went to voicemail. I furrowed my brow. That was strange. I didn't think she would leave without saying goodbye.

After our time up in my suite tonight, I thought maybe we had sorted everything out. I knew we hadn't gotten a lot of talking done, which we probably should have, but she was just as eager as I was on that bed. I thought she would stay the night with me tonight after she was done working.

An hour later, the charity event was starting to wind down. I texted Heart again, but received no reply. Disappointed, I said my goodbyes and went upstairs to my suite. I thought maybe she would come join me, but when midnight came around, I realized she wasn't coming.

The only explanation I had was that maybe she had gotten sick. I knew she would still get bouts of morning sickness, even at night, which was weird. Why did they even call it morning sickness?

I took a hot shower and climbed into the plush bed that still smelled like her. I breathed her in as I closed my eyes and fell asleep.

The next few days, I tried calling Heart again, but all I got was her voicemail. I left a few messages, but then gave up wasting my breath. I didn't understand why she had disappeared at the charity event and why I was now getting the silent treatment.

Repeatedly, I replayed the conversation we had in the hallway. She had been so angry. She hardly ever cussed, but harsh words flowed off her tongue easily then. All the things she had said were true. I didn't know what I was doing, and I knew that it was taking a toll on her. I wished I would have told her how I was feeling rather than taking her to bed.

Well, I didn't regret that part completely. I just knew we had things to fix, and now it felt like I tried to slap a Band-Aid on it with sex. I just couldn't help myself around her. I knew the feeling was mutual, or we wouldn't have wound up having wildly angry, passionate sex that night.

Whatever flip switched, clearly my texts and phone calls weren't working. I picked up the phone at my desk and dialed Margaret at the front desk.

"Yes, Mr. Jacobs?" she answered.

"I need you to put an order in at the florist on Fifth Ave. I want three dozen red roses. And they have to be delivered today."

"But it's already four o'clock…"

"Pay double. Triple. I don't care. It has to be today."

"Okay. Where should they be sent?"

"Ms. Heartly's home address."

"Yes, sir."

I ended the call and wondered if it would be enough to fix whatever I had done.

It wasn't.

Three days had gone by and I didn't hear from Heart. I was starting to go crazy. It had been a week since the charity event, and nothing. I didn't realize how much I needed her until now. I was completely infatuated with her. Perhaps even falling for her, which was something I did not do.

That night, in my apartment, I poured a generous serving of whiskey on ice. Images of Heart and our first night together flashed through my mind, as they usually did in this space. I took a sip and gripped the counter's edge as I studied myself in the mirror.

The word "asshole" was all that came to mind when I saw my face.

Had I really lost her again?

I thought back to what she said in the hallway, trying desperately to retrace my footsteps and see where I had stumbled. She said she didn't know if I was in this or not. Being without her for the past week made me realize I was. I was all in, and I decided to finally show her that.

I took my drink over to the couch and sat down, sinking into the plush sage green cushions. Getting my laptop from the concrete coffee table, I started Googling the best baby stores in Manhattan. I scrolled through website after website, reading reviews for cribs and safety ratings for car seats.

I was completely lost in all things baby. No wonder Heart had been so overwhelmed. She already had so much to learn about being pregnant, and so many adjustments to make to her life. And then you throw shopping for everything on top of all that. It was no wonder she was pissed at me.

After two hours of browsing, I purchased a crib from Bergdorf Goodman and a car seat from Nordstrom. I ordered some wooden toys from a little boutique on Warren Street. The one where all the celebrities go. I even ordered a few newborn onesies in neutral colors. I had everything gift wrapped and sent to her apartment in Brooklyn. I wanted our baby to have the best of the best, and I wanted Heart to know that I was trying.

I wondered when Heart would find out if we were having a boy or girl, or if she knew already. Then, I wondered if she would tell me. I never thought about what I would want because I was never with someone where starting a family was on the table. Hell, it wasn't even on the menu.

Kiera and I had been together awhile, but she wasn't exactly maternal. I saw her hold her baby niece once. It was so unnatural. She held the poor thing out like it was a dog who had just left a doodoo on her expensive fur rug. Come to think of it, when a baby would cry, she seemed to instinctively twitch. As if she were malfunctioning.

Somehow, I knew Heart would make a good mother. I sighed as I leaned back into the couch and thought about everything she was going through. I should have asked her more questions. I should have offered to go with her to her doctor appointments. Now that I thought about it, I should have done a lot of things, including picking up that ultrasound off my desk and looking at our baby together.

I knew buying things wasn't going to fix everything, but I hoped it was enough to show her that I was really in this. I might not know how to be a father, but I was going to give it all I had. I wanted to. And I wanted to do it with Heart.

Chapter 31

ADDISON

M onica pushed her way inside my apartment, avoiding the large boxes wrapped in bows and the bags stuffed with tissue paper.

"Uh, did you have a baby shower without me?" she asked, scratching her head as she took in the mess that was my apartment.

"Of course not," I replied as I plopped down on my couch.

It was the only thing that wasn't covered in all the deliveries that had been showing up for the past few days. My apartment could hardly hold the minimal amount of furniture I owned, let alone all of these boxes and gifts.

I looked around and sighed. Monica stared at me with so many questions dancing around in her eyes.

"They're from Daniel." I shrugged.

She walked over to one of the huge white boxes that was tied with black ribbon. She ran her fingers over it and looked at the tag.

"Bergdorf Goodman?" Her eyes grew wide.

"Ridiculous, I know."

"This baby is going to have nicer things than me."

I let out a soft laugh. It was true. One quarter of this stuff was probably enough to pay my rent for the month.

Monica came and sat on the couch next to me.

"So, the handsome CEO sent you all this stuff for the baby you're having together and you look like you've just tasted a lemon. What is up with you?" she asked, crossing her arms and leaning against the arm of the couch.

"He's not the man of my dreams..."

"Uh-oh. What now? I can't keep up with you two."

"Well, you know I went to that charity event the other night. The charity auction one."

"Yes. I went shopping with you for the dress. I bet you were a knockout."

"Well, Daniel was there."

"Of course, he was, and he probably couldn't keep his hands or eyes off of you."

"He was totally inappropriate when I was trying to do business. It was like he was jealous or something."

"No duh." Monica rolled her eyes.

"Well, we got into an argument over that and then it led to an even more heated argument about the baby and us."

"And then it led to..."

"Mind-blowingly good makeup sex," I said, covering my face with my hands.

"Of course, it did. You guys are like a walking, talking romance novel."

"Yeah, except I don't get the happy ending."

"What are you talking about? The guy is clearly into you and you're having a baby together. And that baby is going to be born into the poshest life. It's like a modern day Cinderella story. Just with morning sickness and cravings for jalapenos."

"I don't care about all of that." I shook my head. "Not when the man I was starting to see a future with turned out to be a big, fat liar."

"What are you talking about?" she asked, scooching closer.

"After we, you know..." I paused.

"Had sex..." finished Monica.

"Yes, well, we came back down to the silent auction and I overheard him saying some ugly things."

"Like what?"

"About how he wasn't into marriage or the white picket fence thing. About how he didn't want to be tied down."

"What the actual hell?" screeched Monica.

"I know."

"Then what's all this for?" she asked, waving her hand around the room.

"I've been ignoring him, but he doesn't know why. He doesn't know I heard what he said. I ran out of there as fast as I could."

"Sheesh. I'm so sorry, Heart. What a mess."

"I know…"

She stood up from the couch and slapped her thighs. "Well, what can I do to help? Should we start unboxing all of this?"

"I can't keep it," I said, shaking my head.

"Like hell you can't. It's not like you're going to use store credit at Bloomingdales or Bergdorf Goodman on yourself. You're going to need all of this for your baby. I say, keep it."

She had a point.

"Okay," I said hesitantly. "But I'm not ready to open anything. It feels too soon. Too real."

Monica nodded. "Right, well, I'll just push it all to the back wall."

"I'll help."

"Nope. No heavy lifting. You sit and relax."

I smiled as I sat back on the couch and watched as my best friend grunted and groaned as she pushed the heavy boxes across the floor. I was damn lucky to have her.

The next morning as I got off the subway to walk into work, I spotted Daniel's face on the front page of the tabloid papers at the newsstand. My heart leaped to my throat as I considered what would be written inside. Had someone found out about us? Had someone found out about the baby? I swiftly walked over and grabbed one of the magazines, flipping through the pages frantically.

"Excuse me, you're going to have to pay for that," said the attendant.

"Right. Sorry."

I pulled out my wallet and slid him a few bucks before turning my attention back to the magazine. I finally landed on the centerpiece spread that was collaged with photos of Daniel and a slew of Victoria's Secret models after their runway show. I swallowed hard as I studied each photo. I couldn't believe he was back to being his old self. How could I have been so stupid?

"Miss, this isn't a library. Please take your magazine and move along," said the attendant impatiently.

"I paid, didn't I?" I snapped.

"Okay, okay. Just don't crowd the counter," he said, putting his hands up in defense.

I stepped aside and read the article, trying not to get distracted by Daniel's dazzling smile and his carefree attitude about being photographed. He was never like that with me. Everything was always so secretive. Always sneaking out back doors or dressing down in sweats and a T-shirt. God forbid, someone recognized him in Brooklyn or with a nobody like me.

It seemed like a stupid thing to be upset about, especially when I had no interest in being in the papers or being hunted by paparazzi. That sounded like a nightmare. I guessed I just couldn't help feeling like he was embarrassed of me. That was what hurt the most.

I scanned the article and read that these photos were from last year but had just now surfaced. I let out a mixture of a sigh of relief and laughter, knowing that this was not present day. Clearly, the tabloids were having a slow news day and were trying to hook their readers with misinformation. For a moment, I felt bad for him, but then I remembered everything that had happened.

I stuffed the magazine in my bag and walked around the corner to my work. When the elevator doors opened to my floor, I was met with a slow applause that quickened as I walked into the room. I looked around feeling very confused. I looked behind me to make sure they weren't clapping for someone else.

Brian approached with a wide grin.

"There she is," he said, clapping along with everyone.

"What's going on?" I asked.

"I'm surprised you didn't know, since you're the one who landed Daniel Jacobs in the first place. He just doubled his donation."

I stood there speechless as I tried to process what he was saying to me.

"When did this happen?"

"All of fifteen minutes ago."

"But Shelley..." I said, looking for her.

She was the one who I had take over for me. Didn't she deserve the credit?

"It's all because of you, girl," she said sincerely, walking up and giving me a hug. "I just finished up the fine print. You're the one who got the deal in the first place."

"Thanks, Shell," I said shakily as I gave her a squeeze.

She let me go and everyone started to dissipate to their offices and cubicles, leaving me feeling dumbstruck. The original donation amount had changed the entire trajectory of our company, and now it had doubled. We now had more money than we knew what to do with.

I smiled meekly at everyone as I walked to my office, trying to hide the shock on my face. Once I was in the safety of my office, I closed the door and sat in my desk chair. What a whirlwind of a Monday morning. And another way of Daniel trying to get my attention. The man was persistent, if anything.

He was either trying to impress me or he was trying to paint himself in a good light after this morning's tabloids. It wasn't because he actually cared about the nonprofit or what we were doing, which suddenly made me angry. What was it with this man and thinking he could just buy his way out of any trouble he was in? Life didn't work that way.

I had half a mind of telling him off, but decided to text Monica instead. He wasn't worth wasting my breath.

Me: *Mr. Moneybags is at it again.*

Monica: *What now? A car for when the baby turns sixteen. I'm sure we could find room for it in your loft.*

Me: *Haha. I wouldn't be surprised, but no. He freaking doubled his initial donation with Leading to Learn.*

Monica: *Shut up. That means it's...*

Me: *Yep. A million bucks.*

Monica: *Holy shit.*

Me: *I know.*

I heard a knock at the door.

"Come in," I said, placing my phone on my desk and looking busy.

Brian peeped his head in. "Are you free for a meeting in an hour?"

"Uh, sure. What's up?"

"Mr. Bradley from headquarters is driving in from Philly. He heard about the deal and wants to meet with you."

I looked at Brian warily.

"It's a good thing, Addison." He drummed his fingers on the doorframe. "One hour."

I nodded and he walked out the door, closing it behind him.

A wave of nausea rushed through me and I leaned over my desk trash can, thinking I was going to hurl. Mr. Bradley was the Executive Director of Leading to Learn. I'd met him a few times, but never had a meeting with him. I started feeling anxious.

An hour passed too quickly and I made my way to Brian's office. I knocked softly and he invited me in. Brian sat at his desk and across from him was Mr. Bradley, in a navy suit with a leather briefcase by his side.

He stood and shook my hand firmly.

"Hello, Mr. Bradley," I said, taking the seat next to him.

"Ms. Heartly. I hear you've been doing great things here. Things this nonprofit could only dream of."

"Oh, I wouldn't say that."

"You made a deal with the largest donor we've ever had or probably ever will have."

"We're very proud of her," said Brian, smiling at us both.

"Thank you," I said softly.

"I think your invaluable people skills and negotiation tactics should be recognized," said Mr. Bradley.

Those were two things I didn't have. I was put on this deal because someone else was busy. It wasn't because I had a knack for small talk or was even a little persuasive. Daniel just saw something he thought he liked and threw money at it. Just like he did with everything. I felt like an impostor.

"We would like to give you a promotion to head up the donation team," continued Mr. Bradley.

"Oh, but..." I started.

"It comes with a generous raise and it will be a good internal move within the company. Who knows? Maybe you'll have my job one day," said Mr. Bradley.

I chewed on the inside of my cheek as I thought about what he was saying.

As if sensing my hesitancy, he said, "You don't need to decide now. Just think about it."

"I will, sir."

He stood and shook my hand firmly before I walked out of the room in a dreamlike state. All of this was happening because of Daniel. I wanted to thank him and punch him at the same time.

Chapter 32

DANIEL

By lunchtime on Monday, I was growing anxious knowing I still hadn't heard from Heart. It had been three days since the silent auction where we bumped into each other. I thought it was something like fate that had brought us together that night after she asked for space. Now, I wasn't so sure. We seemed to be back where we started.

I felt like I was on a rollercoaster that I didn't want to get off yet. The highs felt limitless, and the lows felt bottomless. If it were any other woman, I would have brushed this off, but there was something about Heart. And it wasn't just because she was carrying our baby. Or that the sex was the best I had ever had. She was different.

Impatiently, I drummed my fingers on my desk as I stared at my computer screen. All my gifts had been delivered over the weekend, but I still hadn't heard from her. I became desperate this morning and phoned Leading to Learn to let them know I wanted to double my donation, hoping it would get her attention. It was a ridiculous ploy that clearly didn't work.

I let out a sigh of frustration. Clearly, she wasn't one who responded to gifts. Again, different from other women I had been with.

I wondered what the hell could have happened in the course of an hour for her to leave the hotel and not hear from her again. I had been racking my brain for three days and couldn't figure it out. It was eating away at me—I had to know.

Standing, I quickly grabbed my jacket from my chair, sliding it on. I walked out of my office and swiftly through the lobby, pressing the button for the elevator.

"Mr. Jacobs?" asked Margaret from her desk.

I looked over and she stood looking nervous.

"Yes, Margaret?"

"You're stepping out?" she asked.

"I have somewhere to be."

"But what about your meeting?" she asked, glancing at the clock.

Shit. I had a meeting in fifteen minutes with a representative from London.

"Reschedule it," I said.

It wasn't the smartest move, given that this deal with London had been a pain in my ass. I knew it would be worth it, but the time I had poured into making sure all the details were right had been exhausting. This fight, or whatever this was with Heart, wasn't making it any easier.

"O-okay," she replied.

The elevator doors opened and I stepped inside as I watched Margaret frantically look through her papers and pick up the phone. London would just have to wait.

On the curb, I texted Armand and he pulled the car around. I gave him the address for Heart's work, and we were on our way. Her building wasn't far from mine and I could feel my uncertainty start creeping in as we got closer. It was probably a bad idea showing up at her place of work, but she had really left me no choice.

The car pulled up to the curb and I stared up at the building, wondering what my next move would be.

Armand cleared his throat. "Sir, we're here."

As if I didn't know.

"Thank you, Armand." I nodded.

He got out and came around to open my door. I stepped out and smoothed my suit before walking inside. I rode the elevator up to her floor, trying to come up with some excuse as to why I was there to see her. We hadn't been working together on the donation paperwork, but surely it wouldn't be odd for us to have a meeting. She was the one I initially wanted to work with before things got complicated.

The elevator doors opened and the girl at the front desk looked up sleepily, only to be brought to life suddenly.

"Um, hello. Mr. Jacobs. Welcome."

"Hello," I said, placing my hands on her desk.

"What can I help you with?"

"I am here to see Ms. Heartly. Is she in?"

"She should be. Do you have a meeting?"

"Yes," I lied.

"Right this way." She stood and I followed her down the hallway, feeling the watchful gazes of the staff. I had almost forgotten about the phone call I had made this morning that would change their entire company. They must have heard the news.

"I just wanted to say we are just so excited about your generous contribution to our nonprofit. It truly is amazing. The whole office has been talking about it," said the girl as we walked.

They definitely all knew.

"I like being able to help. Ms. Heartly made it clear the important work you do here. It's admirable, and I'm happy to do my part."

"Well, here we are," she said, knocking softly on the closed door.

"Come in," Heart called.

My heart rate picked up a few paces as the door opened and I walked inside. Heart was looking down at her desk, focused on writing something on a post-it. She looked so effortlessly pretty in a pinstriped button-down and a makeup-free face. I suddenly felt very anxious.

"Mr. Jacobs is here for your meeting," said the girl from the front desk.

Heart's face snapped up and she saw me standing in the doorway. I suddenly felt very hot. The looks that crossed her face were a dance of panic, confusion, and anger.

"Thank you," said Heart coolly and dismissively.

The door closed behind me and we were alone.

"What are you doing here?" she asked pointedly, sitting stiffly in her desk chair.

"I had to see you," I said, taking a step closer. "You disappeared the other night…"

"I had to go." Her words were clipped as she crossed her arms.

"And then you wouldn't return my calls or texts."

"I guess I was busy."

"Well, did you get the gifts I had sent over?"

"Yes, I got your exorbitant number of packages that were delivered." She sighed.

"I just wanted to help out…"

"More like you wanted to buy my attention when you weren't getting it."

"That's not true," I said, even though it partly was.

"I'm not that kind of girl, Daniel. I don't know how many times I have to tell you that. I can't be bought with expensive dinners at French restaurants or gifts from Bergdorf's. Maybe the other women in your life were easily won over with that, but I'm not one of them."

"I know that. That's why I like you."

"But you don't like me enough to be seen with me in public. Would it hurt your image?" she asked with a sarcastic pouty face.

"Is that what this is about?" I asked, feeling exasperated.

"I saw this morning's tabloids. You have no problem parading around someone half my size wearing next to nothing."

"Those pictures were from last year!" My voice rose an octave.

"It doesn't matter. I'm not who you're meant to be with. I'm not like those girls. I don't know what sort of games you're playing."

"How many times do I have to tell you that I'm trying to protect you from the cruelty of the press? They'll hunt you down. They'll dig up your past. You don't need that stress. Not with the baby."

"Oh, the baby that you don't even want?" she asked, shooting me a look.

"What the hell are you talking about?"

"I heard you the other night. Talking to that man about how you had no interest in marriage or babies."

I swallowed hard. I didn't know she had heard that awful conversation that I had to smile through like I believed what I was saying. I must have sounded like such an asshole. No wonder she left.

"Yeah, what a fun conversation to walk in on..." she snapped, noticing my surprise.

"Heart, I didn't mean any of it."

She crossed her arms and looked at me as if my nose was growing.

"I'm serious. It was all business. I was just trying to schmooze that guy and tell him what he wanted to hear so we could possibly do business together in the future."

"That's the most ridiculous thing I've ever heard," she muttered.

"I know, but it's true."

"Even if it's true, it's ridiculous, Daniel. Why would you pretend to be someone you're not to impress some asshole? Unless, that *is* who you are."

"It's not. It was stupid. But it's just how business works. You have to understand."

"I don't have to do anything. I don't know what is true or what's for show with you. If I was doubting you before, now I know I can't trust you at all. Not to be a father. Not to be a boyfriend. Not be in my life at all."

"You don't mean that," I said, walking behind her desk.

"Don't," she said, giving me a look that could have killed me right there if I took another step closer.

I put my hands up to show I meant no harm. "Please, just listen to me."

"No, I don't need you trying to get out of talking like you did Friday night. You can't just pretend there's nothing wrong by getting me into bed with you," she said, getting to her feet.

That wasn't fair. We both got lost in each other in that hallway. In that suite.

"It takes two," I reminded her.

She rolled her eyes, and that pissed me off.

"Don't act all high and mighty when you're the one who came up with me to that hotel room. No one forced you."

"How dare you." Her face turned a bright shade of pink. I wasn't sure if she was blushing or angry.

"Face it. You're scared too. That's why it's easier to fuck than to talk."

"I never wanted any of this!" she cried, shaking her head.

"Really? Because that first night at my place, you were singing a different tune. In fact, you were screaming my name on the bar of my counter."

My frustration was fueling the words that were coming out of my mouth quicker than I had time to process them.

"I-I..." she stammered.

"You what?" asked a voice from the doorway.

I looked up suddenly and saw Heart's boss, Brian, standing there. He looked between the two of us with his head cocked and his questioning brow raised.

"Brian!" Heart exclaimed loudly, pushing past me. "It's not what it sounds like."

"Really? Because it sounds like you had sexual relations with a business associate."

"I can explain," I said.

"Don't," said Heart sharply, whipping her head around.

"Addison?" asked Brian.

She turned to face him and I could see her body tremble as she took a deep breath.

"I'm so sorry, Brian. I just...lost my head for a second."

"Well, unfortunately, that is not a good enough reason for going against our ethical business practices here at Leading to Learn. I'm so disappointed in you, Addison."

"But, if you'd just—"

Brian held up his hand and shook his head. "I think it's best you start looking for another job," he said. "One that doesn't trade sex for money or donations."

He turned to leave, but not before looking to me and giving me a solemn nod.

"Mr. Jacobs," he said, closing the door behind him.

Heart kept her back to me. She was so still, I couldn't tell if she was breathing or not.

"Heart," I said softly, reaching out and putting her hand on my shoulder.

"Don't touch me," she said.

I removed my hand. "I'm so sorry. Let me talk to him or—"

She turned quickly and faced me. "No. Haven't you done enough?"

Tears welled in her eyes and I wanted nothing more than to wipe them away, and pull her into my arms. I had made such a mess of this. Of everything.

Chapter 33

ADDISON

It felt like all the tears I had been holding back the past few months because of this man in front of me came pouring out of me. I didn't bother stopping them or wiping them away. I just let them come. I didn't care what I looked like or how I sounded. I didn't care if I looked weak. I let everything go right there in my office, while Daniel stood close by and watched because that was all I would let him do.

My whole life had changed in the course of a few minutes in this office that I had worked so hard to earn, and wouldn't be able to call mine anymore. I wished I could put all the blame on Daniel, but he was right. It did take two, and I was every part to blame in this tangled web we had weaved together.

I wished I could go back and change the trajectory of where we had ended up. I would have called in sick the day of the meeting. If I did, he would never have recognized me at that fancy bar and ordered another round of drinks that would continue back at his place. If I did, I wouldn't have got so caught up in him and let go of my inhibitions, resulting in a very real baby that was growing inside me now.

But I couldn't go back in time. Instead, I had to live in this moment.

This moment of my boss knowing everything, or at least enough to know that this was bad. Really bad. I was mortified that Brian knew some of the most intimate details of my life. Even more so, I was devastated that it had cost me my job.

It was all too much. I leaned my back against my desk and slid down to the floor, putting my head in my hands. I felt Daniel sink to the floor beside me. He wasn't leaving, and I wasn't sure if it pissed me off or if I found it slightly endearing.

I lifted my head from my hands and looked at him. "Why did you come here?" I sniffled.

"I was desperate to see you. To know what was going on."

"And you thought coming to my work was the best idea?"

"Like I said, I was desperate," he answered softly.

"You've ruined everything," I whispered, anger making my voice wobble.

"Let me fix it."

"You can't. I know you think you can get away with everything in life, but you can't."

"Let me just talk to your boss again."

I shook my head and looked down at the ground. I couldn't believe Daniel thought he could just sweep this under the rug, as if it wasn't his life that had been turned upside down. There was no way Brian would let this go, and even if he did, I wouldn't feel right about working here knowing what he thought of me.

While his assumptions about Daniel's and my relationship, if that's what you could call it, were off-base, I knew how it looked. It looked like I wasn't good enough at my job, so I took other measures to secure a deal. The thought made me sick.

I felt a wave of nausea roll through me, causing me to double over.

"Are you okay?" asked Daniel, putting his hand on my back.

"I'm fine," I said, pushing his hand away.

"We can figure this out."

"*We?*" I snapped.

He gave me a sad look, which just further pissed me off.

"Don't look at me like that."

"Like what?"

"Like you've just lost one of the things that mattered most to you. Like you've just lost your future. Like you have no idea how you're going to afford your rent."

He thought for a moment. I could see on his face that he had never had to worry about anything like that. It wasn't his fault that it made him so out of touch with the reality of most people.

My reality was I had hit rock bottom. I had nowhere to turn to. My parents had already made it clear they wouldn't help me.

"You can find another job. I can help you," said Daniel.

I laughed loudly, a smile never reaching my eyes. "Yes, please, help me find a job where people will speculate on how I got it."

"You have to let me help somehow," he said.

"How?"

"I know you haven't cashed the check I gave you..."

"You think *that's* the solution?"

"It will help, until you can find another job."

"I don't need your money."

That was a bald-faced lie.

He sighed frustratedly before getting to his feet and walking toward the door.

"Where are you going?" I asked, not sure if I wanted to know the answer.

He could be leaving, which deep down I didn't want, or he was going to make a further mess of the situation.

"I'm talking to your boss," he said with certainty before opening the door and stepping into the hallway.

I scrambled to my feet as quickly as I could, which was difficult, as my bump was already twice the size it was. I had done my best trying to cleverly conceal it, but was still surprised no one had noticed. Maybe they were just being polite.

Hurriedly, I followed Daniel out into the hallway, but he was already at Brian's door. I felt everyone's eyes on us, even though they were trying their best to be conspicuous. I tried to walk calmly with a forced smile across my tightly pressed lips, but my heart pounded against my chest. Daniel was already in Brian's office.

I opened the door and quickly closed it behind me.

"Please. I can double the donation," said Daniel.

His back was turned to me and Brian sat at his desk with his fingertips pressed together. He didn't bother looking at me when I entered the room.

"You mean the donation you've already doubled this morning?" asked Brian, raising an eyebrow.

"Yes. Whatever it takes."

"Don't you think that will raise some questions?"

"Not if it's kept private."

"Mr. Jacobs, nothing with you is private," replied Brian, his tone harsh.

I leaned against the wall, feeling like a child who wasn't invited to the adult table. I didn't know what to say. I just let it all unravel in front of me.

"Yes, I agree that questionable choices I've made in the past have found their way to the pages of the press. But never with my business practices. Those are held with the highest morale. Please don't let my reputation skew the standards I have for my company or skew your opinion of Heart."

Brian looked at him questioningly.

"I mean, Addison," said Daniel quickly.

I squeezed my eyes shut for a moment as I realized how this situation had gone from bad to worse.

"Mr. Daniels, while I admire the business you've built for yourself with the morals you are trying too hard to convince me of, I can't allow Ms. Heartly to continue working here. If, and when, this gets out to the press, the nonprofit would have to close its doors. I can't have that happen."

I swallowed hard. He was right. If word got out that Leading to Learn was getting donation money through questionable practices, it would be forced to close. There would be lawsuits. It would be incredibly messy. I couldn't let that happen. Even though I was losing my job, what we had built still meant so much to me.

"I understand," I said, finally saying something.

I pushed myself from the wall and took a step next to Daniel.

"Brian, I want to apologize for putting you in this compromising situation based on my poor choices. I hope you know that what transpired between me and Daniel, while it was wrong, it was real. It had nothing to do with furthering my position here at Leading to Learn."

Brian studied me for a moment before speaking. "I'm sorry to see you go, Ms. Heartly. But it has to be done."

I gave him a solemn nod before turning toward the door.

As I left, I heard Daniel say behind me, "You're making a big mistake letting her go."

I ignored it and walked toward the elevators. I didn't have any of my things with me. I just had to get out of there. If only for a little bit.

As the elevator doors started to close, Daniel put his hand through and pushed his way inside. I didn't say anything. Didn't look at him. We rode in a silence that seemed loud because all the words that had been exchanged were bouncing off each other in my mind.

When we were on the first floor, I quickly walked past him and out onto the sidewalk. There, I finally felt like I could finally breathe. I sucked in the fresh air and closed my eyes, feeling the sunlight on my face.

"I'm sorry," said Daniel, stepping beside me.

I shook my head and kept my eyes closed.

"Can I take you back home?" he asked.

"I don't have any of my things."

"Well, I could..."

"No, you're not going back in there. You're not doing anything. Haven't you done enough?" I asked, my eyes snapping open and really focusing on his face for the first time today.

That was a mistake. The sincerity I saw in those blue eyes was almost enough to make me forget the entire mess of my life and let him save me. But life didn't work like that. *I* didn't work like that.

"I know things look bad right now, but we'll figure something out."

There he went with the "we" again.

"You mean, *I'll* have to figure something out."

"No. I'm here. I'm in this. I haven't left yet. That's what people do when things get hard, they leave. Hell, I've been that person. I've never gotten close to anyone because I was afraid of the *hard*. Of the messy. Of the complicated. But I'm here. And things are pretty damn hard, aren't they?"

His words dug into me like nails, and as much as I wanted to reject them, I let them leave their impressions on me. It was the first time he had really ever opened up about anything. But it was too little, too late.

"Why?" I whispered.

"Why what?"

"Why are you still here?"

"Because of you. Because of the baby. Because it's the right thing to do."

I thought of the baby. Of what a messy life he or she had already found themselves in and they weren't even earthside. It made my heart break.

Of all the things I wished I could go back and change, I ultimately knew that changing anything would mean I wouldn't have this baby inside me. The baby that had changed my life with a single heartbeat and convinced me that I was ready to be a mom, despite everything. A good mom.

Nothing with Daniel had been easy up until this point, and I would hate to have the baby brought up in a world that was so unsteady. I couldn't let that happen.

I took a deep breath before delivering the words that I knew would change us forever. A lie that felt like poison leaving my mouth.

"There is no baby, Daniel," I said.

He gave me a double-take as his mouth fell open.

"I think it's best we never see each other again."

I turned and walked back toward my building. A single tear fell down my cheek. I quickly opened the doors and entered the elevator, hoping he wasn't following me. I looked out the window and saw he hadn't. His back was toward me and his head was hung low. It was the last image I saw before my tears blurred my vision and the doors closed.

Chapter 34

DANIEL

Heart left me speechless on the sidewalk. I felt like I might cry or throw up or punch something. After everything we had been through over the past few months, I was ready to be together. I was ready to be a father. Well, almost. Was anyone really ready to become a parent? Ready or not, I wanted to be a part of that baby's life. I wanted to be a part of Heart's.

Now I was left with nothing on the sidewalks of Manhattan. I felt like everything I had fought for was ripped away from me in seconds. I felt empty.

Not only had I lost Heart, but we had lost the baby too. I tried to grasp at what could have possibly happened in the course of a few days. I couldn't imagine Heart having an abortion without telling me, no matter how angry she was about the miscommunication a few nights ago. I also couldn't bring myself to imagine her having a miscarriage and going through that pain and loss all by herself.

Both possibilities broke my heart. She had been alone for both. I should have been there holding her hand.

I felt tears burn at the back of my eyes. A feeling I hadn't felt since I was a child. I blinked quickly to prevent them from falling.

"Sir?" a voice said.

I looked up and through watery eyes saw Armand standing there.

"Let's get you in the car," he said, putting his hand on my back and guiding me into the backseat.

Never had I been more grateful for him.

"Thank you," I said before he closed the door.

He didn't ask any questions. He didn't even glance back as if he wanted to give me privacy to work through the clear set of emotions running through me. He didn't drive me back to work. He drove me home, which was a decision I wouldn't have made, but a decision I needed.

I couldn't work right now. Not when my heart was angry and breaking at the same time.

Fifteen minutes later, the car pulled into the parking garage and Armand came around to let me out. I gave him a nod that said thank you before going up to my apartment.

I took off my suit that felt like it was suffocating me and climbed into bed. It was barely 2 p.m., but all I wanted to do was sleep. I hoped when I woke up, I would realize this was all a nightmare. There had been too much loss.

Heart lost her job, which was something I would never forgive myself for. If it weren't for my desperate impulsivity, she would still work there. And the other loss, which was almost unfathomable. The loss of our baby. I had gotten lost in looking for cribs and strollers and onesies, and really saw the joy in it all. I was going to be a dad. Was being the key word.

I closed my eyes and settled under the covers, falling into a deep sleep. My emotions had worn me out.

My phone trilled loudly. I groaned as I searched for it blindly, feeling around the bed and my nightstand until my fingers wrapped around it. I brought it close to my face and opened one eye. It was Brody calling. It was 5 p.m.

"Hello," I answered groggily.

"Oh, I'm sorry. Did I disturb you?" he asked sarcastically on the other line.

"Hey, Brody."

"Are you fucking sleeping?" he asked.

"Yeah, I am."

"So, you left work after bailing on a meeting with the London rep to go take a nap?"

"Seems that way."

"What the hell is wrong with you?" he asked, his voice rising.

"Look, I don't really need my little brother babysitting me," I said irritably.

"Uh, you do, when you're dropping the ball. We could have lost the whole London deal. You know that, right?"

"Well, did we?" I asked, uncaring.

"No, thank God. Margaret called me frantically to let me know you left. I had to run the meeting myself."

"You're a big boy, Brody. You can handle it."

"Okay, *Dad*."

"It's about time you stepped up. I can't do everything for you."

I knew I was taking my bad day out on him, but it felt good to unleash on someone. Anyone.

"Call me back when you're not such an asshole," muttered Brody before he hung up.

I turned off my phone and tossed it back on the nightstand. I rolled over onto my stomach and closed my eyes again. I just wanted to go back to sleep again.

And I did. I slept until five the next morning. The sunrise coming over the buildings served as my alarm clock. I stretched my arms and let out a long yawn. It felt like I had been asleep for days.

I rolled out of bed and padded the cool, wooden floor of my bedroom to the bathroom. I ran a cold shower and stepped inside, letting the frigid water wake me up. I brushed my teeth and threw on a pair of gray sweatpants and a hoodie. I put on a pot of coffee and as I waited, my stomach growled loudly.

Yesterday, I had skipped lunch and dinner in favor of sleep. Sleep was my only escape from what had happened, but now I was awake and moments seeped into my thoughts like I was remembering a dream.

I opened my fridge and pulled out a carton of eggs and a package of bacon. I fired up a pan, and soon my kitchen was filled with their savory scent combined with freshly roasted coffee beans. I brought my plate of food and mug of coffee to the large, ten-person dining room table in the large room next to the kitchen.

Putting my food down, I then sat at the head of the table and began eating. I looked around my large penthouse and listened to the silence that surrounded me. In that moment, I realized just how alone I was. And just how much I wished Heart was here, and how much I wished the room was filled with her laughter and the squeals from our baby.

I really thought maybe our life would end up here. Toys on the floor, bottles on the counter, diaper baskets. Figuring out how to do a new life together as we brought up a new life. I should have told her sooner. I should have told her that night at the charity event. Instead, we let our emotions get the best of us and it led to what we always did. Being tangled up in one another.

It was the first time in my life that I wished we would have talked rather than had sex. That was saying something. Now there were too many words left unsaid and too many realized dreams that had shattered.

My phone buzzed on the table in front of me. I picked it up quickly, hoping it might be Heart, but knowing deep down it wasn't.

No. It was Brody:

Has my brother reentered his body?

Me: *Not yet. I'm not coming in today. Can you handle it?*

I watched the three dots bounce on the screen and waited for the angry response to follow, but it didn't. He didn't say anything.

I took the day off and spent most of it on the couch or in bed. It was very out of character for me, as someone who had never even taken a personal day. I just couldn't focus on work or business deals. All of that seemed so flippant in the grand scheme of things.

I went back to work the next morning, and barely spoke to anyone. I didn't see Brody all day, which was what I preferred. Margaret seemed to be wary around me, like I might flip a switch at any second. I was glad they avoided me. I just wanted to go through the motions at my desk alone.

For weeks, I carried on like that. I knew I was being an asshole. Even in meetings with potential clients, I didn't have my usual charisma. I passed them on to Brody, who took them without question. He probably knew I would just screw them up.

One afternoon, after another big meeting with the London representative, Brody came by my office. He knocked and entered at the same time, as he normally did. I never understood what the point of him knocking was.

I looked up from my papers and gave him a nod. He closed the door behind him and sat across from me in one of the armchairs. He watched me silently for a moment, which was irritatingly uncomfortable.

"Yes?" I asked finally.

"We need to talk," he said.

I sighed and sat back in my chair. "What is it, Brody?"

"I don't know what is going on with you, but things can't keep carrying on like this. People are wondering where you are. You're the head of the company for God's sake, Daniel. You can't just keep hiding away in your office and having me run your meetings. People are starting to ask questions."

"No, they're not," I said.

"Yes, they are. It's a miracle the London deal finalized today after I had to win their trust over the past few weeks. No one likes being passed around like an appetizer. They were wary to continue."

"But you did it, didn't you?" I asked.

"Yes, I did. No thanks to you."

"Then I don't see the problem."

"The problem is you are the CEO of this company. I thought we were a team. I can't keep running my position when I'm doing yours too."

I stayed silent. I knew he was right. I just couldn't snap out of this stupid funk.

"I'm worried about you," said Brody seriously.

"I'm fine," I said.

"You're not. But I think I know what will help."

"What's that?" I asked curiously.

"Getting away from New York. I don't mind taking over for a little bit longer if it means you going on a trip, feeling refreshed, and getting your head back in the game."

"I can't just up and leave," I said, exasperated.

"Yes, you can. You've already been mentally checked out for weeks."

He wasn't wrong.

"Here's what you do," he said. "You go and find Kiera—"

"Kiera?" I asked in surprise.

"Yeah. Go find her and patch up whatever went down that has you being the asshole you are. Then you invite her on an exotic vacation."

I snorted. He thought this was about Kiera. It was laughable. But it also wasn't surprising. I had let him and everyone else in the world think there were wedding bells in our future because I was trying so hard to protect Heart. In the end, she still got hurt.

I hadn't confided anything in my brother. Maybe I should have. Too late now. There was no point in telling him when everything had ended. It would be easier for him to assume something else, then dig up the pain that I'd been trying to bury the past few weeks.

"You know she'd love it," continued Brody. "The girl lives for selfies on the beach at five-star resorts, and she looks good doing it."

"I'd rather go alone," I said.

"It would be better with her. Think about it, you can fuck her in every orifice. She'd let you. Happily. Then you can release some of that stress that is clearly pent up."

I rolled my eyes. Maybe he was right. Not about Kiera. But getting away for a while. It would be good to clear my head and get out of a city that had so many reminders of Heart.

"Where would I go?" I asked.

Brody grinned, knowing I had given in. "I hear Bora Bora is nice this time of year."

Chapter 35

ADDISON

"Are you sure you want to do this?" asked Monica.

"I'm sure," I said, forcing certainty to my voice.

"I just don't want to see you getting hurt. Again. Haven't you been through enough?"

I had been through more than enough. I had lost my job. I had lost the man I thought I knew, and lied to him in the process. Knowing the baby was still growing inside of me when I had told him it was gone was too painful to think about. It was wrong. But at the time, it felt like it was my only choice. I wanted to protect this baby.

I felt weepy just thinking about it. Monica noticed and pulled me into her arms.

"Look, if you think going to see your parents will help, then I support you," she said.

"Thank you, Monica," I said between tears. "For everything."

She squeezed me tightly as I tried not to sob in the middle of the airport. I had been a mess for the past few weeks. My heart had felt like someone had taken a sledgehammer to it, pounding it until there were no good feelings left. Only the sad ones. Only the broken ones.

"Text me when you land, okay?" she said.

"Okay. Thank you for coming."

"Of course," she said.

She gave my belly a little rub before turning and heading for the exit to the transfers. I smiled as I watched her go. If I didn't have her, I didn't know what I would do. Maybe she was right in thinking flying home to see my parents was a bad idea. I had gotten by just fine without them over the years, but me becoming a mother only made me want mine. I wanted my baby to have more family than just me.

I got through security quickly and found a café to sit in while I waited for my flight. There was a little table that was vacant, and I propped my feet up on my little suitcase. I ordered a cup of chamomile tea and a cheese Danish, and hoped it was enough to tide me over on the flight. It was a short flight, but I was always hungry. Maybe there would be a snack served.

As I waited, I read one of the pregnancy books I had bought. With the visit home to my parents looming in my mind, it was hard to focus on sleep routines. It was even harder to focus whenever a man in a suit passed by. They all made me think of Daniel.

I didn't hear from him again after that horrible day in my office. I had told him I never wanted to see him again, so I shouldn't be so surprised. But still, Daniel had proven his persistence in the short time I had known him. He was either hurt by the thought of losing the baby, or he was relieved he had no obligation to me anymore. Both hurt like hell, but the first one made me want to cry every time I thought about it.

It was wrong to lie to him. I knew it was. Every day, I thought about calling him and telling him the truth. I was sick to my stomach just thinking about it. But like Monica said, there was no going back now. The damage was done.

I heard the boarding call for my flight being announced and placed cash on the table, enough to cover my pastry and tea, and a decent tip. I thought for a second about becoming a waitress. Maybe I could find a serving position at an upscale restaurant in Manhattan. The tips had to be good. At least until I found a new job. Although, I doubted anyone would hire someone who was clearly pregnant.

Since being fired, it was like my mind was always in overdrive, trying to find ways to survive as I entered motherhood. Brian said I could stay on until the end of the month, which was generous, considering what had happened. It had been so awkward in the office though. I wasn't sure how much my coworkers knew, if anything. The thought made my stomach turn. It was bad enough having Brian know. Which was why I was glad to use some of my remaining vacation time to go home to Pittsburgh.

At the gate, I did as Monica instructed and let the front desk know that I was pregnant. She said I would be able to get preboarding, and she was right. I found my seat and settled in before the rest of the passengers. There were some perks to being pregnant. I patted my belly lovingly and looked out the window at the tarmac.

I tried to remember the last time I had been home. It had been too long to recall.

Soon we were up in the air. I spent most of my flight reading and listening to classical music on my headphones. Thankfully, there were crackers and pretzels to tide me over.

The flight was fast, and as we started our descent, I thought about my parents down below. I wondered who had come to pick me up. If they were waiting at the gate or on the curb outside. If they looked the same or older. I took a deep breath as the wheels touched down on the tarmac, as I was about to find out.

I rolled my suitcase off the plane and through the tunnel that spit me out at the gate. I looked around timidly and spotted my father leaning against a pillar. I was relieved he had come alone. He and I had always been closer than my mother and I.

I studied him for a little bit before he got the chance to notice me. His hair had more gray and looked like it was thinning slightly. There were more wrinkles sprinkled around his eyes and carved into his forehead. He had put on a little weight in his belly. We were the same in that regard.

My heart swelled, realizing how much I missed him over the years. But then I remembered why I even had to miss him in the first place.

His eyes found mine and I gave a nervous wave before walking over.

"Hi, honey," he said with a single nod.

"Hey, Dad."

His eyes fell to my belly and I held my breath, but he didn't say anything. Instead, he silently took my suitcase and began rolling it toward the elevators for the parking garage. I slid into the sedan he had been driving since I was a teenager. He refused to sell it. I laughed softly as I closed the door. My parents were nothing if not stubborn.

The ride home was silent, if not for small bouts of awkward small talk. The weather. Brooklyn. His beloved Pittsburgh Penguins. Everything but my protruding bump and what it meant.

When my father pulled into the driveway, the sun was beginning to set. I saw Mom sitting on the porch on the swing I remembered from my childhood. She didn't stand up when she saw us park. Her lack of acknowledgment didn't hide the coldness in her eyes that I could feel from twenty feet away. I swallowed hard. Maybe this had been a bad idea.

I walked up the steps as my father pulled the suitcase behind me.

"Hey, Mom," I said, trying to hide my nerves.

Her hair was shorter and darker than I remember. Her skin had more spots on it and I couldn't tell if her brows were furrowed or if her wrinkles were just prominent.

"Addison," she said, standing and giving me a stiff hug.

"Thanks for having me." I gave her my best smile.

"You didn't really give us a choice when you said you were coming."

"Right," I said, ignoring the dagger she had just thrown. "I just thought it would be good for us."

"Well, come in." She led the way through the front door.

As I stepped inside, it felt like I had entered a time warp. Everything looked the same. Smelled the same. I took it all in as I spun in a slow circle.

"Dinner will be ready in an hour," said my mom. "You can get settled upstairs in your old room."

"Thanks," I replied.

Up in my room, I realized nothing in there had changed at all. It still looked the same as it did in high school. My posters were still on the walls. The same floral sheets were on the bed. My jewelry box was still on the dresser and I opened it, listening as it played the familiar tune. I watched as the ballerina spun. I found it odd they had kept the room the same after our falling out.

An hour later, right on time, my mom announced from downstairs that dinner was ready. I met my parents at the small dining nook in the kitchen. The table was set for three and a big bowl of spaghetti sat in the middle of the table. My mother's signature dish.

"Looks great, Mom," I said as I sat down.

She gave me a tight smile and began serving the spaghetti on our plates. We began eating our meal in silence, as if we were playing the silent game. The first person who spoke lost.

"So, what brings you all the way home?" asked my mom after a few minutes.

"I just didn't like how we ended things over the phone," I said. "I hoped we could make things right before...you know."

"The baby." My mother's tone was unenthused.

"Right."

Her eyes fell to my bump. There was no love or excitement behind them. I instinctively covered my stomach with my arm as if to protect the baby.

"How far along are you?" asked my father curiously.

"Almost five months."

"Wow." His eyes grew wide. He seemed more interested than my mother.

"I know. It's going fast."

My mom looked from me to my father as if she didn't like what was going on between us.

"And the father?" she asked pointedly.

"I thought I told you he won't be in the baby's life."

"Jesus Christ," muttered my mother.

"I know you're disappointed..." I started.

"Why are you here, Addison?" asked my mother sharply. "I thought we already told you on the phone we won't be financially supporting your poor decisions."

"I know that. I'm fine financially. I actually just got a raise," I lied.

My mother looked appeased for only a moment before digging back into me.

"Probably not enough to support you and a baby. Do you know how much raising a child costs?"

"I know, Mom. I'm going to make it work."

"And the father...he can't support you?" asked my father.

"I don't really want to talk about him," I said softly.

"Probably because he is a deadbeat," said my mother with disgust.

Hardly, I thought.

"You don't know the situation," I argued.

"I know enough to know that you've made a terrible mistake and are here for us to bail you out."

"That's not true," I said.

"Now, now," said my father, looking at my mother.

"Don't 'now, now' me, Roger. Your daughter has made a mess of her life."

"Look, I just came to try and fix things between us. Please, can we just—"

"Can we just what?" my mother interrupted. "Pretend you haven't ruined your future? I thought the nonprofit had been bad, but this...I don't know how we could ever look at you the same."

My eyes stung with tears, but I refused to show her that her words affected me. I would not appear weak in front of my mother. If I could even call her that. Here, I thought seeing her would make things better. That maybe seeing my growing belly would make her soften. Instead, seeing her made me realize I wanted to be nothing like the mother she was.

Chapter 36

DANIEL

"Welcome to the St. Regis, Mr. Jacobs. I am Reva," said the woman in the crisp, white linen suit.

"Thank you," I said as I looked behind her at the crystal-clear, teal-blue waters sprinkled with little huts with straw roofs. I couldn't believe I was here. Just over twenty-four hours ago, Brody was in my office convincing me that a vacation would be good for me. Then we were booking a first-class flight from New York to Bora Bora that night. It was all too surreal.

"I hope your flight here didn't feel too long," said Reva.

"It wasn't too bad."

The eighteen-plus hours were spent drinking Bloody Marys and watching in-flight movies, or sleeping in my private compartment. I felt bad for anyone who wasn't in first class. I didn't know how anyone flew that long in economy. That would be hell on earth. Or hell in the sky.

"Please, enjoy some complimentary champagne as our welcome to you." Reva waved over a server who quickly arrived, balancing a tray with a single glass of champagne and an array of tropical flowers.

"Thank you," I said, taking the glass. I took a long sip, the bubbles dancing down my throat.

A bell attendant came around with a gold cart and began carefully putting my luggage on the red velvet surface.

"We will have your luggage taken to your suite, but in the meantime, I would like to give you a tour of the grounds," said Reva.

"Thank you, Reva." I nodded.

She walked me through the expansive lobby with its white walls and woven ceiling. Bright tropical flowers were arranged in large vases. She introduced me to the concierge where I could make reservations or schedule excursions and activities. We walked to the open-air spa with views of the lush vegetation and the smooth ocean.

Reva and I continued making our way down the winding wooden paths until we arrived at my room, which was really a bungalow. It was the last one on the wooden path.

Reva opened the door with a keycard and pushed the door open.

"Welcome to the Royal Suite, Mr. Jacobs. I hope you find it to your liking. This is where I leave you. I hope you enjoy your stay with us. Please, don't hesitate to ask for anything."

"Thank you," I said, slipping her a fifty-dollar bill.

I stepped past her into the room and heard the door click behind me. I walked into the living room, which looked out over a large deck and a rectangular pool. The doors were open and the ocean breeze met my face. To my right was the master bedroom with a large king bed covered in crisp, white linen in the center of the room, facing an unobstructed view of the ocean. I noticed the walk-in closet to my left was open and my luggage was already arranged neatly inside. The master bathroom had a jacuzzi tub and his and her sinks.

I was surprised how deceivingly small this bungalow looked from the outside.

I stepped out onto the deck with my champagne and looked out over the ocean. This was truly paradise. It was strange to be here by myself. Lonely even. I wished Heart were with me. This could have been our babymoon. I read that was a thing. Along with a push present, which I had already been thinking about. I guess I didn't have to anymore.

She was always on my mind. I wanted to reach out to her again after the mess I had made at her work, but the way she looked at me made me not even try. I had seen her angry before, but not like that. There were sharp edges behind her words, and they cut deep.

I think it's best we never see each other again.

I downed the rest of my champagne and shook my head, trying to get the echo of those words out. Trying to forget the pained look on her face. I kept blaming myself, but we both made choices we couldn't take back.

I realized now that I didn't really know her that well at all. It had only been a few months since we met on the terrace at my work. Little did I know that our lives would change after that day. In those months, nothing had ever been smooth. The waters of this ocean were smoother than anything between us.

We spent our time either fighting or fucking. There really wasn't anything in between. We never took the proper time to get to know each other, and maybe that was partly my fault. It wasn't what I did with women. I never spent enough time with one to get to know them. Maybe Heart was always that moody, or maybe the pregnancy hormones made her that way. Really, the whole time I had known her she had been pregnant. I never really knew her at all.

On top of everything, she had lost the baby. Whether naturally or planned, it was a lot for her. That would drive anyone into a pit. I just was sorry I wasn't there to help her through it.

I was also sorry for us and what we could have had. The thought was almost too much to bear. I never even knew what we were going to have—A boy. A girl. There was no point in thinking about it now, and that was heart-wrenching.

I pushed my hands from the railing of the deck and walked back inside my room. I took off my travel clothes and changed into swim trunks. Then I called the front desk to have some appetizers and a cocktail delivered to the room. After I hung up, I walked back to the deck and launched myself off, landing in the clear, blue waters below.

That afternoon, I ate fresh fruit and French fries from the deck and sipped on Mai Tais, as I floated in the warm waters. It felt like I was on my own private island. Brody had been right. This was a good idea. A *really* good idea. I couldn't remember the last time I had taken a vacation. I had traveled for work, sure, but not for leisure in a very long time. Maybe this was what I needed to forget everything.

I pulled myself onto the deck, water dripping off of me, and faced the sun. I heard my phone ring on the deck chair. I reached over and grabbed it. It was Brody. I accepted the video call.

"Hey, bro," I said, grinning.

"Wow. Is this my brother actually smiling?" he asked.

He was in his office, and for a second I felt guilty for not being there, but he had been the one to insist on this trip.

"Yeah, yeah. You were right. This place is amazing."

"Wait, wait. What was that?" He cupped his hand to his ear.

I rolled my eyes. "You were right," I said.

He gave me that annoying triumphant smile of his.

"I told you it would be just what you needed to get out of whatever funk you've been in."

"I'm already feeling better. Look at this place," I beamed, as I turned my phone and showed him the view of my room and the ocean surrounding.

"Wow. Maybe I should have gone instead. It has been tiring doing *all* your work for you."

"Ha ha," I laughed sarcastically. "How is it going over there?"

"We're moving forward on the design process with the London offices. Thank God. I never thought we would actually get anywhere with them. But enough talk of work. You are there to relax."

"How do you do that again?" I asked with a smirk.

"You'll learn," he replied. "Now get back to paradise. I'm just about to go to lunch. Enjoy, bro."

"Thank you, Brody."

I hung up and pulled myself to stand, my body already dry from the sun. I padded into my suite and into the bathroom. I took a long shower and got dressed for an early dinner. The travel days had caught up to me and I was ready to eat and then crash until morning.

I walked down the winding path toward the lobby, passing other guests on the way. It was mostly couples walking hand in hand, their hair wet from the ocean and a frozen drink in their other hands. I smiled and nodded as I passed, trying to be happy for them when they were a reminder that I was alone here.

I found the restaurant just off the lobby. It was open air, much like everything here. I sat at a table on the patio that overlooked the white sand beach. I ordered a whiskey on ice and sipped on it slowly as I watched other guests enter the restaurant.

I did a double-take as I saw a woman with long, dark hair sit at the bar. As if Heart would somehow be here. I laughed to myself, but couldn't tear my eyes away at the possibility it could be. When I saw her partner join her and she turned toward him, I saw the profile of her face and knew I was out of my head. I took another sip of whiskey and began studying the menu. A moment later, a server came by.

She wore a purple floral halter dress that hugged tightly to her breasts before flowing down to the floor. Her bright blonde hair was pulled into a low bun and her tan skin contrasted against it perfectly. She was probably in her early twenties.

"Hello, Mr. Jacobs. We are so pleased you could join us tonight," she greeted with a heavy French accent.

"Hello,"—my eyes fell to her name tag—"Collete."

I let my eyes explore a little more without bothering to hide it. I noticed her cheeks turn a shade of pink as if she were sunburnt. She gave me a knowing smile. She was game to play along.

"Have you had a chance to look over the menu, Mr. Jacobs?" she asked.

"Please, call me Daniel."

She let out a small giggle.

"I have, but I would love to hear your recommendations. It's my first time in Bora Bora."

"Well, how do you like it so far?"

"I like what I see so far."

She batted her eyelashes and bit her lip as she tapped her pen against her pad of paper. "I'm happy to hear that. And I would be happy to share some of my favorites on the menu."

She leaned in and pointed out her favorite items. She smelled like coconut and saltwater. I ordered her recommendations. Crunchy pork salad. Samosas. Chicken with coconut rice.

"I'll get that right in. Let me know if you need *anything* at all." She walked away, her hips swaying, holding my attention until the moment she disappeared into the kitchen.

She could be fun, I thought. A little vacation fling. Waking up naked in the sheets to the ocean air drifting in the open doorway. Taking a dip in the water to wake us up. The saltwater on our tan skin as we drank too many fruity cocktails before we tumbled back into the king-size bed. Having someone to fuck this pain away would make this trip even better. No strings attached.

The idea was tantalizing. When she came by and served my food, I almost asked her when she was off, but decided against it. I knew in the end, I only really wanted to be with Heart. Anyone else would just be a Band-Aid.

So instead, I ate my food, which was insanely delicious. And with a full stomach, I walked back to my room and passed out alone.

Chapter 37

ADDISON

The sunlight streamed through the purple curtains hanging in my bedroom, casting a violet hue over my childhood bedroom. I felt the warmth against my eyelids as I rolled from my side to my back. I opened them slowly and stared at the ceiling, which still had glow in the dark stars from when I was little. Yawning, I sat up in bed.

I looked around the room, at the boy bands' smiling faces on glossy posters and the book series I used to read lined up on the shelves. I once had been such a happy kid in this room. Playing and learning and not having a care in the world. Having parents who liked me.

I knew deep down my parents loved me. I loved them. But over the years, we just stopped liking each other.

Things would be different if I had a sibling. They would have another child to look after and cast their dreams onto instead of putting all their faith in me. It's funny because I don't know what their expectations were for me. I just know that I hadn't lived up to them. First, with my job. Second, not finding a husband. Third, having a baby without said husband.

The rest of last night's dinner had been wildly uncomfortable in a silence that was only broken by forks scraping against the plate. I helped my mother wash the dishes while my father went to the living room to watch the nightly news. A tradition I had known since childhood. Except, back then, he would let me climb into his lap and let me ask question after question about what the newscaster was saying.

There was none of that last night. Instead, I stood by the sink, watching my mother inspect the dishes I had washed with scrutiny. After we were done and my handwashing skills passed her standards, I went up to my room and stayed there for the rest of the night. I called Monica, let her tell me, "I told you so," and then started to look for flights home.

But then something incredible happened that turned the whole night around. I felt the baby kick. Up until then, I thought I had maybe imagined the little flutters that the baby books had described, but this was real. This made me sit up in bed, wide-eyed. I pressed my hand gently to my stomach and felt another kick. Immediately, tears came to my eyes.

"Hello there," I had whispered.

It was as if the baby was telling me I wasn't alone. Not anymore. I was about to build my own little family, and it would be filled with love and warmth. It wouldn't feel anything like this. I took comfort in knowing that, and was able to fall asleep cradling my bump.

I had no desire to stay here last night after the conversation at dinner took a turn for the worst, as I knew it would. I should have known better than to come back home. Too much time had passed. Too much damage had been done. I would never be the daughter they wanted me to be, and I had to accept that.

I only stayed because it was already a stretch in my budget to fly to Pittsburgh. Adding a last-minute hotel stay was not in the cards, but I didn't have to worry about where I was staying tonight. I already had a flight booked back home to New York in a few hours.

Quickly, I rolled out of bed and changed out of my pajamas and back into my travel clothes from yesterday. I had thought I would be here long enough to maybe do a load of laundry, but here I was. I pulled the leggings over my bump and looked at myself in the small full-length mirror. It was an odd juxtaposition to be becoming a mother as I stood in the bedroom I grew up in, when everything looked the same.

I went to the bathroom to wash up and splashed water on my face and brushed my teeth. The smell of bacon and eggs wafted up the stairs, and my stomach grumbled hungrily. I would rather just get to the airport early than endure another meal with my parents, who had no idea I was even leaving yet. What else did they expect, though?

I grabbed my suitcase from my room and said a silent goodbye to the childhood I once knew, before gently closing the door behind me. I walked downstairs and into the kitchen. My mother was at the stove and my father was at the table reading the paper. When they heard me enter the room, their eyes went from me to the luggage in my hand.

"Are you leaving?" asked my father, surprise in his voice.

"Yeah, my flight's in a few hours," I said, rocking back on my heels nervously. "I just think it's better this way."

My mother pursed her lips and turned back toward the stove without saying a word.

"Addison..." my dad started.

"Let her go, Roger," said my mother, her back to us.

"At least let me take you to the airport."

"And waste a perfectly good breakfast? I don't think so," snapped my mother, whipping her head around.

"Really, it's fine," I said, waving my hand at him.

I knew he was trying. I knew this hurt him. It hurt me, too, but I would never let it show. Not in front of my mother.

"I'll call an Uber." I pulled out my phone.

"Nancy, I'm taking Addison to the airport," said my father, standing from the table.

It wasn't a question. It was a statement. I was taken aback by him standing up to her, for once. I fought back tears as I gave him a thankful nod. He gave me a smile before grabbing the keys off the hook by the garage door.

"I'll be back soon." He opened the door and slipped out, leaving my mother and me in the kitchen.

"It was good to see you, Mom," I said softly.

I could see her stand a little straighter as she continued to stir the eggs in the pan. I started walking toward the door, rolling my suitcase behind me.

"Goodbye, Addison," I heard her whisper.

I closed my eyes for just a moment, trying to soak in her words because they might be the last ones she would speak to me, and headed out the door to the car.

My father and I rode in silence to the airport. It was comfortable, though. I knew there wasn't really anything left to say. He would have to side with my mother and veering away from that would practically be treason. Instead, we listened to classic rock on the radio like we did when I was little. I wanted to wrap my hands around that moment and keep it forever.

When we pulled up to the curb at the airport, my dad came around and helped me get out of the car before grabbing my suitcase from the trunk. We looked at each other for a long moment, as if trying to get our words across in the quiet air between us. Finally, he pulled me in for a hug. A real hug that was filled with tenderness and goodbye. It nearly broke my heart.

I pulled away and gave him the best smile I could before walking into the terminal. I didn't think I could handle any more goodbyes in my life.

On the flight home, I started writing down a list of my current finances and then added everything I could think of that the baby would need. I realized I would have to come up with an entirely new budget. One that included medical insurance and diapers and probably daycare for when I hopefully found a new job. And that job would have to pay a lot more than the one I was about to lose.

I suddenly started feeling very warm as the plane started to descend and we approached New York. My breath felt like it was short and it was hard to fully fill my lungs. I wondered if I was having a panic attack. I gripped the armrests tightly and closed my eyes as I tried to slow my breath. I counted *one, two, three, four, five* in my head. It seemed to be working.

But then I felt my stomach tighten in a way I had never felt before. After a few seconds, it released, giving me some relief before tightening again a minute later. I put my hand on my bump and felt it harden and soften. It was an unusual sensation, and it started to worry me when they grew more painful. I took a deep breath and willed for the plane's wheels to meet the runway quickly.

Finally, the plane bumped up and down slightly as it steadied itself, moving quickly down the runway until it began to slow down. I breathed a slight sigh of relief. At least we were on the ground now, but I wasn't out of the woods yet. It seemed to take forever for the plane to park and open its doors. I may have had priority boarding getting on the flight, but I was just like everyone else in the herd trying to get off the plane.

I winced as I waited in the slow-moving line, gripping the handle of my luggage tightly to try and help with the pain. As soon as I was off, I quickly found an exit and hailed a cab.

"I need to get to a hospital," I said.

The driver's eyes grew wide as he eyed me clutching my stomach. He gave me a nod and pulled the car away from the curb, stepping on the gas.

Twenty minutes later, we arrived at the hospital. The driver was so worried about me that he helped me out of the car and pulled my luggage into the hospital. He made sure I was helped before he left. As a nurse helped me into a wheelchair, I thanked him profusely, wishing I could tip him more. He pressed his hands together and gave a little bow before leaving out the sliding doors.

The nurse wheeled me up to triage to see if there was a room available. On the way up, I texted Monica to let her know what was going on. Within minutes, she told me she was on her way. Thankfully, there was a room available. The nurse helped me out of my clothes and into a hospital gown. Everything felt so surreal. So scary. It was too early to be here. I felt panicked. The nurse must have sensed it.

"Everything is going to be okay," she soothed.

I gave her a grateful look as she helped me into the bed.

"I need to wrap this around your belly so we can monitor your contractions."

"Contractions?" I asked, my voice shaky.

"Yes, you're more than likely having Braxton Hicks contractions. They're normal, but we need to be sure."

She helped me sit up and wrapped a belt around my stomach before covering me with cool white sheets.

"I'll have paperwork sent up soon, but in the meantime rest."

Resting felt like the last thing I could do.

Forty-five minutes later, the nurse led a very frantic Monica into the room.

"Oh, my God, Heart! What is going on?" she asked, rushing to my side.

"Your friend is having some pretty severe Braxton Hicks," said a man's voice.

I looked up and saw a doctor in the doorway. He gave me a warm smile before walking over to my bedside and studying the computer.

"We've been monitoring your contractions, which have most likely been brought on by stress. Is there a lot going on in your life at the moment?"

"A little," I murmured.

A little if you count being pregnant, losing your job, your parents hating you, and you lying to the man you could have one day loved.

"Well, we need you and baby to be healthy. You need to take it easy. No unnecessary stress. Okay?"

"Okay," I said.

Easier said than done.

Chapter 38

DANIEL

I gripped the edges of the surfboard as I looked back over my shoulder for incoming swells. There were a few other guys out on the water, much better than me, who were riding in almost every wave. I had been studying their movements and trying to catch on, only getting lucky a few times.

It had been a spontaneous decision to rent a surfboard from the activity shack this afternoon. I wanted to do something adventurous. Something active. Now, here I was trying to stay balanced as I sat on the glossy wood that rocked beneath me.

I heard a couple of the other guys shout. There must have been a good one coming. I looked back and saw the swell. The others were beginning to paddle fast, so I joined them. When I felt the board begin to dive down, I hopped to my feet and spread my arms out like unsteady wings.

I felt the wave catch beneath my feet and the board went from wobbly to smooth. I had caught it. I gave a triumphant yell as I rode the wave close to shore before jumping off. That was exhilarating. I could see why people fell in love with it. The challenge of it. The thrill. I picked up the board and tucked it under my arm, dragging it onto the sand before plopping down. I shook the saltwater from my hair and watched as the other surfers continued picking and choosing the best waves to ride.

This was the fourth day here in Bora Bora, and I was starting to feel more like myself again. Everything about this place was so different from New York. The beach replaced the damp asphalt. Crystal-clear waters replaced the brooding waters of the Hudson. Straw huts replaced the glass skyscrapers. It was a completely other world, and I had been soaking it all in.

"Can I get you a drink, Mr. Jacobs?" said a voice.

I looked up, squinting against the sun, before I made out the face of Colette, who stood above me in her usual floral dress, the uniform for the female staff at the hotel. It looked best on her young body. One that I had yet to explore.

"I thought I told you to call me Daniel?" I said with a grin.

"That's right. You looked good out there, *Daniel.*"

"Were you watching me?"

"Maybe," she answered, biting her lip.

We were back at our usual flirting game that hadn't gone anywhere because I hadn't allowed it to go any further. Every day, I would see her in one way or another. Up at the restaurant or down here on the beach where she would serve drinks. We would banter back and forth, pass some sexual innuendos, exchange a few suggestive glances. That was it.

"It was my first time." I shrugged, looking out at the water.

"Really? I wouldn't have guessed that. You looked like a pro."

"*You,* my dear, are a fantastic liar."

She giggled. I watched as her eyes took me in and wondered what she was thinking. I knew I could easily find out. I still had a few days *to* find out. She would be willing. That much was clear. I just couldn't seem to pull the trigger.

"You know what sounds good? A pina colada," I said.

"We make the best," she quipped, jotting it down on her pad.

"Can you add a little extra rum?"

"Sure. I'll even add an extra umbrella." She winked before walking down the stretch of sand, taking orders on her way.

I watched as the men on their honeymoons looked at her, careful not to be caught by their wives who were lying on a beach chair next to them. I couldn't help but laugh to myself. Men were so predictable, myself included. At least, I used to be. Before Heart.

I lay back on the board and closed my eyes, letting the warm sun dry the saltwater against my skin. I wondered what Heart was doing now. It had been nearly a month since I had seen her last. It might as well have been a year for how long it felt. I just hoped she was okay.

A few minutes later, Colette brought over my pina colada. It had an extra umbrella, as promised, and an extra shot or two of rum. I took a sip and my eyes grew wide as the rum burned my throat. It was deliciously strong.

"Are you trying to get me drunk?" I asked, raising my brows.

"You asked for it," she replied before slinking away and begging my eyes to follow.

I finished my drink and Colette returned with another one, without me asking. She was definitely trying to get me drunk. I smiled at the thought as I took a sip of my second drink. It felt good to have a woman's attention. Even better to let the sweet taste of alcohol blur the pained edges of my memories with Heart.

After my second drink, I returned my surfboard to the activity shack, feeling the buzz of that cocktail running through my veins. I walked up the steps of the beach to the wooden pathway back to my room. My head felt fuzzy and my limbs loose. I was properly tipsy.

I held the keycard to the door and it clicked open. I stepped inside and lay face-down on the bed. The afternoon of sun and rum had me spent. I passed out quickly.

A few hours later, a knock at the door stirred me from my drunken slumber. I opened one eye and groggily rolled onto my side. Outside, the sun had just set and the sky was purple and sprinkled with a few stars. I had really conked out. I still felt a buzz from my drinks.

The knock at my door sounded again and I remembered that was what had woken me in the first place. I rolled off the bed.

"Coming," I called.

I padded toward the door, assuming it was room service. They liked to come by some mornings or nights with complimentary fruit or chocolate. I opened the door to see it wasn't room service. It was Kiera.

I blinked a few times to make sure I was seeing things correctly.

"Kiera?" I asked.

"The one and only," she said, as she put her hand high on the doorframe and leaned her body against it.

She wore a skimpy hot pink bikini. The bottoms hung low on her hips, held in place by thin strings, and the top was stretched across her voluminous breasts. It was pointless in trying not to look. My eyes were drawn up and down every inch of her long body.

"What are you doing here?" I asked.

She stepped inside the room and the door closed behind her. "I'm here to make you feel better."

"But how did you..."

"Brody."

Of course my brother would do something like this. Send a little plaything to make me feel better.

"You do want to feel better, don't you?" Kiera asked suggestively.

I watched as she reached up and untied the strings of her bikini top with one hand, letting it fall and her breasts spill out before me gloriously. They were tan and her pink nipples were erect and just inviting my mouth to taste them. Then her fingers pulled at the strings at her hips, the hot pink falling to the floor and leaving her slender body completely naked in front of me.

I swallowed hard as she moved her hands down her breasts to her stomach to between her legs. She began to move her fingertips against herself in slow, circular motions. Her eyes never leaving mine.

"Kiera," I whispered, my throat scratchy.

She threw her head back and let out a pleasure-filled moan as she continued massaging between her legs, her fingers disappearing from view. I felt myself growing hard against my board shorts as I watched her play with herself. There was no denying Kiera's beauty or her sex appeal. She knew exactly how to work a man.

Unable to deny her, I took a step toward her and placed my hands on her hips gruffly, digging my fingertips into her. Her skin was soft and warm. She brought her head up and looked me in the eyes before putting her mouth against mine. My mouth opened eagerly. I wanted to taste her. Her tongue lashed against mine desperately, as her hands wrapped around my neck. I pushed her toward the wall, pressing my body tightly against hers. The only thing between us was the thin material of my shorts.

My hands moved from her hips to her breasts, cupping them in my palms as she spread her legs so my erection was pressed against her just so. I let out a throaty moan as I felt her wet warmth seep through my shorts.

I could have her right here. Right now. I could fuck her right here against this wall. Anywhere I wanted. One swift motion, and I could be inside her. Filling her. Slapping into her hard and fast until there was nothing left to give.

But then I thought about Heart, and the thought sobered me up. It brought me back to reality. I wondered how she would feel about me being in this hotel room with my ex naked against me. And that made me pull away from Kiera's kiss.

She opened her eyes and searched mine. "What are you doing?" she asked breathlessly, before trying to kiss me again.

"I can't," I said.

"Yes, you can."

Her hands slid down the front of my shorts until they met my erection. She smiled coyly as she began massaging me slowly. I closed my eyes and lost myself again, but only for a second, before I reached down and removed her hands.

"No. This isn't right," I said.

"What the hell is wrong with you?" she snapped, shoving at my chest.

"I don't know," I muttered.

"Brody was right about you. You're not yourself."

She crossed her arms and glared at me.

"I'm sorry," I said, running my hand through my hair frustratedly.

She was right. Brody was right. I didn't know what the hell was wrong with me. Why did I care how Heart felt when she clearly didn't care about me? It was stupid, but I couldn't help it.

"Yeah, me, too," said Kiera. She picked up her bikini and quickly slid it back on. She struggled to tie the strings that were tangled.

"Let me help you," I said.

"Don't touch me," she snapped.

"Okay. Look, I'm sorry you came all this way."

"Me too."

She opened the door and slammed it behind her.

"Fuck!" I yelled.

I paced the entryway of my suite for a minute to cool down before walking out to the deck. It was dark now. I looked out at the water, which gently lapped against the stilts that held up my little bungalow.

If Kiera was a test to see if I was back to my old self, I had clearly failed. It was clear that I wasn't over Heart. I started to wonder if I ever would be. Maybe I should have had my way with Kiera just to get Heart out of my damn head. I looked back toward the door, as if I had any chance of getting her back here. I knew it would be futile, though.

Heart would still be there in my mind. In my heart.

I sighed and pulled out my phone. I started looking for the next flight home from Bora Bora. I was cutting my trip short.

Chapter 39

ADDISON

Once I was discharged from the hospital, I splurged and split a cab with Monica back home to Brooklyn. I didn't want to deal with the subway. I just wanted to get home with as little stress possible.

"What a whirlwind twenty-four hours for you," said Monica, reaching for my hand.

"You have no idea," I said.

"I wasn't expecting you back in New York so soon. I'm sorry it didn't go like you hoped."

"You can say 'I told you so' again, if you want," I muttered.

"Oh, no! Did it get worse after our call?"

"Yep. Much worse."

"I take it things didn't smooth over with your parents then."

I shook my head solemnly.

"I'm so sorry, Heart."

"I had to get out of there. My mother. God. She's just so cold. It's like I can't even remember who she was when I was growing up because who she is now has tainted everything."

"And your dad?"

"The same pushover he's always been." I sighed. "However, he did surprise me. He stood up to her and drove me back to the airport. At least he's better than my mom. I just really thought we could make things better, but I was living in some sort of dreamland. They will never accept me or support my choices. Especially not now. Having a child out of wedlock is my mother's worst nightmare."

"Well, she needs to get with the times. It's not the fifties anymore." Monica rolled her eyes.

"True, but I did really make a mess of my life."

"But you have a beautiful baby in there who loves you and needs you," said Monica, placing her hand on my bump.

"I felt her. Him. It. Kick."

"Shut up!" said Monica excitedly.

"Mhmm. Last night. It was like they were telling me I wasn't alone in this."

"You're not."

I leaned my head on her shoulder as we weaved slowly through traffic, until we were in front of my apartment. Even though I had only been gone for one day, it felt like so much had happened that a year might as well have passed. I was exhausted. Between traveling and the unexpected hospital visit, I just wanted to lie down and pass out.

While I paid the driver, Monica grabbed my suitcase from the trunk and waited for me on the curb. When we entered the building, I saw Edna hanging some papers on the community bulletin board. She turned around and when she saw me, her eyes immediately traveled to my bump.

"Oh, my God. You're pregnant?" she exclaimed loudly.

I realized I hadn't bothered to cover it up, like I had been for the past few months. Really, I had grown so much bigger that there wasn't really a way to hide it now. I didn't see the point.

"You know it's rude to assume," said Monica coolly.

"It's okay, Monica. Yes, Edna. There's a bun in the oven."

"Whose is it?" she asked, raising a brow.

"It's also rude to ask that question," snapped Monica, crossing her arms.

"It's that guy in the suit, isn't it?" said Edna excitedly, clearly ignoring Monica. "He is so handsome. And rich too, I bet. I was wondering where all those packages were coming from. It all makes sense now."

Edna kept talking, basically to herself at that point, but I didn't confirm any of her assumptions.

"I'm really tired, Edna," I muttered, looking toward the stairs.

"Oh, of course. Of course, sweetie. Go on now. Let me know if you need anything. Chocolate. Crackers. Tea."

"Thank you." I nodded.

I began walking up the stairs to my apartment.

"You're way too nice to that pesky woman," muttered Monica behind me.

"I know...she's just lonely, though."

"I wonder why."

I laughed as I put my key in the door and pushed it open. My loft was exactly as I left it. Clean, but the back wall cluttered with unopened boxes and gift bags. Just more reminders of Daniel. My heart swelled and shrunk at the thought of him.

"You still haven't opened anything?" asked Monica, closing the door and wheeling my suitcase to my closet.

I shook my head. "I'm not ready yet."

"Okay. Well, I hate to leave you, but I have to get back to writing. I have a deadline."

"It's okay. I feel better now. Thank you for coming to my rescue."

"Always, girl."

She gave me a hug before slipping out the door. Once she was gone, I took a long, hot shower and collapsed into bed.

The next morning, I went into the office to wrap up any loose ends before having to leave. I wore an oversized dress and hoped no one noticed it was ballooning out slightly in front of me. Thankfully, no one looked at me any differently. I had always been a bit on the bigger side, so that worked to my advantage now.

As I walked down the hallway, I wondered if they even knew I was fired, or why I was. It didn't seem like it. Brian probably wanted to keep the entire affair with Daniel on the down-low, so nothing was leaked.

After lunch, he called me into his office.

"Addison, take a seat," he said.

I sat across from him and folded my hands in my lap, not noticing it pulled the fabric tight across my stomach.

His eyes skimmed my belly and he looked at me with concern. "Are you..."

Shit. I nodded solemnly.

"Wow."

"Yeah, it was a surprise to me, too."

"I don't want to know any more," he said, putting his hands up. "The less I know about *that* and *who* is responsible, the better."

"Right."

"I just wanted to check in on your progress of contacting your previous contacts."

"It's going well so far. I'm about halfway through my email list. I've passed them on to other staff."

"Good. Remember, you have until the end of the month."

"Yes, I know."

"And remember, that's me being *generous*." He sat back and crossed his arms.

It took everything in me not to roll my eyes. Brian had kept making it clear how generous he was after my mistakes.

"Thank you, Brian. I appreciate it."

"All right, well, you can get back to work now."

As I walked back to my office, I realized there was really no hiding this bump any longer. My coworkers would know any day now, and I would just have to accept that. I just had to figure out a way to dodge their questions and keep it light.

That night, I went on my laptop and began my job search. I filled out several applications and sent résumés to various companies in Manhattan and Brooklyn. A few nonprofits. A few offices looking for secretarial work. A restaurant or two. I realized I couldn't really be picky at this stage. I would go anywhere that would have me.

The next morning, I had a few callbacks. I was even able to set up an interview that afternoon on my lunch break. It was for a secretary position at a law firm just a few blocks from the Leading to Learn office. I wore my loosest pair of pants, and even then, I couldn't zip them or button them up. To hide that, I wore a long white button-down. It wasn't the best, but it would have to do.

It also did nothing to hide that I was pregnant. I figured it was best to be honest upfront. At least they would know what they were getting themselves into. Maybe they would take pity on me. It was an awful way to think about getting a job, but I was desperate.

The interview would have gone perfectly. I was qualified and had years of experience in the office. But I was also pregnant, and no pity was taken on me. The interviewee was polite, but made it clear they needed someone long term as her eyes grazed over my bump. I thanked her for her time and left, feeling defeated.

The next few interviews I was able to line up were more of the same. They were impressed by my qualifications, but worried about the growing body they saw before them. Interview after interview, I left knowing it was another one I had to cross off the list.

At the Leading to Learn office, my coworkers had definitely noticed. It wasn't hard to when the pants I wore were held together with a safety pin. Shelley was the only one who asked me about it though. She was really my only friend in the office. She had asked me to lunch one day on our break and brought it up then.

"Hey, there's a buzz going around the office, but I wanted to hear it from you before assuming anything," she said.

"Oh?" I asked innocently.

"I'll just come out and ask. Are you expecting?"

I nodded, and couldn't help but smile. I was happy to share the news with her. She had always been so kind.

Her eyes lit up and she rounded the table to give me a hug.

"Oh, my gosh. This is so exciting!" she beamed. "I thought there was something different about you. Must be that pregnancy glow."

"Ha ha. You're being much too nice. I felt like I've been a hot mess."

"Not at all," she came back, returning to her seat.

"Well, thank you."

"So, who is the special guy?" she asked.

"Oh, you don't know him," I waved her off and hoped it would stop there.

Thankfully, it did.

"Do you know what you're having?" she asked.

"Not yet. I think I'm going to wait."

"Eeeeh! I bet it's a girl!" she squealed.

I laughed. It was the first time in a while I had felt genuinely excited to be pregnant. I didn't have to be afraid of what anyone else thought. The people who cared about me would support me.

That night, as I was filling out more job applications, there was a knock at my door. I didn't know why, but for a second I hoped it would be Daniel. The truth was, I really missed him. It felt so dishonest to go through this pregnancy without him, knowing he thought the baby was gone. I still felt terrible about it.

And besides that, even though we had our ups and downs, I missed being with him. I knew it was silly. We had both put each other through hell at times, but the rest of the times were perfect. I wondered if I had never let my insecurities get the best of me, if maybe we would have made it.

The knock sounded at the door again and I opened it to find Monica standing there with Thai takeout.

"Hungry?" she asked with a knowing grin.

"Always." I held the door as she slipped inside.

We took our posts on the couch with our takeout cartons and I gave her an update on the job hunt. She listened intently as she slurped down Pad Thai. After I finished my uneventful and depressing update that still left me with no job, she looked at me intently.

"I was thinking..." she started.

"What?"

"I can move in here for a few months when the baby is born. Relieve you of some of the rent and help out."

"Oh, Monica. I can't ask you to do that," I said.

"Why not? I write from home. I could watch the baby if you do end up finding a job, or if you're just tired. Whatever. I want to help."

I felt my eyes growing watery as I looked at my best friend who was willing to change her whole life to help me out. It was overwhelming. I couldn't say anything.

"You don't have to decide now, but I want to help. I am Auntie Monica after all."

I laughed softly. "Coolest aunt ever."

"I know," she said proudly.

She looked over at the wall of boxes and gift bags and seemed to think for a second.

"And don't forget...you still have that check. If things got really bad."

I shook my head. That would be my last resort.

Chapter 40

DANIEL

The next morning, I woke up and reluctantly packed my suitcase. I was leaving. The night before had felt like a dream with Kiera showing up here, but I knew it wasn't. She had been here. I had tasted her. I had almost taken it too far. The thought made me sick to my stomach because somehow it felt like a betrayal to Heart.

Heart, the woman who told me she never wanted to see me again. I owed nothing to her, but my heart was still with her. It was frustratingly painful.

I got dressed and walked down to the restaurant to eat breakfast. My flight wasn't until later that afternoon. It was the soonest one I could find that would get me out of here. As I approached the restaurant, I could see Kiera's back to me as she waited at the hostess stand. She wore a sheer coverup over another skimpy bikini, turning everyone's heads. She hadn't seen me yet. I stopped in my tracks and made a quick turn toward the steps of the beach.

She was still here. Obviously. It wasn't like she was going to pass up on a vacation at a five-star resort simply because she didn't have her way with me.

It was good I was getting out of there soon. I didn't want to risk seeing her again.

I would order some breakfast on the beach. It would be a nice sendoff to this beautiful place. A server came down who wasn't Collette, and handed me a menu. I studied it for a moment and ordered eggs, bacon, and fresh fruit.

I settled into a lounge chair to wait for my food. The waves crashed gently against the shore, filling my ears with the calm sounds of the ocean. I was disappointed I had to leave today. This place was truly paradise, until my brother ruined it all.

"Mr. Jacobs, I have your food."

I opened my eyes and saw the server standing over me with a bucket of champagne and a tray of food. I sat up and made room for him to set it down on the lounge chair.

"Thank you," I said.

I was ravenous. I realized I hadn't eaten dinner last night after my afternoon surf and too strong of cocktails that Collette had served me. Then I had passed out and Kiera was at my door. The whole night was a blur.

I dug into the eggs and took a bite of crispy bacon, watching as guests passed by hand in hand enjoying their morning at the beach with sandy toes.

"Daniel?" I heard someone say.

Shit. I knew that voice.

I looked to my right and saw Kiera walking toward me, trying to balance a mimosa and walk in heels. Not the best choice of footwear for the sand. I shook my head at how ridiculous she looked.

She plopped down in the lounge chair next to mine, her mimosa sloshing out of her cup and spilling on her tan skin.

"Oops." She giggled.

"Kiera, you shouldn't be here."

She rolled her eyes. "Are you still playing hard to get?"

"I'm not playing anything. I meant what I said last night."

"Fine. Whatever." She put her hands up and reclined in the lounge chair.

She was not getting the hint. This was why I was leaving today.

I finished my breakfast in silence and saw my server approach with a bucket of champagne.

"Mr. Jacobs. I was just informed it's your last day here. We wanted to thank you for staying with us with a complimentary bottle of champagne," he said.

"Oh, that's not necessary."

"Champagne?" said Kiera, sitting up and smiling at the server.

I sighed frustratedly as the server set the bucket between us and began working at the cork. There was a pop and a fizz, and he began pouring two glasses. Kiera clapped excitedly.

I wanted nothing more than to get out of there, but I didn't want to be rude to the server. After he handed us our glasses, I thanked him and took a sip as I watched him leave.

"Well, this is romantic," said Kiera, stretching back into the lounge chair.

Her bikini was desperately clinging on to her, threatening to expose the intimate parts of her I had seen the night before.

"This isn't anything," I said, standing up. I set my glass in the sand and put my sunglasses on. I began padding down the beach toward the steps, with Kiera calling after me. Thankfully, the waves drowned her out.

I called for a shuttle to take me to the airport. I didn't care if I was entirely too early for my flight. It was better than being here and having another run-in with Kiera. *Damn you, Brody.*

The airport was busy with flights coming in and going out. It was probably good that I was early so I could get through check-in and security. Once I was through, I found a bar and ordered a whiskey on the rocks. And then another. What else was there to do at airports?

A few hours passed, and the announcement was made that my flight was boarding soon. I grabbed my luggage and rolled it down to my gate. Being first class, I was able to board first and settle into my seat, but I couldn't get comfortable. Not before takeoff and not for the actual flight.

The flight home was brutal. Nothing like the first. I couldn't get settled in my seat, even though it was my own private compartment with a full-on bed. The Bloody Marys weren't strong enough. The movies didn't hold my attention. Sleep didn't come. It was a hellish eighteen hours back to New York.

I kept tossing and turning in my seat thinking about how my getaway had gotten cut short with Kiera showing up the way she did. I could have stayed, but knowing her, she would be back. That was clear at breakfast this morning. I didn't want to feel like I was on edge the whole time or that my resolve would eventually break and I would succumb to her. *Would it really be the worst thing?* I thought to myself.

Falling back into our usual pattern of fucking and fighting and playing games. It's what I knew with Kiera. It's what we were both comfortable with. It certainly would be a distraction from Heart.

But eventually I had to let that go. Heart. Kiera.

I clearly wasn't the same person I was a few months ago before Heart came into my life, or I would be in bed with Kiera right now. Her hot pink bikini on the floor and her long limbs tangled around me. But that wasn't me. Not anymore.

Which was why I was on this plane back to New York to try and piece my life together, and not run from it anymore. I was grateful for the days I had in Bora Bora because they brought some clarity, and much needed relaxation. My brother had the right idea in suggesting it, but then he ruined it all by sending a human package to my door.

When my flight landed, I went through customs and waited for my luggage at baggage claim. Armand was outside on the curb waiting when I emerged out of the sliding doors.

"Mr. Jacobs." He nodded before taking my bags.

"Armand."

"How was your trip?" he asked.

"Fantastic," I said. "I will definitely be back."

"Good, sir. I'm happy to hear that."

He opened the back door and I slid inside.

"Home?" he asked.

I looked at the time. It was nearly 7 p.m. I should have gone home, but I had matters to take up with Brody. I felt like the entire flight I was just seething at his presumptuousness in sending Kiera as some sort of quick fix when he knew absolutely nothing.

"No, actually. I'd like to go to my brother's place."

"Yes, sir," said Armand, putting the car into drive.

Thirty minutes later, he pulled the car up to Brody's red brick townhome on the Upper East Side. I looked up and saw the third-floor lights were on, so he must be home.

"Thank you, Armand," I said as I got out of the car, not waiting for him to do his job.

I walked through the black iron gates and rang the doorbell impatiently. I rang it three times before I heard Brody's voice call from inside.

"I'm coming. Jesus Christ," he said.

I heard the door unlock and then he opened the door.

His eyes grew wide when he saw me. "Daniel! What the hell are you doing here?"

I pushed past him without him extending an invitation.

"Please, come in," he said sarcastically behind me as he closed the door.

I started pacing the entryway of his place, the wooden floors creaking slightly under my feet.

"I thought you were supposed to be in Bora Bora for like another week," he said.

"Yeah, I was," I said heatedly.

"So, why are you here?"

"I'll give you one guess."

"Uh, the waters weren't clear enough?" he asked with a raised brow.

"Kiera, you idiot," I snapped.

"Oh! You got my little surprise!" He chuckled.

"You think it's funny sending her halfway across the world to *surprise* me?"

"Hey, she was willing. She got a free vacation out of it." He shrugged.

"And in doing so, she ruined mine."

"Oh, come on. Don't try to tell me you two didn't have any fun."

"We didn't. Clearly. Which is why I'm here and not back on the beach."

Brody rolled his eyes. "What is your problem, man?"

"My problem is *you*. Thinking you know me and what I need."

"I do know you. You're my brother and you're just as much of a fuckboy as I am."

"Well, maybe I'm not anymore," I muttered.

"Oh, look who is all high and mighty now," he replied, putting his hands up and pretending he was impressed.

"People change. They grow up. Clearly, you wouldn't know anything about that."

"Clearly because you never tell me what the hell is going on with you anymore!"

I could tell that this went deeper than I thought. Brody and I had always been close growing up and in business. We had shared our ventures with women like they were trophies to impress each other with. I couldn't blame him for thinking we were still those same brothers, when one of us was not.

Still, my anger was too hot to admit any of that. And it wasn't the right time to share what exactly had gone on in my life the past couple months.

"Well, until you do know, butt the hell out of my life." I held up a threatening finger.

Brody didn't say anything as I turned and walked out the door, slamming it behind me.

Armand waited outside of the car and opened the door without saying a word. The look on my face must have made it clear I wasn't in the mood for pleasantries.

When I got home that night, I should have been tired. I had just flown for eighteen hours and had a massive blowout with my brother. But instead, I was wired.

I took a hot shower, unpacked my suitcase, ran my laundry, and placed a grocery order for delivery for the next day. As I was ordering groceries, I realized how hungry I was. I threw on a sweatshirt and a baseball cap, not wanting to be recognized by anyone, and rode the elevator down to the lobby. I didn't need Armand. I just wanted to walk the streets of Manhattan in the late hours and find some greasy pizza to eat by myself.

Chapter 41

ADDISON

"I can't believe we're finally doing this," said Monica, her hands on her hips.

She stood in the middle of my loft and looked at all the boxes and bags we needed to open—the gifts from Daniel I had refused to go through. But after my trip to the hospital, and realizing how real this pregnancy was, I knew it was time to start setting up my apartment for baby's arrival. Even if I was only just over five months pregnant.

"I'm tired of looking at the boxes. I figured it's time to just rip the Band-Aid off." I shrugged.

"I'm glad you decided to keep everything. It's the least the jerk could do," she said.

"He's not a jerk."

"Did you forget what he said at that charity event?" she asked, raising an eyebrow.

"No, I didn't forget," I replied softly. "I just know he didn't sign up for this. You know?"

"And you did?"

"We both made choices we might not have thought through, but I'm happy, Monica. Really, I am. I know this isn't the best place to raise a baby, and my current circumstances seem pretty unoptimistic, but I want to be a mom. I want to be a good mom."

Monica knelt down and sat beside me on the wood floor. She put her arm around me. "And you *will* be," she said with certainty.

I nodded and looked at all the pretty gift bags and wrapped boxes. They made me think of Daniel.

"You miss him, don't you?" she asked.

"I try not to," I admitted.

"It's okay to. I know you really liked him..."

"It was more than that. I felt like I might be falling for him. I had this whole silly vision of us being one big, happy family."

"That's not silly. That's what anyone would want for their baby."

"But now I know he never wanted that."

"You don't need him," she said.

I looked around at all of the packages and laughed softly. Clearly, I did. I would never have been able to afford all of this.

"Enough of that. It's time to get into baby prep mode!" said Monica, slapping her hands on her thighs and reaching for the first bag.

She untied the dainty ribbon bow and pulled the tissue paper out. She reached in the bag and pulled out a cream-colored stack of onesies. She unfolded one and held it up in front of me.

"It's so tiny," I said, running my fingers over the soft fabric.

I could feel my heart swell. They were perfect. If baby were a girl or a boy.

"These are newborn size," she said, looking through the tags. She reached in the bag again and pulled out another stack of the same onesies, followed by another stack.

"Oh, he got you 0-3 month too! And 3-6 month!"

I started removing the tags and stickers, and stacking them against the wall as Monica started opening another bag.

"Awwww," she said, holding up a little pair of white and cream striped pants.

It felt like such a bittersweet moment, folding these tiny clothes and feeling the soft material, *ooh*ing and *ahh*ing over the different colors and prints. I felt excited and scared and sad and happy. I was a mess of emotions. Most of all, I just wished Daniel was there with me. Of course, I was happy to have Monica here. She had done so much more and been there for me. But Daniel, the father of my baby, was hard to replace, especially now.

"I think that's it for all the clothes," said Monica, folding up another gift bag.

I looked at the stack of clothes lined up against the wall and shook my head in awe.

"You're set for an entire year," she said, following my gaze.

I placed my hand on my bump and rubbed it gently.

"You are going to be one well-dressed baby," I said softly as I bent over and talked to the baby.

"Very posh," laughed Monica. "These onesies cost more than the shirt I'm wearing."

"That pile of clothes is probably three months' rent," I said, shaking my head.

"Ready for the next one?" she asked.

I nodded and she got up and walked over to the biggest box. She grunted as she started to slide it over.

"Do you need help?" I asked, attempting to get up.

"Sit the hell down. Did you not hear what the doctor said?" she said shrilly.

I laughed and settled back on the floor.

She grabbed a pair of scissors and started working at the tape on the box. Finally, she popped open one side and peered inside. She reached in and pulled out a pamphlet.

"Looks like you have a crib," she said.

"Really?" I asked excitedly.

She handed me the pamphlet that included the instructions. On the front was a picture of a beautiful gold railed crib. I sucked in a breath when I saw it. It was so beautiful.

"Wow," I said, mostly to myself.

"It's really pretty, Heart," said Monica.

"He did a good job."

"Why don't you start unboxing the smaller boxes, and I'll start putting the crib together," offered Monica.

I gave her a skeptical look. Monica wasn't exactly the handiest person. Neither was I. But I at least knew the difference between a Phillips and a flathead.

"What?" she asked with a shrug. "How hard can it be?"

I handed her the instructions and she started pulling out the different pieces and hardware. Once she had everything laid out on the floor, I watched as she flipped through the pages, scratching her head.

"I think I might need some wine," she said.

"Oh, yeah. That's a great idea," I said sarcastically.

"Hey, it couldn't hurt!"

"Top left cabinet," I said with a laugh.

"As if I don't know where you keep the booze." Monica rolled her eyes.

While she was in the kitchen, I opened another gift bag. This one was from Saks Fifth Avenue and was wrapped beautifully. I carefully tore open the tissue paper and wrapped inside was a small, white teddy bear. I sucked in a breath as I pulled it close and clutched it against me. It was such a beautiful little bear. One that baby would probably keep forever. I started to cry softly.

"Hey, hey, hey. What's wrong?" asked Monica, walking over with a glass of red wine in hand. She set it carefully on the floor and looked at me intently.

"It's just. Everything. This bear. The crib. The clothes. It's all beautiful. Perfect, really."

"You and baby deserve it," she said, putting her hand on my back.

"It just all has Daniel all over it. I can't believe he did all of this."

Monica seemed to think for a second. "Maybe you heard him wrong."

I gave her a look.

"I don't know. A guy who does all of this..." She waved her hand around the room. "It doesn't make sense."

"I heard what I heard."

"Well, maybe it was a misunderstanding?"

"I don't know how you can misunderstand that."

"Yeah, I guess you're right," said Monica. "You know what will make you feel better though?"

"What?"

"Pizza!"

"Yes, I'm starving." I wiped tears away from my cheeks.

Monica called and ordered an extra-large pepperoni pizza with jalapenos, and I continued making my way through more baby toys and diaper caddies and different types of bottles. It was going to take us all night to get through everything, and we still had to assemble some things, like the crib Monica hadn't even started. Thankfully, it was the weekend, and we had two whole days to do it.

The pizza arrived just as I had finished unboxing not one, but two strollers. Monica had finally put together about a quarter of the crib and finished one glass of wine. As I brought in the pizza, I started to worry about the size of my apartment and how I was going to fit everything in here.

I set the pizza box on the floor in the middle of everything and we started to eat straight from the box, looking around in amazement.

"Thanks for spending your Friday night with me," I said to Monica.

"I wouldn't want to be anywhere else," she replied, swallowing a bite of pizza.

After we were finished eating, we laid back on the floor with full stomachs. I was so uncomfortably full and as much as the jalapenos were delicious, they were also making my heartburn flare up. Damn those spicy cravings that I kept giving in to.

I clutched my chest and winced.

"Heartburn again?" asked Monica, looking over at me.

"Always," I answered.

"You know...I heard that having frequent heartburn means your baby has a lot of hair."

"Well, it must be a wooly mammoth," I said.

Monica laughed and sat up. "Do you want me to go get you some antacid?"

"No, I can go."

"Are you sure?" she asked. "Remember what the doctor said."

"I can walk, Monica," I said, rolling my eyes. "Plus, some fresh air sounds nice."

"Fine. Well, I'm going to pour another glass of wine and get back to the crib."

She stood and held her hands out to help me up. I grabbed my purse from the kitchen counter and walked out into the hallway.

Outside, the night air was cool against my skin as I walked to the corner store. I grabbed a box of antacid from the shelf and stopped by the freezer aisle to grab a pint of cookie dough ice cream. I carried both to the front counter and waited in line. As I waited, my eyes skimmed the magazines. That was when I saw him.

Daniel's face on the cover of one of the entertainment magazines. My stomach leaped to my throat as I carefully took it from the magazine rack. He wasn't alone on the cover. He was with a woman. The same awful woman he had brought to my office. It looked like they were on vacation together, sitting together on a white-sand beach.

I ignored her for a moment and only looked at him. He looked handsome sitting on a beach chair, his skin tan and his toned body shirtless. My eyes then reluctantly glanced at the woman. Kiera, I think her name was. She looked like a freaking goddess sprawled out on the chair next to him with perfect beach waves in her hair and a teeny bikini only she could pull off.

The line in front of me moved forward slightly. I had time to flip through the pages to find the full story. The headline read:

A Pre-Honeymoon for the Lovebirds?

I swallowed hard as I kept reading.

It said that the two were spotted at the St. Regis Resort in Bora Bora enjoying a romantic getaway as rumors of their engagement swirled around them. They looked cozy on the beach as they enjoyed a bottle of champagne together.

I looked through the other pictures that surrounded the text of the article. They were all of the same day, on the beach, with a server pouring champagne. I didn't see any pictures of them holding hands or kissing, but it didn't mean that didn't happen. Hell, they were in Bora Bora together.

"Next," the cashier called, breaking my focus.

I quickly put the magazine back on the rack and handed him my items.

After I paid, I walked out to the sidewalk and felt like I was going to throw up or scream. Instead, I just started sobbing. People passed by me with curious expressions, but I didn't care. I had just seen the father of my baby, the man I had fallen for, with another woman. I was crushed.

And I had no right to be upset. I was the one who pushed him away. Instead of talking things over, I lied to him in the worst way possible. I should have told him the truth. I should have told him how I felt when I had the chance.

Chapter 42

DANIEL

When I got home from grabbing pizza at the corner joint a block away from my apartment, I saw I had several missed calls from Brody. Plus, one call from Kiera. I had left my place without my phone so I could completely clear my head. Now I had to come back to that. I rolled my eyes. Those were the two people I had the least interest in talking to.

Brody might not have known just exactly what he was doing by basically wrapping her in gift wrap and sending her halfway across the world, but *she* knew exactly what she was doing in coming. I had made it clear that I didn't want anything with her, but she was stubborn and she was too proud to ever give up that easy.

I turned off my phone and tossed it on my nightstand before climbing into bed. I was suddenly hit with a wave of exhaustion. The travel day and the drama with my brother had finally caught up with me. I closed my eyes and was asleep within minutes.

The next morning, I made a pot of coffee and began getting dressed for work. Even though I was not quite ready to face reality, I couldn't stay on vacation forever. I had to man up and run my company. I had taken enough time off, both physically and mentally. It was time to get back on my game.

I rode the elevators down to the parking garage and saw Armand was waiting for me. He looked a little uneasy, but I wasn't sure why.

"Hello, Armand," I said.

"Hello, sir." He nodded and opened the car door.

I slipped inside. I watched him take a seat up front and adjust the mirror so he could see me better. He looked like he had something to say.

"Everything okay, Armand?" I asked.

"Oh, yes. Yes, sir. Everything is fine."

I nodded, unsurely. He put the car into drive and drove up the dark ramp of the parking garage and into the sunlight. I looked out the window at the city that was so different from the paradise I had just been. The concrete and glass were a major juxtaposition from the white sand and crystal-clear waters. It was too bad I had to cut the trip short.

Armand pulled up to a stoplight and eased the car to a stop next to a newsstand. I did a double-take as I looked at the row of magazines with my face staring back at me.

"What the fuck?" I whispered.

"Sir?" asked Armand.

"Let me out here," I said.

"But we are in the middle lane..."

"Fuck it. I'll get out myself," I said, opening the car door and almost had it ripped off by a taxi flying by.

I checked for oncoming traffic before running to the sidewalk. I grabbed a magazine from the rack and looked at my picture printed on the glossy page with a bold headline underneath it:

A Pre-Honeymoon for the Lovebirds?

The letters popped out at me as if they were punching me in the face. My eyes scanned the cover and spotted Kiera's photo printed next to mine. She wore the little white bikini she had been wearing when I ran into her on the beach that day.

Fuck. Fuck. Fuck.

I turned the pages quickly and found the full, two-page spread in the middle of the magazine. There were photos of me surfing, of Kiera topless on the beach, of her leaving my hotel room the night she had showed up and surprised me. Worse than that, there were photos of us together on the beach, a bottle of champagne between us. They painted a completely different story than what had happened.

I shook my head, as if trying to shake the images away, but the magazine was there in my hands staring straight at me. The press had done it again. They had taken something and spun it into another completely different story. Now the whole world thought we had gone on that trip together, and they were just feeding into the narrative that we were going to get married.

"Excuse me, sir?" said a voice.

"What?" I barked.

The woman at the newsstand looked taken aback, but then she took a good look at me and I saw the gears in her head begin to spin as she registered who I was. Her eyes grew wide.

"I... uh... are you going to pay for that?" She eyed the magazine in my hands.

The last thing I wanted to do was support the publications that had made my life a living hell for years, and continued to do so.

"No. I'm not," I said. "And no one should. This is complete bullshit."

I put the magazine on the rack, the back cover facing out, and walked to the car. Armand had pulled the car to the curb and waited there illegally, the hazard lights on. I opened my door and slipped inside before slamming it behind me.

"Sir?"

"You saw this morning's tabloids?" I asked, irritated.

"Uh, yes, sir. My wife was reading it this morning."

"Well, it isn't true."

"Of course, sir," he replied quickly.

"I'm not getting married. I wasn't even on vacation with that woman. I can't go anywhere without being hunted like a goddamn animal." I was more so talking to myself at this point.

"I'm sorry, sir."

"Work. Now," I snapped.

"Yes, sir." He nodded and quickly put the car into drive.

I felt bad for talking to him that way. He didn't deserve it. The newsstand woman didn't deserve it. The person who deserved my wrath was Brody, who had gotten me into this goddamn mess in the first place. I had no desire to see his face today or any day soon.

Deep down, I knew I could try and blame everyone else, but this was my doing.

My phone trilled in my jacket pocket. I answered without looking at the caller ID.

"Hello?" I asked, irritation in my voice.

"Well, hello to you, too," cooed Kiera in a babyish voice.

"What do you want, Kiera?" I asked with a sigh.

"Did you see this morning's papers? We are a hit!"

"*We* are nothing."

"Oh, come on. America loves us. Hell, Bora Bora loves us. The whole staff was abuzz. We put that place on the map."

"You're still there?"

"Of course, silly. Did you really think I was going to pass up on a tan and strawberry daiquiris? Courtesy of Brody, of course."

I rolled my eyes.

"They actually gave me your suite. Can you believe that? I loved it so much. I had to have—"

"You tend to get what you want," I cut her off.

"That's true," she replied breathily. "You know, while I'm in here, I keep thinking about our night together. That was hot."

"There was no night together. Nothing happened."

"Pretty sure I can still taste you, Daniel."

"I stopped it before it got too far."

"You're no fun at all." I could picture her ridiculous pout.

"Kiera, is there something that you need?" I asked, exasperated.

"I just thought we looked cute in the magazine and wanted to celebrate our little debut."

"Goodbye."

I ended the call and shook my head, frustrated. She was loving this and was now probably having her publicist put together another statement for the press.

Sighing, I leaned my head against the back of my seat and stared up at the ceiling of the car. I felt like someone had punctured a hole in me and I was slowly deflating. I felt helpless. The press and their stories were something I had dealt with before. Usually, I could brush it off. But knowing Heart could see this was gut-wrenching. I hated to think she actually believed this shit. I hoped she knew me better than that, especially after I explained to her what my life was like with the press. But still, those photos were pretty incriminating.

I so badly wanted to call her and tell her the truth. Tell her that nothing was going on with me and Kiera. Tell her that I couldn't stop thinking about her. There was so much to say. But I didn't think she wanted to hear it. She had made it painfully clear that she never wanted to see me again.

I had already caused enough mess in her life. The thought that I caused so much hurt and stress made my heart feel three sizes too small. If she had lost the baby, I wondered if I was to blame. I had been so preoccupied with my work that I hadn't given her the time she deserved. And then I was so desperate to win her back that I did something selfish and erratic by showing up at her work, causing her to lose her job. Had I caused so much stress that it had hurt the baby? I hadn't even thought about it until now, causing me to feel like I was about to spiral.

Reaching into my jacket pocket, I pulled out the ultrasound photo. I had been carrying it around with me ever since her friend had given it to me that day. It was a reminder of a new beginning. A beautiful little being. A new life I could have had with Heart, raising a family together. Things I never knew I wanted until my eyes fell on this little black and white shape printed on this glossy paper.

There were so many things I should have said. So many things I should have done differently.

I should have listened to her at the charity event. She was so angry, and instead of hearing her out, I tried to fix it in one of the two ways I knew how. Sex. And the other times, I had tried to fix everything with money.

I should have picked up the damn ultrasound when she came by my office. I should have given her the time of day. She and the baby should have come first before business. Before everything else.

And I should have been there for her when she lost the baby. I wish she had trusted me enough to tell me what was going on, so I could have helped her. So I could have supported her. So I could have held her.

I would give anything to hold her again.

I ran my thumb over the photo and felt my eyes sting with tears. I had lost so much. So had Heart.

"Sir...we're here," said Armand cautiously, breaking me from my thoughts.

I hadn't even noticed the car had come to a stop. I looked out the window and realized we were at work. I quickly tucked the photo back in my jacket pocket as Armand walked around to my door. He pulled it open and I stepped out onto the sidewalk. I took a few steps toward my building, but turned around before I reached the door.

"I'm sorry, Armand," I said.

"It's quite all right, sir."

"It's not. I'm just going through it."

He nodded knowingly. "You miss her, don't you?"

I opened my mouth, surprised by his question. We had always kept it professional and private. But I realized that Heart had been a constant in my life for the past few months and Armand had been there for a lot of it. All the long drives from Manhattan to Brooklyn and back. Heart had always been so kind to him. Kinder than any other woman I had been with. She saw everyone simply as they were. Human.

I gave him a weak smile and walked inside the building, his question still ringing in my ears.

He was right.

I missed her so much.

Chapter 43

ADDISON

I applied a quick coat of lip-gloss and inspected myself in the floor-length mirror hanging in my closet. I turned sideways and looked at my growing belly that was on full display in the black sheath dress I had tugged on. Lovingly, I rubbed my stomach. Rather than being ashamed of it, I was proud. That was my baby.

I gave myself a quiet, feigned, confident nod of approval and walked to the kitchen where a pot of decaf coffee waited. I needed it. Even though there was no caffeine, I swore that it tricked my mind into thinking it was giving me the energy I needed after my sleepless night.

I couldn't get comfortable lately. I was used to sleeping on my back or my stomach. My comfort positions, but those weren't an option anymore. I tried using one of the large pregnancy pillows Daniel had gifted me. It helped a little, but mostly because it felt like someone was in bed next to me and I didn't feel so alone.

But then I would wake up and realize I was holding something that resembled a stuffed pool noodle rather than a human being. Rather than Daniel. He was the first man I had woken up to in a very long time. Really, the first man I had been with in a while. I missed that morning we had together when he stayed the night here in my little loft apartment. Even though I had washed the sheets several times since then, I could still smell his cologne on them. Maybe it was just my imagination. A cruel little memory my heart wouldn't let go of.

Since reading the tabloids a few nights ago, my pain was still raw. The pictures of him on a tropical vacation with his soon-to-be-fiancée were imprinted in my memory. Since then, I had tried avoiding the newsstands and the corner store. I didn't want to see any other pictures or read any updates on him or his relationship.

I couldn't believe he had moved on so quickly. But I didn't have any right to be upset. I had pushed him out of my life. I had told him I never wanted to see him again. And really, how serious were we? We had only known each other for a few months, and really, the only thing that tied us together was the baby.

At first, it had just been a one-night stand. I thought I would never see him again, but life had other plans. If I had never gotten pregnant, I wouldn't have called him or invited him back into my life. He would have just been some hot billionaire guy I once slept with.

Except, he wasn't just that.

He was so much more, and that was why it was so hard to let go.

I took a sip from my *I heart New York* mug and glanced around my loft. It was cramped in here, but it was ready to welcome the baby whenever he or she came. At least that was one part of my life that was sorted out. Sure, everything was a constant reminder of Daniel, but it was also a reminder of how I was about to become a mother. I was both terrified and elated.

Monica and I had spent all weekend unpacking and assembling furniture, including a cream glider that we put near the window where the morning sun hit just right. I imagined sitting there in the early mornings and nursing the baby. I smiled at the thought.

My phone rang on the counter next to me. I picked it up and saw Monica's name on the screen.

"Hello?" I answered.

"Happy last day of work!" she exclaimed.

"Is it really something to celebrate?" I groaned.

"Yes! Because the way your boss handled everything is bullshit and you deserve better."

"True, but after today, I'm jobless."

"Well, I have some good news..."

"What is it?" I asked, my ears perking up.

"I found someone who will give you some freelance work in the meantime. At least until you find a job."

"Are you serious?" I asked in surprise.

"Now, it doesn't pay much, but it's something. *And* you get to work from home. No more commuting to the city."

"What would I be doing?"

"You'd be writing articles on nonprofit work."

"I'm not a writer, though. I'm not *you.*"

"You don't have to be! It's not like you're writing a novel or something. You're just writing short articles about something you already know."

"You really think I can do it?" I asked hesitantly.

"Of course! Why do you think I put you up for it?"

"Wow," I said softly. "Thank you, Monica. Really, you've done so much for me."

"That's what best friends are for. I know you'd do the same."

"I would."

"Look, I gotta get to the coffee shop to meet my editor. I'll send you the contact information so you can touch base and get started on your new gig."

"Okay, thank you!"

"Ta-ta!"

I hung up and felt an overwhelming sense of relief wash over me. I might be losing my job today, the only real place I had ever worked, but at least I had something lined up. While I was terrified and not completely sure I knew what I was doing, it was something. And I got to work from home, which meant less stress on me and the baby. It seemed like everything was working out.

Hurriedly, I finished my coffee and grabbed my purse, heading out the door. As I walked down the stairs to the subway, I thought about how I wouldn't have to do this anymore. I smiled to myself as I waited for the train to come through. Here I was, thinking today was going to be absolutely awful, and things were looking up. Now, I just had to actually get through the workday.

I walked into my building and rode the elevator up to my floor. When the doors opened, it seemed like a hushed silence washed over the room. A few people gave awkward waves, and the rest pretended to be busy at their desks. I noticed Brian leaning against the doorframe as if he was waiting for me.

"Addison, will you come in here?"

I nodded, a bad feeling coming over me.

I followed him into his office.

"Take a seat."

I did.

"Clearly, there's no hiding *that* anymore," he said, eyeing my bump. "People have been talking."

"Oh?" I asked.

"Have you told anyone about your situation with Mr. Jacobs?"

"No. No one."

"Well, I guess they're just speculating then. Rumors have been wafting around since people found out you lost your position here."

Honestly, I didn't care. What did it matter? I was gone after today.

"Okay?" I said, more as a question than a statement.

"It's just messy, Addison. You see that, don't you? If word gets out…"

"I no longer work here after today." I shrugged.

I didn't know what else he wanted from me. It wasn't like I could go back in time and change anything, and even if I could, I no longer wanted to. I was going to be a mother, whether anyone else liked it or not.

"Yes, well, now that has even raised some eyebrows as to why you're being let go."

"Look, Brian. I don't know what you want me to do…"

"Well, I want you to think about the mess you're leaving me with." He sighed dramatically.

"You *fired* me," I snapped.

"Because *you* decided to sleep with someone for money."

I felt my face burn.

"How dare you!" I stood up suddenly.

"Don't make a scene, Addison," he warned, his voice low as he looked toward the door.

"You know me. I've worked my ass off for years, and *this* is how you treat me? That's what you accuse me of? You *know* me, Brian. I would never."

"Calm down. I didn't mean it. I'm just...worked up," he said.

"No, I won't calm down. I don't appreciate you accusing me of a behavior that is so far from what I'm capable of. How dare you."

"People are starting to stare," said Brian, looking behind me and through the windows of his office.

"Let them. Let them see the giant mistake you're making in letting me go. I have brought in more money than any of my coworkers. I have always done what you've asked of me, and then some. You won't find a replacement who even holds a candle to me."

Brian put up his hands as if to calm me down, but I wasn't having it.

It was as if everything I had been holding in for years suddenly gushed out of me and it felt so damn good. It was all true. I had poured everything into this job, and had hardly ever received the recognition I deserved. It wasn't until I landed the deal with Daniel that people started to take notice, but before that I had been busting my ass here. I never so much as got a thank you or a raise, until a few weeks ago.

"I know I'm supposed to finish out the workday, but I don't think I can spend another minute in this office with someone who casts judgment on something they know nothing about. Goodbye, Brian."

I opened his office door and slammed it behind me, not caring that the entire office was staring with open mouths. I held my head high as I walked down the hallway and began packing my things. Quickly, I put my personal belongings in a cardboard box and said a quiet goodbye to my office before closing the door behind me.

Upset, I balanced the box in my hands as I walked through the floor to the elevators. I pressed the button and waited impatiently, ignoring the murmurs behind me. Finally, the doors opened and I stepped inside, pressing the button for the ground floor and not looking up. I wasn't going to look back. I was only looking forward now.

I carried the box down the stairs of the subway and waited for the next train back to Brooklyn, where I would happily stay. For now.

Back at my apartment, I set down the box that held so many memories from the past several years. Rather than feeling angry, I felt proud. I had accomplished so much, and while things ended messily, I knew I had done a lot of good for people around the world. That was what made this all worth it.

I suddenly felt empowered. I dug out my phone from my purse and scrolled through my contacts until I found the number I was looking for. I pressed send.

"Hello?" I heard my mother answer.

"Hi, Mom."

"Addison? I didn't think I would be hearing from you again," she said coolly.

"And you won't again. Not after this."

"Oh?" she asked coolly.

"Yeah, I wanted to tell you that I don't *need* you. I don't need one thing from you. Not money. Not love. Not approval."

"Excuse me?"

"I'm going to be just fine on my own."

"I very much doubt that," she muttered.

"Doubt all you want. You see, I don't care anymore. I don't need you to believe in me because I believe in me. I'm going to be a great mother to my baby. And he or she will grow up knowing they are loved and supported in whatever they choose to do. They'll always be more than enough for me."

"Addison..."

"Goodbye, Mother."

I hit the red button and set my phone on the counter. I noticed my hands shook as I took a deep breath. It felt good to get that off my chest, but I couldn't shake the feeling of sadness that was creeping in.

That was enough goodbyes for one day.

Chapter 44

DANIEL

I decided to walk home from work, which was something I rarely did. Armand was following close behind, even though I told him he could head home early. I had no plans that night. I had every intention of holing up in my living room and ordering takeout, which was something that was becoming more and more common for me.

Ever since the tabloid came out with the story about Kiera and me enjoying a tropical vacation together, I felt more exposed than ever. I had dealt with paparazzi and lies from the press in the past, but this time it might have hurt the one woman I cared about.

Or maybe it didn't hurt her at all. That was even more crushing.

There was no way she had avoided seeing the story, or the spins that came afterward. There were several photos that came out over the following week. Photos where Kiera and I weren't even together, but the press cleverly pieced them together to look as if we were.

The night she came to my room, we almost were. I had almost let it get too far. It still went further than it probably should have, which was eating away at me. I felt like I had been unfaithful in some way, even though I knew I hadn't. Heart and I weren't together anymore, if we ever even were.

The press had placed a photo of my leaving the restaurant days before Kiera had arrived next to a photo of Kiera leaving the same restaurant after I had left back to New York. A photo of me at the beach surfing was placed next to a photo of Kiera lying topless on a beach chair and looking out at the ocean. It was all so predictable. I knew how it looked, even though I knew what was true. To anyone else, we did look like a happy couple.

Stupid me didn't even notice any photos being taken. The damn paparazzi were sneaky. It felt eerie looking back to know I was being watched, maybe from behind a bush or from a long lens from a boat. I should have been used to it.

I wondered what Heart thought when she saw the photos. *If* she saw them. Again, they were hard to avoid.

I figured it was better to stay home than risk being photographed and having those photos comprised into a story that fit the narrative of someone else. It was a risk just walking these few blocks home, but I had to get fresh air. I had to clear my head, which was covered with a Mets baseball cap in hopes it would help conceal me.

When I arrived home, I opened the drawer of takeout menus and blindly selected one. I wasn't sure what I was in the mood for, so I left it up to fate. It looked like fate had chosen Chinese. I dialed the number and placed an order for Mongolian beef, fried rice, egg rolls, steamed vegetables, and honey shrimp. They said it would be about forty-five minutes.

I decided to take a shower and wash away the day, which had been spent mostly in my office, avoiding my brother. Thankfully, most of my meetings were video calls with our associates in London as we moved forward with our deal. The deal that Brody had landed on his own, while I was dropping the ball. I knew I couldn't avoid him forever. He was my CFO, after all. And my brother.

I knew my anger and resentment was wrongly placed on him, but he was the closest one to me right now. And for being the closest one to me, he knew absolutely nothing about me or the mess of my life.

After my shower, I threw on some black sweats and a large Mets tee. I sunk into my couch and scrolled through my phone to see if my nights at home had paid off. I didn't see any new photos of me, and the story of Kiera and my engagement seemed to be dying down. All they had were recycled photos from Bora Bora or photos from years back of Kiera and me at certain engagements when we were actually dating.

The buzzer on my intercom rang. The Chinese food must have gotten here early. I buzzed them up and listened to the whir of the elevator beginning to descend. I grabbed my wallet from the entry table and fished out some cash for a tip.

The doors opened and I was surprised to see Brody standing there with a pack of beer in his hands.

"What the hell?" I asked in surprise.

"Nice to see you, too," he said, walking past me.

He went to the kitchen and set the beer on the counter. *Make yourself at home,* I thought. He opened the box and pulled out a beer and then another. He tossed it to me and I almost fumbled it before steadying the cold can in my hands.

"A peace offering," he said, popping the tab of his beer.

I stood there, unsure if I wanted to kick him out or let him stay.

"Thanks," I said, opening my beer and taking a sip.

I guessed it was time to stop being an asshole.

We stood there drinking our beers in silence for a moment. It was awkward and uncomfortable, but I was the one to blame for that. The past few months I had been in my own world and shutting everyone out.

"So..." Brody started, "I don't know what's going on with you, and not to be soft, but I care about you. You're my brother, and I'm here for you."

I took a deep breath before nodding toward the couch. "Come. Sit. Chinese food is on its way. I ordered way too much."

"Junzi's?" he asked hopefully.

"Where else?"

He smiled and followed me toward the couch.

We both plopped down and sunk into the large plush cushions that I had fallen asleep on more times than my own bed in the past few weeks.

"Well... I'm listening," said Brody, taking another sip of beer and raising a brow.

I gazed out the large glass windows and thought for a moment. As I looked out at the skyscrapers towering nearby, I spoke about something I hadn't thought about in years. Something I had blocked out.

"Remember Danielle?" I asked.

"Danielle, *Danielle?* From college?" asked Brody, a note of surprise.

"Yeah."

"God, yes. That was a fucking mess." He shook his head.

"I know. I feel like ever since then..."

"Ever since she tried to completely screw you over?"

I gave him a look.

"Okay, okay," he said, putting his hands up.

He was right, though. Danielle was my girlfriend through college and I thought she was *the one*. We had been together for four years. She was beautiful, bubbly, and fun-loving. I really thought I had our lives all figured out. But then I found out she was cheating on me with the teaching assistant in one of her classes.

I was crushed. Pissed. Sick. She said I never had any time for her, which was partially true because I was trying to get my tech start-up off the ground while juggling my senior year. She had always said she supported me. She was rooting for me. But I guess she got tired or lonely. She found comfort with someone else.

I broke up with her and threw myself into my start-up even more. I had a vision for AI long before AI had even become what it is now. Some say, I was the founder of artificial intelligence. After graduation, my start-up got noticed. Major tech giants wanted to get their hands on it, but I refused. I never wanted to sell it. I wanted to *be* one of those major tech giants. By me holding onto it and the buzz surrounding it, the value shot up and I eventually landed where I am today.

I lost Danielle in the process, but I couldn't say I regretted it. Especially after what she did to me. Months after our breakup, when the buzz around my start-up becoming a full-fledged company was all over the press, she called me. She told me she was pregnant and that it was mine. I was shocked. We had broken up months ago.

I was scared to death, but I was also ready to step up and do whatever she needed. But Brody wasn't convinced. He said things weren't adding up and to be cautious. He insisted I take a paternity test. Danielle was pissed, but legally she had to allow me to.

It turned out, the baby wasn't mine. She was actually only a few weeks pregnant, so it couldn't possibly be my baby. I never found out who the father was. I didn't care. I wanted to get as far away from her as possible. To know that someone could lie and use someone for their own personal gain was scary, but when it was someone you once loved. That was a whole other level of fucked up.

"Well, since everything went down with Danielle, I feel like I've had a really hard time trusting people," I said.

"Rightfully so," said Brody.

"I thought I had blocked that part of my life out, but I think deep down it's always been there. Maybe that's why I haven't settled down yet. Maybe I used this whole playboy lifestyle as a way to protect myself. You know, never letting anyone get too close." I shrugged.

"Then what's my excuse?" Brody smirked.

"You're young. It's what you're supposed to do."

"And you're, what? A grandpa?"

I hesitated a moment before speaking again. "No, but I was going to be a dad... for real."

"What?" asked Brody skeptically.

"I was involved with someone for a few months. It started off as a one-night stand, but then she got pregnant."

"What are you talking about? When was this?" asked Brody, his voice jumping an octave.

"A few months ago. I never told anyone. Well, except Freddy."

"Freddy?!" Brody's voice raised an octave. "You told Freddy and not me?"

"I know. I just got scared. I'm your older brother. I should be a good influence..."

"Ha. Hardly." Brody laughed. "So, what happened?"

"I was scared at first. Scared shitless. Once I got past that, I felt like we could be the real deal. You know, the whole shebang. I was really starting to see myself as a dad."

"And you believed her? After everything..."

"Yeah, for some reason I did. I still do. But I messed it all up."

"Okay, then fix it."

"I can't. She overheard something I said that was misconstrued. It was bad. And then all this stuff with Kiera came out."

"So, that's why you were so pissed," said Brody, putting it all together.

I nodded.

"Well, I can explain it to her..."

"No," I shook my head. "It doesn't matter now. The baby is gone."

"What do you mean, gone?"

"I don't know. She either lost it or... took care of it."

"Wow..." said Brody softly.

"I've been really torn up about it."

"Well, it all makes sense now. Fuck. I'm so sorry, bro."

He put his hand on my back and we sat in silence for a moment.

"Baby or no baby, it sounds like you have feelings for this woman."

"Heart," I said.

"What?"

"That's her name."

"Fitting."

I laughed softly.

"Well, get Heart back. Just talk to her."

"I tried."

"When?"

"I had all these gifts sent to her apartment. Everything she could need for the baby. I even wrote her a check that would set her up nicely for a few years."

"I missed the part where you talked."

I gave Brody a questioning look.

"Money isn't everything, Daniel. There was a time you didn't have it. You used to have to actually use your words. It sounds like Heart needed to *hear* you."

I chewed on my cheek. Brody was right. I had tried to fix everything with money. I should have known Heart didn't want that. She was different, I knew that, so why had I treated her like everyone else?

Chapter 45

ADDISON

"Are you sure you want to go out with me tonight?" I asked Shelley over the phone.

I held the phone between my shoulder and ear while trying to shove my swollen feet into shoes that would give a little. So far, I had been unsuccessful.

"Of course. Whatever went down at work doesn't mean you and I can't still be friends," she said.

"You're the only one from that place who wants to even be associated with me," I said.

I held my breath as I tried a pair of black ballet flats, as if doing so would somehow help my foot slide in with ease. I felt ridiculous even going out to a bar at seven months pregnant, but I owed Shelley birthday drinks from all those months ago. She wanted to go to Bemelman's again.

While I had tried to get out of it or try to change the destination, she was insistent. I wasn't sure if I was ready for all the memories that would come with it. That night had changed the entire trajectory of my life.

"Don't let them get you down. They're just trying to save their asses with Brian, who is a complete asshole for letting you go."

I couldn't disagree with her.

Since I had left my job a few weeks ago, I had realized how much better off I was. It had been an adjustment and the significant decrease in pay had been a blow, but I was making it work. Thanks to Monica, I had been doing a few hours a day of freelance work for the publishing house she had set me up with. While I wasn't a writer, I knew enough about nonprofit work to make it seem like I was.

Working from home was a whole new world. I woke up later, which was a luxury now that I didn't have to make the train to Manhattan. I needed the extra hours in bed since the baby seemed to be running marathons every time I lay down and closed my eyes. It was practically impossible to get comfortable when it felt like someone was doing jumping jacks inside of me.

When I did wake up, I stayed in my pajamas. There was no need to dress up or try to look remotely presentable. I stayed in my favorite flannel pajama pants and a sports bra, my round belly on display as I made a pot of decaf coffee and fired up my laptop for the day.

It was the break I hadn't realized I needed after years of busting my ass at my old job. While the work was rewarding, I never felt like I received the recognition I deserved. Well, not until I landed the biggest donation we had ever had. But that was short-lived.

"I better get going if I'm going to meet you on time, Shell," I said, assessing myself in the mirror.

"Oh shit. Is it 6:30 already?" she asked frantically.

"Yes." I laughed.

Shelley was never known for her punctuality.

"I'll see you soon!"

I heard the phone click on the other line. I walked to the door and grabbed my purse from the small entryway table. Before I closed the door behind me, I looked around my apartment, which had now become baby central. Every time I looked at the beautiful gold crib, or the small clothing rack that was adorned with tiny onesies, my heart swelled. Baby's due date was getting closer every single day.

I was excited, but I would be lying if I said I wasn't scared. As much support as I received from Monica and the small amount of relief I had because of my new job, I knew I was in over my head. It would be so much easier to do this with a partner. With Daniel. While everything he had bought for the baby had been more than enough to bring new life into this world, I wanted so much more. I wanted the loving home that a baby needed. That a baby deserved.

It wasn't even just about the baby. *I* needed him. I missed him more than I liked to admit. I found myself Googling him or flipping through magazines as if I enjoyed the torturous words and pictures that the press published. It hurt, but at least I got to see him. At least I got to get a glimpse into his life.

The story about him and Kiera had died down, much to my relief. They were focusing more on his business deal with London, which I was proud of him for. I knew that his business deals were what he wanted to be known for.

I also realized how big the deal was, and maybe that I had expected too much from him that day in his office when I had showed up unexpectedly. Looking back, I should have been more understanding, now that I knew the kind of stress he must have been under. I had let my insecurities rear their ugly head. The ones that always told me that I wasn't enough. Maybe it's something my parents had ingrained in me when I started to make choices they didn't approve of.

I walked down the stairs. Actually, I more so waddled down. I noticed Edna's door was open and I knew I wasn't getting out of there without her striking up her usual curious conversation.

"Addison!" she called from the doorway.

I smiled at just how predictable she was. She stood at the door, stroking Beatrice in her arms.

"Hello, Edna," I said cheerfully.

I couldn't really be irritated with her. She was who she was. An old, lonely landlord who lived vicariously through the tenants of her building.

"You look very nice tonight. Hot date?"

"Oh, yes," I said sarcastically. "Everyone is lining up to take me out." I rubbed my bump and winked at her.

"You know...I haven't seen that handsome guy in the suit in a while," she commented.

"Neither have I," I replied with a shrug.

"I really thought you two might have something," she said.

"Oh?" I asked.

"I guess I was wrong." She sighed before nuzzling Beatrice.

So was I, I thought.

"You know, if you ever need anything. Just holler, okay? I absolutely love babies."

"Really?"

I was surprised. As old as Edna was, I never saw any children or grandchildren visit. She really was just the old cat lady. Or so I thought.

"Oh, yes. I have five grandkids, but they live across the country and I'm scared to fly. My daughters don't make it out to New York as much as I'd like. They're busy with their own lives. I get it..." She looked down at Beatrice and stroked her soft fur.

I couldn't help but feel bad for her.

"You can come visit us anytime," I said with a reassuring nod.

A hopeful looked passed through her eyes. "Thank you," she said softly.

I thought she might cry, but she just smiled and stepped back into her apartment, closing the door gently behind her.

As I rode the subway into Manhattan, I thought about the friends that would become the baby's family. They might not be blood, but they had a lot of love to give. That was more than my parents or anyone else would give.

When I walked into Bemelman's my eyes shifted toward the end of the bar where Daniel and I had sat all those months ago. I half expected him to be there. Sidled up on a barstool in a dark, expensive suit with whiskey in his hand. But he wasn't there. The empty seat just made it even more clear how vacant he was from my life.

"Addison!" said Shelley, waving me over from a nearby table.

I smiled and made my way over.

"Wow. You look fantastic." She stood and gave me a big hug. "How far along are you now?"

"Seven months," I said, taking a seat once she released me.

"Incredible."

I picked up my menu and scanned it quickly. I had already looked it over online and decided what I could afford, which was an appetizer. I made sure to eat a light dinner before I left. Since I wasn't drinking, I was saving money by not getting an expensive cocktail.

Shelley and I placed our orders and began catching up about work and everything that had been going on since I left. I was happy to know she had taken over my position. I couldn't think of anyone more deserving.

When our food arrived, she asked about my pregnancy, but never snooped as to who the father was. She was genuinely curious about symptoms and baby names and birth plans. While I still didn't know the half of it, it was nice talking about it with her. She was so non-judgmental.

After we paid our bill, Shelley excused herself to the restroom. I looked around the restaurant and let the memories flood in. The taste of that cosmopolitan on my tongue, my leg brushing against Daniel's, his eyes intent on me when he asked me back to his place. It was that night that changed everything. I glanced over at the corner of the bar once more, but this time there was someone in his seat. Someone I knew.

I did a double-take as I realized it was Kiera. She looked irritatingly stunning in a sapphire blue strappy dress. A dazzling smile was plastered on her face as she talked animatedly with the man in front of her. A man who wasn't Daniel. I sucked in a breath as she leaned in and whispered something in his ear, her hands straying dangerously far up his legs.

I couldn't believe what I was seeing. This was supposedly Daniel's fiancée—or soon to be. As much as I hated the idea of them being together, he didn't deserve this.

I suddenly felt angry. Erratic. Without really thinking, I picked up my water glass and walked over without a real plan in my head. As I approached, I heard her asking him back to her place and that's when I lost the little bit of control I still possessed. As I walked by her, I poured my drink down her back, pretending I had tripped.

She shot up out of her chair, the ice water running down her back and darkening the color of her dress to a dark blue. She whipped around and faced me, a look of discomfort and irritation on her face.

"What the hell?" she asked shrilly.

"Sorry about that," I said, biting back a smile as best as I could.

"Oh, my God, you fat freak! Did you do that on purpose?"

I realized she didn't recognize me from the one time we met in my office. I didn't expect her to remember a nobody like me, especially now that I was pregnant.

"Of course not. I don't even know you," I lied.

"My dress is ruined!" she said, her voice shrill.

"It's water," I said smugly.

"Get the hell away from me! I'll call security on you!"

Her date tried to calm her down, but she pushed him away as she searched for napkins and started to try to dry herself off. He looked at me sympathetically, and I realized I had gotten away with it. No one would ever blame a pregnant woman for being clumsy.

I noticed Shelley was back at our table and looking over curiously. I backed away from Kiera, who was having a full-on meltdown, and made my way over to Shelley to grab my purse that hung from the chair.

"What's going on?" asked Shelley, looking from me to where Kiera was still fuming.

"No idea." I shrugged innocently as I pulled her with me toward the front door, feeling victorious.

Chapter 46

DANIEL

"Margaret says you're not coming tonight," said Brody, peeping his head in my office.

"I didn't realize my secretary was such a narc." I rolled my eyes.

"Oh, come on. She has probably just been worried about you. Just like I was."

"Well, I'm fine now."

"Are you?" he asked, taking a seat in front of my desk and eyeing me curiously.

"I'm better than I was..."

It was partly true. Ever since I had opened up to Brody the other night and told him the truth about Heart and the baby, I felt like I was no longer holding everything in. It felt good to get everything out and not feel like I was going to explode at any moment. I realized I should have just told him in the very beginning. Despite being my younger and mostly immature brother, he was still a good confidant.

"I don't see why you don't just call her up..." said Brody.

"Who?"

"Addison. Heart. Whatever her name is."

"I can't."

"Why the hell not?" He looked at me, incredulous.

"She said she never wanted to see me again. Maybe the loss of the baby gave her the finality she needed."

"If you two had something between you, and it sounds like you did... Hell, you were going to have a baby together. Then it can't be over."

"Since when did you become such a hopeless romantic?" I raised an eyebrow.

"I don't know. Since I watched *The Notebook.*"

"When did *you* watch *The Notebook.*"

"Oh, I've watched it multiple times. I put it on when I have a girl over. I find it gets them in the mood." He wiggled his eyebrows.

"You're ridiculous." I laughed.

"What? It works. You should call up Heart and watch it together."

"Okay, we're done with this topic."

"Fine." He rolled his eyes. "But you're not off the hook for tonight. It's one of the—"

"Biggest charity events of the year," I finished sarcastically.

"Exactly."

"We say that about every fucking one."

I was all for charity, but I was tired of the endless events you had to go to in order to prove that you cared. I did enough behind the scenes and donated enough money. The ridiculous auctions and expensive dinners were just for show. By the time the event space was paid for, on top of the pricey champagne, caviar dinners, and waitstaff, what was really left for these organizations?

These things were just an excuse to buy new dresses and tuxedos and talk about anything but the cause. The only person who had ever seemed actually invested in the work was Heart. I admired her for it. I wondered if she had found another job where she could throw her passion into it, since I had cost her the last one.

"Okay, but you're the face of the company and one of the largest donors..." said Brody.

"Can you go? Please. Just this once. I don't want to deal with the whole red carpet thing and the schmoozing. Plus, I have no interest in running into Kiera."

"Yeah, I guess I kind of made a mess of that."

"You think?"

"Fine. But this is the last time I cover for your ass. Okay?"

"Thank you, bro."

He got up and stretched.

"I guess I better go pick up my tux and get ready. There's nothing like walking down the red carpet looking like a fucking penguin."

"I owe you."

"Yeah, yeah." He walked toward the door.

"Have fun," I called after him.

He gave me the finger before slipping out into the hallway.

I chuckled to myself as I looked out the window. I did feel a little guilty for making him pick up my slack again. The sun was beginning to set, casting an orange glow through my office. I closed my laptop and stood from my chair. I slipped my jacket on and walked down the hallway.

"Have a good evening, Mr. Jacobs," said Margaret, giving a little wave from her desk.

"You too, Margaret," I replied. "And just so you know. I'm fine. I don't need my little brother babysitting me."

She opened her mouth nervously, but no words came out. I immediately felt bad for calling her out. She was always so timid.

"It's okay, Margaret." I winked, trying to soothe her worries.

I knew she did it because she cared. I had thrown her a few curveballs over the past few months, like canceling important last-minute meetings and disappearing to Bora Bora.

"I'm so sorry, Mr. Jacobs," she said after me.

I gave her a little wave and stepped into the elevator.

On the ride home, I caught up on the news on my phone. At the top of the business page, I noticed my name. I clicked the link, hoping it was an article covering the latest developments with our London partner, but was disappointed to see it was really just entertainment news disguised as business.

The headline read: *Will Daniel Jacobs and Kiera Shipley Make Their Public Debut?*

I continued reading.

As reported, the two were getting steamy on the beaches of Bora Bora just weeks ago. While we haven't received any commentary from Jacobs' team, Shipley's publicist did release the following statement:

"The two are enjoying their reunion and excited for what the future holds."

I rolled my eyes and kept reading the bullshit in front of me.

The two were in a relationship years back, but broke up stating irreconcilable differences. While Shipley has married twice since then, Jacobs has continued enjoying the bachelor life. Will this be the second chance that will end in forever?

Only time will tell, but we are eager to see if the two show up at tonight's Angel Ball.

I closed the browser on my phone and slid my phone back in my jacket pocket. That was just another reason not to go tonight. Kiera would definitely be there. I heard she was back in town and she never missed an event to dress up and be seen.

The last thing I needed was the paparazzi to snap our photos and the press to put them together, while they spun whatever story they wanted.

Up in my apartment, I took a shower and slid on some flannel pajama pants and a Mets T-shirt. I ordered a burger and fries from Lucky's and flipped through the channels on TV for a movie to watch while I waited for my food to be delivered. I settled on an action movie and poured myself a glass of whiskey at the bar.

Four hours later, my stomach was full and my brain was comfortably fuzzy from the whiskey as the sequel to the first movie wrapped up. I checked the time on my phone. It was nearly 11 o'clock. I took the takeout containers to the kitchen and threw them in the trash, and then rinsed out my whiskey glass.

I was about to head to bed when my intercom buzzed. Who the hell was showing up now?

I hit the button.

"Hello?" I asked.

"Hi, Mr. Jacobs. There is a woman here to see you..." said the front desk attendant down in the lobby.

For a second I thought it might be Heart.

"Who is it?" I asked hopefully.

"Ms. Shipley," she said.

I sighed.

Half of me wanted to send her away, while the other wanted to make it perfectly clear to her that we were nothing. That we were never going to be. As if I hadn't tried that before.

"Send her up," I said reluctantly.

A few minutes later, the elevator doors opened and I saw Kiera standing there in a long champagne gown and a fur stole around her shoulders. Her neck was dripping in diamonds. She stepped off the elevator carefully in her strappy heels that she seemed unsteady in. *Probably tipsy from champagne,* I thought.

"Daniel," she said, spotting me sitting on the couch and not bothering to get up to greet her.

"Kiera," I said, my voice clipped.

She stepped down into the living room and stopped at the edge of the couch. She crossed her arms and pouted as she looked down at me. She looked ridiculous. Like a grown baby. I tried hard not to laugh.

"What is it Kiera?" I rolled my eyes.

"Where were you tonight?"

"Where was I supposed to be?" I asked innocently.

"The Angel Ball. Duh."

"Oh that..." I replied dryly.

"Yeah. *That.* We were supposed to be there together."

"I don't remember that agreement."

"You always go," she whined.

"I didn't feel like it tonight." I shrugged.

She sat down on the other end of the couch and removed her stole, revealing the top of her strapless dress. Her breasts looked like they were about to bust out. I shook my head. She would always try to do *this* to get what she wanted.

"I don't know why you're being so stubborn," she said, kicking off her heels and nuzzling her feet in my lap.

I gently lifted her ankles and pushed her aside.

"I don't think I'm the one who's being stubborn here," I replied, raising an accusing eyebrow.

"Everyone wants us to be together. Have you seen the press? They're gaga for us."

"We had our shot, Kiera. You and your beloved press need to let it go."

"Think about it, though. It would be good for your business."

"How so?"

She put her hands up dramatically, as if she were spelling out the words.

"New York's Most Eligible Bachelor is Finally Dropping His Playboy Reputation."

"Wow. Sounds riveting," I deadpanned.

"Who better than to do it with me?" She smiled.

She slid across the couch and leaned in, playing with the collar of my shirt before putting her lips against my neck. I pulled away quickly.

"Kiera, I don't know how to make it any more clear, but I don't want to be with you. There was a reason we didn't work out, and I have no interest in treading that same water again."

"I'm different now..."

"You're the same Kiera you've always been. Don't fool yourself."

"And what Kiera is that?" she asked.

"The one who likes to be pampered and spoiled and drunk and in all the papers."

"You used to like that Kiera..." she reminded me. "Enough to be with her for a few years, mind you."

"Well, I've changed. Plus, I've found someone else."

Her lips pressed into a hard line as her eyes shot to mine. "Excuse me?" she said.

"I've met someone else. Someone I want to settle down with, and I'm sorry, but it's not you."

"I don't believe you."

"It's true."

"Who the hell is she?" she asked, her voice rising.

"You don't know her," I lied.

Kiera did meet Heart that one time in the very beginning, but I doubted she remembered. The only people she remembered were the ones who could offer her something.

"I can't believe you've strung me along!" she yelled, standing up quickly.

"I haven't. If I have, I didn't mean to. I already told you that what happened in Bora Bora was a mistake, and I stopped it before it went too far."

"You will never find anyone like me," she said, snatching her stole from the couch and covering her shoulders.

That was true. I had found something better.

"You'll find someone, Kiera," I said gently.

"*Don't*," she yelled.

"I'm sure there is another billionaire out there. They say the third time's a charm."

"You are an asshole," she snapped pointedly.

I was, but I had to be if it meant she would finally get the hint.

She slipped on her shoes, wobbly on her feet, and strode quickly toward the elevators. I watched as she disappeared behind the doors and I breathed a satisfying sigh of relief. She was gone. And I hoped it was for good.

Chapter 47

ADDISON

"Baby looks really healthy. He or she is growing at a normal rate," said the tech as she glided the wand over my belly, the jelly cool against my skin.

I smiled as I looked at the baby on the screen. The nurse said it was safe for me to look given the position of the baby. Since I had decided not to find out the sex of the baby, the ultrasounds would become trickier. Today though, I was happy I got to see the baby.

I didn't know what made me want to wait to find out. I knew Monica so eager to know if it was going to be a girl or a boy. She was practically internally combusting with each appointment that passed and me still choosing not to find out. I just felt like the moment the doctor tells me if it's a boy or a girl will be something I treasure for always.

As I looked at the video on the monitor, the moving picture on the screen actually looked like a baby. I could see the nose and the lips and fingers and toes. It was so surreal. Every time I cried, but today I really cried. I had a little human who was growing and growing by the day and would soon be earthside.

"Wow," I whispered through tears.

"It's pretty surreal, isn't it?" The tech placed her hand on my shoulder and gave me a gentle squeeze.

"Very."

"I'm going to take a few photos and get those printed out for you, okay?"

I nodded and she began typing on the monitor and positioning the wand for clear photos. Soon, I had a new set of ultrasounds in my hands. I couldn't wait to hang them on the fridge and compare them to the last ones.

"Let's get you all cleaned up and then the doctor will see you." She reached for a paper towel and handed it to me before excusing herself from the room.

I wiped the clear jelly from my stomach and quickly got dressed. This was my first appointment alone. Monica usually came with me to all of them, but she had another meeting with her editor she couldn't miss. I didn't mind, of course. She had already done so much for me.

I heard a knock at the door.

"Come in," I said.

The nurse peeped her head in. "The doctor is ready for you."

I followed her down the hallway to an exam room and hoisted myself onto the exam table. A few moments later, the doctor came in.

"Ms. Heartly. It's great to see you again." She smiled warmly before looking down at her papers.

"Good to see you too, Dr. Halquist."

"How is everything going? How are you feeling?"

"A little restless at night, but I just try to go to bed early to make up for the lack of sleep. Or I take naps during the day."

"Ahh, you have a little night owl in there, don't you?"

"More like a kangaroo."

The doctor laughed. "Well, it looks like baby is doing just fine in there. How are your stress levels?"

"Better. I'm working from home and it's a less demanding job."

"Good. After the scare you had last month, I want to make sure you're taking care of yourself."

"I am," I assured her.

"Well, I'm going to have you lie back and I'll give baby's heart a listen and do some measurements of your belly."

I nodded as I lay back on the table.

Dr. Halquist took the doppler and held it against my stomach, moving it until she located the baby's heartbeat. We listened together for a quiet moment before she gave a nod of approval.

"Sounds great in there. Now, let's measure you."

She walked her fingers up the sides of my stomach, causing me to squirm slightly.

"Sorry, I know it tickles," she said.

She then walked her fingers up to the top of my abdomen and pressed gently.

"Baby is measuring right on track," she said, jotting a few notes on her clipboard.

"Thank you, doctor."

"Do you have any questions for me?"

"No, not today."

"Well, then head to the front and we'll get you checked out, okay?"

"Thank you."

I watched her slip out of the room. I felt so grateful to have her as my doctor and the nurses on staff here. It was night and day from that nightmare of an office in Manhattan. That seemed so long ago. I was thankful Freddy had recommended someone else. Someone I felt like I could trust and not feel judged by.

I lifted myself from the exam table and walked out into the hallway. At the front desk, I let them know that I would have a change of insurance soon. I was dreading the day when I would have to pay out of pocket for these appointments. I needed to find a new insurance company quickly, as I only had until the end of the month with my benefits from my old job.

I thanked the girl at the front desk and walked out of the office, staring at the new ultrasounds in my hands. As I smiled down at them I walked directly into someone, and the photos floated to the ground.

"I'm so sorry," I said, kneeling down to pick up the photos.

"Heart?"

My heart leaped to my throat as I quickly looked up to see Daniel towering over me.

"Daniel," I said softly, not really believing what I was seeing.

He stood there with a dumbfounded look on his stupidly handsome face. The same face I had imagined for so many nights over the past month, trying to hold onto every detail. Every little expression that I considered was just for me.

"What are you doing here?" I asked, looking around.

"I'm here to meet Freddy for lunch," he said.

Of course. I should have known there was a chance I would run into him here one day. Freddy worked in the same office, and while I hadn't seen him, I felt foolish for thinking I could avoid him or his best friend forever.

Daniel kneeled down to help me, reaching for the photos.

"What are you doing—" he started to ask.

He paused as he looked at the ultrasounds scattered on the floor. His eyes floated up to my round belly. I sucked in a breath as I watched him process what he was seeing. The lie that was crumbling between us.

"Wait... are you..." His brows furrowed as he looked down at the ultrasound in his hand. He ran his hand over the image of the baby. It was such a tender motion. My heart felt like it might break in two.

I quickly snatched it back and struggled as I tried to stand up. He stood up swiftly and held out his hand. I reluctantly took it before he pulled me to my feet. The same electric feeling I always felt passed through my whole body. Once I was steady, I pulled my hand from his and looked down at the floor.

I had been caught in a lie. A lie that was so big and so painful that I didn't know what to do in this moment. I couldn't bring myself to look at him, even though the only thing I had wanted was to see him over the past month. I had missed him so much and now he was here in front of me, but this was far from a happy reunion.

"Heart... you're still pregnant," he murmured, looking at me intently.

"Yeah, I am."

"But you said..."

"I lied, okay?"

He looked taken aback and I saw a flash of pain in his eyes. Pain I had caused.

"But why?"

"Because I just wanted you to go away," I blurted out.

He remained silent.

"It was the only way for you to move on with your life. I know you never wanted this." I rubbed my belly.

"You don't know what I want," he said sharply. "Do you even know what I've been going through? Ever since you told me the baby was gone..."

I kicked at the ground. I knew it was a horrible thing that I had done, but I never knew the full damage it might have caused. Until now.

"I've been tearing myself apart, thinking of all the things I should have done and the pain you went through. Heart, I've been a wreck. And here you are..."

"You and I were never going to work. You know that."

"Do I?" he asked.

I looked away. "Don't do that. Don't act like we were going to be some happy little family."

"I wanted that, Heart. I told you I did. I told you I was in this. For you. For the baby."

His words were everything I wanted to hear, but then I thought of what he had said at the charity event. And about the tabloids with Kiera. I couldn't let myself fall for it, even though I so badly wanted to.

"Look...*this*"—I rubbed my bump—"doesn't change anything."

"What are you talking about? This changes *everything.*"

"I can do this on my own, Daniel."

"But I don't want you to." He looked at me sympathetically.

"It's not really up to you."

"I'm the father. Of course, it's up to me."

"Oh, now you want to be a father?" I snapped.

He closed his eyes and looked pained, but only for a moment. He then released a slow breath through his nose before looking at me. His blue eyes piercing.

"I'll admit I was shocked at first. There were things I didn't handle well. I'm so sorry for everything, Heart. But you have to understand that what you overheard was a lie, and one I regret every day. No business deal is worth lying about who I am, or hurting you in the process. You have to believe me."

His voice was pleading as his eyes searched mine. It was so hard not to get lost in him. The little spray of wrinkles around his eyes. The iciness of his gaze. The slight stubble along his sharp jawline. The way he looked at me like that. It was all too much.

"And so what if I did believe you?" I asked. "What about your new fiancée? I don't think she would be happy to know that her soon-to-be husband has a baby on the way."

He sighed. "She's not my fiancée."

"Really? Because you looked awfully cozy on the beach."

"It's not what it looked like."

I laughed sarcastically. "Please, explain how you ended up at the same resort halfway around the world at the same time."

"It's a long story..."

"*Of course* it is." I rolled my eyes. "You know, you seem to have an excuse for every little thing, Daniel. I'm surprised you haven't used them all up yet."

"I know I've lost your trust, but if you would just hear me out—"

"I'm good. Really. I've heard and seen enough."

I slipped the ultrasound photos in my purse and walked toward the door. I heard his footsteps behind me. His hand slipped around my arm gently, pulling me to a stop. I whipped my head around and he lowered his forehead to mine. For a moment, I thought he was going to kiss me, and wondered if I had enough strength to stop him.

"Please, don't do this again. Please, Heart," he begged.

"It's for the best. Now you can live the life you wanted before you met me," I whispered.

I pulled away from his grasp and pushed open the doors, sucking in a deep breath outside in the sunshine. How many times would I have to say goodbye to this man? And how did it hurt more and more every single time?

I hailed a cab and quickly clambered inside as Daniel ran after me. I sat there stoically as the car pulled away from the curb, leaving him behind.

Chapter 48

DANIEL

I watched as the yellow cab drove away with Heart and our baby inside. She never once looked back, even as I slapped my hand against the window as the car pulled away from the curb. There wasn't a cab to follow her and Armand had gone to lunch. I had no choice but to watch her go.

I couldn't believe it. I couldn't believe I had run into her. Outside of her OB office, nonetheless. It was the last place I expected to see her again, since she would have no business being there. But it turned out, she did.

Our baby was alive.

I felt like I was dreaming when I turned around and saw her. She was as beautiful as ever, if not more. She wore a white dress that hugged her bump snuggly. Her hair seemed longer as it fell around her face, her makeup-less skin glowing. Only she would be able to get more beautiful the more pregnant she became.

She still smelled the same intoxicating way. It took everything for me not to pull her into my arms. The only thing that made me realize she was real was when I offered her my hand and she took it. That same electric feeling ran up my arm before she quickly pulled away, breaking the connection and bringing us back to the reality that we were there together again. And she was still pregnant.

Pregnant. The word echoed in my head as I watched the cab turn the corner. This time I had gone after her, quickly following her as she fled from the office. I didn't want her to get away again, but for being pregnant she was quick. It felt like a scene from a movie where I was chasing after the cab down the streets of New York.

Now, standing here on the sidewalk, I felt like I was having déjà vu from the last time she had left me and said she never wanted to see me again. I had felt helpless then, after causing her to lose her job. But now, I didn't know how to feel. I was hurt. Angry. Sad. Still helpless.

"What are you doing out here?" I heard Freddy ask behind me.

"Heart..." I said softly.

"What?" he asked, confused, as if he wasn't sure he heard me correctly.

"Heart was here."

"Really?"

"Why didn't you tell me she's still pregnant?" I whipped around to face him.

"What? She's still pregnant?" The look on his face was pure shock.

I realized he had no idea. I nodded.

"She was just leaving her appointment. Seven months, if I'm counting correctly."

"I, honest to God, had no idea, Daniel," he replied, shaking his head. "You know how it is. We're always coming and going with labor and delivery. Either here or at the hospital. Plus. we don't discuss our patients with other doctors."

"Yeah," I said understandingly.

"Wow. Just wow," he murmured.

"I can't believe she lied to me," I shook my head.

She had so badly wanted nothing to do with me that she came up with a lie so deceitful. For as good and honest Heart was as a person, I realized how much I had hurt her for her to go through that length to end whatever we had. It damn near broke my heart.

Freddy put his hand on my back as I stared down the block, willing the yellow cab to turn back around the corner with Heart inside. I knew it was wishful thinking. She was gone.

"Why don't we get out of here and go to lunch?" asked Freddy. "We can talk more there."

"Okay." I nodded.

"Where do you want to go? You choose."

"Ocean Prime?" I suggested.

"My man!" He slapped me on the back and we began walking the few blocks to the restaurant.

We stepped through the large glass doors and were met by the hostess, who seemingly recognized us. She gave us a warm smile and stood up a little straighter.

"Freddy," she said, opening her arms wide. "It's been awhile."

"I know, sweetheart. Been busy delivering babies."

She giggled before looking to me. "Mr. Daniels," she nodded and gave me a shy smile.

"Hello," I said.

"Table for two?" she offered.

"Yes, please. Usual spot if you have it," said Freddy, looking toward the window.

"You got it." She grabbed two menus and gestured for us to follow her.

Freddy's eyes fell exactly where I expected as her hips swished in a tight skirt. I rolled my eyes at how obvious he was and nudged him with my elbow.

"What?" he asked, oblivious.

"She's like twenty-one."

"I'm just looking," he whispered with a sly smile.

"Here we are," said the hostess, pulling our chairs out slightly.

We both sat and she handed us our menus.

"Your server will be right with you," she said before walking away.

Freddy's eyes followed.

"So, how is Virginia?" I asked, breaking his focus.

Freddy sighed heavily. "Everything was going great. Really damn good. I mean, you met her. She was a firecracker."

"She definitely kept up with you," I recalled.

"Until she couldn't…"

"Uh-oh. What happened?"

"She got tired of the doctor life and me being on call at every hour of the night. It's not like I can predict when a baby will be born. I thought she knew what she signed up for."

"I'm sorry, man," I said.

"I just can't stop thinking about her. I thought she really might be the one. After we went to dinner with you and…"

"You can say her name," I said.

"Heart. After that dinner, I realized how well she fit into my life. It felt like she had always been there."

"Well, maybe it's not over yet. I wouldn't give up so easily," I suggested.

"Look at us," mused Freddy. "Who have we become?"

"A bunch of old softies," I muttered.

He laughed as our server came and asked for our drink order. I ordered an old-fashioned, and Freddy ordered a Coke. It was still the afternoon and there was a possibility he would be delivering a baby in the next couple of hours. I, on the other hand, had nothing that serious going on.

"So, tell me about Heart…" he started, taking a sip of his Coke and looking at me intently.

I sighed and looked down in my drink. "I can't believe she still has the baby. That was a double shock for me today. Seeing her, and then seeing her still pregnant."

"Why did she lie?" asked Freddy. "That's kind of fucked up."

"I must have really hurt her. I'm not exactly good at this whole relationship thing, you know."

"That's an understatement," said Freddy with a grin.

I rolled my eyes at him.

"The whole time I feel like I've been saying the wrong things. Doing the wrong things."

"That can't be entirely true. Hell, she let you get her pregnant. You must have done something right."

"When I met her for the first time, something in me told me I had to have her. I used the usual 'Daniel Jacobs' charm I always do. It was never meant to go past a one-night stand."

"But then..." Freddy started.

"The baby came along," I said.

"But I saw you two together at that dinner. Baby or no baby, there was something there. Even Virginia commented on it at the end of the night. She said the two of you were like magnets. I would have to agree. I've never seen you like that with any woman. Not even with..."

"Kiera?" I muttered.

"Yeah. What's going on with that, anyway?"

"It's over. For good. I was harsh, but I think she finally got the hint."

"So, she won't be showing up here in a hot pink bikini?" asked Freddy with amusement as he looked toward the door.

"Ugh, don't remind me." I took another sip of my drink. "Heart saw the tabloids."

"Who didn't?" Freddy shrugged.

"It only made things more complicated. She thinks we are really engaged or something. I just wish she would listen to me..."

Freddy thought for a moment as he studied me.

"What?" I asked, raising an eyebrow.

"When was the last time you *actually* talked?" asked Freddy.

"We talked all the time..."

"I mean about your relationship."

I started to say something and then stopped. Freddy had a point. Heart and I never really talked about us. Never established what we were. If things got tough, we would either fight or fuck, and it never led us to any sort of resolution.

"I guess we never really did," I admitted.

"Why?" asked Freddy curiously. "Clearly, this girl means something to you."

"Maybe, that's why. I don't know how to do this. I haven't been in a relationship since Kiera and that was all so surface level. I look back and wonder if the years we were together were all just part of one big publicity stunt. We never shared anything really *real,* you know?"

"Not surprising. It's Kiera. But you both were young and she was fun. Always up for a good time. It's what you needed at that time." Freddy shrugged.

"Heart is different, though."

"So, are you."

"How do I get her back?" I asked.

"Well, what have you done in the past?"

I thought for a moment.

"Let me guess," he started with a shake of his head. "You bought her extravagant gifts."

"They were for the *baby*," I said defensively.

"Daniel, I know your intentions are pure. But that's what you've always done. Dresses from Bloomingdales. Jewelry from Tiffany's. Now, apparently cribs from Nordstrom. Different, but still the same."

"It's what's worked." I shrugged.

"On *other* women. You, yourself, just said that Heart is different."

She was. She really was, and I had just let her get away again.

"So?"

"So, try something different."

"Like?"

"Oh, I don't know...why don't you try *talking* to the girl."

"She won't give me the chance."

"You haven't tried."

I thought back to when I would make the drive out to Brooklyn every morning just to possibly have the chance to ride with her back to Manhattan. It had been a risk showing up like that with cold herbal tea in my hand, but she had agreed. Maybe it really was that simple.

"You have to stop trying to buy her, and start trying to earn her," said Freddy.

"Holy shit," I said, looking at Freddy in surprise.

His eyes widened. "That *was* pretty good," he admitted.

"You're like Dr. Phil or something. Are you sure you're in the right profession?"

We both laughed.

Freddy was right, though. I had been going about this whole thing with Heart all wrong.

She wasn't like the other women I had dated in the past, if you could even call it that. I needed to start treating her differently. That meant actually talking, and not deflecting with sex. That meant showing up, and not sending gifts.

I had to earn her trust back, which I knew wouldn't be easy, but I had to try. It wasn't just because she was still pregnant with our baby. I missed her as a person. The past few months had been hell not having her in my life.

The rest of my lunch with Freddy, we enjoyed oysters and steak and lobster. We didn't talk any more about relationships or Virginia or Heart. We were both tuckered out from matters of the heart. Things we weren't used to.

Instead, we talked about work and the stock market and the usual things, but the whole while I was thinking about Heart. How I could win her back. The right way. I knew it would take time. Something big. But I was going to do it. I had to.

Chapter 49

ADDISON

When the cab dropped me off at a subway station a few blocks away, I walked down the stairs, still shaking from seeing Daniel at the doctor's office. I couldn't afford a cab ride back to Brooklyn, but it was the quickest getaway I could find to escape him. Part of me wanted to stay. To hear all the excuses he would muster up and the sweet words he was so smooth at delivering.

But the other part of me doubted everything, and it caused me to flee. I had heard him say he never wanted to be a father with such confidence, and while he had an excuse to say it, it sounded all too convincing. And then there was Kiera. I had seen the photos. I had read the tabloids. I had done a deep dive into their relationship when I was suffering from pregnancy insomnia the other night. It was stupid, really. I supposed I just wanted to torture myself more.

She had been his only real relationship in recent years, and that said something right there. There must have been something special about her for him to commit to her for those couple of years. I looked through all the press photos. All the paparazzi photos. She looked like a damn supermodel in every single one, even the caught off guard ones. And he looked like a GQ model right next to her. They looked perfect together. It was no wonder the public was rooting for them.

I realized as I scrolled through the photos that I would never fit into his world. As if I didn't know before. What I realized even more was that a baby would never fit into his world. It was a harsh realization to have at three in the morning when the baby was doing somersaults in my stomach.

Then to see him today, looking every bit his best self in a custom suit that hugged him just right and those damn icy blue eyes boring into me as he realized I had lied straight to his face. It was too much. I started to cry right there on the subway steps, people busily passing by me and too concerned with their next destination to care about the crying pregnant woman.

I didn't care. I didn't want anyone to notice me as I grieved all that could have been with the man I had once again left on the sidewalk. The driver had looked concerned in the rearview mirror, which was all I could look at as Daniel ran after the cab, his hand against the window. I felt bad for leaving him in such a state of desperation, but I had to.

I thought about his muffled voice through the window, yelling my name. The name that I only ever let people close to me call me. He had once been that person, but now the word "Heart" sounded so sad on his tongue. It made me cry even more.

The stairs were getting more crowded as people walked up and down them, bumping into me as they went. I had to get moving. I wiped my tears away and took a step down toward the platform. Suddenly I felt unsteady on my feet. I reached for the railing to steady myself. The stairs in front of me looked as though they were warped, moving in and out. People moved in swift blurs around me.

I gripped the railing tightly and blinked a few times, trying to get my focus back, but it was no use. My legs felt weak underneath me, as if I had been sitting on them for hours and now they had fallen asleep. I let out a little gasp as I slid to the floor.

People were starting to notice me now. I wasn't just some emotional pregnant woman. I was in trouble. I felt dizzy and out of breath.

"Ma'am, are you okay?" asked a man in a business suit, crouching down next to me.

"I-I don't know," I stammered, still gripping the railing as if it were the only thing holding me here on this planet.

"Can we get some help over here?" he yelled over his shoulder.

I didn't want to make a scene.

"Oh, that's not necessary," I said, trying to get to my feet and failing.

"You stay right there," he said, putting his hand on my shoulder.

"I need some help," he called again.

A woman came down and crouched next to him, looking at me worriedly. She looked like she was a server at the nearby 50s themed diner. This must have looked like quite a scene to everyone around us. Like something out of a movie.

"How far along are you, honey?" she asked.

"Seven months," I said.

"Are you having contractions?"

"No," I said, shaking my head. "I just feel..."

I then keeled over and threw up right between the two of them. They both quickly jumped away before looking at each other worriedly.

"We're going to get you to a hospital," said the woman. "Help me lift her."

The man and the woman wrapped their hands under my arms and hoisted me to my feet, guiding my arms around their shoulders. We walked up the few steps back to the sidewalk, and the man quickly hailed a cab. They both helped me inside, the woman following in behind me. The man checked his watch and looked slightly perplexed.

"I can take her from here," said the woman assuredly.

He nodded and gave a little wave as she closed the door behind her.

"Please take us to the nearest hospital," said the woman urgently.

I felt like I was having déjà vu from my last trip to the hospital after I flew home from Pittsburgh, except this time I wasn't having contractions. I just couldn't catch my bearings. Everything seemed to be blurring in and out, and breathing felt like a task on a to-do list that I couldn't quite check off no matter how hard I tried to get to it.

"What's your name, sweetie?" asked the woman.

She was probably old enough to be my mother.

"Addison," I replied, holding my belly woozily. "You?"

"Sandra. You're going to be just fine, Addison," she said, taking my hand and giving it a squeeze.

"Thank you, Sandra. Can you call my friend? Her name is Monica," I said, reaching for my purse.

"I'll get that for you," she said. "You just rest."

She reached over and grabbed my purse for me, searching for my phone. I quickly typed in my password for her and she scrolled through my contacts to Monica's name. I closed my eyes as the cab weaved through the traffic of Manhattan.

"Hi, Monica?" asked Sandra.

She waited for a reply.

"Yes, this is Sandra. I'm with your friend Addison. We are on our way to the hospital. Can you meet us there?"

There was a brief silence as Sandra listened. I could hear Monica's frantic voice on the other line.

"No, no. Everything is fine. I think she's just a little out of sorts, but I think it's best she see a doctor."

Sandra gave me a reassuring smile.

"Yes, yes. I'll text you the hospital once we get there."

She hung up.

"Thank you," I said. My mouth felt dry and tasted sour from throwing up.

Ten minutes later, we were pulling up to the hospital. Sandra paid the cab driver, even though I protested. She waved me off and walked me inside.

"I'll text your friend which hospital we ended up at," she said as we walked to the front desk.

Sandra explained what had happened and the nurse brought over a wheel-chair, helping me sit down.

"We are going to take her up to triage and get her check out," said the nurse.

I looked up at Sandra gratefully. "Thank you so much. Please let me repay you for your kindness," I said.

She waved me off. "Oh please, sugar. I believe in paying it forward. You just get better, okay? For you and that precious baby."

I nodded, feeling teary-eyed.

"I better get going. My shift starts soon." She bent down and gave me a quick hug before walking toward the door.

The nurse wheeled me toward the elevators and we rode up to triage, where she found me a room. She helped me into a hospital gown and got me settled in a bed where she hooked me up to the machines. The same one as last time, although I wasn't having contractions. She brought me some water and said she would be back.

I lay back in the bed and closed my eyes. I must have dozed off because I soon woke up to a knock at the door. Monica quickly strode in and her eyes took me in, a worried expression on her face.

"You have to stop doing this to me," she said, putting her hands on her hips.

"I'm sorry," I said. "I don't know what happened. I ran into Daniel and then it was like my body went into some sort of shock."

"Excuse me? Daniel?"

"He was at the OB office to meet his friend. I literally ran right into him and then he saw all this." I motioned to my belly.

"Jesus, Heart."

"I know," I said softly.

"What a mess. This is exactly what the doctor told you to avoid. All this stress isn't good for you."

"Clearly," I said, gesturing to the machines and my hospital gown.

Monica took a seat beside me and reached for my hand. We sat there and I told her everything that had happened with Daniel. How I had to tell him the truth and how he had run after the cab.

"Girl, you're like a walking, talking book just waiting to be written," she said, wide-eyed.

"Tell me about it," I muttered.

"Which, by the way, there's something I want to talk to you about…"

There was a knock at the door and the doctor walked in.

"Hello, I'm Doctor Patel. I realize we don't have any intake information for you yet, but I will have some sent up. What's your name, miss?"

"Addison Heartly."

"And you are…" She eyed my belly. "Seven months pregnant?"

"Yes. Just over," I said in amazement.

She nodded knowingly.

"It looks like your blood pressure took quite a drastic drop leading to a dizzy spell and the nausea. Have you eaten enough today?"

"Yes, plenty," I said, before listing off everything I ate.

"Good. And how are your stress levels?"

Monica gave me a pointed look.

"Not so good lately," I admitted.

"It's not the first time she's been in the hospital, doc," said Monica, crossing her arms.

"I see," said Doctor Patel. "Well, I'm sure your doctor has already told you, but this stress is not good for you, and especially not good for the baby. You need to get it under control."

"Yes, doctor."

"I'd like to keep you here overnight just to be sure everything is okay."

"Okay," I said softly.

I felt guilty for the craziness of my life because of how it could be potentially harming the baby. It wasn't like I asked to lose my job or run into Daniel, but I couldn't help but feel like everything was my fault.

The doctor gave me a reassuring smile before slipping out of the room.

"Heart..." started Monica.

"I know, okay?" I said, my eyes watering.

I didn't need another lecture when I was already feeling bad enough.

"Okay." She put her hands up and backed off.

We stayed silent for a few moments.

"What were you wanting to talk to me about?" I asked, remembering our conversation from before.

"Well...I kinda started writing a book that's loosely based on your life lately..."

I sat up in the hospital bed and looked at her curiously.

"Please don't be mad," she blurted out.

I laughed. "I'm not mad. I want to hear some of it."

"Well, lucky for you"—Monica leaned over and pulled out her laptop out of her bag—"I have some of it right here."

I settled back in the bed and she began reading the first few chapters. I closed my eyes and listened to her storytelling, which made my life sound so much more magical than it really was. She really knew how to write.

When she was done reading, I opened my eyes and looked at her.

"How does it end?" I asked softly.

"I'm still waiting to find out." Monica winked.

Chapter 50

DANIEL

"How does it feel to be an old man?" asked Brody as we strode down the sidewalk to our usual coffee spot.

The air was crisp and the leaves were starting to change to shades of burnt orange and warm brown. It was just another reminder of how much time had passed. Another reminder that the baby was growing and readying itself to enter the world, and I would have no part in it. It was shattering.

"Hello? Earth to Daniel," said Brody, trying again.

"Sorry. Uh, it feels good." It came out more as a question.

"Oh, come on. You've gotta do better than that."

"What do you want from me, Brody?" I snapped harsher than I intended to.

He put his hands up defensively, as if to ease me before looking ahead. We still had another block to go and on every corner I tried not to look for Heart. Every long-haired brunette made my head turn, until I realized they were missing her round stomach.

How many kicks had I missed? How many sleepless nights had I failed to soothe Heart back to sleep? How many doctor appointments did she have to go to alone? Had she found out if it was a boy or a girl? So many questions that I felt I would never have answered.

Time was passing too quickly and my birthday was just another cruel reminder of that.

"Sorry," I muttered. "Thirty-four just feels..."

"Old." Brody smirked.

"You're a real ass." I shook my head, as I finally gave him the laugh he was chiding me for.

He smiled as he pulled open the door to the coffee shop. The warm air and smell of freshly roasted coffee beans wafted through the doorway, welcoming us in. The tables were crammed with people. Men on their laptops. Women on their phones. Typical Manhattan. We stood in the short line and ordered two Americanos to go.

"It's his birthday," said Brody to the barista, nudging me.

I rolled my eyes.

"Well, happy birthday," she said with a warm smile. "This one is on the house."

"Thank you," I said as I watched her write our names on our cups, adding a few birthday doodles to mine.

I left a twenty in the tip jar and followed Brody to the end of the counter to wait for our drinks. It was early. We still had about thirty minutes before we needed to start the workday at the office. It was Brody's idea to go for coffee beforehand.

"So," he said, eyeing me cautiously as we waited.

"What?" I asked, raising an eyebrow.

I knew that look. That tone. He wanted something, but was afraid to say what.

"Since it's your birthday...Freddy and I..."

"Nope." I shook my head.

"You didn't even let me finish."

"I don't need to. I have plans tonight. My couch. Pizza. Beer. The last thing I want to do is go out and party with you two."

Brody groaned. "Come on, man. You never go out anymore. You're so mopey. In fact, Freddy and I call you that. You're like the eighth fucking dwarf, except instead of being holed up in a cottage with a hot chick, you're holed up in your penthouse."

"I like it." I shrugged.

The barista called my name and slid our drinks across the counter. Brody grabbed his and I wrapped my hand around the paper cup covered in balloons and confetti. A slightly embarrassing display that I was one year older.

Birthdays never bothered me before. I enjoyed the parties. The attention. Every year seemed to get better and better. I felt like I had my life figured out. I could have retired five years ago. Hell, maybe even ten. To everyone else, I'm sure I looked like I had it made. I thought so too at one point.

But then I met Heart and everything got flipped on its head.

I had a taste of what a real relationship was like. I saw a glimpse of what my future could possibly look like as a father. While it had scared me shitless at first, now it was all I could think about. Now my life didn't seem so full.

"What if we just keep it low key?" asked Brody, taking a sip of his coffee.

He wasn't letting up. Knowing him, he already had the night booked and planned. This coffee date was just his way of trying to get me to go. Freddy probably put him up to it.

I looked up at the ceiling, exasperated. "You're not going to let this go, are you?" I asked.

He shook his head. "Fine. Low key. Just the boys. Whatever you probably already have planned, cancel it. I don't need strippers popping out of cakes or bottle service girls coming home with us."

"Aww. But it was so fun last year," he chided.

I shot him a look. "Fine." He rolled his eyes and headed toward the door as I trailed behind him, feeling annoyed.

The workday was filled with mostly meetings and going over the final designs for the launch of our product with London. It wouldn't be out until next year, but we had to finalize the colors and fonts for our newest AI software. The tech magazines were already talking about it, since we purposefully leaked bits of information. Our plan worked, and the hype was already building around it. It was the most anticipated release in the tech world.

After the final meeting of the day, I sat back in my chair and sighed triumphantly. We had finally nailed down the final look of everything, and come to a solid agreement with our associates in the UK. Not an easy feat when there was an ocean and a drastic time change between us.

Brody rolled in a bar cart with a bottle of champagne on ice and two glasses.

"What's this?" I asked, leaning back in the chair of the conference room and eyeing him curiously.

"Just a little celebration."

He popped the cork from the champagne, the sound echoing through the empty room. He was careful not to let it spill on the floor or the conference room table as he poured two generous glasses before handing me one.

He raised his glass.

"To London. Our biggest launch ever. And to you, brother. One of the youngest billionaires in the country, even with it being your birthday."

He really was trying. I couldn't fault him for that.

"Thank you, bro," I said, raising my glass to his. "I couldn't have done it without you."

We both downed the champagne and I looked around the large conference room where we had just led a meeting with about twenty people. I never thought my life would be where it is now. I should have been proud. I was, but the nagging hole in my heart felt like it was pulsing.

"Let's cut out of here early. The night awaits," said Brody with a sly smile.

"Low key," I reminded him.

"I know, I know." He waved me away.

We had another glass of champagne before leaving it with Margaret at the front desk. She looked at us like we were crazy.

"Work is done for the day," I said, handing her a glass.

She took it carefully from my hands, looking from me to Brody as if we were playing some sort of trick on her.

"Birthday boy's orders," said Brody, pointing a playful finger at her.

When we got downstairs, Freddy was waiting outside a limo.

Low key my ass, I thought.

"Happy birthday, Daniel!" he said loudly, patting me on the back and ushering me inside the limo.

There was another bottle of champagne waiting and thankfully no women in sight. I settled into the seat as Freddy and Daniel clambered in. As the limo pulled away from the curb, Freddy popped open the bottle. It was even more expensive than the last.

"Where are we going?" I asked hesitantly, taking a full glass from him.

"Nobu to start."

"And then?" I asked, raising an eyebrow.

"Calm down," said Freddy innocently. "It's chill. Just us boys."

I nodded and took a sip of champagne.

Freddy wasn't lying. We did go to Nobu and had a private room just for us. We ordered a round of sake and practically everything on the menu. When I didn't think I could eat any more, the server arrived with a small cake with a sparkler candle lit, emitting sparks as she brought it over. Freddy and Brody both sang the birthday song, horribly might I add, and for the first time in many birthdays, I actually made a wish.

After I blew out the candle, Freddy asked, "What did you wish for?"

I gave him the best smile I could muster up and lied about making any wish at all.

After Freddy paid the bill, we got back in the limo. I would have been perfectly content with going home then, but Freddy and Brody had other plans. On the drive, I expected the limo to pull up outside a club, but instead it pulled up outside a pool hall. I looked from Freddy to Brody shocked.

"What?" Brody shrugged, knowing full well I was impressed.

"Thank you," I said.

We headed inside and found a seat at the bar. It was dimly lit and not too crowded. Just the kind of low key thing I wanted.

Freddy ordered a round of beers and Brody found a nearby open table for us to play. I grabbed two pool sticks and began chalking them.

"Cut throat?" I asked, handing them their sticks.

"You're on," said Freddy.

After we played a few rounds, I leaned against the table and took a long sip of beer. I could feel Freddy and Brody's eyes on me, as if they had something to say.

"Out with it," I said, putting my beer down on the edge of the table.

They look startled, like they had been caught.

"We're just worried about you," said Brody with a shrug.

"I'm fine," I said.

"Are you?" asked Freddy.

I thought for a moment before letting out a sigh. I had been shutting them out for months, and where had that got me? Being alone with my thoughts wasn't getting me anywhere. In fact, it was driving me crazy.

"I never thought I would say this," I started. "But I really want to be a dad."

Brody looked at me wide-eyed and took a long sip of beer.

"I know. Weird, right?" I said.

"Nah," offered Freddy.

"I had never really thought about it, but then once there was a possibility and that possibility was ripped away from me, it's all I can think about," I said, grabbing the eight ball and rolling it across the table mindlessly.

"Well, you still have time," offered Freddy. "It will happen one day when you meet the right one."

"I already did," I said softly.

"Right..." Brody's voice trailed off as he stuffed his hands in his pockets.

We didn't talk about this kind of stuff. Not because we didn't want to, it's just neither of us had been in any sort of relationship in a long time. Not one that was serious enough to have parenthood on the table.

"What are you going to do about it?" asked Freddy, raising an eyebrow.

I looked at him curiously.

"She's still pregnant with your baby. You're obviously crazy about her. Maybe you can have it all."

"I want to..." I admitted. "I just don't even know where to start."

"Well, let's get another round of beers and we can come up with something," said Brody, slapping me on the back.

I laughed as I followed him to the bar. I really should give my friend and my brother more credit. For the first time in a while, I felt hopeful. Like maybe my birthday wish might come true.

Chapter 51

ADDISON

I rolled onto my other side, trying to get comfortable in the hospital bed, but deemed it impossible. I felt like a boulder ping-ponging slowly between the guard railing. I let out a heavy sigh and reluctantly sat up, although the only thing I wanted to do was sleep. The baby had been kicking all night, and while I loved the feeling, I didn't love it as much at 4 a.m.

Monica sat slumped in a chair, her chin resting on her chest as she slept. I had told her she could go home, but she had insisted on staying after the doctor told me I needed to stay not one, but two nights to be monitored. Just to be on the safe side. I smiled sleepily over at her and realized that the hospital bed didn't seem so bad in comparison to the chair she was in.

I lay back and stared at the ceiling, feeling the baby do somersaults inside of me. I placed my hand gently on my stomach and closed my eyes, soaking in this moment. To know the baby would be earthside soon made me realize these kicks were fleeting.

I couldn't help but feel a little guilty that Daniel was missing these moments. I shook the thought away and tried to focus on something else. Like Monica's book.

While it was a little weird to hear a version of my story typed in her poetic prose, there was a magic to it. It wasn't my reality, but it was a version of it that I had so badly wanted at some point. She depicted my character perfectly. Stubborn, fiercely loyal, and independent. And even though she had met Daniel once, she seemed to have written his character effortlessly. Ridiculously handsome, smart, and scared.

I couldn't blame him for that last part, which was also why it was better to do this on my own. As much as I wished we could have a happy ending, there were too many messes that were made along the way. Too much uncertainty. I wanted to give the baby stability. While I didn't really have the financial means, I could at least give him or her the emotional stability. I could give them love. Unfaltering love.

"Whatchya thinking about?" asked Monica groggily.

I looked up and saw her staring at me curiously with a sleepy expression on her face.

"Just the baby," I said.

She rubbed her eyes and stretched before looking at her phone for the time. She groaned.

"Christ. It's barely 4 a.m.," she said, settling back in her chair.

"I know."

"Baby kicking?"

"It's the witching hour." I laughed.

"At least when the baby is here, I can relieve you so you can get some rest. There's not much I can do out here." She pointed at my belly and back to herself.

"Go back to sleep," I said with a chuckle, settling back in the bed. I turned on my side and shut my eyes tight, willing sleep to come.

But it never did.

Three hours later, a different doctor knocked softly on the door, waking Monica from a deep sleep that I was jealous of. I sat up slowly, hoping I could go home. I looked at him eagerly.

"Hello, Ms. Heartly. How are you feeling this morning?" he asked, clicking his pen and readying himself to write on the clipboard in his hands.

"I'm feeling much better," I said.

"Any nausea?"

"No."

"Dizziness?"

"No."

"Cramping?"

"No."

He jotted a few notes down before looking back at me.

"Well, it sounds like you're feeling much better. I was able to go over your charts from the night, and it looks like things are normal."

"Does that mean I get to go home?" I asked eagerly.

He laughed. "I take it you want your own bed?"

I smiled and nodded.

"I will have a nurse come by with your discharge papers. But before I do, I need to remind you that stress is not healthy for you or the baby. I don't want to assign you bed rest."

I gulped. I couldn't imagine being bedridden for the rest of my pregnancy.

"We're not at that point yet," he continued, "but I do need you to take it easy."

"Yes, doctor," I said sheepishly.

I couldn't believe I had gotten myself to this same place again because of the mess that was my life. I wanted to kick myself for putting the baby under any stress. It wasn't fair.

"I'll make sure she takes care of herself, doc," said Monica, standing up and giving him a firm nod.

"Good," he said. "Now, you do need to schedule a follow-up with your OB. I will make sure to put in my notes that it's urgent so you can get scheduled in a timely manner."

"Thank you," I said.

"I better not see you back here, unless that baby is being born."

He said it so seriously that it made my stomach drop, but then he gave me a wink, which sent a flood of relief through me.

"Trust me, I don't want to be back here," I said.

"Have a good day, Ms. Heartly," he said before slipping out the door.

An hour later, Monica and I were in a cab back to my apartment. I told her she should go home, but she again insisted she stayed.

"I have my laptop. I'm good. I can write from anywhere." She drummed her fingers on her laptop case and gave me a reassuring smile.

"Thank you. I don't think I've said it enough."

"You've said it plenty. I'm your best friend and I know you would do the same for me."

I nodded and rested my head on her shoulder as the cab weaved in and out of the morning traffic of the city. I must have fallen asleep because the next thing I knew, we were out front of my apartment. I lifted my head groggily as Monica paid the driver.

"You really were tired," she said, opening the door and stepping outside.

She offered me her hand and pulled me out of the cab with a grunt. I gave her a grin as I hoisted myself out of the seat.

"I can't imagine getting much bigger than this," I said, rubbing my belly.

"You have two more months, missy." She raised a brow and led me to the door of my building.

Once we were up in my loft, I collapsed slowly onto the bed. Exhaustion hit me hard. Hunger too. My stomach grumbled loudly.

"How about I whip up some pancakes?" asked Monica.

"That would be great."

She nodded and started opening cabinets in the kitchen, pulling out a bowl and whisk and pancake mix. I watched as she moved around the small kitchen, feeling so grateful for her. Fifteen minutes later, she brought over a steaming plate stacked high with four buttermilk pancakes drizzled with syrup. My mouth watered just looking at it.

I eagerly took a bite.

"Thank you," I said as the sweetness danced on my tastebuds.

"Of course," said Monica, sitting beside me. "Look, I think I'm going to move in sooner than later."

I looked at her, confused. We had agreed she would move in after the baby was born to help out and ease the rent. I already felt like enough of a burden to her. I couldn't let her do more for me.

"Monica," I said, my voice thick with emotion or syrup. I wasn't sure.

"You need someone here with you to make sure you and the baby are okay."

"But…"

"No buts. I'll gather some of my things today and slowly get the rest this week. We're officially roomies."

I laughed, but also felt tears forming in my eyes.

"Hey, hey," she said, pulling me close. "Don't cry. We're in this together. Okay?"

I nodded and wiped a tear from my cheek.

"Now, I'm going to call your OB and see if she can squeeze you in today. 'Kay?"

"Okay."

Monica spent most of the morning and afternoon making trips from her apartment back to mine. My loft was small as it was, and having her few things and the baby's things made it feel even smaller. Especially when I felt as big as a house. I knew we would soon outgrow this loft, but for now we would make it work.

I wasn't much help with the heavy lifting, but I did help her set up a little work station right next to my small desk. A place where she could write alongside me. I felt grateful that I had the freelance job she got me because I knew I would go stir-crazy without having anything to do.

Plus, we needed the money.

I had been avoiding looking at my finances since I had left my old job. My final paycheck had already hit my bank account, and now I relied on the small paychecks from freelancing that weren't nearly as big or stable.

After I ate my pancakes this morning, I opened my nightstand to grab my journal and saw Daniel's check folded in the dark corner of the drawer. It would make life so much easier if I just cashed the check. But I was stubborn. I didn't want to rely on him. I knew deep down the baby needed me to check my ego at the door and accept his help. He was the father, after all.

Until that day, I would just have to figure it out. Day by day.

Monica was able to get me an appointment with my OB at four that afternoon. I felt my nerves creeping up my throat as the cab pulled up outside. Just a few days ago, I had seen Daniel here, and while the chance of seeing him again was slim, I was still absolutely terrified.

"You're shaking," said Monica softly as she grabbed my hand.

"Ridiculous, huh? I'm being ridiculous," I said, looking out the window of the cab, up and down the sidewalks.

"You're not, but you need to calm down. Okay?" said Monica worriedly.

I nodded and opened the door of the cab. I paid the driver before I heaved myself out of the car. I hated spending money on cabs when I had a perfectly fine subway pass, but Monica didn't trust me not to go into labor down in the tunnels or the train.

Anxiously, I glanced at the spot where I had left Daniel on the curb before he chased me down the street. I sucked in a deep breath and walked by it and into the building.

My OB didn't tell me anything I didn't already know. The doctor from the hospital had sent over my charts. The doctor from the first hospital a few months ago had done the same. She knew everything about me, inside and out, and the look of concern on her face made me clutch my stomach tightly.

"Addison," she said, narrowing her gaze and grabbing my hands firmly.

I slowly looked up at her.

"If you want this baby to come out healthy, I need you to rest. Stay home as much as possible. Let people help you. Okay?"

It was like she was trying to tell me something, even though she knew nothing about Daniel or our history.

"Okay," I said softly.

I tried not to get frustrated by what she was saying. Or when the other doctors had said the same thing. I didn't ask for my world to collapse around me or for my heart to be shattered.

Still, I promised her and myself that I would do as I was told.

Chapter 52

DANIEL

I woke up surprisingly early, despite the night out for my birthday. While it wasn't the normal party I partook of each year, we still had a risky combination of alcohol. Champagne. Sake. Beer. It was a true boys' night out and I was surprised and grateful that my brother and best friend actually listened. I'm sure they were originally planning bottle service or a hotel suite, but the pool hall had been perfect.

We had stayed until closing, shooting pool and talking about my next move with Heart. For all being bachelors, I realized we did have some romantic bones in our bodies. They made me face the harsh reality that if I really wanted to be the man I said I wanted to be, which was a father and a husband, I needed to realize that money couldn't buy that. And if it could, then it wasn't the right woman.

We came up with various scenarios where I could win her back. I'm sure if anyone were listening to our conversation it would be ridiculously humorous. Three guys at a pool hall with pints of beer and talking about romantic gestures.

"You could write her letters," suggested Brody.

"Letters?" I asked, raising a questioning brow.

"Yeah. A letter every day—"

"You've been watching *The Notebook* too many times."

"*You* watch *The Notebook?*" interjected Freddy, casting Brody a surprised glance.

"The ladies love it," said Brody, puffing his chest out.

"I think *you* love it." Freddy laughed.

"Whatever. That romantic shit works."

"Letters would make sense if we didn't live in the same city..." I mused.

"Brooklyn and Manhattan are basically different cities," said Freddy.

I rolled my eyes and took a long sip of beer before we started coming up with different alternatives.

Now that I was awake at six in the morning, all the alternatives seemed a little hazy now thanks to the pints of beer. I do know they had just become more and more ridiculous as the night went on. Talks of ginormous cakes and flying storks and hiring a band to play outside her window. They were all laughable now. I lay in bed trying to remember them all, but gave up. None of them were right.

There was a part of me that wondered if I was stalling out of fear. Fear of rejection. Fear of losing the little bit of a dream. So much had already slipped through my fingers like sand. I felt like I was desperately grappling to hold on to it, but more time was passing and I was losing the real possibility of being a part of Heart's life. The baby's life.

I sat up suddenly in bed and made the mental decision that today was the day. No letters. No grand gestures. No frills. I would simply show up as myself.

Quickly, I washed up in the bathroom and was about to get dressed when I realized it was barely past six in the morning. As much as I wanted to see Heart, I figured I should at least show up to her place at a more respectable hour.

I padded down the hall to the kitchen to put on a pot of coffee. As it brewed, I settled into a barstool at my kitchen island. I unlocked my phone and began scrolling through the news as a way of distracting myself from the day ahead. A day that could end in a true goodbye, or a day that a new life would start.

I read the latest business articles for tech and smiled to myself as I saw my company at the top of the morning's headlines. They were teasing what the new product might be. They didn't know what we were launching, but everyone had their guesses. Some were right. Some were way off. Either way, it had everyone talking, which was increasing the company's market value, which was where I browsed to next to see how my investments were doing.

As I browsed and scrolled, I realized it had been a few weeks since I had seen my face in the tabloids. While I hadn't gone looking, I would usually hear from my publicist if something was off color. Kiera had been surprisingly quiet. She hadn't released any more statements about upcoming nuptials or our time in Bora Bora. Maybe she had really gotten the hint after all. She had to eventually. We were through.

Just out of curiosity, I clicked the tab for the gossip pages. Most of the headlines were about a celebrity affair and a major divorce. I kept scrolling and then I saw a picture of Kiera looking drunk off her ass, leaving a benefit event with a man twice her age. The headline read: *Do We Ship Shipley's New Romance?*

I chuckled to myself and shook my head. Some things never changed. I was just glad I wasn't any part of *that* anymore. I walked over to pour myself a cup of coffee and went to the living room and looked out the large windows at the city below. The steam from my coffee warmed my face as I watched the light change from purple to an orange glow as the sun began to rise.

It really felt like a new day.

I texted Brody, who I was certain was still asleep and probably hungover. I had gone home after the pool hall, but who knew what Freddy and him got up to afterward. They were in the mood to party more, but I had Armand drive me home, much to their disappointment.

Probably not coming in today. I'm about to go full Notebook.

I hit *send* and sat on the couch to drink my coffee. The minutes felt like they were dragging on. When it finally hit seven in the morning, I went to shower and change. I slid on a pair of dark denim jeans and a black crewneck before texting Armand to meet me in the parking garage.

It was still early, but I figured I could make a stop along the way and the traffic to Brooklyn would probably tack on another hour. I just knew I couldn't be in my apartment anymore. I had to keep this momentum going before I lost my nerve.

"Where to, Mr. Jacobs?" asked Armand as he slid into the driver's seat.

"Is there a nearby florist?"

"All the florists are closed at this hour."

Disappointed, I chewed on my cheek as I thought of an alternative.

"But the flower market should be open. It's where the florists get all of their supplies," offered Armand with a smile.

I wondered if he knew what I was up to.

"Great. Take me there, please," I said.

Twenty minutes later we pulled up to a long stretch of sidewalk that was lined on one side with black awnings hanging over fresh greenery and colorful flowers. As I stepped out of the car, I was immediately hit with sweet and earthy smells. I had never seen anything like it. I began walking up the sidewalk, feeling slightly overwhelmed. I usually had a florist put something together.

I stopped and looked at the selection of roses, rubbing my chin with my fingers.

"May I make a suggestion?" I heard Armand say.

I turned around and saw him standing there hesitantly. I thought he had stayed in the car, but here he was trying to help me.

"Please do," I said.

"Well, blue hyacinths are a representation of 'making peace' and they are slightly more unexpected than roses, although when mixed together can make a beautiful bouquet."

I looked at him in surprise.

"I've had a few bicker matches with my wife." He shrugged before giving me a smile.

He knew *exactly* what I was up to.

"How did you fix it?" I asked.

He sighed and looked thoughtful for a moment.

"Communication," he said. "It seems so small. Such a small gesture. But talking to each other is what really works. What really matters."

I nodded as I thought about his words. Everything I had done in the past had just been a Band-Aid. A monetary quick fix. A large check and prettily wrapped boxes wouldn't get us to the heart of the issue. I realized I had relied on my money out of fear. Fear that the words wouldn't come out right or that they wouldn't be enough. I wondered when I had become that person.

"Flowers help, too," said Armand with a wink.

For the next twenty minutes, I followed him through the flower market and he began explaining the different ones to me. He told me the meaning behind each one, and I started to wonder if he was a florist in a previous life. We began pulling various flowers from their fresh water containers. With Armand's help, we put together a bouquet of blue hyacinths, pale pink roses, and white orchids. While each had their own meaning, they all had the same message of "I'm sorry." And I owed Heart a big one.

As I looked around the market at the bustling morning crowd, I wondered how many of these people were trying to make things right too. I knew flowers wouldn't be nearly enough, but I hoped they would be a beautiful reminder of how I wanted to be in Heart's life. And in our baby's life.

As we walked back to the car, I put my hand on Armand's back, making him turn to face me.

"Thank you, Armand. Really. I mean that," I said gratefully.

"Of course, Mr. Jacobs." He nodded.

He looked hesitant for a moment before speaking again. "If I'm not being too bold, Mr. Jacobs..."

"What is it?" I asked.

"That one was special. I have never seen you like that with any other woman."

I gave him a soft smile, realizing we had never really ever talked about anything personal. In all the years he had worked for me, this was as deep as we had ever gotten. I guessed I never realized all the time we actually spent together. All the things he knew about me and had witnessed over time.

"She was special. *Is* special," I corrected myself.

"Let's go get her," he said, putting his hand on my shoulder.

I laughed and got in the car. This man was getting a big bonus at the end of the year.

As we began our drive to Brooklyn, I suddenly thought of something as I realized where we were.

"Armand," I said, leaning forward in my seat hurriedly.

"Yes, Mr. Jacobs?"

"One more stop, please."

"Where to?"

"The coffee shop. The one with the tea. You know the one."

He nodded and made the necessary turn before it was too late. I hopped out of the car and stood in the long line of morning commuters. I tapped my foot impatiently, feeling a mix of anxiousness and excitement bubbling in me.

When it was my turn to order, I ordered an herbal tea. The same tea I had taken to Brooklyn all those months ago when I would drive Heart into the city for work. It felt like a lifetime ago, if I were being honest. When things were better. When things were right.

I held the cup in my hands, its warmth seeping into my skin as we approached the Brooklyn Bridge. The tea brought me back to all those long car rides as we really got to know each other.

I solely concentrated on the heat on my hands and the smell of the flowers because it was all I could to not lose my nerve.

My phone buzzed. I slipped it out of my jacket pocket. It was a text from Brody: *Go get her back, bro.*

I smiled down at my phone before returning it to my pocket. I hoped more than anything that I could.

Chapter 53

ADDISON

"Do you need anything while I'm out?" asked Monica. She applied a nude shade of lipstick to her lips as she stood in front of the small floor-length mirror next to my closet.

She looked fantastic in a cream skirt and a flouncy silk blouse that was tucked into her waistband, revealing her petite figure. I looked down at my flannel pajamas and sports bra that did their best to contain my body that was growing at a rapid pace.

I couldn't help but feel a little envious of her. She wasn't a ball of emotions, or an actual ball of a human, for that matter. She got to work her dream job and leave the apartment as she wished. It felt unfair that she would have to stay holed up in here with me.

I sighed as I thought about how different I looked and how different life looked.

"Hey," said Monica, walking over to the bed and plopping down next to me. "What's wrong?"

"I feel like a whale. I look like a whale. I'm only two days into being on house arrest, and I'm already going crazy," I said, lying back in the bed dramatically.

I knew I was being dramatic and emotional and all "woe is me," but I couldn't help it. My hormones were playing a game of which one could make me break down first, and seemingly, they were all winning.

"Hey now," said Monica as she put her arm around me. "You do not look like a whale. You put other pregnant women to shame. You're weeks away from delivering a beautiful baby. What did you expect? To look like Heidi Klum?"

"Ha!" I laughed sarcastically. "She looked hot even pregnant."

"So do you. Look, I know this isn't how you imagined pregnancy to be."

"Or life..." I rolled my eyes.

"But, you're kicking ass. You have a job that lets you stay home in your pajamas. People would kill for that."

I nodded. Leave it to Monica to try to make me see the bright side of things when I could only see the shaded areas.

I should feel lucky that I even had a job at all, let alone one that I could do from the comfort of my home. And one that followed my doctor's orders of resting as much as possible for the health of the baby.

"I feel so selfish," I said softly, my eyes welling up with tears.

"What? Why?"

"Because I'm complaining about all the things that I should be grateful for. I should be thinking about the baby and how to keep him or her healthy as they come into this world. I'm already a bad mom."

"Oh, hush," said Monica, squeezing me tight. "Your hormones are playing tricks on you. I won't hear any more of it."

She released me from her hug and stood up quickly.

"Get up," she said, or more so demanded.

I groaned.

"Now."

I sat up slowly and rolled out of bed.

"Now stop feeling sorry for yourself. You're going eat the breakfast I made you. It's on the kitchen counter. Then you're going to get dressed and start your workday. Okay?" Her hands were on her hips and it looked like she meant business. Sympathetic Monica had left the building, and here stood bulldog Monica.

"You're bossy," I said, giving her a slight smile.

"Someone needed to snap you out of this," she said, eyeing me up and down.

"Well, thank you," I replied.

And I meant it.

I had been in such a funk the past few weeks, and it was taking a toll on not only me, but the people around me. Which was really only Monica and she deserved better.

I followed Monica to the kitchen and grabbed the plate of bacon and eggs that was still warm on the counter. I picked up a fork and took a big bite of eggs as Monica watched me triumphantly.

"Thanks for breakfast," I said after I swallowed another bite.

"Auntie Monica wants to make sure her niece or nephew is well fed," she said.

She reached over and gave my belly a little rub.

"Now, my meeting with my editor shouldn't be too long. She's just proof-reading the last few chapters. Call me if you need anything."

"I'll be fine," I assured her.

She eyed me warily. This was the first time she had left my side since we left the hospital. I knew she was worried about me, but I had no plans of leaving my apartment that day.

"Go!" I said, shooing her toward the door.

She grabbed her purse from the counter and walked out the door, closing it behind her. I breathed a little sigh of relief. I need a little alone time.

I finished my breakfast and put the empty plate in the sink. Since I was working from home, I knew there was no point in really getting dressed, but I decided to follow Monica's orders and change. Being in pajamas would make me just want to crawl back in bed, anyway.

Slowly, I rummaged through my closet and found a pair of black bike shorts that were stretchy enough to fit. I opened my dresser drawer and pulled on an oversized T-shirt that wasn't so oversized anymore. As it slid over my belly, I studied myself in the mirror for a moment and gave myself a discontented smile. This was as good as it was going to get.

In the bathroom, I brushed my teeth and splashed my face with some cold water. I was still a little sleepy from another restless night. I looked forward to when my body would once again be mine again, even though I doubted I would get much more sleep with a newborn. I wondered which sort of insomnia was worse.

I pulled my hair into a messy bun and then padded into the living room, which had really become a nursery. I had a little time before I needed to start working. No one was clocking my hours anyway. I just had to make sure I met my writing deadlines.

I walked over to the gold crib that shone in the morning sunlight and ran my fingers over the cool metal bars. It really was a beautiful crib. I imagined the baby sleeping peacefully in it, although that wouldn't be for a while. The baby books all suggested a bassinet close to the bed for the first few months.

Daniel had made sure to get the best one and it already sat in the corner of my bedroom. Everything in this apartment that had to do with the baby reminded me of him. I wondered if I would ever stop seeing his face whenever I looked at the baby clothes or the rattles that sat in a wicker basket or the small teddy bear in the corner of the crib. They were all such joyful things, but they were all little reminders of pain.

Would I feel that way about the baby? I wondered if the baby would look like him, and if it would break my heart every time I saw their piercing blue eyes and dark hair. I wondered if it was a boy or a girl. Most days, I was content with not knowing. The surprise of it made it that much more special and exciting. But some days I was so curious to find out. I would know soon enough.

After spending a little more time looking through the baby's things, I finally sat down at my desk and fired up my computer. I opened my web browser and today's news stories popped up. I read up on the nonprofit work going on in Uganda and the newest start-up charity that was making waves on the West Coast. I scrolled to the business page and saw Daniel's name in the top headlines. My breath caught as I hovered my mouse over the link.

Hesitantly, I clicked and was brought to the article about his newest product launch. It was probably the one that had him so stressed that day I dropped by unannounced with the ultrasounds. The day that really changed everything because it shook the confidence I had in him right out of me. Everything had gone downhill from there. The charity event. The things I heard him say. The tabloids I read about him and Kiera. The pictures I had seen.

I sighed as I closed out of the article. Then my curiosity got the best of me. I clicked the tab for the tabloids, which was something I had been avoiding ever since I saw the pictures of Daniel and Kiera in Bora Bora. I scrolled down a ways and was relieved when I didn't see Daniel's name.

Then I saw Kiera's right next to a photo of her and that older man I had seen her with at Bemelman's a few weeks ago. I quickly read the headline and skimmed the article. It seemed as if she was in a new relationship. My stomach turned as I looked from her to her new beau. He could be her father. Gross.

I felt a faint smile cross my lips as I closed out of my browser. Maybe Daniel had been telling the truth about him and Kiera. How nothing was going on. Still, those photos were pretty incriminating. And yet, they shouldn't be. We weren't together anymore. He was free to do whatever he wanted. I didn't have a say in that. My feelings shouldn't matter. I told him I never wanted to see him again.

They were words I often regretted. Because they were a lie. I would do anything to see him and fix things, but my stubborn pride and insecurities kept me pushing him away. It was too late now anyway, especially after the other day outside the doctor's office. He had found out about the biggest lie I had ever told. How could he ever forgive me after that? Moreso, how could I forgive myself?

The time on my laptop read that it was close to 10 a.m. I really needed to get to work. I had a deadline of five this evening, and had several articles to research and write. I tried my best to push out the lingering thoughts of the baby and Daniel out of my head so I could focus.

I opened my latest doc and picked up where I had last left off. When I first started this job, I felt like I wasn't qualified. I had never really been a writer, but I did know nonprofit work. The ins and outs of it, and that was what helped me. It wasn't like I was writing fiction like Monica could with pretty prose and fanciful stories of love. I simply had to write the facts.

I began typing and finding my rhythm, which was why the knock at the door broke my stride, irritating me. I looked at the time again. It was barely 10:30 now. I knew Monica had said her meeting wouldn't take long, but she hadn't left that long ago and she had to commute back and forth to

Manhattan. Maybe it really had been quick. I figured she must have forgotten her key.

"Coming," I said softly as I pushed myself out of the desk chair, which I was surprised I hadn't gotten stuck in yet. I should probably start working from the couch from now on. It would be more comfortable, anyway.

I walked over to the door and opened it. I was taken aback when I saw it wasn't Monica. Instead, it was the last person I expected to see standing there with a bouquet of flowers and a familiar paper cup in his hands. I looked into his icy blue eyes and felt everything else fall around me.

Chapter 54

DANIEL

I watched as Heart's deep brown eyes found mine and widened in surprise. Her lips slightly parted as if she was about to say something, but nothing came out but a slight breath of air. We stood there staring at each other for a minute that felt like an eternity. An eternity I could stay in because it meant she was here with me.

I wondered what her next move would be. Would she shut the door in my face? Would she let me in? Would we hash it out right here? I stood tensely just outside her doorway with her familiar vanilla scent wafting into the hallway, captivating me even more. It felt like I was in some sort of dream.

She looked so effortlessly beautiful in an oversized light blue T-shirt that hugged her round belly and a pair of black bike shorts. Her hair was pulled into a messy bun on the top of her head and her skin was flawlessly makeup-free. She clearly wasn't expecting company, but it didn't make her any less perfect.

She tucked a strand of hair behind her ear as if realizing what she looked like, which was more than enough for me, but I could see her self-conscious-ness get the better of her. I wished I could reach out and touch her face. Make her see what I saw. Instead, I stood there and watched as her eyes fell to the ground, her hands moving to her stomach protectively. It broke my heart in that moment.

"Heart..." I started.

"What are you doing here?" she asked softly, still looking at the ground.

"I couldn't stay away. I can't stay away."

"But I said..."

"I know what you said," I interrupted, "But I don't believe you. I refuse to believe we are better off apart and out of each other's lives."

"How can you say that?" she asked, raising her eyes and meeting my gaze.

I shifted my feet as her pointed gaze penetrated me. I couldn't tell if she was about to yell at me or cry. Either one, I was ready to take. I knew that I deserved it.

"My whole life turned upside down after I met you. I got pregnant, lost my job, and found out the father of my baby was practically betrothed to someone else. It's a mess. Us together is a mess. Why can't you see that?" she pled.

"I know life didn't go according to plan. Does it ever? I had no idea I would find you on that garden terrace and become completely enthralled with a stranger who was badmouthing me straight to my face. Believe me."

Heart shook her head at the memory, a flush of color rising to her cheeks.

"But I wouldn't take any of it back. Not one thing. Well, maybe a few things...but only where you got hurt. But meeting you, taking you home that night, realizing I was going to be a father. All of that I would do one hundred times over."

She remained silent for a moment.

"Why?" she asked finally. Her eyes searched mine.

"Because this is the life I want." I pointed between me and her.

"But you said..."

"What I said at that party was a lie. A stupid one to tell for the sake of my company. It was selfish and wrong, but most of all, it was a lie. A big, fat lie."

"Then what's the truth?" she asked.

"I want to be a dad. I want to be a dad more than anything, but I want to be one with you."

My eyes fell to her stomach, which was even bigger than I remembered after our run-in at the doctor's office. My heart swelled just thinking about the baby inside. How close it was to entering the world and how I might not have a chance to see it. It broke me.

Her hands clutched her stomach even tighter as my eyes remained where they were. How could I make her see?

Then I thought of something. I set the bouquet of flowers and the tea on the ground.

"What are you..." she started.

I reached in my jacket pocket and felt the glossy photo against my fingertips. The same photo I had been carrying around since I found out she was pregnant. The one her friend gave me that day just a few feet away from this very spot.

I pulled the ultrasound carefully out of the pocket and heard Heart audibly gasp when she saw it. The baby was just a little speck on the paper. It was probably just over twelve weeks old.

"Where did you get that?" she asked, her voice breathless.

"Your friend gave it to me."

She looked at me questioningly. The look on her face told me she didn't know I had it or that her friend had given it to me.

"Short. Dark hair. Fiercely protective."

"That would be Monica," she said with a hint of a laugh.

She gently took the ultrasound from my hands and looked at the picture. Her eyes welled with tears as she looked at it.

"This was from so long ago..." she said, almost to herself.

"I've had it ever since."

"But why? You've just been carrying it around with you?"

I shrugged. "Yeah, I guess I have. I don't know why. I just felt like it needed to be close to me."

She twisted her mouth as she looked from the photo and back to me.

"Is this a bad time?" said a voice from the stairs.

Heart and I both looked over simultaneously to see who was interrupting this moment. I saw her landlord standing at the top of the stairs, clutching the banister as she looked between the two of us. An expression of amusement and enjoyment was on her face, as if she had just walked into a soap opera as a live audience member. Her cat weaved between her legs and purred at us with the same curious expression as its owner.

"Yes, Edna. Not a good time," said Heart, a hint of annoyance in her voice.

Edna nodded, but didn't take any initiative to leave.

"Can it wait?" asked Heart, sighing.

Edna's eyes widened as she realized she was indirectly being told to leave. Clearly, the lady could not take a hint. Heart had told me how nosy she was. As I looked at her in her pink fuzzy robe and matching slippers, I realized she must just be lonely. I kind of felt bad for her.

"Yes, yes. Sorry. I'll be going," said Edna as she scooped up her cat and held it to her chest. She began walking down the stairs and Heart waited until we heard her door close to continue our conversation.

She let out a sigh of a laugh before bringing her hand to her head.

"Are you okay?" I asked worriedly, reaching my hand out and wrapping my fingers gently around her arm.

"Oh, I'm fine. It's just Edna. Sorry about that."

I nodded, but didn't let go of her arm. She looked down at my hand, but didn't pull away. I took that as a good sign. It was time to go *Notebook* on her. With no speech planned, I just let every feeling I had do the talking.

"When I first met you, I wasn't looking for anything. Relationships weren't on the table for me. I wanted to believe I was too busy for one or too disinterested in the same women who only wanted my money or status. But I think I was also scared. But then I met you. Somehow, those fears just kind of washed away. It was so easy with you, like I had always known you or something. Like you had known me before I became 'the Daniel Jacobs'—and I say that in the most humbling, embarrassingly way."

Heart's lips lifted into a smirk and it took everything in me not to lean in and kiss her, but I knew I had to get everything off my chest. If our past had proved anything, it was that we needed to learn how to talk to each other. *Really* talk to each other.

"At first, it was just about the sex. I never thought it would turn into something else or that you would become pregnant."

I saw her mouth open as she was about to say something, but I continued.

"And I want you to know before you start jumping to assumptions, I didn't want to be with you just because you got pregnant. Yes, it's the commendable thing to do, but it was more than that. *You* were more than that."

Her mouth snapped shut. I knew her well. Better than she probably knew.

"You are as determined and strong as you are beautiful. Your kindness is too pure to believe sometimes. I've never met someone whose true passion was to help others when it didn't lend them any advantages. You put me in my place when I need it, and you don't tiptoe around my feelings. You also don't tiptoe around yours. You tell me how it is and your needs. You're stubborn as hell, which is annoyingly endearing."

I could see her holding her breath as she took in my words, and I only hoped that she was really absorbing them. Believing them. It seemed like no one had told her just how incredible she was, and that was a cruel revelation to me.

"While I know you can raise this baby on your own, and you'd fight tooth and nail to give it the best life you could all while being a loving mother, I don't want you to do it alone."

She looked down at her stomach that she couldn't even see her feet over, and the look in her eyes showed the love she had for the baby. I could see right then and there the kind of mother she would be. The baby was so loved already, and that's what mattered. It didn't matter the kind of crib the baby slept in or what clothes it wore or what stroller it rolled around in. What mattered is that it had loving parents.

I took a chance and gently placed my hand over hers. We stood like that for several minutes, just embracing the silence and this moment that felt all too fleeting. I felt a tear fall on my hand and drip off my knuckles. I looked up and saw that Heart was silently crying. Her eyes found mine and then she did something that made my heart feel like it was being put together.

She slid her hands from under mine and my palms were then pressed against her firm stomach. She placed her hands over mine and pushed against them slightly. That was when I felt it. A kick. The most incredible feeling in the entire world. I felt my eyes burn as tears began to form behind my eyes. Then there was another kick. And another. As if the baby was saying hello. As if the baby knew who I was.

I leaned down and whispered, "Hello."

After a few moments, the baby became still again, and I stood slowly as if in a trance-like state. How could someone I had never met have me wrapped so tightly around their finger? I had never loved someone so fiercely, except maybe for the women who stood before me silently weeping.

I slowly raised my hand and brushed her tears away with my thumbs. She nestled her cheek into the palm of my hand and looked at me with a soft smile. I could see she was scared. I was too. We could be scared together, just as long as we were together.

"Heart. I love you," I said. "Fiercely, loyally, and passionately."

She sucked in a shaky breath.

"It would be an honor to raise our baby together. If you'll let me."

Chapter 55

ADDISON

I stood in the doorway of my apartment and let Daniel's words soak into me as if I was stepping into a warm bubble bath. They surrounded me with warmth and a comfort that I didn't know how badly I needed until this moment.

I felt like I was in a movie or one of Monica's romance novels. It felt so surreal to be delivered a speech like that. One you only saw on the screen or read in books. But the words were for me. I had a quick, satisfactory feeling thinking about how Monica's book just might have that happy ending after all.

Daniel's eyes were looking at me expectantly. The icy blue of them had somehow danced into a deeper shade, and I found myself lost in them. Lost in this moment. I knew he was waiting for me to say something. It took everything I had not to start sobbing and try to formulate a sentence. My gaze fell to the floor.

At my feet was the most beautiful bouquet of flowers. I had never seen anything like that. The hues of blues and pinks and soft whites kissed in a soft array of pastel colors. Roses. Orchids. Hyacinths. And next to it, a white paper cup of herbal tea that was probably lukewarm by now.

I laughed softly at the gesture. The memory. Of a time when things seemed so simple and new. Even then, he was trying to be a part of my life by showing up to Brooklyn each morning and driving me into Manhattan. A commute back and forth that not many would want to take first thing in the morning.

He really had been trying all along. And maybe he didn't get it right sometimes. I sure as hell hadn't. But he was here at my door and he was fighting for me once again.

I took a deep breath.

"When I first met you, I thought I had you pegged. I knew your type. A rich, spoiled playboy. I told you as much, until I realized who you were. I'm still mortified by that," I said.

Daniel laughed softly.

"But even through having my preconceived notions of you, I felt something on that terrace. It's like you actually *saw* me. Someone most people look over. I couldn't shake the way you looked at me or the way you made me feel out on that terrace. It's like you somehow crept into my mind without me knowing, and you stayed there."

"And you've stayed in mine," said Daniel.

"I had a hard time believing that someone like me would be of any interest to you. I let everything I had read about you and everything I had seen about you tell me I wasn't enough."

"You *are* enough," he started, but I put my hand up.

I had to get this out. He nodded and put his hands gently down at his sides, signaling he was listening.

"I've never had a real sense of confidence. I never felt pretty enough or smart enough or successful enough. It could be because of the relationship with my parents. While my childhood was wonderful, when I moved out, it was a different story. I felt like I could never keep up with the plan they had plotted out for me. One I never wanted. When I chose a different path, they were more than willing to let me know it was the wrong one."

I realized this was really the first time I had shared anything this personal with Daniel. My estranged relationship with my parents was something I didn't open up about with anyone. Besides Monica. I wondered if we had been this open and honest and deep from the beginning, if things would have played out differently. But there was no sense in thinking about the would have, could have, should haves. We had this moment now.

"I feel like I've spent years trying to prove I was worthy enough in the choices I made in my life, and I never succeeded. Because of this, my self-esteem has been about this big," I said as I held up two fingers and pinched them together, leaving a small sliver of space between them.

"I've seen the women you've been with. Beautiful, successful, thin. I let my intrusive thoughts and my own insecurities push you away because I didn't feel worthy."

I could tell he was restraining himself from saying something, but I continued.

"But I feel worthy now. I don't know if it's this pregnancy or meeting you or finding my true independence, but as hard as these past months have been, I've never felt stronger. I have my days…a lot of them, but at the end of the day I know I'm strong."

It hadn't really hit me until then just how strong I had grown. Yes, a lot of days I had been weepy and felt sorry for myself. But I had also done things I never thought I would.

I had stood up to my parents, once and for all, and gained my freedom from their judgments that had eaten away at me over the years. Not many people could do that, especially to family. The people who raised you.

I had stood up to my boss, who unfairly looked at a situation and judged me before even hearing what I had to say. I had worked for him for years and had been one of his top employees, yet I was rarely acknowledged for that. I deserved better and I made sure to tell him as much.

And then there was this pregnancy and all the ups and downs I had gone through. All the appointments. The scary hospital visits that no one would ever want to take. The building of furniture and preparation of my loft. I had Monica through most of it all, but I knew she couldn't be with me forever. I knew in the end, I would be raising the baby by myself. And I had come to terms with that. I was determined to be a good mother, despite the circumstances.

But as strong as I was, it didn't mean I had to push away this man in front of me.

"I know I can do this on my own..." I started.

I could see Daniel's face drop.

"But I don't want to," I finished.

His eyes lit up as quickly as they had just faltered. A small smile began to form on his lips.

"You mean..."

I nodded eagerly.

He took three quick steps toward me and pulled me into his arms, his hands wrapping around me as my body melted into his. I had missed him so much. His steady breath. His strong hands. His smell, a mixture of sandalwood and something sweet I couldn't put my finger on. I closed my eyes and breathed him in as the familiar electric current ran through me.

This was everything I had wanted, but would never admit to myself because of my stubborn pride. I suddenly felt overwhelmed with emotion. And something else. I let out a breathy moan and pulled out of his embrace, keeling over.

"Heart?"

I closed my eyes and waited for the pain to pass.

"Heart, what is it?" asked Daniel worriedly, putting his hand on my back.

After a few more seconds the pain passed and I stood upright, blinking a few times as I tried to regain my bearings.

"I'm okay. I just..." I stopped.

I felt pressure between my legs and a bursting sensation, followed by the sound of water spilling on the floor.

"Oh, my God," said Daniel, looking at me wide-eyed.

I looked at him and down to the floor where a puddle lay between my legs.

"My water...my water broke," I said in disbelief.

"We have to get you to the hospital," he said.

I shook my head. "No, no. It's too soon. I'm not even eight months yet. It's too soon," I cried, my eyes watering as I clutched my stomach.

It felt like a shadow of doom passed over me as I stood, realizing what was happening. The baby was coming and there was no stopping it. I couldn't naively refuse to go to the hospital out of disbelief that the timing was wrong. I knew I had to go.

This was all my fault. Everything I had put the baby through had finally had the most unfortunate consequence I had dreaded. I started sobbing as the guilt took over.

"This is all my fault," I said, mostly to myself.

"Hey now. Don't talk like that. No one knows how these things are going to go. Babies have their own timing and ours just wants to meet us sooner than later."

Daniel pulled my hands from my stomach and gripped them tightly, pulling me to face him. His eyes were intent, but somehow calm. I found a fragment of relief in them.

"We have to go to the hospital now, okay?" he said, more as a statement than a question.

I nodded.

"I'm going to text Armand. He's just down the street. He can take us."

"Okay," I said.

"Now, do you have a hospital bag packed?" he asked, the same steady calmness to his voice.

"Mhmm," I said.

"Okay, let's go get it," he commanded as he typed a quick text on his phone.

He followed me into my apartment and I pointed next to my bed where my black duffel bag sat. It was the one Daniel had bought me and it was packed with all the essentials the baby books had recommended. He picked it up and slung it over his shoulder.

"You ready?" he asked, raising his eyebrows.

I wondered how he could be so calm. I also wondered what I would have done if he wasn't here. I would have been a hundred times more scared than I was now. I didn't know if I could be doing this without him. What a stroke of luck that timing would bring him to me at this exact moment.

"Yes, I'm just going to change really quick," I said as I walked into my closet.

I peeled off the soaked shorts and took off my shirt and underwear before slipping on a fresh pair of underwear and a roomy dress over my head. I remembered something I read, so I ran to the bathroom quickly and put on a maxi-pad and grabbed a towel. Apparently, I was going to keep leaking.

"Okay, ready," I said.

He grabbed my hand gently and we quickly walked out of the apartment and down the stairs. Edna's door was open.

"Edna," I called, knowing this would make her day. "It's happening!"

I heard her slippers move quickly across the wood floor and saw her peep her head out. Her eyes bulged when she saw me and she clapped her hands excitedly together.

"Oh, my stars!"

"Wish me luck," I said with a wink.

She gave me a warm smile and I swear I saw tears forming in her eyes. I didn't have time to make sure because another wave of pain came over me, causing me to bend over again. They were contractions. More painful than anything I had ever felt. They put the Braxton Hicks to shame.

"I'm going to start timing your contractions," said Daniel, pulling out his phone.

He waited for me to stand upright before placing his hand on my lower back and leading me to the door. He nodded to Edna, who watched us go.

Outside on the curb was Armand, who stood by the car with the back passenger door open. He looked nervous, but excited.

"Heart, it's good to see you," he said as he took my hand and helped me into the car, Daniel bringing up the rear.

"Good to see you too, Armand," I said breathlessly.

He closed the door behind us and jogged to the front of the car, slipping quickly into the driver's seat. I told him which hospital and he peeled away from the curb, faster than he ever had before.

Chapter 56

DANIEL

I didn't let go of Heart's hand the entire car ride to the hospital. It felt useless because she was in so much pain, but I wanted her to know I was there for her. Every time a contraction came, she squeezed my hand until it was turning purple, but it was nothing compared to what she was going through.

I could see the worry in her eyes. I felt it too, but I didn't want to show it. I didn't want to show any fear in this moment because I knew she needed reassurance that everything was going to be okay. That was what I kept repeating to myself internally, as my heart felt like it was frantically beating out of my chest.

In the baby book I had read, I barely skimmed what would happen if the baby was born prematurely. Now, I was kicking myself because I felt so unprepared. The baby wasn't supposed to arrive for *at least* another four weeks. I tried not to think about the chance that their health might be at stake.

Heart groaned beside me as she doubled over in pain. Her contractions were coming faster now, spaced out at about two minutes between each one.

Each one seemed to be more painful than the next. I felt helpless as I continued to hold her hand and rub her back with my other hand.

Armand looked nervous in the front seat, but he kept his eyes on the road and expertly weaved in and out of traffic. It was a good thing Heart had chosen a hospital in Brooklyn. We wouldn't be so lucky with time if we were heading into Manhattan. I could see the build-up of traffic on the bridge, and there was no way we were taking the subway.

"Ahhhh," Heart cried out.

"I'm right here with you," I said, giving her hand a squeeze and letting her squeeze back until again my fingers turned purple and blue.

"We need to call my doctor," she got out breathlessly.

"She's already on her way," I said. "I texted Freddy as soon as we got in the car. He filled her in."

Heart nodded as we pulled up to the hospital. We had made it there surprisingly quick. I wondered how many illegal moves Armand did to get us here so fast. It was just another thing I owed him for. Another thing to tack onto his end-of-year bonus.

He ran around the car and pulled open the car door. I quickly slid out of the seat and he helped me pull Heart from the car. She slung her arms over our shoulders and we walked her through the sliding doors of the hospital. A nurse saw us coming in and ran over with a wheelchair.

"How far along is she?" she asked.

"Almost thirty-three weeks," said Heart.

The nurse nodded and helped Heart into the wheelchair before looking to Armand and then me.

"And you are?" she asked.

"I'm the father," I said with a stern nod.

"Come along," she said, gripping the handles of the wheelchair and steering Heart toward the elevators.

"Thank you, Armand," I called over my shoulder as I tried to keep up.

"Good luck," I heard him say.

We rode in the elevators for what felt like one hundred floors until we reached the labor and delivery floor. The nurse asked questions as we rode about when Heart's water broke and how far apart her contractions were. Heart was in too much pain to answer, so I took over.

"We're not bothering with triage," said the nurse. "There's a good chance this baby will be here within the next hour."

"It's too early," said Heart, crying.

"It's okay, sweetheart. They're coming today whether it's early or not, but we are going to help you through it. We are going to take care of you and the baby."

Heart looked back at me in a panic, but I gave her a reassuring nod and the best smile I could muster.

The nurse helped Heart strip and change into a hospital gown. She talked her through everything, including the catheter and the machines she was being hooked up to. Everything was moving so quickly, but I did my best to try to keep up. Once Heart was settled in bed and the nurse was done with the wires and the IVs, she began writing information on a nearby whiteboard.

I took my chance and walked over and stood by Heart's bedside, taking her hand in mine.

"I'm scared," she whispered.

"Me too," I finally admitted. "But it's going to be okay. I promise."

I hoped that promise wouldn't be broken.

We heard a knock at the door and a woman in scrubs walked in.

"Addison," she said with a big smile. "It's the big day!"

She looked over at me and introduced herself. "Hello, I'm her doctor." She held out her hand.

"Daniel," I said, shaking her hand firmly.

She gave a knowing nod before snapping on a pair of gloves and turning to Heart.

"Now, let's see what we have going on here," she said, pulling up a rolling stool and taking a seat at the foot of the bed.

I stayed at Heart's side, her hand in mine as the doctor did a quick examination. She called out a few numbers to the nurse. Something about effacement and dilation. My mind tried to grasp the numbers and make sense of it.

"Well, the good news is, baby is face-down. I can feel the head right there. The bad news, depending on what your birth plan was, there's not time for an epidural."

Shit, I thought to myself. I knew nothing about Heart's birth plan or if she made one or what her thoughts were on an epidural. All I knew was from what I had read was that natural births were painful and I was scared for Heart.

"Okay..." said Heart nervously.

"You can do this," I reassured her.

She pressed her lips into a tight smile and gripped my hand as another contraction ripped through her, causing her to cry out.

"Is there nothing you can give her?" I asked the doctor worriedly.

"Unfortunately not. This baby is coming and coming soon. She's too far along in active labor. The epidural will only slow things down. But I assure you, she *can* do this," said the doctor. "Did you hear that, Addison? You *can* do this."

"Okay," whimpered Heart, breathing out.

"I'm going to get my tools prepped and I'll be back soon," said the doctor, slipping out the door.

And soon it was. It hadn't even been ten minutes before she was followed in by a nurse rolling a table full of metal tools. I swallowed hard as I took everything in. It was all happening so fast.

I followed the doctor's directions and helped Heart get positioned on the bed, with a nurse at her side and the doctor at the foot of the bed.

"Okay, Daniel. Do you want to come down here to the edge of the bed? You can just hold her leg and coach her through it, okay?" said the doctor.

I looked to Heart to make sure that was what she wanted, as we had never discussed my role in the hospital. Hell, I didn't even know I would be here, let alone actually watch our baby being born. Heart gave me a warm, pained smile that said to do as the doctor told me.

The next thirty minutes, I watched as Heart cried and yelled through the pain, but all the while showing strength I had never seen in anyone. Between the doctor's orders of when to push and when to relax, I stroked her leg and held her hand, giving her my own words of encouragement.

"Okay, Addison. I want you to push now. Give it everything you've got," said the doctor.

Heart bore down in the bed and gripped my hand harder as she closed her eyes. I watched as her face scrunched together and she let out a cry.

"Breathe," I said. "Breathe, baby."

"One more push, Addison. You've got this," said the doctor.

Heart pushed once more and squeezed my hand again. I felt her leg shake as she put everything into it. And that was when my eyes fell to the most beautifully strange thing I had ever seen in my life. Our baby was born. After a few seconds of silence and the doctor skillfully moving, I heard a shrill cry fill the room. My eyes welled with tears immediately.

"It's a beautiful baby girl," said the doctor triumphantly.

"Oh," Heart sobbed, trying to sit up and see.

"Sit back, Mama. I'm bringing her to you."

The doctor carefully cradled our baby girl as she brought her over to Heart and placed her gently on her chest. I came and stood next to Heart and the baby, running my fingers through Heart's damp hair.

"Dad, would you like to do the honors?" asked the doctor, holding up a pair of scissors. I swallowed hard, knowing what was coming next. I felt like a bundle of nerves as I shakily took the scissors from her.

"Just cut right here," she instructed reassuringly, pointing to the umbilical cord.

I did as she said, holding my breath the entire time.

"Good job," she said.

Then Heart and I cried softly together as we took in our baby girl. She was absolutely beautiful. So tiny. I tried to push my concerns over her size out of my head and just enjoy her first few moments in our world.

After several minutes, the doctor broke the magical spell we were under.

"Daniel, if it's okay with Addison, why don't you hold her and assist me in weighing and measuring the baby?"

Heart gave me a nod and carefully held up the baby for me to take. If I thought cutting the umbilical cord was scary, this was next level. I carefully wrapped my hands around the baby's head and body, bringing her to my chest. She was so light. It was so unreal. I breathed her in as I followed the doctor to a nearby table.

She swiftly took the baby's measurements and weight.

"Four pounds, five ounces. Sixteen inches," said the doctor as the nurse jotted it down.

"Now, I need to get her to the NICU. From the looks of everything, she's perfectly fine, but given her age and size, we need to keep her there for monitoring to make sure she's healthy. Don't worry. These are standard procedures for any preemie," assured the doctor.

"When can we see her again?" asked Heart frantically.

"Why don't you rest up a little bit while we will get her settled? Then you can come visit her. You can visit her anytime. I promise," said the doctor, looking from Heart to me.

"Okay," Heart whispered in disappointment.

I handed our baby carefully to the doctor, who placed her gently into a little bed on wheels. They wheeled our baby out of the room, leaving Heart and me alone with what felt like a hole in my heart.

"She'll be okay, right?" asked Heart, looking at me teary-eyed.

"Of course. She's strong, just like her mama," I said, walking to her.

"We don't even have a name for her," laughed Heart softly.

I grabbed a chair and pulled it up beside her. "Well, let's think of one," I said, sitting down.

We went through a list of names, me vetoing some and Heart vetoing several others.

"This is something we should have talked about before," she said, shaking her head.

I knew she was right. There was so much we should have done and talked about before this enormous moment in our lives, but we couldn't dwell on that now. I was just happy we were together.

I kissed her knuckles softly.

"Let's not think about that now," I whispered. "I love you. I'm here. We are figuring it all out now. Just know, I'm not going anywhere."

She reached her hand up to my face and caressed my cheek. The love I had for her swelled in my heart.

A thought came to me. "What about Bridgette?" I offered.

Heart rolled the name off her tongue as if she was trying it out.

"It was my grandmother's name," I added.

She thought for a moment. "I love it," she said.

I leaned in and kissed her.

Chapter 57

ADDISON

"What do you want for breakfast?" asked Daniel, as he perused the small hospital menu in his hands.

"I feel like I could eat the entire cafeteria," I answered sleepily.

My stomach grumbled loudly in agreement and I placed my hand on it to quiet it. The bump that was there twenty-four hours ago had deflated like a balloon and left me feeling empty. Although Bridgette was here, she had to spend tonight and many more nights in the NICU. It was a hard idea to grapple with and I missed her so much, even though she wasn't far and I had already visited her several times.

I must have looked sad, because Daniel stood from his chair and walked over to me. I scooched over and made some room for him on the small hospital bed. He slowly lowered himself next to me. He was in his navy flannel pajama pants and Mets shirt from the night before from when he slept on the small couch against the window of the hospital room.

"You okay?" he asked, wrapping his arm around me.

"I just miss her," I said softly.

"Me too," he said.

"She's the most beautiful thing I've ever seen."

"I know. Well, she's tied with you."

I nudged him playfully and laid my head on his chest.

"I just keep thinking I did everything wrong. She needed a few more weeks to grow and..."

I felt my throat closing up as the tears started forming in my eyes. Ever since Bridgette was born I had been playing the blame game with myself about all of the things I could have done differently to not have us in this situation. Last night, it kept me up for hours as Daniel slept soundly just a few feet away.

"Hey now," said Daniel, stroking my cheek gently. "This wasn't your fault. She was just excited to meet us."

I laughed softly. He had been so comforting this entire time, from my water breaking at my apartment to the car ride here with Armand, to the delivery of our beautiful baby girl. As strong as I thought I was, I didn't know if I could actually do any of this without him. Not now that I could feel the solidness of his body next to mine or the calmness in his voice as he soothed all of my fretful thoughts.

"You're really something, you know that?" I asked as I looked up at him.

"*You're* the one who just had a baby. You're practically Wonder Woman. Now, let's get some breakfast in you."

He read off the breakfast items from the menu and I chose scrambled eggs with cheese, bacon, and pancakes with extra syrup. Daniel chose the same and called down to the cafeteria to place the order. I watched him sit at the edge of the bed so serious as he held the phone, like he was taking a business call rather than ordering eggs. I laughed softly to myself and my heart wrapped around him like a warm hug.

Last night he had ordered two gigantic subs from my favorite Italian deli and had them delivered to the hospital, along with a mini bottle of sparkling cider to celebrate. The cold cuts I had been missing through pregnancy tasted so good and the sparkling cider was close enough to champagne that it made me think I was actually tipsy. I wasn't comfortable yet celebrating with real champagne, since I was breastfeeding and I was overly cautious since Bridgette was so small. We ate our dinner while we watched a marathon of *Friends*.

It felt like we were having a date night in, which was something we had never done, and I loved every second of it. Laughing and stuffing our faces with spicy pepper sandwiches and greasy potato chips. It felt like we hadn't lost any time at all. It felt like we had known each other for years. Last night was the most reassuring thing I had felt our entire relationship.

Having Bridgette. Going through all of that had brought us closer. Not once during the delivery did Daniel waver. He stood by my side with not one shake in his body or squeamish look on his face. He held my hand as he coached me through the most exhaustingly rewarding moments of my life. Our lives. He listened to the doctor and did as she said without any hesitation. I had no doubt in my mind that he was ready to be a father now.

We hadn't talked much about us yet, or where we were going to go from here. I wanted to, but we had to take it one thing at a time.

Our breakfast arrived twenty minutes later and I shoveled the food in my mouth hungrily and impatiently. I wanted to go up and visit Bridgette as soon as possible.

"Wow, you were hungry," said Daniel, eyeing my empty plate as he took probably his second bite of eggs.

"I want to go see Bridgette."

He stood up and took the tray from my lap. "Of course you do," he said, placing the empty tray on a nearby table.

He helped me out of bed and into my fuzzy hospital slippers. He went to put his on, but I stopped him, knowing he had a full plate of food to eat.

"Stay," I said. "Finish your breakfast."

"Are you sure?" he asked, raising his brows.

"Of course. You need to eat."

"Okay," he said hesitantly. "But make sure you tell her daddy says hi!"

Those words soaked into my heart like a sponge.

Daddy.

I gave him a soft smile and a nod before walking out into the hallway. One of the nurses spotted me and came walking swiftly over.

"Do you need a wheelchair to go visit baby girl?" she asked.

"No, no." I waved her off. "I'm feeling strong today. Plus, she's not far."

The nurse smiled and went back to the nurses' station. All of the nurses had been so wonderful and helpful, especially in the NICU. I walked down the hallway to the room of incubators where Bridgette was. I checked in with the nurse and washed my hands before I eagerly made my way to her and saw that she was on her back and looking up with curious eyes.

"Hey, baby girl," I whispered as I sat down in the chair beside her.

Bridgette turned her little head toward me and her grayish-blue eyes found mine. I sucked in a breath as I took her in. Every single time I saw her little rosy cheeks and dark brown hair, I felt completely taken aback. She was so beautiful. So tiny. So perfect in every way. If I had thought I loved her before, then my heart had grown one hundred times since the doctor placed her in my arms.

I didn't know how long I was staring at her when I heard a voice behind me.

"Ms. Heartly."

I turned around and saw the same nurse who stopped me in the hallway and offered me a wheelchair.

"Yes?" I asked.

"Your parents are here to see you. They're in your room."

"My parents?" I asked in surprise.

"Yes. Would you like me to tell them to wait?" she asked. If she was confused, she didn't let it show.

I twisted my mouth as I looked from Bridgette to the nurse, debating what I wanted to do. Debating if this was real. My parents?

"I'm coming," I said.

I followed her down the hallway to my room and heard voices inside. Daniel's and my father's. I felt my heart quicken as I stepped inside the room. I saw my mom first, sitting on the couch where Daniel had slept and nervously clutching a familiar little white lamb plush. Dad stood next to Daniel, who was looking at me with a nervous excitement.

"Mom? Dad?" I asked, looking between the two of them.

"I'll let you all have a moment," said Daniel, giving me a kiss on the forehead before walking out the door.

I watched him go before turning back to my parents. My mother was now standing and my father had his arm around her. They both looked at me with glossy eyes. My mother spoke first.

"I know earning your forgiveness is a vague possibility after everything we've done. Everything *I've* done. But I owe you an apology. A million apologies." Her voice broke as a tear rolled down her cheek.

I wanted to go to her and hug her, but it felt like such a foreign thing to do. I couldn't remember the last time I hugged her. Or saw her cry.

"When Daniel called us to let us know the baby was born..." started my father.

"Wait, he *called* you?" I sputtered.

Daniel didn't know much about my parents. He didn't know their names or where they lived. Didn't know how truly complicated everything was. Yet, I was completely touched by his gesture and how he had tracked them down to share the news of Bridgette. This man truly cared about me. I suddenly felt overwhelmed with emotion.

My father nodded. "Last night. We took the first flight out. We wanted to see you. Meet our grandbaby."

I looked from my father to my mother.

"I know we have no right to see her or have a place in her life, but..."

She clutched the little lamb in her hands even harder and then I remembered. That lamb used to be mine as a baby. I put my hand to my mouth as I registered it all. She had kept it all this time. Even after everything.

"I thought Bridgette would like to have him..." said my mother.

I held back tears.

"Would you like to meet her?" I asked.

My mother and father looked at each other and back to me, nodding enthusiastically.

I led them down the hallway to the NICU. We checked in, washed our hands, and walked over to Bridgette. We found Daniel sitting in the same chair I had been in and holding Bridgette against his bare chest. He looked up as we approached and smiled warmly.

"Skin to skin," he explained nervously as he realized he was half naked in front of my parents.

I laughed softly as I shook my head. The sight was too precious.

I heard my mother suck in a breath as her eyes took in Bridgette, who lay curled up, her little fingers pressed against Daniel's chest.

"She's so... so beautiful, Addison," said my mother as she wrapped her arm around me gently. At first, my body didn't know how to react, but I soon melted into my mother's embrace, now realizing how badly I had missed it.

"Look at her tiny toes and fingers," whispered my father in awe.

"She's perfect in every way," said my mother.

"She looks like you," my father added.

"And you," my mother commented to Daniel.

We spent the next thirty minutes admiring every inch of Bridgette, and there weren't many. I couldn't get over how small she was, but the doctor said she was strong and healthy, which were the most reassuring words I could hear.

"We should probably let you have your time," said my mother, not able to tear her gaze away from Bridgette.

I nodded and gave Daniel a thankful look before I led them out of the room. We walked in silence down the hallway. As we approached the elevators, I stopped and looked at them both.

"I want you to be a part of Bridgette's life. Of my life. *But...*"

I saw my mother's face bristle as she waited for what was coming next.

"We have to promise we won't drop out of each other's lives again," I continued.

My mother let out a sigh of relief and she pulled me in for another hug. My father came from behind and wrapped his arms around us both.

Chapter 58

DANIEL

Calling Heart's parents had been a bold move. I had never met them before, but was the father to their grandchild. I was sure that wasn't the way they had planned things to go for their daughter. Her mother had sounded surprised on the phone, but said they would make the necessary arrangements to get out to New York as soon as possible.

When the nurse brought them to the hospital room this morning. I was taken aback. I wasn't expecting it to be so soon, but it was probably better for them to take me off guard. My nerves of waiting to meet them would probably eat me alive. I would be practicing how to introduce myself and how to share the story of Heart and me meeting. I knew it would be a mess of a story. Now that I was a father, I would keep Bridgette far away from a guy like me. At least, the guy I used to be.

While Heart was with her parents, I decided to do another bold thing. I called her best friend. The bulldog otherwise known as Monica. I had swiped her number from Heart's phone while she was sleeping. I held my breath as the phone rang, not knowing if this was going to go well or not. We hadn't exactly gotten off on the right foot and I knew how fiercely protective she was of Heart.

I looked around the empty NICU to make sure I wasn't disturbing anyone. Bridgette was still asleep on my chest, breathing calmly and soundly. There wasn't a more soothing feeling than her little body against my chest. It felt like my whole world was right here.

The phone rang a few more times and I finally heard a click on the other line.

"Hello?" answered Monica.

"Hi, um, Monica?" I stammered.

I didn't know which was more nerve-racking. Facing Heart's parents or her best friend.

"Who is this?" she asked skeptically.

"It's Daniel. Daniel Jacobs. Heart's..." I didn't know what to call myself. Boyfriend. Baby daddy. Friend.

"I know who you are. What's going on? Is everything okay?" she asked in a panic.

"No, no. Everything is fine. I'm sorry to alarm you. I'm with the baby right now—"

"Wait," she cut me off. "She had the baby? It's too early! Is she okay?"

I smiled and looked down at my daughter. "She's perfect. Heart is perfect. She's with her parents," I reassured her.

There was a pause on the other line and I checked to see if she hung up. She hadn't.

"Her parents?" she asked skeptically.

"Yes, her parents came to meet the baby. I called them last night," I said, trying to keep the confusion out of my voice.

"Well, shit," said Monica.

"Excuse me?"

"I'm just surprised after her last visit with them."

"Oh?"

"You don't know, do you?" she asked.

Clearly, I didn't. I wondered if I had made a big mistake in calling them last night. Were they even welcome here? I felt heat creep up my neck.

I realized I didn't know much about Heart's family life, nor did she know much about mine. The time we spent together, it never came up. It felt like we had skipped go and gone straight to the finish. The baby on my chest was proof of that.

I knew in my soul that I loved Heart, though. She loved me. Maybe we had done things backward, but I would spend my life getting to know her. I couldn't wait for that.

"What don't I know?" I asked. I might as well get started on knowing Heart from the person who knew her best.

Monica chuckled. The cockiness that she knew and I didn't was palpable, but I ignored it. I deserved it.

"Heart and her parents hadn't spoken for years before you came along and changed everything."

Years. Shit. What had I done inviting them here? No wonder her mother had sounded so taken off guard on the phone. And Heart had seemed in a daze when she brought them into the NICU. It all made sense now. But why? I had to ask.

"What happened between them?" I asked cautiously.

"Oh, I'll leave the details for Heart to fill you in. But let's just say they haven't been the most supportive parents of her decisions. From her major in college, to her career, to getting pregnant before marriage."

I swallowed hard. They had seemed more than kind to me. A stranger who they clearly knew nothing about who had gotten their daughter pregnant. Would it be wrong to say I was relieved they didn't know all the details of the past few months? They would probably be much cooler to me.

"Heart had spent so long trying to live up to their expectations of her. To earn their love. Nothing was ever good enough. Those two are a real piece of work," continued Monica.

"Wow," was all I could say in barely a whisper.

No wonder Heart was so guarded. So unsure of how wonderful she was. No one had told her in recent years how special she was. So stubbornly strong in thinking she could do everything. She hadn't needed to rely on anyone else. The thought broke my heart. It all made sense now.

"But they came..." said Monica musingly. "That's a good sign."

"They did. Things actually seem good."

"Good. Good for Heart. Good for them. I had hoped they would come around, eventually."

"Thank you for filling me in," I said. "I know I have a lot to learn about Heart, but I want to be here to know her. I want to be here to raise the baby. I love your best friend fiercely, and I know I've screwed up too many times to count, but I promise I plan to make it up to her. To Bridgette," I said.

"Bridgette." Monica sucked in a breath.

Now, I knew something she didn't. To say I wasn't a little satisfied would be a lie.

"We chose the name last night."

"It's beautiful," said Monica.

A silence settled between us for several seconds before she spoke again.

"If Heart is giving you another chance, then I am, too," said Monica.

I smiled as I looked down at Bridgette. She had good people in her life.

"Then maybe you can help me with something," I said.

"Sure. What is it?"

"Well, I saw that everything for the baby was already built and set up. I'm guessing that was you."

"Let's just say I'm a pro at the Allen wrench now."

I laughed. "Well, thank you. Thank you for everything you've done for Heart."

"It's what best friends do."

"Well, since that's all done thanks to you. Maybe we could put together some sort of welcome home party for her and the baby. I don't know when we are getting out of here yet. We will know more in the next coming days. But I'd like to put you in touch with my assistant, Margaret, to help plan the party."

"I'm sure Heart would love that," said Monica.

"I think so, too. She needs it after everything she's been through."

"Okay. I'll get right on it. Just keep me posted on when," said Monica.

"I'll text you Margaret's number. She has all my contacts for florists and caterers and anything else you need."

"Okay," said Monica.

Just then, I saw Heart walk in the doors of the NICU.

"Hey, I gotta go," I whispered. "Keep it a surprise."

"I will. Thank you, Daniel. Glad you're back," said Monica before hanging up.

I locked my phone and slid it back in the pocket of my flannel pajamas before looking up at Heart, who wore a smile on her lips.

"Hey," I said softly.

"How is she?" she asked, looking to Bridgette.

"Been sleeping like a—well, a baby." I chuckled.

She laughed softly and pulled up another chair.

"Do you want to hold her?" I asked.

"No, no," she waved me off. "Let her sleep. She looks so peaceful."

"You think she'll always be this good of a sleeper?"

"Don't get your hopes up."

She placed her hand gently on Bridgette's back and ran her fingers softly up her spine.

"Thank you for calling my parents," she said, keeping her eyes on Bridgette.

"Of course. I hope you didn't mind I found their contact in your phone while you slept. I knew you were so tired that phone calls weren't the first thing on your list."

"For being so small, she sure kicked my ass," said Heart with a smirk.

There was a moment of silence, then she added, "No, but really. You don't know how much that meant to me. How much I needed it." Her eyes held a happiness that was new, as if she was fulfilled. I hoped it meant she found peace with her parents.

"Will they be here for a while?" I asked, not wanting to pry too much or reveal anything Monica had just told me.

"I think so," she said, a smile spreading across her lips.

I reached over and took her hand, giving it a squeeze. "I know we have a lot to learn about each other, and you don't need to tell me everything now. But I want to know you. All the parts of you, the good, the bad, the sad, the scary. All of it."

I brought her hand to my lips and kissed her smooth knuckles. Her eyes closed at my touch.

"I want to know you, too," she whispered.

"Our life starts now," I said, placing her hand on Bridgette's back.

She opened her eyes and smiled lovingly at our beautiful baby.

"What's it going to look like?" she asked dreamily.

"Well, I'm hoping it means you're my..."

"Girlfriend?" she asked playfully.

"God, this is so weird. I feel like I'm in middle school, except I'm thirty-something with a baby."

Heart let out a loud laugh and Bridgette stirred in my arms.

Heart covered her mouth and her eyes widened as we watched Bridgette fall back asleep.

"Yes," I whispered. "I want you to be my girlfriend. Will you?"

She looked at me, her eyes dancing. "I'd love that."

"And another thing," I said, hoping I wasn't moving too fast.

"I'd like you and Bridgette to move in with me," I said.

Heart's breath caught as she looked at me. Her mouth opened, but no words came out.

"I want us to be a proper family. I want us to go to sleep together and I want to wake up to help with her. I want to set up a nursery where she can play, and learn, and grow. I want to dance with you and laugh with you, and show the baby what a loving home is," I said.

"You mean it?" she asked.

"With every part of me."

She looked thoughtful for a moment before nodding slowly.

"Is that a yes?"

"Yes," she said, her eyes glazing over with tears.

I reached over and placed my palm gently against her cheek before pulling her in for a kiss. Her eyes fluttered closed as her lips met mine. In that moment, I couldn't tell if the taste of salt was from her tears or mine.

As we kissed, with our baby between us, I thought back on how much my life had changed in the course of less than a year. I never thought it would turn out like this. So extraordinarily different from the life I had lived before. I didn't realize how empty I had been until all those hidden parts of me were filled. Filled by these two girls right here.

As Heart pulled away and rested her head on my shoulder, I smiled to myself. My birthday wish had come true.

Chapter 59

ADDISON

"I'm outside," said Daniel through the phone. I smiled and walked swiftly to the window.

There he was, leaning against the town car in that effortlessly casual way, but instead of his suit, he wore jeans and a sweater. He must have felt my eyes on him because he looked up and grinned, making my heart pitter-patter. I wondered if I would ever get used to the sight of him, or if I would permanently feel this combination of goosebumps, jitters, and a racing heart.

"Be right down," I said before hanging up.

"You going to go see baby?" asked Monica from the couch that had been her bed for several weeks.

I nodded.

After Bridgette was born four weeks ago, Daniel and I were able to stay a few more nights at the hospital, but eventually we had to leave to make room for other patients. I wished we could have stayed there forever, or at least until Bridgette was released, but that wasn't how things with preemie babies worked.

It was the most painful thing ever to leave the hospital knowing she wasn't coming with me. Daniel practically had to pry my hands off of her incubator and held me as I sobbed through the hallways. He took me back to his place to comfort me and I stayed for a few nights before going back to my apartment in Brooklyn with Monica. He only let me because he knew I wouldn't be alone.

Since then, it had been a waiting game. Daniel came and picked me up from Brooklyn every morning with a cup of coffee, instead of tea. It felt so reminiscent of our first weeks together that it made me smile as we drove the long stretch back to Manhattan. Almost the entire time we would talk about Bridgette and wondering if that would be the day she could be released. In the other moments, we got to know each other more.

I learned more about his childhood. His vivacious mother and his serious father. A match that was likely to combust and everyone betted on it, yet it worked. Their wildly different personalities meshed well together like a pair of hands that were meant to hold each other. I could tell from the way Daniel spoke about them that he was very fond of them, but since they lived in Europe, he didn't see them very much.

Little by little, I was discovering the different pieces of Daniel, and he was discovering mine. It was as if we were putting together our own puzzles, even though we fit together seamlessly.

When Daniel saw me step out of the building, he walked swiftly toward me and wrapped his arms around my lower back as I looked up at him. He just stared at me for a moment before gliding his hand up the length of my spine to the back of my head, gently tilting my face up toward him before meeting my mouth with his. I felt the breath leave my body as I leaned into him.

He pulled away and stroked my cheeks with his thumbs. "Are you ready to go see our girl?"

"Mhmm," I said, still trying to right myself after his kiss.

Armand opened the car door and Daniel and I slid inside the backseat. As the car pulled away from the curb and began its journey to Manhattan, I lay my head on Daniel's shoulder.

"Do you think today is the day?" I murmured.

"I have a good feeling," he said.

I did too, but I was trying not to get my hopes up. Last week, Bridgette was able to be taken from the incubator and weaned into an open crib. It was a huge development and the doctor had told us it wouldn't be long now. Today she was just past thirty-seven weeks and had already grown so much. She didn't even look like the tiny baby we had met all those weeks ago. Her fingers were plumper and her cheeks were rounder. The doctor said she was strong. A tough cookie. Daniel made sure to let the doctor know that she took after me.

Instead of our usual chatter on the drive, we remained mostly silent. A bundle of anticipation. When we arrived at the hospital, we walked hand in hand up to the NICU. The nurses all said their hellos. They had grown used to us being here every day.

When we arrived to the special care nursery, we rushed over to see Bridgette, who was playing with her fingers and looking up at a cloud mobile that hung above her crib.

"Good morning, beautiful girl," said Daniel.

Bridgette turned to him and cooed.

I gently picked her up and gave her a hug, swaying as I held her and breathing in her perfect newborn scent.

"Ahhh. Addison. Daniel. You're here," said the doctor, walking in with a smile that I tried to dissect. Hoping today was the day.

"As always." Daniel chuckled as he ran his finger over Bridgette's cheek.

"I have good news," said the doctor.

My breath caught. I looked at her hopefully.

She nodded, as if to answer my question. "Today is the day."

I could already feel the tears streaming down my face as Daniel held Bridgette and me to him. I barely registered what the doctor was saying because my head kept echoing...

Today is the day.

Life could begin for us three. Really begin.

We spent the next several hours waiting to be discharged. It was a lengthier process given Bridgette's history. The nurse also had to take us through care instructions. I didn't care though. We got to take our baby home today.

Around 4 o'clock, we carried Bridgette out of the hospital for what I prayed would be the very last time. Armand had insisted on setting up her car seat in the town car and was waiting at the curb for us. When he saw me holding

Bridgette, I could have sworn his eyes had teared up. I positioned her so he could get a better look.

"She's beautiful," he whispered.

Those were definite tears.

"Thank you, Armand. Thank you for everything," I said, and I leaned in to give him a quick kiss on the cheek.

His face turned red as he opened the door for Daniel and me. We gently eased Bridgette in the car seat and took too long making sure everything was just right before we began our drive to my place in Brooklyn. The whole time we stared at our beautiful girl who sat between us, drifting off to sleep by the lull of the car.

When we got to my building, Armand came around and helped us out of the car. We unstrapped Bridgette from the car seat and Daniel scooped her up. She looked like a pink fuzzy teddy bear in his strong arms. The contrast was the sweetest thing I had ever seen. She yawned and blinked a few times as she realized the change of scenery.

"Welcome home, baby girl," I said.

I opened the door to the building and we carried Bridgette up to the second floor. I unlocked my door and pushed the door open. I slightly stumbled backward as I saw what was inside.

There were pink roses everywhere. On the tables, the counters, lined against the walls. There was a white balloon arch above every window. There was an array of desserts on my small dining room table. Powdered donuts, chocolate croissants, berry tarts. But besides all of that, there were friends and family. Monica stood in the center of the room with a glass of champagne in hand, grinning cheek to cheek. Next to her were my parents, and on the other side of her was who I could only assume was Daniel's brother. Shelley was also there, and a few old coworkers from the nonprofit. Freddy and Virginia.

"Since you never had a baby shower," said Daniel softly in my ear.

I looked up at him and just shook my head in awe.

"Is this... is this...okay? For..." I looked to Bridgette.

He nodded reassuringly. "I talked to the doctor today. She's strong enough."

I felt a wave of relief.

After I greeted everyone and gave them all hugs, Daniel placed Bridgette gently in my arms and put his hand on my lower back as he guided me further into my small apartment. I went to Monica first, who cried when I handed her Bridgette. She cradled her in her arms and rocked her back and forth, taking her all in.

"She's perfect. Just perfect," she murmured.

"Did you do all of this?" I asked, looking around.

Monica nodded. "With a little help." She looked up at Daniel and winked. "It was *his* idea."

"You two?" I pointed between them in surprise.

"We're besties now," said Daniel with a laugh.

My mouth dropped open slightly as Daniel went to grab two glasses of champagne from a table nearby. He returned quickly and handed me one.

"I'd like to make a toast," he said.

Everyone turned their attention to him.

"To Heart. Er, Addison. The strongest woman I know. I don't know how I deserve you, but I will never take one single day with you for granted. I love you for the woman you are, and now for the mother you are. Cheers everyone."

He raised his glass and everyone followed suit.

I looked up at him with teary eyes as we both took a sip of champagne.

"I love you," I said, standing on my tiptoes and kissing him on the cheek.

"I love *you*," he said.

He stared at me a moment longer before looking around the party proudly. I saw his eyes land on Brody and Freddy. I knew he was eager for them to meet Bridgette. I scooped her from Monica's arms and handed her to Daniel.

"Go," I said, giving him a nudge. "Go introduce her to her uncles."

He looked at me and down at her before walking over proudly to his friends.

"The whole dad thing looks good on him," said Monica.

"It does, doesn't it?" I sighed, taking another sip of champagne.

I admired him for a moment, already thinking about getting him alone later tonight. If we would have a chance for that now that we were a family of three. We had so much to navigate, but I was eager to do it together.

I turned to Monica. My best friend who had done so much for me during everything. I wanted to thank her, but I stopped myself when I caught something in her eye. I hadn't seen that look in a really long time.

"Monica?" I asked curiously.

"Hmm?" she said dreamily.

"Whatcha thinking about?" I asked, nudging her.

She giggled. Actually giggled. Monica, the bulldog acting like a giddy character from one of her novels.

"Monica..."

"Okay, okay. I met someone..."

"Oh, my gosh!" I squealed. "When? How? What? Who?"

"Calm down, calm down." She laughed as she put her hands up.

"This is crazy," I whispered, after I realized people were looking.

"I know. At first, I thought the whole thing between you and Daniel was crazy, but then..."

I waited for her to finish, but she shook her head.

"I'll tell you everything later. This is *your* day," she said.

I pulled her in for a hug. "You better."

We made our way over to where Daniel was now surrounded by his brother, Freddy, and my parents all admiring Bridgette. Never would I have ever pictured all of these people in a room together, but here we were. It was one of those moments you wanted to take a mental snapshot of and keep forever. I would never forget this.

Epilogue

DANIEL

My eyes slowly blinked a few times as they adjusted to the stream of morning light cascading through the window, its warmth only making me more comfortable in the cloud that was my bed. It was Saturday. No need to wake up yet. I closed my eyes and tried to go back to sleep, but I felt a hand trail down my chest and move slowly down my torso.

I opened my eyes and found Heart looking at me with a sleepy but mischievous grin on her face. I let her hand wander as my eyes explored her naked body that peeked out from underneath the silky white sheets. I held my breath as her fingertips met my length, stroking gently up and down, waking me up. Her eyes locked with mine as I grew hard against her touch.

I reached under the sheets and gripped her hips, pulling her quickly toward me. She let out a little squeal and reached one hand up, wrapping it around the back of my neck, while the other continued moving with more intent now. She leaned her forehead against mine, our breaths growing heavy as we stared at each other.

My mouth met hers. My tongue ran across her lips, coaxing its way inside. She accepted and let me taste her, her tongue meeting mine. As we kissed, my hand moved down her breasts, grazed her stomach, and found what it was looking for between her legs. I felt her suck in a breath while we kissed, as my fingers trailed against her.

As my tongue moved inside her mouth, I dipped a finger into her and it was met with a slickness that made me hungry for more. I moved to the rhythm of our kiss, which was growing more desperate. Her hand gripped my erection harder and began moving faster, matching my desire.

Her hand on my neck moved to my lower back, her fingers digging into me as she pulled me closer. I rolled onto her, one hand still moving against her while the other supported me against the mattress. Her eyes trailed down to my erection she gripped in her hand. She bit her lip as she spread her legs, an open invitation.

I slowly eased my finger from her wet walls and placed my hand on the mattress so I now hovered over her. She positioned herself underneath me, so that my tip was against her wet opening. She massaged it against her, continuously moving up and down the length, her eyes watching as she pleasured herself, never letting me fully inside.

I groaned with pleasure and the desperate desire for more, but she just gave me that teasing smirk that I would never get used to. The one that sent me over the edge. I watched as she moved her hips under me, her legs spreading further.

"Heart," I whispered somewhere deep in my throat.

Her eyes found mine and I needed her right then. She knew it. She put her hands up by her head and my hand wrapped around them, pressing them into the bed. My other hand positioned myself against her. I could already feel myself throbbing with lust. I eased myself into her, inch by inch, feeling her walls surround me. She let out a cry of pleasure as she writhed underneath me, but I didn't free her hands.

I eased out and smiled down at her. Her eyes were desperate; hungry. Two could play this game.

I brought my mouth down to her beautiful breasts that were mine for the taking. I flicked my tongue against her nipple lightly before taking it into my mouth completely. I massaged my tongue against her, swirling it around her erect nipple. I felt her breath quicken.

"Daniel," she said, her voice breathy. "Please."

I looked up at her as my mouth moved to her other plump breast.

"Please," she said more desperately.

She pressed her hips up to meet mine.

I smiled, knowing I had this power over her. I pushed her hips back down on the bed and held them there. Her legs opened wide and I plunged inside of her swiftly. She cried out and broke her hands free, meeting my back and digging her fingers into me as I pounded into her again. And again. Until we both were at our peak and crashed into each other, releasing everything we had.

"Fuck," she said as I fell on top of her.

"Ditto," I said.

She nipped my shoulder playfully with her teeth as we tried to catch our breath. A moment later, we heard a cry on the baby monitor. Bridgette was awake.

Heart groaned.

"I've got her," I said, kissing her softly on the forehead.

I peeled myself off her and grabbed my sweatpants from the floor, sliding them on. Heart propped herself up on her elbows to watch. I shook my head at her and laughed.

"What? I can't help it." She shrugged.

I strode over to the bed and pressed my lips against hers before walking out of the room. Most of our mornings started like this. Mind-blowing sex and then tending to the baby. We were practically hormonal teenagers with how much we couldn't keep our hands off each other. Thank God she lived with me or it would be torture.

Heart had moved in shortly after Bridgette was born. It just made more sense that way. We didn't want to be apart, and we wanted to raise our baby together as a family. Plus, she had gotten a job in Manhattan at my friend's firm. She was able to work from home and in the office. I started working remotely some days too. We traded off on who took care of Bridgette.

We made one of the spare bedrooms a nursery, and we had done it all just us two. I didn't hire anyone. I wanted it to be *our* thing.

I quietly opened the door to the nursery and walked inside to see Bridgette sitting up and looking at me expectantly.

"Good morning, beautiful girl," I said as I scooped her up.

She let out a little giggle as I led her to the glider in the corner of the room. I sat down and rocked her gently.

"Did you know what today is?" I asked.

She tilted her head curiously.

"It's your first birthday."

"B-b-deh."

"That's right!" I exclaimed as I kissed her cheeks.

"Mama," she said, looking toward the door.

I looked up and saw Heart standing in a pink floral robe. She looked just as beautiful as the day I had met her. If not more.

"Hey, birthday girl," she said, walking over and sitting on the armrest of the glider.

She leaned in and gave Bridgette a kiss. We sat like that for a few minutes, exchanging cuddles and kisses and coos. My whole world was in this room.

"We should probably get ready for the party," said Heart.

"Coffee first?" I asked.

"Obviously. After last night and this morning, I might need a pot all to myself." Heart winked as she strode out of the room.

I laughed softly as I stood up and walked Bridgette to the changing table to get her cleaned up. I loved being a dad. Even the diaper changes or the middle of the night feedings that I often did to let Heart sleep. It was all more than I ever thought it would be.

I met Heart in the kitchen where she was waiting with a steaming mug of coffee for me. I leaned in and kissed her before taking it from her. She took Bridgette from my arms and snuggled her. I smiled at the sight of them. Heart was such a good mom. I loved her even more now.

"You're incredible. You know that?" I asked, after taking a sip of coffee.

She looked at me curiously.

"You are. I just thought you should know." I shrugged.

She gave me a soft smile, her cheeks turning a rosy shade of pink.

"I love you," she whispered.

"I love *you.*"

After several cups of coffee and setting up the party with Monica and the party planner Margaret had hired, the place looked party ready. There was a large pink balloon arch that hung over the entire living room that was filled with cocktail tables and chairs covered in pink tablecloths. There were white, glittery streamers hanging from the ceiling. A dessert table sat in the center of the room, filled with every miniature sweet treat you could imagine. The kitchen was bustling with the caterers preparing the food. The face painter had just arrived, along with the princess we hired for story-time and dancing. Bridgette sat in the small ball pit we had bought and was looking around at everything in awe.

"Is it too much?" asked Heart, leaning her head against my shoulder.

"Maybe, but she's worth it," I replied as I looked around.

The doorbell rang just then and the party began. A few coworkers from Heart's new job came, along with everyone from my office. Brody and Freddy. Monica. Heart's parents. Even my parents flew in from France for the party.

They had already met Heart and Bridgette a handful of times over the past year. They said they had been away too long and wanted to be a part of their granddaughter's life. All our lives. I didn't realize how much Bridgette had brought everyone together, and she wouldn't even be here if it weren't for Heart coming into my life.

She had changed everything for the better.

I watched as she danced around the living room with Bridgette in her arms, the party crowd clapping in sync with the music as they watched. I reached into my pocket. My thumb brushed over the velvet box that was nestled inside. I smiled knowing what was to come by the end of the day.

"You ready for this, bro?" whispered Brody, slapping me on the back.

I removed my hand from my pocket swiftly. "Will you shut up?" I laughed.

"What? No one heard me. No one knows."

I shook my head at my brother who looked like a kid on Christmas morning.

"I'm ready," I said with a nod.

He had come with me to pick out the ring at Tiffany's a few months ago. I was waiting for the right time, and today felt like the perfect occasion with all of our friends and family here to witness.

"I'm happy for you," he said.

"Thanks, Brody."

After Bridgette opened her gifts and dug her hands into her smash cake, it was nearing time for everyone to go home. It was almost her naptime, anyway, and she made it known by the long yawn she let out that everyone *awwe*d over.

It was now or never.

I pulled Heart to the center of the room, where Bridgette sat at our feet playing with wooden blocks my mom had got her from Paris. Heart looked at me curiously as everyone made a circle around us.

"I want to thank everyone for coming," I said, holding her hand tightly in mine. "I especially want to thank this woman right here. Heart, you have turned my life upside down and made everything right. I love you for the woman you are. The mother you are."

Heart's eyes glazed over with tears as she looked at me.

"I can't imagine life without you," I said as I reached into my pocket and pulled out the velvet box.

I heard the crowd gasp and a few squeals emerge from our mothers, but I kept my eyes on Heart, who looked as shocked as anyone. Her hands flew up to her mouth as she watched me get on one knee.

"Will you marry me?"

I opened the box, revealing the solitaire oval diamond that sat on a thin gold band. Effortlessly beautiful, just like Heart.

"Yes," she cried through her tears.

THE END

Craving more?

Want another addictive romance read at an amazing price?
Check out my other books on amazon!
Or sign up for my newsletter and receive a **free romance novel for your
Kindle Reader:**
https://www.subscribepage.com/rebecca-baker-english

Made in United States
North Haven, CT
29 August 2025

72278291R00219